WHITE
DARKNESS

Other books by Steven D. Salinger

Behold the Fire

WHITE DARKNESS

A NOVEL

STEVEN D. SALINGER

Crown Publishers
New York

For Daniel and Diane Heftel, treasured friends, sorely missed

Published by Crown Publishers, New York, New York.
Member of the Crown Publishing Group.

Random House, Inc. New York, Toronto, London, Sydney, Auckland
www.randomhouse.com

Crown is a trademark and the Crown colophon is a registered trademark of Random House, Inc.

Printed in the United States of America

Design by Susan Maksuta

Library of Congress Cataloging-in-Publication Data

Salinger, Steven D.
      White darkness / by Steven D. Salinger.
         1. Haitians—New York (State)—New York—Fiction.   2. Inheritance and succession—Fiction.
      3. Brooklyn (New York, N.Y.)—Fiction.   4. Jewelry stores—Fiction.   5. Immigrants—Fiction.
      6. Jewish men—Fiction.   7. Voodooism—Fiction.   I. Title.
      PS3569.A459527 W48   2001
      813'.54—dc21   00-050905

ISBN 0-609-60728-6
10 9 8 7 6 5 4 3 2 1
First Edition

ACKNOWLEDGMENTS

The author wishes to express his gratitude to the following people, who provided valuable insights and invaluable encouragement during the creation of this book:

Henry Dunow
Bob Mecoy

Lynn Baier
Barbara R. Ezell
John H. Gardner
Ted Goldman
Helene Hovanec
Donna and Ken Kuchtyak
Estelle C. Ladrey
Alexander J. Londino
Allyson, Ana, Gretel, Lillie, and Tony Salinger
Paul Stern
Bonnie, Fred, and Josh Waitzkin

. . . a white darkness . . . floods up through my body,
reaches my head, engulfs me.

—Maya Deren,
Divine Horsemen

PART ONE

WANGA

At the top of the hill, framed by countless stars, the elegant house shimmered in the Haitian moonlight. As the colonel climbed toward it, the ground came alive with night creatures scurrying to avoid the crunch of his boots.

A young maid in a starched pink uniform answered the door. She had the flat nose and prominent cheekbones of the colonel's home district, though her skin was several shades lighter than his. He informed her that he wished to see Mr. Dalwani. In response to the requisite question, he replied that no, he was not expected. His eyes followed the sway of her firm young rump as she went in to announce him. Another foolish child seeking an escape from those scrabbly hills, he thought, removing his cap and wiping his forehead. There were some things about his job the colonel did not enjoy.

The dining room tingled with cool air and the sharp smell of curry. The Dalwanis were all at dinner: father, mother, three daughters. There was a cook somewhere, the colonel knew, but no houseboy.

Mr. Dalwani rose and introduced himself. He was a balding, naturally slender man onto whose narrow frame prosperity had appended a potbelly. "I bid you welcome," he said affably, "Colonel . . . ?"

"Ferray," the colonel replied, nodding his thanks and taking the indicated seat.

The women were skittish, but Mr. Dalwani exuded the easy confidence of a man accustomed to purchasing his way through the world. The colonel accepted his offer of coffee. When the maid went to fetch it, he observed that her legs were slightly bowed, a condition common among the undernourished hill children. She was well fed now.

"A nice child," Mr. Dalwani remarked, noting the colonel's interest.

"Yours seem nice as well," the colonel responded amiably. "May I guess their ages?"

"Please," his host encouraged.

Ferray pretended to guess, surprising everyone with his accuracy. The eldest girl was fifteen, the middle one fourteen, the youngest twelve. The twelve-year-old was just beginning to bud. All three girls had their mother's long, straight, lustrous hair, delicate bones, and sorrowful, dark-rimmed eyes. The colonel doubted that his men would appreciate such refinements.

When the maid delivered his coffee, the flowered cup rattled against its matching saucer. Her long fingers were marred by small, whitish scars.

The colonel was startled when the middle daughter thrust a thick, multicolored arm toward him from across the table.

"Would you like to sign my cast?" she asked him.

Her mother admonished her impertinence. Her sisters giggled. Her father smiled indulgently, shrugged, offered the colonel a pen.

He waved it off and leaned toward the girl. "My work is very secret," he confided impishly. "I must not leave even the slightest trace of where I have been."

"Are you like a spy, then?" she asked delightedly.

He scanned the room theatrically before raising an index finger to his lips. The girl's eyes widened and her cast retreated back beneath the table. Everyone smiled politely.

While the Dalwani women sipped their tea and nibbled on sugar cookies, the two men talked. Mr. Dalwani steered the conversation to the long-term outlook for tourism, wondering if the colonel agreed that political stability was a prerequisite for large-scale foreign investment.

Ferray demurred. "We are so far from the capital, and I am but a simple soldier."

"Not so simple, I suspect," his host suggested with a sly smile.

The colonel shrugged and finished his coffee. The maid reached in and removed the crockery. She smelled of sweat: fresh and pleasantly pungent. That was something his men would appreciate.

"Did you wish to speak privately?" Mr. Dalwani inquired.

The colonel stood and took his cap. After nodding to the women, he followed his host into a dimly lit den of dark leathers and polished woods. An overhead fan gently stirred the fragrant air.

After seating his guest in a leather easy chair, Mr. Dalwani slipped in behind a writing desk. Its green-shaded lamp cast exaggerated shadows on the walls. Ferray carefully extracted a small paper bag from his jacket and dropped it into the upturned cap resting on his knee.

"Now," Mr. Dalwani said warmly, clasping his hands on the desk, "as you see, Colonel Ferray, I am at your service."

"Thank you, sir, but regrettably, my mission here is not a happy one." Ferray paused. "Mr. Dalwani," he said formally, "I am instructed to inform you that you have been designated by the government as a profiteer."

Mr. Dalwani remained unruffled. "A profiteer? My, my, Colonel, that does not sound good at all."

"I am afraid it is even worse than that," Ferray told him, absently fingering the sweat band of his cap.

The clasped hands on the desk tightened. "What does it mean, 'worse than that'?"

"It means, Mr. Dalwani," Ferray explained calmly, "that I have received orders to eliminate you."

"Eliminate me? I'm afraid I—"

"A euphemism," the colonel apologized, displaying an upright thumb and then slowly reversing its orientation.

A shadow on the wall jumped. Mr. Dalwani cleared his throat. "And when, may I ask, is this 'elimination' scheduled to take place?"

"You may assume," Ferray replied, the leather creaking as he casually shifted his position, "that my presence here tonight is not entirely social."

Mr. Dalwani's posture stiffened. "Who issued these orders?" he demanded.

"Those with the authority to do so."

"I will make a phone call."

"I regret that it is too late for that."

Defiantly, Mr. Dalwani lifted the receiver and brought it to his ear.

The colonel watched impassively. "You see," he said after a few seconds, making a snipping motion with two fingers, "too late."

"I am a businessman," Mr. Dalwani declared, replacing the receiver with some difficulty. "I employ many people. I pay large sums in taxes. I love this country."

"No doubt."

"Surely, a few minor currency infractions . . ."

"I would not know." Ferray shrugged. "I am merely a soldier."

"Now look here, my friend," Mr. Dalwani said, trying to reason, "this is a mistake. I have powerful friends in the capital. At the highest levels, I assure you. You must allow me to contact them."

"I am afraid not," the colonel sighed, taking his cap from his knee and maneuvering to his feet.

"And what of my family?" Mr. Dalwani cried, jumping up. "My wife? My daughters?"

"Ah, yes." The colonel reached into his cap and held out the paper bag. "I nearly forgot."

"What is this?" Mr. Dalwani asked, refusing to take it.

"Lubricant." The colonel placed it on the desk. "For the women."

It took a moment for his words to sink in.

"I have twenty men outside," the colonel explained, putting on his cap.

"Colonel Ferray," Mr. Dalwani croaked, "please sit down."

"I would like to, Mr. Dalwani. Truly. But I am already behind schedule."

"Please."

"All right, if you insist." The colonel glanced at his watch and frowned.

Mr. Dalwani hurried around the desk. "Take her," he whispered urgently.

The colonel looked up at him quizzically.

"The girl. The maid. Take her with you, Colonel." Mr. Dalwani came closer. He smelled of old tobacco. "Force her to do things," he whispered, wringing his hands. "Filthy things. Beat her if she disobeys." His lips were quivering. "Spank her very hard, Colonel. Very hard. She likes it. Believe me, she likes it."

Ferray stared at him evenly. Mr. Dalwani retreated a few steps, his balled hands pressed against his chest, his eyes darting about the room.

"If that is all . . . ," the colonel said, making to rise.

"No, no, no," Mr. Dalwani exclaimed, rushing over and anxiously patting the colonel's shoulder to resettle him in the chair. "No indeed, Colonel," he giggled. "That was a joke. A poor joke. Please forgive me." He hurried across the room and pulled away a framed painting, revealing a wall safe. As he turned to the combination dial, he continued, "Marie, her name is, Colonel. The girl. If you want her, you will simply take her, of course." His speech was becoming manic. "She is only a maid, after all." He cursed, spun the dial, and began again. His hand was shaking. "I saw you looking at her and I thought, naturally, well, we are both men. So, I offered my recommendation, that is all. A common girl, yes, but willing, anxious even, so that even you, my dear Colonel Ferray, a man of refined tastes, even you— Ah, there it is, here we are, open at last. Now you shall see. Remain seated, Colonel, please. Stay exactly where you are. I have gifts for you, many gifts."

"What a lovely surprise," murmured the colonel.

When Mr. Dalwani finished, Ferray's lap was filled with stacks of banknotes, kilo bars of gold, glassine envelopes with loose gemstones: a small fortune.

Mr. Dalwani stood by the safe mopping his face. "Well, Colonel," he asked hopefully, "are we now friends?"

"I know so little about jewelry, but your wife was wearing a ring . . ."

"The colonel has a discerning eye," Mr. Dalwani said, beaming. "Please wait right there. It would be my pleasure . . ."

"Mr. Dalwani," Ferray called, "take the bag. In case you do not return quickly enough."

The man hesitated a moment, then grabbed the paper bag and rushed from the room. The colonel rose carefully, located an attaché case behind the desk, emptied its contents on the floor, and filled it with his new treasure. When Mr. Dalwani returned with the diamond ring, the colonel took it and slipped it into his pocket.

"The house is surrounded," Mr. Dalwani said. "My wife and children are frightened."

"Yes. Naturally."

"But you are leaving now, Colonel Ferray, my good friend, are you not? We have an understanding. Is that not so?"

"Yes, Mr. Dalwani."

"And you will not return? I have your word as an officer?"

"As an officer," Ferray confirmed solemnly.

Mr. Dalwani grasped the colonel's hand with both of his and pumped it vigorously. His face was drenched with relief. He smelled rancid.

The maid scurried ahead and opened the front door. As Ferray left, he felt her eyes scratching at him like a drowning cat. At the base of the stairs his lieutenant stepped from the shadows, stamped his foot on the gravel, and delivered a crisp salute.

The colonel switched the attaché case to his other hand and returned the salute. "Total of seven," he said softly. "Husband, wife, three daughters, a maid, and a cook. Do nothing until you hear my Jeep pull away."

"Sir!"

The colonel flicked a small moth from his sleeve. "Follow standard procedure. Kill the husband immediately. Make certain that all the women are dead before you burn the house."

"Sir!"

"Carry on," Ferray said, walking off into the night.

TWO

Following a ritual he had been performing six mornings a week for the last ten years, Moe Rosen paused to check the street before reaching for his store keys. It was all clear to the right. One door down to the left, about twenty yards away, the chubby, middle-aged Haitian lady everybody called Miz Ark was standing outside her restaurant rummaging through her bag.

A voice spoke inside Moe's head: *Look what this woman is doing.* Moe smiled at the memory of his father's gruff affection. *That is something you never do, you hear me?* the voice warned. *Never ever. With her back to the street, no less. Are you listening to me, Moses? Are you hearing what I'm saying?*

"Yes, Dad," Moe murmured, humoring him the way he'd done as a kid. Moe Rosen was thirty-nine. His father was gone ten years now. Ten years . . .

You're drifting, the voice scolded. *This is no time for drifting. Not when you're out here all exposed. This is Brooklyn we're in, Moses, not Saint Moritz.*

"Okay, Dad," Moe chuckled, shaking his head nostalgically as he reached for the keys.

Something caught the corner of his eye. His hand froze. Trouble. Yes, but where? There! Crossing the street, coming this way. A big man. Black. Taller and thicker than Moe. Younger too. Moving like a stalking cat.

The man glanced over, saw Moe watching and changed direction. Now he was heading toward Miz Ark. Uh-oh. Moving a little too fast. Moe wondered, should he say . . . ? Moving even faster now. A mugger, almost guaranteed. Miz Ark still fumbling in her purse. Oh, no! She's a woman, you no-good—

The mugger swung his arm like a club and struck Miz Ark in the back, dropping her to her knees, making her cry out. Then, almost in the same motion, he stepped back and kicked her viciously in the side. She toppled over and hit the pavement hard. As the mugger bent over her, Moe, charging down the street like a madman, launched himself into the air and landed on the mugger's back.

There were screams, a crash, the sound of breaking glass. Things hit Moe's head, his shoulder, his back. He was struggling to get his arms around the man, to hold him for the police, but it was like trying to ride a Brahma bull. Everything was spinning. Moe clung on desperately, shocked by the man's strength, frightened by his raw animal smell, terrified of what would happen if he got loose. Moe was trying but he couldn't seem to—his fingers were slipping and—

Oh, God!

—⦅∽∽⦆—

Moe heard voices, then felt hands all over him, helpful hands, lifting him, pulling him this way and that. The sounds got louder. He heard birds. His legs wouldn't work right. He couldn't seem to get his balance. Where were his keys? Where was his pocket? His hands were shaking. His ears were ringing.

They got him into a chair. Everything was blurry. One of the buttons on his suit jacket was hanging by a thread. It must have— His shirt was a mess. Little pieces of glass were all over him. How the— My God, the store!

"My keys!" he cried, trying to rise.

"Here," a voice said, and someone grasped his wrist, held him down, pressed the cool, heavy key ring into his hand.

Moe clutched the keys and looked around. Big, brightly colored fish were swimming above his head. His heart was racing. Where was he? Who were all these black people? What was that smell?

He squeezed the keys hard, and things began to click into place. The smell was curry, itchy and cloying, the same alien smell that seeped in all day through the walls of his shop. So this had to be the restaurant next door: Miz Ark's place. These black people had to be her workers. He looked up. The fish were a decoration: painted wood, hanging from strings. The bird sounds were probably a tape.

"How is she?" he asked the nearest face, that of a middle-aged woman who was busy picking flecks of glass from his tie.

"Miz Ark?" the woman replied without looking up. "Miz Ark bruised up some. But she'll be okay, thanks to you, Mr. Rosen."

"You know me?" Her nails were a fiery red. She was chewing gum. It smelled sweet, fruity.

"You're the gold man," she said, her long nails pecking at him like a hungry bird. "You own the jewelry shop right next door."

"That's right," Moe said, amazed. He had never set foot in here. How—?

"You single too," she said, then paused and made a strange chirping noise with her teeth. "Big, strong, good-lookin' young man with all that gold." She chirped again. "An' that fella had a knife."

"Knife?" Moe exclaimed. "What knife?"

Moe's arm began to twitch. A knife? He could have been killed! He saw himself lying facedown in a pool of blood.

The nails lady was staring at him. They were all staring at him. Moe felt trapped: a captive in a jungle clearing, surrounded by an unknown and curious tribe.

"I have to go," he said, grasping a nearby chair and pulling himself to his feet. "My store," he explained, so as not to hurt feelings.

"You sure?" the nails lady asked, brushing off his sleeve. "When you wouldn' go to the doctor with her, Miz Ark say we best fix you a big breakfast."

Moe didn't remember any of that. He didn't want to be rude, but he wasn't hungry and he was dying to pee.

"Thank you, but no," he said, straightening up, cautiously taking a deep breath. He seemed okay. It occurred to him that he should say good-bye. "Is, uh, your boss, uh, back from, uh . . . ?" he asked, struggling to put together a sentence.

"Miz Ark still off gettin' x-rayed," a new, younger woman said, lifting a breast and pointing to her ribs.

"Nice," Moe said, forcing himself to look away. The walls were covered with travel posters, lush and exotic: palm trees and waterfalls and bikini women. "The mugger," he said, locating the door, "did they catch him?"

"Not to worry," a man answered. "Plenny people see he face before him run off."

"So the police, they've been notified and—"

"Not to worry," the man assured Moe.

"Good. That's good, because—"

"I goin' to fix you a cup a tea, Mr. Rosen," the ribs woman said. "Miz Ark blends it her own self. Calms the nerves somethin' wonderful."

"No, thank you," Moe told her, trying not to stare. "You've been very kind. All of you," he said, glancing around. There were about ten of them. Nice people. All nice people. A nice, clean restaurant. Nice fish. He took a tentative step. His legs didn't feel right.

"Mr. Rosen, he leavin'," someone announced.

Moe looked down and carefully slipped the keys into his jacket pocket. Then he hitched up his pants, tucked in his shirt, felt for his wallet. When he looked up, all the workers were clustered by the door.

"Tonk you, Missa Rosen," the first one said in a singsong accent. "Tonk you fuh savin' Miz Ark." He put out his hand.

Moe felt himself turning red, but he had no choice but to shake hands and mumble some response. Then, taking small, sideways steps, he had to shake every hand and accept all the thanks before making good his escape.

The street seemed different: brighter somehow, and mercifully quiet. The storefront speakers wouldn't start blasting their infernal music until about eleven. He looked back over his shoulder. Several of the restaurant workers were watching him from their doorway. When they saw him looking, they waved.

Moe checked around again before opening the big locks and pulling up the steel curtain. He just hoped the police would catch that mugger and put him behind bars. Fast. Today. Before he decided to get a gun and come back.

Moe secured the steel curtain, turned around to make sure he was alone, and then, the appropriate key already in his hand, unlocked the front door, slipped inside, and closed the door behind him. He unlocked the second door, reached up to the little plastic box on the wall, punched in the security code, and waited for the red light to blink twice. It felt safe inside the store.

Black, white, Moe told himself, making his way toward the office, people were people. He felt good, clean, alive: the kind of feeling he used to get in the locker room after a tough high school basketball game. At five eleven, he'd usually been the shortest guy on the court. He shook his head. It didn't seem possible that had been twenty years ago. Well—he smiled, recalling how he'd leaped on the mugger's back—maybe he still had a few moves left in him.

Don't be so proud of yourself, his father cautioned. *What was that, Moses, the Good Neighbor Policy? You think you're a Roosevelt instead of a Rosen?*

Moe shrugged, fighting off a grin.

And that surprised you, didn't it, Moses, that girl knowing that you're single? You liked that, right? And the ribs girl with the big chest. Don't

*think I didn't see you looking. Well, here's something to think about, Mr.
Eligible Crime Fighter: These people next door, with their dark skins and
their sexy posters and their secret teas, what else do they know?*

Moe reached up, flipped on the lights, and saw all the hands in the
showcases. Women's hands, with long, graceful fingers, sheathed in
fuzzy black velvet skin; some of them lying palm up with their fingers
bent; others standing straight up, their fingers stretching toward the
sky. Most days these spectral hands were Moe's only companions in Eli
Rosen & Son, a store once noted throughout Brooklyn for taste and ele-
gance, for fine European design and old-world craftsmanship: a store
that used to attract a steady stream of discerning customers, people who
appreciated quality and had the means to pay for it, even if they sometimes liked to hondle over price.

Twenty-five Piagets a year they used to sell, Moe recalled. The finest
watches in the world. Right here in this store. He looked down at the
faded carpet. A minimum of twenty-five Piagets a year, every year, like
clockwork. How long ago was that? Ten years? Fifteen? Losing the Piaget
line had brought on his father's heart attack, the first one, the one that had
torn Moe from his new life in California and dragged him back here to
Brooklyn to help run the store. What had kept him here was his father's
second attack, the one that had prompted Moe's desperate promise to
keep the store going, to make it a success again. As if that would heal his
father's heart.

Water under the bridge, Moe counseled himself, anxious to change
the subject. The question had been, What else did they know, these
mysterious black people next door? Moe looked around the empty shop.
Did they know how bad business was these days? Did they know how
much it pained him to have to stock the store with junk: gaudy,
machine-made pendants and hollow chains and earrings stamped from
gold so thin they could blow away in a stiff breeze? Did they know how
much it hurt him to see the neighborhood deteriorate right before his
eyes, to witness the "white flight" firsthand, to watch as one by one the

classy old stores were replaced by open-air fruit stands and greasy-spoon takeouts and blaring record shops and check-cashing joints and discount travel agencies and smelly hair salons and basement churches with strange names, and to sit here day after day and watch an endless flood of people from the West Indies—legal, illegal: who knew?—Haiti and Jamaica and Santo Domingo mostly, but also Antigua, Saint Kitts, Nevis, Anguilla, Barbados, Barbuda, Trinidad and Tobago, Tortola, Saint Martin, Curaçao, Guyana: scrappy, happy people who, Moe was the first to admit, hustled and worked hard, but who—God should forgive him—swarmed like insects and bred like rabbits?

Moe caught himself: What was the use of beating himself up again? Life was what it was, and that was that.

He entered the office and went to the safe. He had done something good, jumping in to protect that woman. Done something good: that was the bottom line. And if that bastard really had a knife, it could be that Moe had saved Miz Ark's life. That was a nice thought. What was that line from *Schindler's List,* that Talmudic saying engraved on the ring the Jews made for Schindler? Oh, yes: "He who saves a single life saves the world entire." Which only proved that even the Talmud could be wrong; Moe Rosen was not about to save the world entire; he'd be satisfied selling a few gold chains.

THREE

The faint splash from the back of the house told Fabrice that Madame Jouvier had entered the pool. He pulled a weed and smiled; Madame rarely called him with chores while she was taking her swim.

It was a lovely morning. Hazy sunshine angled in from the east above the capital, warming Fabrice's head, encouraging his dreams. Squatting comfortably in the grass, he stared at a flowering hibiscus and imagined that the gently waving, bright red blossoms were happy people lining the streets of New York, America. The people were all waving to Fabrice as he drove by in his new Japanese Mercedes taxi, a taxi whose hard metal skin sparkled with every color of the rainbow, a taxi whose name— *Erzulie*—was painted in big, beautiful letters across the back. Yes, Fabrice thought with satisfaction, absently working the machete around a stubborn root, his taxi would carry the name of the goddess Erzulie, the most desirable of all creatures: Erzulie, the l'wah of love.

And who, Fabrice wondered, gazing wistfully into the clear blue Haitian sky, who would be the passengers in his shiny new Erzulie? The Huxtables from TV? It would certainly be nice to meet them, especially the daughter. But, no, he decided, his passengers would be the Jouviers: the young Madame herself, the gray-haired Monsieur, and the two ti-Jouviers. And why, he asked himself, why would the Jouviers be in America? To visit Madame's relatives? To make business for Monsieur's newspaper? No, it had to be something more important than that. Of course! They would be there to see Fabrice's fine new American house! A house three stairs high, with a TV dish on the roof, and a garage with a magic-eye door for Erzulie, and a big refrigerator that would make ice without being told. All that and more!

Fabrice used his machete to shoo away a pesky, iridescent horsefly. And where, he asked himself, returning to his weeding and his fantasy, where would he be driving the Jouviers in his beautiful Erzulie? He tapped the blade against the ground, thinking hard. Perhaps the Jouviers would be returning home and he would be driving them to New York's famous Charles de Gaulle Airport.

Yes, now he had the whole glorious story. He settled back on his haunches and listened as Madame's gentle splashing blended with the steady hum of Erzulie's powerful engine, the combination suggesting the competing Vodoun rhythms of rada and petro drums, and reminding Fabrice that he had not attended the ceremonies in a long time. Lately, he had been spending all his free hours with Antoinette.

He moved sideways and began digging fresh earth, telling himself that Antoinette was too young to go to America. The heat spilled over the brim of his straw hat, warming his shoulders and making his polo shirt stick to his back. This was the same shirt Madame had given him more than two years ago, on the very day she had brought him here. He had been sixteen when she chose him from a group of boys larking about a roadside stand. The shirt was tight now because he had grown so much since then, but he was still pleased to wear it. Perhaps when Antoinette was older . . .

A gust of wind shook the flowers. Fabrice inhaled the fragrant aroma, closed his eyes, and saw the cardboard bathing girl dangling from Erzulie's rearview mirror: a sexy, perfumed, coffee-colored American lady with long, flowing hair, smiling red lips, and bosoms nearly as large as Madame Jouvier's.

Stung with guilt for thinking of Madame in that way, Fabrice searched his mind for the l'wah responsible for planting such a thought. He looked everywhere, but the culprit eluded him. Many spirits were quick, he knew, and tricky. This one had done its mischief and run away. Then again, the l'wah's appearance might have been a signal that it was time for Fabrice to renew his vows to Les Morts, Les Mystères, and Les Marassa, to return and play the drums at the ceremonies. Soon, he promised whichever spirits happened to be listening.

Fabrice ground his bare heels into the dry grass and imagined his pockets stuffed with crisp, green American money. He saw himself steering Erzulie straight out onto the runway. There was a great crowd. The Jouviers' airplane had flags of many nations flying from its great silver wings.

Fabrice was watching himself politely refusing a hundred-gourde tip from Monsieur Jouvier when Madame's shriek yanked him from his taxi and launched him on a mad scramble around the house.

Another scream! Fabrice clutched his machete as he ran; if anyone was harming Madame—!

She was floundering at the far end of the pool, out where the water was more than three meters deep. Without breaking stride, Fabrice dropped the machete, hurled himself into the pool, and began swimming, frantically begging Agwe, l'wah of the seas, to please please please spare Madame's life.

As Fabrice drew near, he realized that he did not know the proper way to save her. Trusting the spirits to guide him, he dove down and, ignoring the burning in his eyes, grasped her thrashing legs and hugged them to his chest. Then, planting his feet on the concrete bottom, he hoisted her torso high into the life-giving air and held it there.

Her kicking subsided. Fabrice, still submerged and still clutching her legs, lurched to the pool's side and held her aloft until her weight shifted and he knew she was safely out. Only then did he push off the bottom, burst from the water, and gulp in huge mouthfuls of air.

He dragged himself halfway out of the pool, rested his cheek on his folded arms, and listened to the galloping of his heart. His legs swayed weightlessly in the cool, forbidden water. Less than a meter away, Madame was stretched out on her back, a raised forearm shielding her eyes from the sun. Fabrice could tell she was alive by the way her belly was fluttering inside her red bathing suit.

"Madame is safe now. Safe," he whispered in anxious Creole. Then, in the English she preferred: "Is Madame hearing me?"

Her fingers crept across the patio stone toward him. He saw that one of her shoulder straps had fallen down, loosening the top of her bathing suit. Below the suntan her breasts were as white as the meat of a coconut.

"Fabrice," she said weakly, patting his wrist, "is that you?"

"Yes, Madame," he stammered, bewitched by the sight of so much forbidden flesh.

"Come out of there," she said, tugging gently at him.

"Yes, Madame. Immediately."

He hauled himself up into a sitting position and pulled his legs from the water. Servants were not allowed in the pool. Fabrice should not have stayed in there any longer than necessary.

And now his jeans were dripping water onto the patio, forming a dark, ugly puddle. Madame would be angry with him for that too. A breeze came up and he began to shiver.

"It is chill," he said, concentrating on speaking English. "Madame must go to the house."

"You saved my life, Fabrice," she murmured.

Her words embarrassed him. The spirits had saved her, not him. "Madame is making a cold," he cautioned. "I am calling Marie to help Madame."

"Marie has gone to the market," Madame Jouvier said, gripping the top of her bathing suit and wriggling back into it.

Trying to ignore the stirring in his belly, Fabrice offered to call Sophie.

"Sophie has gone to the market with Marie," he was told.

Fabrice did a quick inventory. Monsieur Jouvier was at his office. Antoine would be waiting there with the car. The children were at play school. There was no one else to call.

"Come," he said, standing and offering his hand, "Fabrice is helping Madame to the house."

"Chlorine is bad for the skin," she said distractedly, allowing him to help her up. "Look, your arms are all streaked."

"Madame is please to worry about Madame," he responded, holding her elbow and guiding her delicately toward the living room.

"My room," she said, managing despite her unsteadiness to change their direction.

"Yes, Madame." He was not used to touching her. It felt awkward, improper.

He slid open the glass door, held the curtain aside, and helped her step up into her bedroom. She negotiated the step, but then teetered.

Instinctively, Fabrice jumped forward and let her sag against him. Then, taking both her elbows, he helped her to sit on the edge of her bed. He released her cautiously, taking care she did not topple over.

He glanced about. Women's things were everywhere: soft pink and yellow things. He had been in here twice before: once last year when Marie had called him to chase a bat from the ceiling beams, and last week when Madame had summoned him to kill a scorpion hiding in the closet. He had been uncomfortable in here on both those occasions and was starting to feel the same way now. He began backing toward the door, trying to avoid leaving footprints on the terrazzo.

"Fabrice," Madame Jouvier said, halting his retreat, "would you please go turn on the shower?"

"The shower, Madame?"

"In the bathroom, Fabrice. Do you think you can manage it?"

"Of course, Madame," he grumbled. Only moments ago he had saved her from drowning, and now she was asking if he could turn on a shower? Did she think he was still a child?

He strode into the bathroom, pulled open the glass door, and felt his confidence collapse. Which of these many handles was he supposed to turn? The servants' shower had only one, for the water.

He tiptoed into the white-tiled shower room and examined each handle. None offered a clue as to its function. How was he supposed to choose? And what if he turned the wrong one? Something might break and—

"Give me some room," Mrs. Jouvier said, stepping in and pulling the smoked-glass door closed.

Fabrice retreated into a corner, pleased by her swift recovery but unnerved by her presence. Standing next to him in this suddenly cramped space, Madame seemed smaller but, even in a bathing suit, somehow more intimidating. He reminded himself to speak English.

Responding to a few sure movements from her hands, water began streaming from the nozzle, splattering the tile floor and tickling Fabrice's feet. He looked down and watched mud stains running to the drain. His soaked jeans and T-shirt felt heavy. The water around his feet became warmer. The air began to fill with mist.

"Come here, Fabrice," Madame Jouvier said, motioning to him. "Give me your hands."

Obediently, he stepped forward and held out his hands for inspection, as he had been taught to do before touching valuable things.

"Not like that." She took hold of his wrists and turned herself so that her back was to him and his hands were out in front of her.

Fabrice did not resist, but he was troubled. He should not be in this place, standing this close to Madame. He wondered what the l'wahs were up to now.

"This is the hot," she said, recapturing his attention by tapping one of his hands against a silver handle.

He looked over her shoulder to see which handle it was, but could not prevent himself from peeking at her bosom.

"And this is the cold," she continued, tapping with his other hand. "Now this one in the middle"—tap, tap—"controls the other showerhead."

She got his hand around the handle and helped him to turn it. A jet of cold water splashed his back. He cried out and bolted forward, accidentally bumping her. He regained his balance and was about to apologize when he discovered that his hands were pressed against her breasts. Horrified, he attempted to pull free, but found that Madame's elbows were squeezing down, trapping his arms, and that her hands were covering his. He realized that he was not doing this terrible thing, Madame was!

Fabrice became light-headed. He stopped struggling. The water, the mist, the slippery floor, the softness of her flesh—too many things were fighting for his attention at once. His legs went weak. Water was attacking him from all sides. The air was filling with a thick mist.

Fabrice's attention shifted. Madame was now rubbing his captive hands all over the front of her bathing suit. He was terrified and embarrassed and excited all at once. Madame had gone mad! What was he to do? Why were the l'wahs doing this to him?

She stepped back, forcing him against the wall, and began rubbing her bottom against him with the same rhythm she was using for their hands. He felt a rush of panic; pressing herself against him like this, she could not fail to recognize what her actions were doing to his body.

To his astonishment, her movements became even more pronounced. Fabrice felt helpless and afraid. He knew that the consequences of this would be terrible, but he felt powerless to stop it. The l'wahs seemed determined to destroy him.

Madame Jouvier began to speak. It was hard to hear above the water, but her voice seemed strange, her breathing was harsh, and her words made no sense to him. The circles she was tracing with his hands grew wider, the pressure of her hips more intense, the noises from her throat more threatening. Even in his fearful confusion, it was apparent to Fabrice that Madame was no longer herself and—crazy as the thought was—he began to suspect that Madame had been mounted by a l'wah, possessed by a spirit who was controlling her words and her actions. Fabrice had seen such things before, of course, but never outside the sanctuary, never without the drums and the rituals, and never with an unbeliever. He had never even heard of such a thing taking place. Yet there was no denying the reality of what was rubbing so insistently against him.

Fabrice's fear was approaching panic. He had no idea what was expected of him in such a situation. This was not like being with Antoinette. The muscles in his stomach began to quiver. Warm water was beating on his head and neck and running down inside his shirt and jeans. The mist was so thick it was becoming difficult to see. His hands were sliding, bumping, pressing. Much as he was excited by this, all he wanted was to escape. He begged the l'wahs to stop. If this continued, he was doomed. He would never get to America. He would be dragged off to prison and—

Something new was happening. Madame was trying to use his hands to push down the front of her bathing suit. But without his help it wasn't working. Angry growls were coming from her throat.

Fabrice shuddered. He knew that voice!

This was not Madame!

She failed again and cursed in Creole.

He knew that voice!

It was Erzulie! Erzulie the temptress had taken control of Madame Jouvier!

Fabrice was thrilled to his core. He began to tremble. He had been dreaming about Erzulie and she had decided to appear. Nothing was accidental. Erzulie had come to him!

His fear vanished.

"Here," he said, freeing his hands, grasping the front of the bathing suit, and—with a single sharp stroke—peeling it down to Madame's waist.

She collapsed back against him. He cupped her breasts in his hands. Heavy and soft and slippery, her breasts were like the water-filled balloons he prepared for the ti-Jouviers' pool parties. Except that these were warm, living flesh, and squeezing them was making Erzulie moan.

"Fabrice," called a faraway, throaty voice.

It was the love-hungry voice of Erzulie: the same voice Fabrice had heard many times before, though never without offerings, never without drums. That Erzulie would come to him in the body of his beloved Madame was beyond Fabrice's wildest dreams. But here she was, and he must please her.

He dug a hand deep down inside the front of her bathing suit. She gasped and tried to twist away, but he kept his hand there. Ignoring her feeble protests, he started massaging the springy mound between her thighs and, when all resistance ceased, began gently probing the silken, oily hair with his fingers.

As he had hoped, her thighs parted, her moaning increased. Her hands reached back and began fumbling with the snap on his jeans.

"I know what is expected of me," he assured her, turning her around to face him.

Warm water continued to pour down on them. They were enveloped in a thick, steamy mist. Their eyes met for only a moment, but it was Erzulie's hungry fire he saw, Erzulie's heat he felt, even as Madame's trembling hands were struggling with his jeans. He waited until she had them off and then he wrenched her bathing suit down over her hips and legs, grasped her under her arms and lifted her free of it.

She took his face in her hands and kissed him. Erzulie sent Madame's tongue into his mouth, making it dart about like a frightened bird. It stopped after a while but only long enough to allow Madame to hurriedly pull off his T-shirt.

His hands roamed Madame's soft, wet back, moved down and out across her thick flanks. He heard a satisfied growl as her fingers explored his member and then grasped it greedily with both hands.

"It's too big," she said, placing it between her thighs and grinding herself against him. "I want to," she whispered breathlessly, hugging him, "but it's too big."

"Not too big," he assured her. He could not be too big for Erzulie. No man could be too big for Erzulie.

"I want to," she insisted, hugging him fiercely, "I really do. But it's too big for me, Fabrice. I—"

He reached down and slapped her bottom hard, to stop her teasing. She yelped and wriggled up against him. He smiled, secure in the knowledge that when she was herself again, she would not remember any of this; those mounted by a l'wah never did. He took her buttocks in his hands and squeezed them. "No more jokes," he said.

He felt her whole body trembling as she stroked his chest, took his arm, guided him down on his back, and straddled him.

"If we go very slowly . . . ," she said, grasping his member and raising herself to position it. Water flowed from her breasts in twin, graceful streams, anointing him.

"I'll try," she said, leaning forward, breathing hard, licking water from her lips.

He felt her hand maneuvering him. Inches above his face, her heavy breasts swayed like giant white clouds.

"Promise you'll be patient," she said.

"Of course," he told her, settling back into a watery bliss, reaching up for the clouds.

FOUR

The bell rang. Moe looked up from the old Piaget catalog and saw a man standing outside the front door: tall, white, lanky, thirties, with wheat blond hair. After buzzing him in, Moe put on his jacket and went out to greet him, hoping that the man's cheap blue suit was a sign of eccentric wealth. Moe knew better than to judge a customer by his clothing; over the years he'd sold a five-figure diamond solitaire to greasy overalls and caught an Armani suit shoplifting silver bangles. Life was always playing tricks.

"Detective Beck," the man said before Moe got close enough to offer his hand. "Eighteenth Squad." He produced a wallet with a gold badge. "You Eli Rosen?"

"No. I'm the son."

"Close enough." Beck's blond eyebrows gave him a ghostly appearance.

"Come on back to the office. I've been expecting you."

"That right?"

Moe had assumed this was about the mugging, but Beck's guarded tone suggested otherwise. What else could it be? Moe felt a pang. Some building code violation? With business as bad as it was, that was all he needed.

Beck took a seat, drew out a pad, and started with the standard questions—name, address, home phone, work phone—recording Moe's answers with the studied slowness of a Motor Vehicles clerk. It had taken Moe two seconds to appraise Beck's wedding band—14k, no workmanship: two grams, tops—and he was getting antsy.

The detective closed the pad, unbuttoned his jacket, and reached into his shirt pocket. His tie clip featured a pair of miniature handcuffs soldered to a thin silver bar. Sterling, but schlock.

"You recognize this, Mr. Rosen?" Beck asked, handing a Polaroid across the desk.

As Moe took it, he noted the Timex on the detective's wrist. The photo showed a line drawing—weird, primitive, vaguely familiar: a straight vertical with many branching lines, some ending in curls, others intersecting to form triangles or what appeared to be *A*'s. It was either an abstract nothing or a highly stylized something: tree? Totem pole? Coatrack?

Reminded of his own perpetually fruitless efforts at designing, Moe joked, "Is this a Rorschach test?"

"You want to spell that?" Beck asked, reaching for his pen.

"I was kidding. Actually, the design looks Native American." No response. "Or something Tibetan monks might do." That too drew a blank, "Then again, it could be hand-printed tapa cloth from the South Seas."

"How about Voodoo?"

"How about it?"

Beck slowly unwrapped a stick of Dentyne. "That's a vevay," he said, watching for Moe's reaction.

"A what?"

"A veh-vay."

Moe shrugged. He didn't recognize the word. He didn't care for the way the detective was looking at him.

The bell took Moe by surprise. He looked up. Two black women were out by the front door. Customers. Except that Moe was bound by the ironclad Rule of Rosen: "One salesman, one customer."

He pressed the intercom. "I'm very sorry, ladies," he said, watching them through the glass. "But I'm with someone at the moment. Could you please come back a little later?"

They nodded, but Moe knew the odds of their returning were slim, especially if they had caught sight of Beck's blond hair. Everyone was so sensitive these days. Reluctantly, he turned back to the detective.

"See," Beck said as if nothing had happened, "every one of their Voodoo gods has its own vevay. It's like what we might call a coat of arms."

"Interesting." Moe forced himself to look at the photo again. It pained him to turn away customers, not because of the money, but because he took the store's decline personally, because the lack of business dishonored his father's memory.

"So what you're telling me, Mr. Rosen," the detective said, placidly chewing his gum, "is that you don't recognize this particular vevay." He stopped to brush something from a trouser leg. "Do I have that right so far?"

Moe smiled in lieu of a reply. A uniformed cop might be this dumb, not a detective. But if this wasn't about the mugging or some building code violation, what could it be?

The bell rang, giving Moe a start. A young black couple were standing at the door. Using the intercom, Moe apologized to them and asked them to please return a little later. He watched them walk off. These days, two customers in ten minutes qualified as a stampede. And he'd lost them both.

Beck was sitting back in his chair, chewing contentedly. "So then, if I'm following you, Mr. Rosen, you wouldn't know which vevay this was, am I right?"

"Right." Moe wondered if that young couple might have been shopping for an engagement ring. For cheap, oversize earrings—the bulk of his trade these days—women generally came alone or with a girlfriend. "Look, do you think we could . . . ?"

"So," Beck continued in the same maddeningly slow cadence, "if I told you that this was the vevay of Ogoun Ferraille . . ."

"Oh-who?"

"Oh-goon fur-Aye. The Voodoo god of war."

"Never heard of him," Moe grumbled. Two customers he'd had to turn away. Two. In ten minutes. One a possible engagement. All because of some Voodoo war god?

Beck nodded his head slowly, as if confirming something to himself. "Here"—he offered another photograph—"try this one."

Moe looked at the new photo and chuckled; he'd been right, after all.

"Something funny?" the detective asked.

"It's a mug shot. Isn't that what you call these things with this, you know, the numbers: mug shots?"

"So?"

"So that's why I laughed. A mug shot of a mugger. See what I mean?"

"No."

"This picture," Moe said, shaking it for emphasis. "This is the guy, the mugger, from the other morning."

"What mugger?" Beck asked, sitting straighter.

"The one I tackled," Moe told him, bristling with frustration. "Come on. You know."

"What do I know?"

"About the mugging! Tuesday. Right outside. When the guy jumped—"

The bell rang again. A tall black man, early forties, nicely dressed.

Moe pressed the speaker button, wishing it were a trapdoor that would make Detective Beck disappear. "I'm very sorry," he apologized, feeling helpless. "I'm with someone at the moment. Could you possibly . . . ?"

Three! Three was an avalanche, an aberration. Moe was anxious to cooperate with the police, but—

"Mugger?" Beck prodded.

Moe opened his mouth, but something stopped his tongue. Ideas were swirling through his head. Was it possible that the police really didn't know about the mugging? What was going on? Three customers, one after the other. Maybe, for some reason, Miz Ark's people had never reported it. What reason could they have? Three customers. Boom, boom, boom. Maybe Moe should just shut up. Three—a whole day's traffic—in less than fifteen minutes. No, he had to cooperate, help the police get that bastard before he attacked someone else.

"This man in the picture," Moe said, taking a deep breath, "he's a mugger. He, uh, got into a tussle with me the other day. On the street in front of the store."

"Which day are we talking about?" Beck asked, flipping his pad open.

"Tuesday. I already told you that. Look. Please. Have you—"

"What time did this incident occur, Mr. Rosen?"

"A few minutes before nine. In the morning."

"'A few minutes,' Beck repeated, chewing thoughtfully. "Could you be more specific?"

"Eight," Moe snapped. "Eight minutes before nine. Is that specific enough?"

"Yeah, that's good." Beck nodded, concentrating on making a note. "What makes you so sure of the time?"

The bell rang. Two black girls, teenagers. Moe was as nice as he knew how, but as he watched them go, he was filled with despair: they wouldn't be back. None of them would be back. Four customers he'd had to turn away. Four . . .

". . . before nine?" Beck was asking, studying something in his pad.

"What? Oh, I'm sorry. Look, Detective, I don't mean to rush you, but do you think we could cut to the chase?"

Beck's face swung up. His eyes met Moe's. "What chase is that, Mr. Rosen?"

"Look, I watch *N.Y.P.D. Blue,* I know the routine. I'll come down and pick this guy out of a lineup for you. Sign a statement. I'll testify in court, okay? Whatever you want. But here's the whole story. Please listen." Moe wrung his hands, trying to calm himself. "On Tuesday, I was getting ready to open. I checked my watch. It was eight minutes to nine. Exactly. I wear an Omega: the moon watch—see?—the same one the astronauts wore when— Anyhow, this fellow in the picture here, he showed up. We wrestled outside in the street. I fell to the sidewalk. He ran away. End of story."

The bell rang. A black woman in a stylish leather coat. Five. This was unbelievable. Moe's hand shook as he pressed the intercom and made his abject apologies. She asked if he carried a gold chain called Diamonds by the Yard. The term made Moe wince; he had a whole spool of it collecting dust in the safe. He hadn't sold an inch in more than two years. This was torment, like the ten plagues of Egypt.

"I'm making you nervous," the detective observed after Moe finished with the woman. "Why is that, Mr. Rosen?"

"I've turned away five customers since you've been here. You know how long it's been since I've seen five customers in one morning?"

"Business is awfully important to you people."

"Which people?"

Beck fingered his tie clip. "Business people."

"Look, one simple question: Do you have this man behind bars?"

"Not exactly."

Moe threw up his hands. "Listen to me," he demanded. "This guy tried to mug me. He had a knife. There were witnesses. I have a right to know if he's in custody."

"He's in the morgue."

Moe experienced a moment of absolute blankness. When he recovered, he asked, "What?"

The bell rang. A young black couple with a rottweiler. They asked if the store sold engagement rings. Distracted, Moe sent them away. Morgue? What was going on? It was as if the whole world were upside down this morning. A sprig of blond hair popped up at the back of

Beck's head. It made him look like a cockatoo. Moe didn't know whether to laugh or cry.

"That vevay I showed you before," the detective said. "That was done with chalk. We found it near the body. We think there could be a connection."

Moe was still struggling to comprehend it. Jail, yes; but death? Moe didn't wish that on anyone. He felt a chill; he had seen this man, touched him, two days ago. Now he was dead. How was that possible? "How did he die?" he asked the detective, recalling the vision of himself facedown in a pool of blood.

"That's privileged information. But trust me, it was very unpleasant. We found him in a Dumpster."

"Dumpster?" Moe asked, feeling queasy.

"It happened last night. Right out back. That's why I'm here."

"Oh," Moe said, too confused to think clearly.

"Now, Mr. Rosen, what was that you said about witnesses?"

"Witnesses?"

"To the mugging. Tuesday morning?"

"I didn't—I don't know," Moe mumbled, rubbing his hands together. His underarms were damp. Beck was a German name. A Dumpster? Right next door? That meant—

"Witnesses," Beck prompted.

"Black people." Moe was trying to think and talk at the same time. "A few black people came along, helped me up, dusted me off. Nice people."

"Can you describe them?"

"Black. With accents."

"But you never reported this mugging. Why not?"

"The others—"

The bell rang. A young man in a leather Chicago Bulls jacket. This was pure torture. Moe begged him to come back later. Was that seven or eight? My God, he'd lost count!

"You were about to explain something to me," Beck reminded him.

"No, I wasn't." Moe stood up. "Listen, this fellow in the picture knocked me down," he said, stalking about the small office. "I was groggy. Out on my feet. People helped me. Men and women both. I couldn't even tell you how many. All I know is they were black. With all the different shades these days, I could even be wrong about that."

"This is a murder investigation, Mr. Rosen. You don't seem to be taking this man's death very seriously."

"Here," Moe said, hurrying to the desk. "Please, take your pictures. I'm sorry the man is dead. I didn't know him. We wrestled once, that's all. Now, Detective, if you will please excuse me . . ."

"I only have one more thing."

Moe forced himself to stand still. "Okay."

"What do you know about Sirene Arcenciel?"

"Nothing. Never heard of it," Moe declared firmly. He strode to the office door and opened it.

"*It* is a woman." Beck was still planted in his chair. "Sigh-reen Ar-ken-seal. Are you telling me you don't know the woman who owns the restaurant next door?"

"Miz Ark?"

"That's what she calls herself?"

"I don't know. That's what people call her: Miz Ark. That's all I know. A very nice lady."

"Meaning?"

"Meaning," Moe growled, "that she seems to be a good, hardworking citizen. Look, we're neighbors. That's all. We don't see each other socially. I've never even eaten in there. Why are you asking? Is she a suspect?"

"Here's my card. I can see you're a little uptight, Mr. Rosen. Violent death can do that to a person." Beck stood. "I'll give you a call. We'll set up a time that's more convenient. How does that sound?"

"Come, let me walk you to the door."

Beck snaked his way down the aisle, perusing the showcases on both sides. "You sell any good watches?"

"Not today," Moe said, holding the door for him.

FIVE

Fabrice kept running until he reached the top of the final rise. With his heart thumping like an angry petro drum, he looked out past the blue-green shallows of the cove to the dark, unbroken surface of the open sea. The wind kicked up. Closing his eyes and breathing in the cool salt air, he spread his arms like a great seabird and let his imagination lift him high into the sky and carry him out beyond the curved edge of the sea, all the way to America.

But when he opened his eyes again, the sight of Agwe's restless waters filled him with dread. He looked down and saw giant white blossoms dotting the hillside. The parish women, their white skirts billowing in the wind like sails, were busy gathering flowers for the coming festival. Fabrice wondered if his lovely Antoinette was among them. He pictured the wind lifting her white skirt and tickling her firm, dark legs and he became jealous. Then he remembered that he had not been to see Antoinette even once since . . . since . . .

He forced his eyes away from the women and down to the water's edge. Two long ropes led from the tangled roots of a mangrove and disappeared beneath a thick canopy of sea grapes. Between the rustling branches Fabrice caught glimpses of pink flowers and logs of green bamboo.

The presence of the ceremonial raft, the sight of the parish women, the bittersweet odor of the sea—all combined to soothe Fabrice's troubled spirit. He began picking his way down the steep hill, scouring the ground for a suitable offering.

"Good day, Fabrice."

The familiar voice set his ears tingling.

"Good day, Antoinette."

She was standing a little above him and off to one side. The stiff wind was ruffling her hair and pressing her white dress against her small, high breasts. Her pose fit the picture of her he carried in his mind: her hands clasped behind her back, one sandaled foot turned outward, her big eyes and sweet shy face. Everything was the same; her presence still made him feel strong and clean.

"Have you nothing to say to me?" she asked, staring down at her feet.

"It is good that you are here," he said, unable to think of anything better.

She nudged a stone with her foot and sent it down the hill past him. Her skin was so smooth it pained him to look at it. He wanted to say something clever, but the same foolish word kept spinning in his head: *beautiful, beautiful, beautiful*.

"Yesterday," she said, "was my birthday."

"I did not know," he apologized.

"How could you know?" she asked, her head still down. "You never come to visit anymore."

"Twah," a woman called out to Antoinette from a nearby rise, "let the boy work!"

Fabrice was tempted to hurl a stone at the woman, but he lowered his voice instead. "And how many years did you make?"

"You should know," she murmured, rubbing the ground with the sole of her sandal. "Seventeen."

A sudden gust sent her skirt fluttering. Her hands appeared and began pulling at her dress, but the determined wind kept pressing it back against her soft, round belly. Without thinking, Fabrice reached into the pocket of his jeans and took out the crumpled bill meant for Agwe.

"Here," he said, smoothing the bill against his thigh. "For your birthday."

Her hands retreated behind her back. "What is it?" she asked, staring at the ground.

"This is from America." He clambered up to her and held the prized possession with both hands so it would not blow away. "Look."

But Antoinette would not look.

"It has pictures."

"Pictures?" She inched closer, bringing with her an aroma like the sea.

"Look, this is the president."

She bent, studied the portrait, frowned. "Why is he so old?"

"He was America's first president. During the time of Toussaint-Louverture," he added, repeating the rest of what Madame had told him.

"Why is there only one number? One, one, one, one, one."

"Because America is number one. Number one country."

Her voiced dropped. "And will you really be going there one day?"

"Of course."

She stole a peek at him. Then, embarrassed, she asked to see the bill's other side.

Fabrice turned it over. "See the war bird. See the arrows and the poison leaves."

"Yes, I see the bird. But what is that? The triangle with the big eye."

"That, uh, that—you see the bricks?—well, that is the tomb for the American presidents who have died."

She bent closer, intrigued. "And the eye?"

"To remind the people that the l'wah presidents inside the tomb are always watching them. They look out and see everything. Everything."

"I understand," Antoinette said, nodding her head respectfully.

The slanting light filled the shallow scar on her cheek, making it look as smooth as the sea. Fabrice fought back the urge to run his finger along it.

"Thank you for teaching me all this," Antoinette said, stepping away.

"Here." He carefully took her wrist and pressed the bill into her palm.

"You will need it when you go to America," she protested.

But she did not pull her hand away.

Gently, he bent her fingers around the bill. "Happy birthday, beautiful one," he whispered.

She withdrew her hand, folded the bill carefully, reached down the front of her dress, and tucked it into her bra.

"We must work," Fabrice declared. "Agwe will be angry if we fail to honor him properly."

"You are right," she agreed, checking the buttons down the front of her dress. "Oh, do you remember my house?"

"Of course."

She paused to adjust a button, then said, "My bed is still by the window that faces the sea."

"Yes. And?" he asked impatiently.

"Nothing." She shrugged.

She looked away and started twisting her shoulders. No man could understand a woman. Fabrice had work to do. He turned to go.

"Fabrice?"

He turned back. "Yes?"

She was looking at him with funny eyes. "Fabrice, will you really go to America one day? Truly?"

"Yes. I will go."

The sun, directly behind her, was shooting sparkles through her hair. When she lowered her eyes, the sunlight became a crown, like the pictures of Catholic saints.

"When you go to America," she whispered, "will you take me with you?"

Fabrice felt shafts of light coming off her face and piercing his heart. "If you wish."

She uttered a strange little squeak and hurried off. Fabrice shook his head and began searching the hillside for an offering. Now, without the American money to accompany it, it would have to be something very special. He tried not to think about Antoinette or America or—

An unusual plant caught his eye. Its twin white blossoms were so large that they bent the stem. As Fabrice reached for them, he thought of Madame Jouvier, how she had insulted him today.

He grasped the thick stem and ripped the plant from the soil. Then, angered by the clumps of earth clinging to its exposed roots, he shook the plant furiously, sending dirt and pebbles flying everywhere. Some of the debris struck a little girl gathering flowers nearby.

"Ma-mee!" the child cried, rubbing her tiny fists against her eyes. A moment later she began to wail.

The child's mother hurried over, pausing only long enough to shoot Fabrice an accusing look. He smiled meekly and held up the plant to show that it had been an accident. But the mother's scowl did not soften until she had satisfied herself that there was no serious injury to her child.

Fabrice slouched off down the hill with his limp offering. Shaking it had damaged its petals. He remembered the insulting words of Madame Jouvier. *Surprise,* he thought darkly, feeling the anger rising inside him like hot smoke.

Clutching the plant's stem as if it were a throat, he slid down the final embankment and followed the ropes across a narrow strip of muddy ground. Then, anxious to avoid the water, he jumped directly onto the gently bobbing raft. The fragile craft lurched sharply. Fabrice, waving his arms to keep from falling, heard the slurping of the bamboo logs.

"Have you gone mad?" Marie-Josée cried from the raft's far side.

Fabrice hopped off into the shallow water and grasped the raft's edge to slow its rocking. Discarding the ruined plant, he filled his hand with water and set about wiping his muddy footprints from the bamboo deck.

"What is wrong with you, boy?" Marie-Josée demanded, steadying herself against the mast while she fussed with her white dress. As the parish *la place,* Marie-Josée was responsible for the raft.

Fabrice mumbled an apology and sloshed off through ankle-deep water. He had cut his feet running here through the brambles, and now the salt water burned like the stingers of a jellyfish. Gritting his teeth against the pain, he trudged on through the water, telling himself that he deserved much worse.

—⌁—

"*Surprise,*" Madame Jouvier had whispered to him as they lay side by side in her bed. "That will be our secret word." She reached up and began lazily tracing the outlines of his face. "If I sense danger while we are together, I will say *surprise,* and then you must go quickly and open the trapdoor and hide in the cistern."

Fabrice could not believe his ears. *Surprise?* Hide in the cistern beneath the house? Like a water bug? Or a scorpion? Or a rat?

And then, after speaking to him like that—as if he were some shoe-less child by the roadside—after telling him that he must behave like a rat, she had reached down between his legs and grasped his slack member. "Come on, now," she teased, playing with it as if it were her little pet. He ordered it not to respond, but it stood up for her like an eager puppy. He watched Madame's eyes as Erzulie regained posses-sion of her and had her climb up on top of him. Then Erzulie began speaking in her own deep voice while grinding Madame's sex against him, telling him what she wanted him to do to please her. He did as instructed, but because he was still angry at Madame, he was not able to finish. Erzulie thrashed and gasped, ordering him to do everything harder and still harder, until Madame finally collapsed in a wet heap against his chest.

"One more thing about *surprise,*" Madame Jouvier had said a few minutes later, resuming her conversation as if Erzulie had never inter-rupted it. "If it ever happens that you must hide in the cistern, Fabrice, remember that this house is built on the foundation of an old plantation house. The cistern is full of nooks and crannies you can crawl into and—"

That was her word: *crawl. Crawl!* Like a whimpering puppy dragging its belly. Like a slave. And he had listened to her words and said nothing. Nothing . . .

—*∽*—

Fabrice looked around in confusion. When the world came back into focus, he saw that the sun had become a giant red disk hanging above the horizon. A wide trail of blood stretched out over the sea. The sight made him shiver.

With growing desperation, Fabrice began searching for a suitable offering. He scolded himself for having neglected his duties. For weeks now the people of his parish had been coming to this isolated spot to help prepare for tomorrow's festival. Carpenters had shaped the best bamboo logs. People trained in the art of tying had assembled the logs into a raft. A low, sturdy railing had been built around the deck to prevent any of the precious cargo from falling overboard before reaching its destination. While the raft had been under construction, other parishioners had been hard at work preparing Agwe's favorite foodstuffs, wrapping cakes and cookies in fancy papers and filling brightly painted bottles with his preferred liquors. There was even a bottle of his favorite, champagne. Still others had begun collecting flowers in Agwe's colors of pink and white and weaving them into garlands.

At dawn Saturday all the faithful would gather here for the ceremony. They would fill the raft with the last of the gifts and flowers. Then they would join hands around it and wade out into the shallows, singing Agwe's praises and asking for his blessing for the coming year. Still singing, they would guide the raft into deeper waters and tie it to a boat manned by the best sailors in the parish. When the boat was far out at sea, and the captain was sure that the tide and the current were right, he would release the raft to continue on its own out to Agwe's home in the deepest part of the deep waters, the Island Beneath the Sea. Once it arrived there, the cleverly tied knots would unravel, the raft would come apart, and the offerings of the parish would sink down to the souls of their ancestors who dwelt with Agwe at the bottom of the sea.

Fabrice looked around. It was getting late. The white dresses spotting the hillside were bathed in a golden glow. Knowing that Antoinette was one of them helped bring Fabrice back to himself and remind him that this was his place, that these were his people. He sensed their quiet joy in working for the good of the whole parish. If they succeeded, the Lord of the Seas would bless them with calm days and full nets. But if their efforts displeased him, Agwe's wrath could be terrible. He could order his creatures to avoid all nets, all traps, all hooks. Worse, he could allow them to be caught but fill their flesh with poison. Worse still, with an angry shrug he could stir his waters and suck bathers to watery deaths, destroy the strongest boats, or send waves crashing so far up the shore that even Azaka's crops would be washed away. Worst of all, he could join with the rain-making Marassa and send a storm powerful enough to destroy whole villages as easily as a machete cut dry grass.

In the end, of course, Agwe, like all great l'wahs, would do as he pleased. Fabrice understood that. But all spirits could be influenced, even one against the other. That is why every parish had its houngans and mambos and *la places* and the rest—to intercede with the gods for people like Antoinette Voisin and Fabrice Lacroix. Through offerings and ceremonies, things could be changed for the better. All l'wahs demanded food and drink, respect and devotion. The spirits were always present, always watching, though their intentions often remained a mystery. Why, for instance, had Erzulie chosen to come to Fabrice in the body of Madame Jouvier? Was her choice of him a gift or a curse?

Fabrice gazed out across the darkening sea. He was running out of time. He had to find the loveliest plant, the best possible offering to Agwe. Fabrice understood that he bore a special responsibility for the success of tomorrow's festival; even children knew that Erzulie was Agwe's mistress.

Suddenly Fabrice began to tremble. He retreated from the water's edge and hugged himself against a chill that seemed to be coming at him from deep beneath the sea. Perhaps Agwe was showing his famous jealousy. Even the wind was becoming angry. Fabrice shut his eyes against the harsh, stinging spray. Alone with the darkness, his deepest fears rose up and coated him with a cold, clammy sweat.

SIX

Moe was preparing to close when the bell rang yet again. He looked out, saw a young black woman, and buzzed her in. While waiting for the outside door to lock so he could buzz her into the store itself, he did his usual quick scan and guessed that she was here for a pair of those hideous, ultralight, doughnut-sized earrings. No matter, he would treat her like the Queen of Sheba.

He hurriedly ran a comb through his hair. What a day this had been! And yesterday! This whole week! The sudden upswing didn't make any sense, but Moe wasn't about to question it. The store hadn't seen this much action since the crazy days of '80–81 when he and his mother were working like demons out front while his father manned the office: approving discounts, calling for authorizations, handling the cash. Those were the days when inflation was roaring, the prime rate was soaring, and the gold price was clawing toward $800 an ounce. Those were the days, all right, he reflected. He had been in his early twenties then, and wearing his hair nearly as long as this new customer's. He looked again. Well, maybe not *that* long.

She appeared nervous at Moe's approach so he tempered his exuberance, tepeed his hands at his chest, and bowed slightly, presenting her with a totally nonthreatening welcome.

Her eyes paused at Moe for only a moment before continuing to flit about the store. She was high-waisted and stocky—kind of barrel-shaped—with a dark, round, pleasant face. Her neat white uniform indicated either the medical, nail-care, or housekeeping profession. Her hairstyle appeared to be the result of some horribly misguided experiment, its many tightly wound, asymmetrically swirling coils suggesting a roller coaster that had been firebombed.

She caught him staring.

"Forgive me," he said, "I was just admiring your hair. Did you"—he gave a flourish with his hand—"all by yourself?"

"A fren do it," she replied shyly, reflexively reaching up and patting it. "You likes it?"

"Extremely unusual. It, uh, frames your face in a most, uh, unique manner."

She peered at him. "You tink so?"

"Absolutely," Moe assured her, surprised by her interest in his opinion. "Those little white things woven in among the braids, are those cowries?"

"No. They some kinda shells."

"Oh, I see. Very, uh, nautical, if I may say so. Now, is there something in particular I can help you with this afternoon?"

"I aine shoo." Her eyes wandered again. "Is dis de place fuh de wanga dem?"

He inclined his head. "Ma'am?"

"You de boss, in't it?"

"Yes, I'm the owner."

"You de rose man?"

"The . . . ? Rosen. Yes. Rosen, that's my name."

"The same one what save Miz Ark?"

"The same one . . . ? Ah," Moe exclaimed, flattered and flustered at the same time. "Well, *saved* is a bit . . . Well, I suppose I did, yes, you might say, it's nice if people choose to . . . I'm sorry, what was it you were looking for?"

"I lookin' a wanga. I tole you dat."

"Yes. Yes, you did. But . . . ?"

"Lossa my frens get wangas here. Righ from you. You de rose man."

"Yes. Of course. The rose man. A wanga. Of course."

He stepped back and cleared his throat. As usual, his comprehension was lagging behind his translation. A wanga had to be a good-luck charm. Now why—

A wild surmise, like a blinding flash, sent Moe's mind reeling: all of this, all this business, all these sales, this sudden surge, all of it because—

How stupid he'd been!

"Pardon me," he said, trying to force his mind back to his customer, "what sort of, uh, wanga did you have in mind?"

"I was tinkin' a bracelet." She reached up and brushed shells from her eyes.

"And for this bracelet," Moe inquired, struggling to stay focused, "were you thinking of gold or silver?"

"Gole," she declared firmly.

"This way, if you please," he said, inviting her to walk ahead.

The view from the back was astounding. Her large, high rump moved independently, almost like a beach ball loosely glued to the small of her back. Its bouncing motion cleared his head. Everything suddenly made sense. Now he understood why all his customers these days were so insistent that he fasten their chains for them, that he put on their bracelets for them, that he— Fool that he was, he had flattered himself into believing that it was some newfound sexual magnetism that was making all these dark-skinned women crave his pink-fingered touch.

He hurried around and jerked open the balky old showcase, making the jewelry jiggle and all the hands shake. For a moment he had the odd sensation that they were laughing at him.

He chose half a dozen bracelets and laid them out on a velvet pillow on top of the glass.

The young woman pursed her lips and came closer. As she bent, her shells made a dull clacking sound, like a dysfunctional wind chime. "Wish one you likes bess?"

He pointed to the one with alternating matte and polished links: medium-priced and only slightly gaudy. She offered her wrist—an unexpectedly dainty gesture—and he draped it carefully and secured the clasp. His hands were moving deliberately now, but his mind was still racing. His newfound knowledge was making him positively giddy. If anything bought from his store was a wanga, he reasoned, then it was probably fair to say that he, Moe Rosen, was also a wanga. He found the idea irresistible. He envisioned himself at a class reunion. "What are you doing these days?" a friend would ask. "Oh," Moe would say shrugging, "same old, same old. Still a wanga." He could open a burger franchise: MacRosen's, Home of the Wanga. It was crazy. It was nuts. He loved it.

When the woman paid cash for the bracelet, Moe surprised them both by offering her a free pair of hammered 14k earrings. She insisted that he put them on for her. Perhaps it was the white uniform, but as he reached out to her, he imagined himself transformed into Ben Casey, the TV surgeon he'd idolized as a kid. Yes, he thought, confidently grasping a fleshy lobe: the heart of a lion, the eye of an eagle, the hands of a wanga.

SEVEN

The corporal sprang to his feet and delivered his salute with such fervor that his hand trembled. Colonel Ferray smelled his fear from across the room.

"What's wrong?" Ferray demanded. "Has there been a message from the captain?"

"Uh, yes, sir," the soldier stammered. "He telephoned ten minutes ago, sir."

"Well? Where is it?"

As the terrified soldier fumbled with the desk drawer, the colonel tapped his foot and tried to mask his anxiety with a scowl. What could have gone wrong in Miami? Diplomatic pouches were exempt from customs inspection. The trip should have been routine. Unless . . .

Ferray reached out and snatched the paper from the corporal's shaking hand.

Delivery completed without incident, the message began. The colonel felt the muscles in his lower back relax. *Return delayed. Problem in New York. Sister sends regards. Will advise. Ghede.*

"This is all of it?" Ferray asked.

"Yes, sir. Every word exactly, sir."

But the corporal continued to stare fixedly past the colonel's shoulder. There was something else.

"Out with it," Ferray growled.

"Sir," the soldier began, but his voice broke and he stopped to clear his throat. "Sir, there is someone in your office, sir."

A heavy throbbing began above the colonel's eyes. His voice shrank to a whisper: "What did you say?"

"There is a man in your office, sir. He—"

"And you were here at your post?" Ferray was incredulous. "You allowed this?"

"Sir, I told him, sir, that no one—"

But Ferray was already striding toward his office door, unsnapping his sidearm.

"Sir," the corporal cried. "He's a *blanc!* An American!"

The colonel stopped. His posture changed. He replaced his weapon, then took a moment to smooth his uniform.

When Ferray entered the office, the slim, blue-suited stranger lounging in the visitor's chair turned his blond head and said, "Howdy." He had a toothpick in his mouth.

"Please remove your briefcase from my desk," Ferray said mildly as he walked around to his leather chair.

The man took more time than the task required. "Colonel Ferray, I presume," he said with a cocky grin, adjusting his jacket but not bothering to stand.

The colonel did not respond. Instead, he pulled out his chair, sat down, rolled himself up to the desk, centered his clasped hands on the leather-trimmed blotter, and asked, "Who are you?"

"Bob Townley." The man popped up and thrust his hand across the polished surface. "Surprised?"

Ferray's hands remained clasped. Though he and Townley had spoken on the phone at least a dozen times, they had never met. Townley worked out of the U.S. embassy in the capital, ostensibly as a cultural attaché.

"What are you doing in my office?" the colonel asked, his eyes fixed on the ugly scuff marks left by the man's briefcase.

"Site visit." Townley smoothed his tie. His shirt collar was open. "Just checking to see how our money is being spent out here in the boonies."

Ferray made eye contact for the first time. "You presume too much, Mr. Townley," he said evenly.

"We have another assignment for you," Townley continued, undeterred. "I decided to deliver it personally." He removed a folded paper from his inside jacket pocket and held it out to the colonel.

Ferray's hands remained clasped on the desk. "You have made a series of grave errors, Mr. Townley."

"So educate me." Townley dropped the paper on the desk and sat back down. The toothpick migrated to the other side of his mouth. He reached up and chased a mosquito from his ear.

"Please show me your identification."

The American sighed theatrically, took out a plastic case, and offered it across the desk. The colonel took it, flipped it open, studied the elaborate photo ID, handed it back.

"Three things," Ferray said. "Please listen carefully. First, no one may enter this office without my permission. Second, this desk which you mistook for a luggage rack is my personal property. Finally, and most important, Mr. Townley, neither I nor anyone in my command takes assignments from you, your agency, or any branch of your government." Ferray leaned back in his chair, pulling his clasped hands onto his taut stomach. "Now, is there anything I said that you did not understand?"

Staring directly into Townley's eyes, savoring the man's indecision, the colonel realized that he had never killed an American CIA agent. He found the prospect appealing.

Suddenly Townley's face broke into a childish grin and he raised his hands in mock surrender. Then he stood, pulled out his handkerchief, and carefully buffed the scuff marks from the desk.

"Okay, Colonel," Townley said amiably, returning the handkerchief to his pocket, "how's about we start all over?"

When Ferray nodded his assent, the American loped across the room to the door. His back was turned but the colonel could see that his arms were moving. A faint smell of tangy aftershave hung in the air.

There was a knock on the door.

"Yes?" Ferray said.

The tall American spun around. His collar was buttoned. His jacket was closed. He approached the desk and offered his identification. The colonel took it, examined it, returned it.

"Robert Townley, Colonel. It's a pleasure to meet you."

The hand Townley put out reminded the colonel of an albino starfish, but Ferray rose and shook it. The American's expression was respectful. The toothpick was gone.

"Won't you sit down, Mr. Townley." Ferray made a point of glancing at the paper still lying on his desk.

"Thank you, Colonel." As Townley moved to sit, he retrieved the folded paper and slipped it into his pocket.

"Now, what can I do for you, Mr. Townley?"

"Bob, Colonel. Please."

"What can I do for you, Bob?"

"This is simply a courtesy call, Colonel Ferray. I'm on a cultural tour of the district. After our many pleasant telephone conversations, I was anxious for us to finally meet face to face."

"I am always pleased to meet a representative of your government." Ferray reached into his desk and came up with a box of cigars.

"Jamaican?" Townley asked pleasantly, leaning forward for a better look.

"Cuban." The colonel lifted the lid. "If you don't care to smoke now, take one for later. And please, Bob, call me Hugo."

"Thank you, Hugo." Townley selected a cigar, passed it beneath his nose, and nodded appreciatively before slipping it into his breast pocket. "For later."

Ferray put away the box. "Tell me, Bob, is there some way I can be of service during your visit?"

"Well, as I'm sure you are aware, Hugo, your nation and mine share a long tradition of friendship."

"Oh, yes," Ferray readily agreed, recalling that this "long tradition of friendship" included the unprovoked 1915 American invasion that had ushered in two decades of brutal U.S. military rule.

". . . and if there is anything you need," Townley was saying, brushing away a mosquito, "some computer equipment, say, or anything, really, that would help you do your job better, well, I stand ready to facilitate."

"At the moment, Bob, we have everything we require. But I very much appreciate the offer."

"And we appreciate your efforts here, Hugo. We applaud your commitment to restoring freedom and democracy to your proud nation."

"I am a simple solider," Ferray declared, displaying open, empty hands.

He recognized his own smile on Townley's face. Together they had successfully completed the diplomatic charade. Now perhaps they could be—well, not quite friends, to be sure, but something.

Townley reached up and slapped himself on the neck. "Christ. These damned mosquitoes!"

"Fresh meat," the colonel remarked with a wry smile. "Speaking of which, have you had the chance to sample any of our local delicacies?"

"You mean the local food, Hugo?"

"I mean the local women, Bob."

"Oh." Townley was caught off guard. "Actually, no, I haven't." He cleared his throat, sat up straighter.

Smiling, Ferray reached out, pressed his intercom, and asked for the lieutenant. The lieutenant would see to it that the American was kept happy. Townley would return to the capital and route the identity of his agency's new target through Ferray's superiors. The mission would be carried out. Ferray would obtain the use of another diplomatic pouch. Captain Ghede would take another trip to Florida. The intricate *pas de deux* between their two nations—the richest and the poorest in the hemisphere—would continue: another cycle in their long tradition of friendship . . .

"Hugo," the American asked, interrupting Ferray's reverie, "why are you moving your finger like that?"

Ferray looked down. His index finger was absently tracing little circles in the air, as if spinning a miniature lasso.

"This," the colonel explained, glancing about, dropping his voice, "this is a little Voodoo trick we natives use to keep away mosquitoes."

"Does it work?" Townley tried it himself.

"Who can say?" The colonel shrugged, amused by the sight of their synchronized fingers, one white, one black, making meaningless rotations.

EIGHT

Moe had planned on switching to a local at Times Square, but as the train clattered out onto the Manhattan Bridge, he saw the sunlight glinting on the water and decided that a walk would do him good. It was Sunday. It was summer. He was feeling reckless.

When he turned onto Forty-seventh Street, Moe experienced a rush. It wasn't only being caught up in the bustling jewelry-district crowd and its strange goulash of languages; it was a sense of his own destiny. Things had changed. Business at the store was booming. Moe Rosen had become a player.

The office building still had the WHOLESALE ONLY sign Moe remembered from years ago. He went in and laid his briefcase on the conveyor belt, nodded to the two uniformed guards, emptied his pockets into a plastic tray, and passed through the metal detector. Glancing around the shabby lobby, he recalled walking with his father to that same bank of elevators.

At the reception desk a rumpled young man with a denim shirt, black beard, and bobby-pinned yarmulke sat listening to a Walkman. At Moe's approach, he removed his earphones and looked up.

"Fum?" he demanded, his dark eyes brimming with suspicion.

"Excuse me?"

"You dunt spik English?" The accent was Russian, the tone snide. "For who are you here? Which fum?"

"Oh. F and S. Fishbein and Slovitch."

"You haff appointment?"

"Yes, I have appointment."

He gave Moe a long, dubious look. "Giff me name."

"Moe Rosen."

"Giff me photo ID." He thrust out an arm. He was wearing an Olympic Swatch, the one commemorating the 1980 Moscow games.

After checking Moe's license, the Russian picked up a phone, pressed buttons, mumbled something in Yiddish, listened, hung up.

"You muss vait." He pointed. "Dare."

"Dare" was a backless aluminum bench whose faded plastic cushion had a long, ugly gash. Moe sat carefully, resting his briefcase on the floor between his freshly shined shoes. He was angry, but mostly at himself. Two days ago he had called F&S and asked them to send a salesman to

the store. The woman—after keeping him on hold for what seemed forever—informed him that no salesman was available, that if he wanted to
see the line, he would have to come to the showroom, and that Sunday at
two was available. Dangerously short of merchandise, Moe had ignored
the insult and taken the appointment. Now here he was, waiting downstairs on a torn bench like some delivery boy. It served him right.

The minutes dragged. While Moe read and reread the building direc-
tory, a steady stream of people came in and presented themselves at the
desk. The Bolshevik bastard sent every one of them directly to the elevator. Moe began to seethe. Who the hell did F&S think it was? Fishbein and Slovitch was not exactly Van Cleef & Arpels. Moe recalled
how Piaget's top salesman used to visit the store, hat in hand; how he
would enter the office, set down his display case, and open it slowly and
reverently, like a Fabergé egg.

A fat Hasid with a thick white beard, a long black coat, and a ratty fur
hat swept in, announced in Yiddish that he was here to see F&S, and was
waved right through. Moe looked down at his own pressed gray suit, his
crisp white shirt, his conservative blue silk tie. For what? he asked himself. To sit here on slashed plastic and stare at foam-rubber stuffing?

Fifteen minutes later the cossack at the desk got Moe's attention by
snapping his fingers and jerking his thumb toward the bank of elevators
behind him. Moe bit his lip and walked past him in silent fury.

Most of the glass-doored cubicles that lined the F&S showroom were
occupied. Moe approached the counter and introduced himself. "Moe
Rosen," the clerk called out over his shoulder, and immediately
returned to his computer terminal.

No one reacted. Moe waited. Seconds dripped like saline from an IV.

Finally, a cadaverous old man shuffled up to the counter and
squinted dubiously at Moe. "Eli Rosen's son?"

"Hello, Mr. Slovitch."

The old man cocked his head, stared harder. He looked like the
ghost of Christmas past. "You're really Eli's son?"

Moe smiled, trying to look son-like.

"You had a name," Mr. Slovitch said, rubbing a sunken cheek.

Moe gave him a few seconds, then told him.

"That's it." The old man pointed a bony finger, revealing an ancient Bulova on an alligator strap. "Eli Rosen's son," he mused, shaking his head in wonder. "Come closer, I'll give you a little advice."

Moe bent to listen. The old man's skin was thin and waxy. He smelled of fish.

"Don't get old," Mr. Slovitch whispered, reaching out and squeezing Moe's shoulder with surprising force. "You speak Yiddish?"

"No," Moe lied.

"Not even to understand?"

Moe shrugged apologetically. "Sorry."

"Shlomo!"

A kid in his twenties rushed up.

"Eli Rosen and Son, from Brooklyn," the old man said. "Take good care of him."

"Shlomo Karp," the youngster said, reaching across the counter. Shlomo's hand was damp. His "Rolex" was a cheap Hong Kong knock-off. His tie was stained. "I'm from Israel."

"That neighborhood of yours," Mr. Slovitch remarked to Moe, "I remember it when."

"Me too," Moe said.

The old man sighed. "Now it's all *shvartzers,* am I right?"

Moe forced a smile. The word simply meant "blacks," but the connotation was "trash."

"And they buy gold, these *shvartzers?*" Mr. Slovitch asked.

Someone called out. The old man was needed elsewhere.

"So I'll leave you two youngsters." Mr. Slovitch patted Shlomo's shoulder and murmured to him in Yiddish, "Try to move some of that domestic junk." Mr. Slovitch smiled at Moe and began backing away. "Your father," he said, receding slowly, "I bought a Piaget from him once. For the wife, when she was alive." He waved. "Listen," he called to Shlomo in Yiddish, "be sure to see me about credit before he leaves."

"A glass of tea for Mr. Rosen?" Shlomo offered as Moe squeezed himself into the tiny cubicle. "A bagel? Maybe a Danish?"

Shlomo's curly hair and forced earnestness reminded Moe of a young Richard Dreyfuss.

"Coffee," Moe said. "Milk, no sugar."

"Milk I can't do. Is the powder all right?"

"Forget the coffee." Moe tried to work his briefcase into the sliver of space between his shoe and the wall. "There's no room anyhow. Let's get right to work."

Shlomo beamed. "What would Mr. Rosen like to see first?"

"Chain. Solid fourteen-k Italian."

"Styles? Gauges?"

"All of them. Dazzle me."

Alone in the tiny cubicle, Moe was seized by a thrilling idea: he would hire a salesman for the store. Yes! A salesman was a great idea! The first step in developing a staff. Except that salesmen were expensive.

The Israeli returned with a scroll of gray fabric that he unrolled across the brown Formica tabletop. Chains of various lengths and styles gleamed against the drab background. Moe unsnapped a box chain and hefted it in his palm. It felt a little off. He took out his 10x loupe and examined the manufacturer's stamp.

"You see," Shlomo said with a nervous giggle, "fourteen-k, just like you asked."

"This is domestic." Moe relaxed his eye and let the loupe drop into his hand. "I asked for Italian."

"Yes, okay. But this line is on special, priced below the Italian goods. I thought—"

"This isn't plumb."

"Solid fourteen-k," Shlomo insisted, looking uncomfortable.

"Come on," Moe said irritably, "there's a difference of nearly three percent in gold content between U.S. and Italian chain."

"Yes, you and me, we know that," Shlomo agreed with a smirk. "But your *shvartzers,* they don't know from plumb, am I right?"

"You have Italian chain?"

"Of course. This is F and S. We have the finest—"

"Go get it."

When Shlomo left, Moe looked over into the spacious showroom across the way. Old Mr. Slovitch and the same overstuffed Hasid Moe had seen downstairs were sharing a laugh.

—*ᴏᴠᴏ*—

Moe's arms were tingling all the way up to the elbows. For him, there was no sensation quite like handling first-quality, solid-gold chain: feeling its weight, running his fingers over its magical surfaces, holding it up to the light and admiring its finish, testing the smooth interplay of its perfectly tooled links; enjoying that special buzz generated by nature's most beautiful, most sensuous metal sliding through his fingers: rubbing itself, cool and snakelike, against his skin.

His final selections were laid out on a black velvet pad: seventeen chains, ranging from a featherweight serpentine to a thick and crusty rope. There was a satisfying symmetry to the arrangement, an eye-pleasing progression that appeared logical, proper, inexorable.

"Quantities?" Shlomo asked hopefully, opening his order book and wiping his lip. The cubicle was hot.

Moe pointed to the first chain, the thin serpentine. "Seven-, eight-, fifteen-, sixteen-, and eighteen-inch. One gross each."

"I am thinking you mean dozen," Shlomo suggested helpfully.

Moe moved his finger to the second chain, a narrow herringbone. "Same lengths. Six dozen each."

"Dozen? Are you sure . . . ?"

But Moe was already pointing to the next chain in line and reciting lengths.

Shlomo, writing as fast as he could, had filled three pages by the time Moe was finished.

"Excuse me, Mr. Rosen," the salesman said, anxiously mopping his face, "do you know how much order you have made?"

"I hope you have everything in stock."

"A moment, please." Shlomo contorted himself past the table's sharp corner and into the hall.

A minute later Mr. Slovitch's skeletal head appeared in the doorway. "My dear Mr. Rosen," he crooned. "Would you come this way, please?"

As they crossed the office, they passed an open walk-in safe. The sight stopped Moe in his tracks. Suddenly weightless, he felt himself tumbling backward in time to when he was a little boy of four or five and accompanying his father on a trip to Europe. Moe still retained two images from that distant journey: looking out of the airplane and seeing clouds below him and, what had been even more incredible, standing alone in what he remembered as the Grotto of Gold: a huge room whose every inch was covered with luxuriant gold chain, its high walls an impenetrable jungle of gold, its vast ceiling hung so thick with chain that their number was past counting. He remembered standing there and turning slowly, as if in a dream, the room shimmering around him like petrified sunlight.

Mr. Slovitch's voice wrenched him from the grotto and returned him to the offices of Fishbein and Slovitch. Moe looked around, getting his bearings. The F&S safe was smaller. The Grotto of Gold had been huge. Huge. Ten times this size, at least. And there had been more gold, much more. Tons.

Moe followed the old man into the spacious showroom he'd glimpsed from his cubicle. The Hasid was gone. There was a heavy smell of roses. Someone had sprayed air freshener.

Moe dropped into an easy chair. The old man took the chair opposite. Shlomo closed the door and hurried over to stand behind his boss.

"Shlomo is new," Mr. Slovitch said to Moe. "You know how it is with new. Let's go over your order to make sure he wrote everything correct."

Shlomo located the first item and laid it on a burgundy velvet pillow. Mr. Slovitch recited lengths and quantities.

"I'm just checking here, Mr. Rosen, you'll forgive me," the old man said. "But when you say 'gross,' you're talking twelve dozen, am I right?"

"That's what my father taught me."

"I'm getting a little . . . ," Mr. Slovitch replied with a flutter of his hand and a self-deprecating chuckle. "Okay, fine," he said, making a check mark. "Now the next item." He turned his head. "Come on, Shlomo, Mr. Rosen is a busy man."

"Oh," Moe said, "that reminds me. When I called here the other day, I was told that no salesman could come to the store."

"Who told you such a thing?" the old man demanded, feigning shock. Shlomo laid out the next chain.

"Excuse me," Moe said to Mr. Slovitch, "I didn't mean to interrupt. You're a busy man."

"What busy?" the old man protested, spreading his arms wide. "For Eli Rosen's son I have all the time in the world." He smiled, but they weren't his teeth.

"Let's finish the order," Moe suggested.

—◦◦◦—

"Which brings us to the subject of terms," Mr. Slovitch said, checking off the final item.

"I'm glad you brought that up," Moe said. "Because when I was told that I would have to come up here to the showroom to place an order—"

The old man waved Moe into silence. "Let's not beat horses. I'll tell you the truth. It's not the store, it's the neighborhood: the *shvartzers.*"

He sighed. "Look at that terrible thing last week, right there by you." He shook his head. "To kill a man and toss his body out like so much garbage. One of their own, I know, but still, it could just as easily have been one of us. . . . To cut off a man's hands like that. And his . . ."

He leaned forward and clasped his hands between his legs. "The truth is, Mr. Rosen, I'm frightened to send my people into such an area. You can appreciate that, Mr. Rosen. I don't say it's right, but what can I do? My people have families. You know how things happen; some *shvartzer* gets all loaded up with drugs the way half of them are these days, he sees a nice boy like Shlomo here, an Israeli, walking along with his sample cases . . ."

"Terms," Moe reminded him.

"We'll need something down."

"Something."

"A deposit. Before we can release the goods,"

"I see," Moe said.

"Because this order—here, Shlomo, take this in and have Nusha run the numbers. For the gold price, tell her to use Friday's London P.M. fix." He turned back to Moe. "That price is based on you giving us a check this morning. Otherwise—"

"How much of a check?"

"Your line with us is for maximum twenty-five. That's what's on file with the *gonifs* at the bank. We're locked in to that number."

"So?"

"So we'll need the difference."

"The difference."

"Between the total order and the twenty-five. Don't carve me in stone here, but it looks like we're talking an order here of seventy-three to seventy-five."

"So you're going to need somewhere around fifty thousand."

"Give or take."

"Before you release the goods."

"I have no choice," the old man explained. "Those are the bank's rules. If it was up to me . . ."

"What's my discount?"

"Pardon me?"

"My discount. If I'm paying two thirds up-front I should get a discount."

The old man moistened his lips. "Look, you're a nice young man. If your check is certified, I could give, let's say, two percent. Is your check certified?"

"No."

"Well, then . . ."

"May I ask you a hypothetical question, Mr. Slovitch?" Moe moved to the edge of his seat.

"Please," the old man encouraged, sliding back in his.

"You call a company to send you a salesman," Moe began, as if recounting an anecdote. "They tell you no. They say you have to make an appointment to come to their showroom. Then—please, let me fin-ish—then, when you arrive for your appointment, they keep you wait-ing downstairs for half an hour. When you are finally allowed up, they assign you a junior salesman, stuff you into their smallest cubicle, and try to sell you their worst goods. They insult your clientele and then demand two thirds of the total order up-front. Mr. Slovitch, I ask you, would you do business with a company that treated you like that?"

The old man shifted in his chair. "Fishbein was always better with people," he sighed. "I was always the numbers man. But Fishbein died. Just like the wife. Just like your father. So we carry on as best we can. What else can we do?"

"We can treat people with respect."

"Sure, that would be lovely. In the meantime, we shouldn't cut off our nose to spite our face. No one does business with F and S because of our fancy offices or my wonderful way with people. We carry the best goods at the best prices. Period." Mr. Slovitch paused for a moment, thinking.

"I'll tell you what. Give me a check for one third. Pay me the balance in thirty days. I'll go fight with the bank."

"And?"

"Never bear grudges. You're a smart boy so I'll tell you something. If we Jews ever stopped to worry about what people said about us . . ." The old man shook his head and laughed soundlessly. "I'm happy to see that business is so good." He reached out and patted Moe's knee. "Your father must be pleased."

"And?"

The old man grimaced. "And go ahead," he sighed, "take the two percent. My grandchildren will have to go without heat this winter. We have a deal?"

"Okay." The discount would pay a month's salary for a new salesman at the store. But who could he get? A *shvartzer*, he thought with sudden, malicious glee. And he knew exactly who to ask.

NINE

"Fabrice."

"Yes, Madame. One moment, please, Madame."

Fabrice waited while Monsieur Jouvier returned the carving set to the platter. Then, taking care not to spill any juice, he lowered the roast to the dining table, tugged at his gloves, and went to answer the door.

Fabrice hated these white gloves. Madame insisted that he wear them when serving dinner, but they itched his skin and made everything slippery and—

The front door chimed again. Fabrice quickened his pace, happy to be standing straight after so much bending with plates of food. This inside work was all right, he supposed, but he much preferred the quiet of the garden. Especially these days, what with Madame and . . . everything.

He squared his shoulders and pulled open the door. "Good evening, sir," he said, bowing exactly as Madame had instructed him.

"Good evening," the soldier responded. "Are Monsieur and Madame Jouvier at home?"

"Yes, sir."

"Please inform them that a colonel of the Haitian army would like to speak with them."

"Yes, sir. One moment, sir." As he had been taught, Fabrice closed the door without engaging the lock, to keep out the insects but not offend the visitor.

He had done everything correctly, but as he walked to the dining room, Fabrice had a bad feeling in his belly. He told himself it was the pistol on the army man's belt, but more likely it was this stiff white jacket, the shiny gold buttons, these foolish gloves.

"Show him in," Monsieur Jouvier said.

"Yes, sir."

The colonel stepped through the doorway and removed his fancy cap. Fabrice had never seen such an impressive uniform. He led the way into the dining room and then went over and stood near the door to the kitchen.

Monsieur Jouvier rose and introduced himself and Madame. She apologized for the noise, explaining that the children were inside watching TV.

The soldier smiled. He was standing very straight. "Colonel Hugo Ferray," he said with a sharp click of his heels. "At your service."

The name echoed inside Fabrice's head. There was something about it he did not like. As if reading Fabrice's mind, the colonel glanced his way. Their eyes met for only the briefest of moments, but it was enough to send a chill through Fabrice's heart. While the Jouviers chatted with the colonel in French, the name kept buzzing about Fabrice's brain: Hugo Ferray, Hugo Ferray, Hugo Ferray . . .

The colonel was smiling politely at something Madame had said when suddenly Fabrice felt a terrible, heavy thing enter his body through the soles of his feet. He fought to steady himself as it worked its way up his legs, into his knees, his thighs, his loins, growing steadily as it climbed. He clenched his muscles as it clawed painfully past his stomach and continued upward, straining the bones in his chest and then trying to force its way into his throat. Fabrice was trembling from the effort to contain it. Drops of sweat began dripping from his forehead onto the starched white jacket.

The Jouviers, meanwhile, had invited the colonel to sit with them. They were now speaking in English. Madame Jouvier offered coffee. The soldier accepted. Fabrice watched all this as if in a dream. Then he saw that Madame was looking at him, saying something. The awful thing was clogging his throat. Hugo Ferry. Hugo Ferray. Hogoun Ferr—

A horrible knowledge struck Fabrice with the force of a club. This was no soldier!

He hurried over and bent close to Madame Jouvier. "Tell him to leave," he whispered urgently.

"Shhh," Madame responded without even turning her head. She wasn't paying attention.

A quick glance across the room confirmed Fabrice's worst fears. The so-called colonel was staring at him with eyes like bottomless pits.

Fabrice bent closer and tried again. "Madame, you are in danger," he insisted, his voice rising with his concern. "This—"

"Stop," Madame said, turning to face him. She seemed shocked by his appearance. "Go back to your place."

"But, Madame—"

"This instant," she said sharply.

Fabrice took a step back and nearly lost his balance. His head was pounding. The fear was choking him. He couldn't keep it down much longer.

"What is going on?" Monsieur Jouvier demanded irritably.

"Look there," Fabrice cried, jabbing his finger toward the cold, black eyes. "This l'wah brings death to your house, Monsieur. Make him leave! Now! Please!"

"Fabrice," Madame Jouvier scolded, "what has come over you?"

"Control yourself, boy," Monsieur warned him.

"I tell you," Fabrice said, speaking over the painful throbbing in his head. "Monsieur, Madame, make him to leave. You must do this! This is an evil l'wah, I swear you!"

"Fabrice," Madame soothed, reaching out to him as if he were a child.

Fabrice jumped back. "Here is Ogoun!" he yelled, hopping about in his desperation to make her understand. "Ogoun Ferraille! Look his eyes, Madame! He comes to kill!"

"Has this boy gone mad?" Monsieur Jouvier asked his wife. Then, turning to Fabrice: "Look here, boy, this gentleman is an army officer, not some foolish Voodoo spirit."

Fabrice's head was squeezed inside a pounding petro drum. He glanced over at Ogoun's cold, empty eyes and realized in a flash what he must do. Had he not saved Madame from the pool?

With a fierce cry, Fabrice lunged at the table and grasped the carving knife. His mind raced ahead and he saw himself raising his arm and plunging the long, sharp blade—

But no! It slipped! The knife slipped through his white-gloved fingers and clattered to the floor. Fabrice fell to his knees, crawling for it, tearing wildly at the gloves. He had to—

"Fabrice!"

Madame's harsh cry stopped him. The jangle of silverware rang in his ears. He looked up. She was standing by her chair, her face flushed, her chest heaving, her hand still trembling from striking the table. Fabrice looked around nervously. Ogoun had backed against the wall. He was watching Fabrice. His eyes were laughing. His hand was on his pistol. It was too late for the knife.

Fabrice peeled off the gloves and stared up pleadingly at Madame. The pounding in his head prevented him from speaking. Suddenly, as he watched, the whites of her eyes turned red. Red! A bright, fiery red!

Fabrice pressed his hands together. Sobs of joy came from his throat. They were saved! Erzulie-ge-rouge, Erzulie with the red eyes, the l'wah of love turned fierce warrior queen, had come to save him! He and Erzulie-ge-rouge would fight this Ogoun together!

"Fabrice," Erzulie-ge-rouge cried, the fury in her voice lifting him to his feet. "Listen to me!"

Her red eyes were glowing like embers. Fabrice was listening with all his being.

"Fabrice," she growled, "I am surprised at you."

"Surprise?" he stammered, unable to believe his ears.

"Yes, surprised. Now leave us," she commanded, pointing to the door.

"Yes, Maîtresse," he replied meekly, stunned by the l'wah's instruction. Obediently, he began backing toward the door.

His legs were numb, but somehow they kept moving. A few more steps and the hallway branched; to the right were the laundry room and servants' quarters, to the left the family's wing. Fabrice turned left, grasped a knob, slipped into Madame's bedroom, and closed the door behind him. The next room over was the children's. Their TV was on. Fabrice recognized the brassy music of *Hawaii Five-O*. It was dark in Madame's room. Fabrice stood still and looked around, waiting for the outline of familiar shapes to calm his racing heart. Yes, there was the chair, the dresser, the big bed, the—

A rustling of the curtains! Something was moving outside on the lawn! He tiptoed over to the window and squatted down, aligning his eyes with the bottom louver, the one that never opened. He held his breath and pressed his nose to the glass.

Soldiers! With rifles! Many of them, all moving quietly, surrounding the house! Fabrice's first impulse was to run back and warn Erzulie, but he caught himself. What was he thinking? Erzulie-ge-rouge had nothing to fear from soldiers. What could their guns do to a l'wah? Their bullets would pass right through her. They would shoot each other!

Filled with a wild new happiness, Fabrice hurried to the corner, squatted down, grasped the stone edges of the cistern cover, and dragged it aside. When he sat and draped his legs over the edge, his sneakers brushed the surface of the water. Keeping a firm, two-handed grip on the chalky edges of the stone floor, Fabrice lowered himself into the cistern. With his arms fully extended and his lower half swaying free in the cool water he released one hand and used it to maneuver the heavy cover back into place. It took a long time. His fingers were trembling from the strain, but he could not risk letting the cover make a loud crash. Ignoring the pain in his shoulder, he worked the stone square back and forth, back and forth, until the only thing keeping it from closing was his other hand. Then, with a deep breath and a quick prayer, he loosened his grip and let himself fall.

The cistern cover closed above him with a soft crunch. He swam in place, moving his arms and legs like a dog. A windlike sound frightened him until he realized it was his own breathing. He stretched out his legs but was unable to touch bottom. It was stuffy in here, and a little scary, like being in a dark cave. Something came up and brushed his chin and he spun away from it, making a splash. He found himself facing a faint square of light, which he knew had to be one of the ancient tunnels that now served as runoffs when there was too much rain.

Keeping his hands beneath the surface, Fabrice paddled toward the light. It occurred to him that since entering the cistern he had heard nothing at all from the house above. Perhaps Ogoun did not yet realize he was gone.

Fabrice's fingers struck a plaster wall. It was cold and slimy to the touch. He bicycled with his legs while he ran his hand up along it until, about two feet above the waterline, he felt the rough edge of the brick opening. Then, using all his strength, he squirmed and lifted and pulled and slithered until he managed to haul himself out of the water and into the narrow passage.

He lay there and tried to catch his breath. Behind him he could hear water dripping back into the cistern. He couldn't tell if his face was wet with cistern water or sweat. He did not like it in here at all. It was cramped, it smelled bad, and there were dead things, leaves and twigs and insects and sharp, curly things that felt like dried-up lizards.

Keeping his lips pressed together, he dragged himself along, making himself as narrow as possible but still scraping the dirty walls. It was too bad he had not listened to Monsieur and cleaned down here more often. He used one hand to clear cobwebs while praying that none of the things he was blindly pushing away with the other was an angry scorpion. Each time he moved, the gold buttons scraped on the uneven brick, making squeaks like a mouse. Something was telling him he must get out of here.

Fabrice made slow but steady progress. He knew that all these shafts opened on the side of the hill, and that they were covered with thick wire mesh to keep rats and other creatures from entering the cistern and fouling the water.

He reached the end and lay there sticky with filth, sucking in the fresh air, staring through the wire mesh at the night sky and considering his next move. One hard push would remove the mesh, but he would have to be careful about the noise. There were other problems. How many soldiers were out there? Were they all up by the house? Fabrice had seen guns. He was now quite a ways down the hill, it was true, and on the side of the house opposite the driveway. But would that be far enough to avoid being seen? The moon was only a thin slice tonight and Fabrice's skin was dark, but he would have to remove the white jacket. What a fool he was! He should have done that before climbing into the shaft. He turned on his side and undid the buttons. Then he reached back, grasped the collar, and worked it inch by inch up over his head. After slipping his arms free of the sleeves, he placed the crumpled jacket against the wire mesh. Holding both with the fingers of one hand, he gave a sharp push with the heel of the other and the mesh popped loose. As he had hoped, the jacket muffled the sound.

He stuffed the jacket under his belly and inched forward until his arms and shoulders were out into the cool night and he could reach down and rest the wire mesh on the ground.

His ears filled with sounds. Too frightened to proceed cautiously, he wriggled out, hugged the earth, held his breath, and listened.

Crickets. Wind. The faint noises of a car changing gears, driving off. But no voices, no sounds of battle. The car meant that Ogoun knew that he was gone and had sent someone out to look for him. It was all clear to Fabrice now: Ogoun had come to steal his soul, to turn him into a zombie, and Erzulie had come to help him escape.

Soft light from the house spilled past him down the hill, drawing a path across the open lawn to the safety of the thick bush. He squatted in that direction, tensed his muscles, and waited. Sharp currents of night air hardened his wet skin and set his teeth chattering. From somewhere close behind he heard what sounded like voices, then slow, heavy footsteps coming his way. He couldn't make up his mind whether to run or to hide. The footsteps came closer. There was a mechanical sound, like a rifle being readied to shoot. Fabrice cringed. He pressed his eyes closed and begged Erzulie to tell him what to do, to give him a sign.

A crash of crockery from the house sent him flying down the hill. Tripping, rolling, stumbling, clawing the earth like some mad beast, Fabrice somehow made it to the bushes and kept going. He tried to slow himself but his legs would not be checked. They wanted to run, run, run, to race the wind. Nothing could catch him now. Nothing! Ogoun would not get to steal his soul. It was all he could do to keep from screaming out with joy.

—◦◦◦—

Fabrice brought the heavy bottle to his lips and tried to take another drink. Some champagne went into his mouth, but most missed, dribbling down his chin and neck and into his T-shirt. He shook the bottle and discovered that it was less than half-full. He let his head fall back against the cool bamboo and tried not to think about being out here on the sea where there was nothing holding him up but water, deep deep water, water that was full of shark fish and snake fish and giant fish like the one that swallowed Noah.

Fabrice raised the bottle high up and tried to pour some champagne straight down into his mouth. But Agwe tricked him and shook the raft, and the champagne splashed his eyes and trickled into the sea. Fabrice lowered the bottle to the bamboo deck and began to cry. He fumbled his way up into a sitting position and hugged his knees. The raft was rocking. The air was cold. The breeze was stiff. His skin was crusty with salt. Everything was a blur. The raft was so far from shore that he could no longer distinguish the lights of the land from the stars in the sky. The sea was carrying him, but he had no idea how far he had come or how much farther it would be to the Island Beneath the Sea, the place Agwe and all the spirits of the dead called home, the place where the raft would come undone and everything on it would sink down through miles of water: the place where this life would end and the next one would begin.

A little champagne was left in the bottle and Fabrice drank it down. He was sorry he would never have the chance to take Antoinette to America. Perhaps someone else would take her. Thinking about Antoinette in someone else's arms made him start crying again. He tossed the empty bottle far into the air and heard it strike the water with a plop. He fell over on his side. The smooth bamboo felt cool against his cheek. He would sleep now. Perhaps he would awake at the bottom of the sea surrounded by all his ancestors. They would be surprised to see him. He wondered if they had taxis on the island of souls. If he was very good, perhaps Agwe would let him drive one. He would paint it himself. With all the beautiful colors. Then, when Antoinette arrived, he could drive her around, show her everything . . .

TEN

Tomás Cruz, standing on the bridge, felt *Esperanza* moving beneath
him like a good woman. The thick planks of her old wooden hull
creaked with the sweetness of a fine Cuban guitar. All around them the
swells were large but rounded, and the air had that gritty freshness that
always accompanied a stiff, intermittent breeze. A few scattered, puffy
white clouds hung from a sky of the purest blue. Crisp sunshine
caressed him like the warm hand of God.

A good day for fishing, Tomás thought, scanning the sea's surface for
telltale shadows. It was a pointless exercise: all the fishing gear was
back on shore, in the hut. Just as well, Tomás thought. As he often told
his mate Ernesto, fishing nowadays was only for the very rich and the
very young.

The very young. Tomás smiled. Today was Ernesto's twentieth birthday. It had been more than fifty years since Tomás Cruz had been
twenty years old. The sea had been full of fish then, and all his clothes
had been snug. Fish and muscle, Tomás reflected, those had been
the best things of his youth. And Maria, he chided himself, do not forget Maria.

Well, Tomás thought, his hands sliding over the familiar wheel, he
had planned this departure well. The horizon was clear. The route he
had devised had worked out perfectly: no patrol boats, no fishermen,
not even a freighter. Leaving the note for Ernesto inside the hut had
been a clever idea. And leaving him all the gear had been the proper
thing to do. Besides, Tomás hastily added, not wishing to tempt fate
through conceit, he had needed the deck space.

Tomás twisted his long frame and looked down. Crowded about the
gear-free deck, his fourteen passengers had settled into the rhythms of a
gently rolling sea. The midday sun was working its sleepy magic; those
not yet dozing were lazily arranging their possessions into bedrolls. Off

the port bow a clutch of flying fish burst from the water, skimming the surface in a frantic but graceful effort to elude some predator. Dorado, Tomás decided, noting the nearby patches of seaweed. Dorado were a good sign. Tomás esteemed the dorado above all other fish: their fighting spirit, their acrobatic leaps, their fabulous green and yellow iridescence, their wonderfully sweet flesh. He recalled the way Maria used to prepare dorado for him, with butter and bread crumbs, onions and sweet peppers and—

Stop thinking so much, old fool, Tomás admonished himself, turning the wheel and easing *Esperanza* to starboard. He heard the diesel gurgle and felt her tough old hull slide back down into the center of the trough. *Esperanza* was nearly as old as Tomás, and though she had none of the fancy gizmos that cluttered up the newer boats—the expensive radios, fish finders, Fathometers, radars—she had always served him well. Today Tomás did not need even her trusty compass; the bright sun would show them the way, first to the Dry Tortugas, then to the Marquesas Keys, and from there to Key West, the first link in the long, curving chain leading to Florida itself.

Isn't that right? he asked *Esperanza*, and smiled as the old boat nodded her bow in agreement.

When the stranger had approached him that night in the cantina, Tomás had known immediately what it would be about. Every *pescador* with a boat had received scores of such offers over the years. This man's proposal had been no different, but his timing had been perfect. Perhaps this stranger had heard something. Perhaps he was just lucky (though no sailor—least of all Tomás Cruz—ever discounted the importance of luck). Tomás still could not accept that one morning, after more than forty years of marriage, Maria had simply refused to wake up.

People had come into their house. A storm of people. Tomás had been in a kind of trance, but he remembered them wrapping Maria in white linen and carrying her off. He remembered putting on his wedding suit, shaking many hands, following the priest up the dusty road and then standing there holding his hat and watching the wind ruffle the grass. The day had been hot, the grass yellow and dry.

Their six children and their families had all come and said things to him and then gone back to their homes in the big cities, leaving him with an empty bed and no one to fix his dinner.

But it wasn't only Maria. There had been other things as well. He and Ernesto had continued to go out fishing, but the fish had become scarce, and what was worse, Tomás had discovered that he had lost his enthusiasm for catching them. So he had sat there in the cantina and drunk four of the man's beers and listened politely to his proposal. Though Tomás did not care about the money, he knew that business had to be conducted in a serious manner. Slowly and carefully, he had negotiated a big price, all in U.S. dollars. Like virginity, Tomás had explained to the man, raising his glass to his Maria, this was a voyage that could be taken only once.

Tomás was scanning the empty horizon and daydreaming about the sweet taste of cold beer when he heard something from the engine: a sputter, a cough, a warning. Reflexively, his hand went to the silver medallion around his neck. His first thought was to summon Ernesto, but of course Ernesto was not on board today. Keeping his voice low, Tomás called down and motioned the first man who heard him up to the bridge.

"Here," he said when the man arrived, "hold the wheel with both hands. I must do something below. It should not take long. Steer her exactly as you would an automobile, but more gently. You see the compass here? You see the number two ten on top? Here, by the line. Your job is to keep that number in the same place."

"No problem, boss." The man was grinning. He was missing a tooth.

"Try turning the wheel. See how it feels."

The man jiggled it back and forth, accomplishing nothing. "It feels good."

"Watch the compass," Tomás reminded him, grasping the ladder. The engine sounds were not good. He missed Ernesto. He did not like strangers handling *Esperanza*.

"Both hands," Tomás reminded the man. "Do not touch anything else."

Tomás climbed down and picked his way across the rolling deck. Several people had awakened. The hull was slapping now because it was no longer in the trough. Some passengers were getting splashed.

"Everything is okay," Tomás assured them. "Do not be worried," he soothed, as if they were children. "We are in international waters. Nothing can go wrong."

He set his feet wide apart and unlatched the engine cover. Raising it released a thick black cloud. Oil, Tomás thought unhappily, shielding his eyes from the acrid smoke. When the smoke cleared, he saw that one side of the engine block was covered in oil, and more was spitting out with each stroke. Something was wrong in *Esperanza*'s gut. Fighting back the fluttering in his own, Tomás decided he would have to shut her down.

—◦∾◦—

Five hours later *Esperanza* was still drifting aimlessly in the growing swells, and Tomás, slathered with oil and sweat, his stomach knotted and his arms aching, was still tinkering with the balky engine. Though they were all experts at asking foolish questions and getting in his way, none of the men knew a damn thing about diesels. The women were huddled together in the stern, their frightened chattering as irritating as a swarm of mosquitoes. Every minute, it seemed, someone else was rushing to the side and throwing up. The two babies were competing to see who could cry the loudest.

Tomás dried his hands on a crusty rag, picked up the oil-slicked wrench, and attempted once again to tighten a bolt that—because of old age or poor quality or who the hell knew what—had stripped its threading. The problem was much deeper than this one loose bolt, Tomás knew, but at least this was something he had a chance of repairing. *Esperanza* was bobbing about like a cork, making the task more difficult, but the trick was to turn it gently, slowly, to get it past the bad part of the thread—that's it, that's it—until he could—

"Captain!"

His hand slipped. For perhaps the twentieth time, the bolt came loose. Tomás closed his eyes and rested his chest against the engine housing.

"Captain! Look!"

"What is it?" he grumbled, struggling to straighten up.

What he saw froze his insides. The sun was gone. The sea was jagged. An ominous black curtain had been drawn across the eastern horizon.

Tomás studied it long enough to confirm his worst fears, then turned his attention to his passengers.

"Listen, my friends," he called, raising his voice above the gathering wind. "As most of you have already guessed, that dark cloud is a storm. And, yes, it is coming this way. Quiet! Please!" He spread his arms and flapped them gently up and down, like outriggers. "There is no cause for alarm, my friends. No cause at all."

He could tell by their murmuring that they didn't believe him. "The engine has been repaired," he lied.

That quieted them. They crowded in, straining to listen. He wasn't used to having so many people around him. It reminded him of Maria's funeral.

"But even with the engine repaired," he explained to them in his normal voice, "we cannot outrun this storm. We must use the time we have to prepare. Everyone must lend a hand. *Esperanza* and I have been through many storms together, storms far worse than this one, I assure you, storms so terrible they were given the names of women."

He paused. There was a smattering of nervous laughter.

"This thing is nothing more than a rainstorm," he lied. "Do exactly as I say and *Esperanza* will protect us. Are we in agreement?" He looked around and saw eyes soft with fear staring back at him. "Good. Excellent. Let's get to work."

Tomás estimated that they had less than fifteen minutes. The storm bearing down on them was a monster. The rain would be torrential, the wind ferocious. Everything on board would have to be secured. All the passengers would somehow have to be squeezed inside the cabin. The seas would be huge and treacherous, but *Esperanza* would not capsize as long as her weight was properly distributed and stabilized. The old girl would be fine as long as Tomás kept her bow into the wind so she could take the waves head-on. For that he would need the engine, of course, but he was confident it would keep running. It had to. Because if the engine failed—

Tomás stopped himself. He had no time to waste on foolish thoughts. The engine was American, a Cummins, not some cut-rate Russian junk.

He looked out again, trying to gauge the size of the storm. It was useless; the vast cloud, dark and pitiless as a shark's eye, stretched from one side of the eastern horizon to the other. Lightning crackled deep inside it, filling the air with the sharp smell of ozone. As a thick, dull rumbling shook the sky, Tomás felt his balls shrivel up between his legs. So, he mocked them, you are not dead, after all.

—◦◦◦—

The storm was right in front of them now. Tomás saw it as a huge, malevolent beast preparing to swallow them up. Bracing himself against the wind and spray, he mounted the madly swaying bridge, located the nylon line under the controls, carefully wound it about his waist, and leaving enough slack for movement but securing it on three sides, tied himself in. Things were going to get rough, but now the only way he could be washed overboard was with the entire bridge. Thus prepared, he grasped the wheel, pushed the gearshift into forward, moved the throttle ahead, and began slowly turning *Ezperanza* into the wind.

The sea began crashing over the gunwales and pelting him with spray. The waves were no more than five feet, but oddly spaced and choppy. The wind had a meanness to it. His rain gear flapped against his skin. He looked out and sensed that the storm, though already dangerous, was still gathering itself. As he stared, it took on the aspect of a black cobra, its hood flaring out to the horizon, its eyes crackling with lightning, its head reared back and poised to strike.

Esperanza, bucking rhythmically, was now facing the storm head-on. Down on deck, a wire cable clanged against its metal pole, tolling like a church bell. Tomás ran through a mental checklist. There was plenty of fuel in the tank. The engine would continue to lose oil, but if he kept the rpms down and used it only to steer, it would be all right. As long as he kept Esperanza in a head sea, she would be fine. The tourists would be fine. Everything would be fine. What he had told the tourists had been true; he and *Esperanza* had been through worse than this. Far worse.

Tomás felt for his medallion, licked the salt from his lips, squinted, and looked forward. His throat was dry. Thunder rumbled overhead. Lightning flashed, illuminating the insides of the beast they were about to enter. He was glad Ernesto had not come. Tomás held *Esperanza's* wheel steady as the storm swallowed them up. As he felt its fury against his face, Tomás released one hand and slowly crossed himself: a heartfelt gesture not only for *Esperanza* and her passengers, but for any poor soul who might be caught in this nightmare with a less seaworthy craft.

PART TWO

FERMO

Moe closed the big steel door and gave the combination dial an exuberant spin. It was after six, but he was still bristling with energy. The store had been busy all day; in nine hectic hours he'd barely had time to gulp down six cups of coffee. Now, buzzing with caffeine and emboldened by success, Moe decided it was high time he ventured next door to pay his respects to Miz Ark. Everything had been quiet on the crime front. There had been no further news about the murder. Detective Beck had not returned. Moe was ravenous. He would order chicken: How bad could it be?

After a day spent in the dim confines of a jewelry store, the brash vitality of Wedo's West Indian Kitchen was jarring. Moe took a few tentative steps inside and stood shifting his weight from one foot to the other, craning his neck for an empty table. The music was frantic. The laughter was loud. Everyone was black. Moe began having second thoughts. Any one of these guys could be the killer. The way his business was booming, it would be a shame to be murdered now

A sharp noise made Moe duck, but it was only the smack of a domino. What kind of people played dominoes in a restaurant? What kind of restaurant had people playing dominoes? Maybe coming here hadn't been such a good idea.

A sharp tug, a sudden loss of balance, and Moe was on the move. A waitress had hooked his arm and was dragging him across the room. Fish sailed by overhead.

"You comin' wit me, Missa Rosen," she declared, hurrying him between tables.

The voice was familiar. Moe stumbled, narrowly avoiding a collision. The sinking of elbow into flesh brought a shock of recognition. This was the "Ribs Girl," the one who had lifted her breast to show him where Miz Ark was getting x-rayed. Moe had replayed that thrillingly bawdy gesture in his mind a hundred times since. As she pulled him along, his arm sank into her again, bounced off. Sank. Bounced. She was a trampoline of flesh. People were staring. Moe felt weird but nice. His elbow tingled.

She stopped at a vacant table and stood with her hands planted on her hips while he took a seat.

"You tink some udda girl gonna take care a Missa Rosen?" she proclaimed, issuing what amounted to a territorial challenge. Her accent, thick as molasses, was almost comical.

Moe pulled in his chair and gazed up at her. Her eyes were bright. Her skin was dark. Her chest was magnificent.

"It's nice to see you again . . . Marlene," he said, reading from her name tag.

She beamed, basking in his recognition. Moe was surprised at how pretty she was. Because he hadn't really noticed last time, all his fantasies had started at her chest and worked their way down.

She leaned over and fussed with his place setting. Tiny beads of perspiration trembled along her hairline. It looked like a wig. She smelled sweet. He guessed she was about thirty.

"How you knows to come in on my shiff, Missa Rosen?" she teased.

"It must be fate," Moe suggested, nervously picking up a menu.

"Damn right," she agreed, snatching the menu from his hand. "You aine need dat. Marlene knows juss what Missa Rosen needs."

People at nearby tables began to laugh.

She spun around, presenting Moe with a broad back, a narrow waist, and the scent of musky flowers.

"Missa Rosen a single man," she announced. "He sittin' here wit me cause he got tayse. Aine dat right?" she demanded, whirling back at Moe.

"Absolutely." Framed by colorful dangling fish, she looked mythic, Amazonian. He would have agreed to anything.

"You juss relax," she told him, giving his shoulder a proprietary pat. "I'll go see whass good. Doan let nobody teef you."

Moe was still translating when a man from a nearby table stood up and approached. He had a pink shirt and a big grin. He didn't look like a murderer. His neck chain was familiar.

The man put out his hand. Moe shook it.

"You also bought a bracelet," Moe recalled, inviting him to sit.

"The bracelet for my wife," the man said, politely declining Moe's invitation.

"I hope she liked it."

"Two year. Two solid year she be workin' at dat place and yessaday she gess her firse raise."

"That's great," Moe said, wondering at the change of subject. "Please give her my best."

"Yes, suh. Tonk you, suh." The man insisted on shaking hands again.

Moe smiled as *teef* clicked in. "Doan let nobody teef you" meant "Don't let anyone kidnap you." Which was Marlene's way of saying that she wanted to keep the wanga at her table. Which, Moe then realized, might also explain why the man—

But the man was gone, his place taken by a tiny old woman wearing the pearl earrings with the 14k posts Moe had sold her last week. When he stood and took her twiglike hand, she edged closer and confided that her arthritis was much improved.

People kept drifting over to say hello. Despite the raucous music and the nerve-racking smacking of dominoes, Moe received them as graciously as he could. As he smiled and nodded, listened and shook hands, his feelings about himself kept alternating between shameless fraud and Dalai Lama. Once again he was struck by how genuinely nice West Indians were, how lucky he was to have them as customers.

A break in the music prompted Moe to look around. Miz Ark, her mouth fixed in a pained smile, her walk aided by a cane, was slowly making her way toward him. She was chunky. Her loose, white-trimmed, red dress reminded Moe of one of those European flags. Norway? Switzerland? He rushed around and held a chair for her.

"Thank you, Mr. Rosen," she said over the music, shooing him back and easing herself down.

He began by asking about her ribs.

"Still a bit sore," she sighed, grimacing as she tried to get comfortable. She had a mild lisp, like someone born in France but raised in the States.

"And how are you feeling, Mr. Rosen?"

"I'm fine. I guess we were both lucky, Ms. Arcenciel. I suppose you've heard—"

"My name is Sirene." She offered her hand.

"Mine is Moe."

They shook hands. Her grip was strong. Moe was about to say something about the fate of their mugger when he saw her watch. His mouth fell open.

"A gift," she said, turning her wrist and letting the diamonds catch the light. "Too small for me, don't you think?"

"The bracelet can be adjusted," Moe said absently, staring in awe at the twenty-five-jewel Piaget Principessa, a legendary masterpiece from the 1930s. Moe had never seen one outside a catalog.

"It pinches. But when I heard you were here, I couldn't resist putting it on. Vanity. Could you really adjust the bracelet?"

"I'd be happy to."

"*Bon.*" She reached down, released the clasp, shook it from her wrist. "Here." She handed it to him.

"Thank you." Moe tenderly wrapped it in his handkerchief and tucked it into his jacket pocket.

"Sirene," he said, dropping his voice, "do you know how much this watch is worth?"

"What is it worth if I cannot wear it?"

"Good point." Moe wondered where she could have gotten such a treasure. "By the way, if you don't mind me asking, who is Wedo?"

"Not some rich man who gives me fancy watches, if that's what you are thinking." Her deep-set eyes glittered with mischief.

"Not at all," Moe protested, unnerved by her insight.

"Wedo," she considered, absently clucking her tongue as she thought. "Wedo is the family name of Damballah and his wife, Ayida, two of the most powerful . . . how shall I say this? . . . spirits."

"Haitian spirits," Moe offered, trying to be helpful.

"Spirits have no nationality."

"I guess that's true," Moe admitted, wondering why he'd never thought of that. "So, the restaurant is named for these spirits."

"Not entirely. Excuse me." She looked off to one side, squinted, gave a quick hand sign, returned to Moe.

"Wedo is other things as well," she said, continuing her thought. "It is another name for Ouidah, the capital of the ancient African kingdom of Dahomey."

"Is that where your people are from?

"My people?"

"Your family. Parents, grandparents."

"Not really. My family is Haitian. But your question is quite incisive, Moe."

"It is?"

"Oh, yes." She paused to scratch at a stain on the tablecloth. "For centuries Dahomey was the center of the West African slave trade. Every slave going to the West Indies or the Americas had to pass through Wedo."

The loud song playing in the background had a pleasant syncopation. The voice was sweet.

Miz Ark leaned closer. Moe was surprised to see that her eyes were green. "So, *Wedo* suggests what we Haitians call our *ra-seen*, our roots. In that sense, it is another name for home."

"And home cooking."

"Just so," Miz Ark agreed with a smile.

Marlene arrived with a basket of rolls, a bowl of soup for Moe, and a cup of tea for her boss.

"Marlene," Miz Ark asked skeptically, nodding toward the soup, "Mr. Rosen order this?"

"No, ma'am, but—"

Miz Ark began to chuckle. "You see what this wicked girl is up to?" she said to Moe. She made *wicked* sound like a compliment.

"Up to?" Moe asked. The soup looked good. It smelled fine. He was starving.

"That soup, the young girls call it sexy soup. It makes a man feel all"—Miz Ark gave a little wiggle—"all itchy inside."

Moe looked at her.

"Itchy for a woman." Miz Ark looked up. "Isn't that right, Marlene?"

The waitress pouted, looked away, crossed her arms.

"I'm afraid Marlene is teasing you," Miz Ark said to Moe.

Marlene turned her head and made a strange chirping noise. "I dozen tease. Dis soup fresh an' nice. Try it, Missa Rosen."

Moe dipped his spoon into the thick, copper-colored liquid and tasted it. The soup was gamey, spicy, interesting. He emitted a loud, satisfied "Mmmmm" and watched Marlene's chest expand. She gave an extended chirp before prancing off.

"The soup really is good," Moe told Miz Ark.

"Thank you. Don't worry about Marlene," she said, peeling open a plastic packet and dripping honey into her tea.

"I wouldn't want to hurt her feelings," Moe said, staring after Marlene's hips.

"Eat slowly, then. She gets off at eight."

Moe looked over to see how to take that, but Miz Ark had turned her attention to the front door. A carefree young couple had come breezing in with their arms around each other. Seeing them reminded Moe of California. He felt a pang.

"And how is business these days?" Miz Ark asked, pulling him back.

Moe told her. Though she refused to take any credit for the upturn in his store's fortunes, she seemed delighted with his use of the word *wanga,* which she said was an African term. As they talked, Moe noticed that her eyes were drawn to the front door each time it opened.

She saw him watching. "The authorities," she explained, dropping her voice. "They are always making problems for us."

Moe was tempted to say something about his visit from Detective Beck. But what should he say, exactly?

"Not problems for me personally. I have my green card. But there are others less fortunate." Miz Ark glanced around. "Many others."

Moe scanned the room. Everyone looked pretty much the same.

Miz Ark stirred her tea. "America is a beacon. It draws people like moths."

"I need a salesperson," Moe said impulsively.

"Really?"

"Yes. To work with me in the store. Someone young, bright, good with people. I was hoping you might know someone like that."

Miz Ark seemed intrigued. "How much experience would this person require?"

"None. I mean, I would have to train him and—"

"Him?"

"Or her," Moe quickly corrected. "I have no preference."

"Is that so?" she teased, raising an eyebrow.

"No, no, no," Moe protested, feeling himself redden. "I only meant—"

"*Bon.* I know just the person."

"Really?"

"Yes. A young woman. If you wish, I can send her round to see you."

"That would be great. But is she . . . I mean, does she have . . . ?"

"All the proper documents," Miz Ark assured him.

"Super. Thank you. What's her name?"

"Air."

"Air?"

"Yes. It's short for Air-zuh-lee."

He took out a scrap of paper and a pen. "Would you mind spelling that?"

"E-R-Z-U-L-I-E."

"Air-zuh-lee," Moe said uncertainly. "That sounds African." He imagined tribal scars, distended ears, a long bone through the hair.

"She is a Haitian girl. Is that all right?"

"Of course. Absolutely. In fact, I was hoping for someone from the neighborhood, someone who could, you know, communicate . . ."

"Air can communicate. She's away now, but I'll send her round next week, if that's all right."

"Fine. Great. Thank you, Sirene. Now, in terms of salary . . ."

Moe's eyes followed hers to the front door. A white man slipped inside. His hair was blond.

"Beck," Moe muttered under his breath.

"You know him?"

"He's a cop." Moe watched as Beck turned and signaled someone outside. "He came—"

Her shriek hit Moe like an electric shock. The restaurant erupted. Everyone began running at once. Glass broke. Plates smashed. Chairs overturned. Before Moe's ears stopped ringing, the restaurant was bedlam. Up at the front, men in suits were fighting to get in the front door, trying to force their way through the unruly mass of black people— dozens of them—suddenly blocking their way, all pushing, shoving, struggling to reach the exit but succeeding only in creating a huge traffic jam.

As Moe watched the mad crush around the front door, things began flitting across his vision. Another group of people—ten, fifteen, more—

were moving swiftly and purposefully in the opposite direction, picking their way quickly across the food-splattered floor and disappearing one after the other into the kitchen, following each other so closely that the swinging white doors never had a chance to close.

Moe sat there stunned by the noise, the chaos, the speed with which the restaurant had been transformed into a . . . what?

A sudden scream from up front. Moe turned in time to see a woman come flying backward out of the pack, landing heavily and sliding across the debris-strewn floor. Instinctively, he moved to help her, but something caught hold of his arm. He tried to jerk free and saw that Miz Ark was clutching his wrist with both her hands and shaking her head no. He sat back down.

She patted his hand and leaned back in her chair. Moe was mystified. The battle raging less than twenty yards away was turning her restaurant into a shambles, yet Miz Ark appeared as unruffled as the colorful fish swaying gently above the fray.

Then, as Moe watched, the mob scene at the door took on a new aspect. It dawned on him that all those people blocking the doorway weren't trying to get out; they were trying to keep the invaders from getting *in*.

The police—or whoever they were—continued to struggle against the tide of shoving, jostling bodies. One of the suited intruders burst from the tightly packed mass and stood there in the open, bewildered by his sudden freedom. He scanned the toppled tables and chairs, the broken crockery, the food-splattered floor. His eyes alit momentarily on the only two patrons still seated. Then he got his bearings and ran slipping toward the kitchen. He pushed through the big white doors and disappeared, as if he had passed through some portal leading to a parallel universe.

A short, piercing whistle and, as if by magic, the madness by the front door subsided. Moe looked over at Miz Ark. Her expression was inscrutable as the Sphinx.

The men in suits quickly took control, announcing themselves as "INS," holding up badges, issuing orders, herding all the people into one section of the restaurant. Moe felt a twinge when he spotted Marlene among them, her hair askew, her uniform stained, but apparently unharmed. Resisting the childish urge to wave, Moe instead counted agents: eight of them, not including the one who had disappeared through the double doors.

The restaurant was filled with an eerie, nervous quiet. People were dusting themselves off, pushing away debris. Curiously, none of those being detained looked the least bit concerned about being in custody. Overhead the fish swung about on their strings, placidly surveying the damage.

A lone, dejected agent came straggling out through the big doors to join the others. It took Moe a second to realize what that meant; it meant that all the people who had made it to the kitchen—how many had there been? Fifteen? Twenty? More?—every one of them had escaped. Miz Ark's calm demeanor was starting to make sense.

A heavyset man in a disheveled gray suit picked his way across the littered floor toward Moe's table. He looked like a cheap version of Lou Grant. As he walked, a square plastic badge on a long, base-metal chain bounced against his belly.

"Immigration," Miz Ark muttered, making it sound like some infectious disease.

The big man walked right into Moe's space and stared down at him menacingly. His jacket was open, revealing a long black holster under one arm. "I know who *she* is. Who the hell are *you?*"

"I'm a law-abiding citizen," Moe replied, aware that everyone was watching him.

"I'll bet," the INS man said sarcastically.

Moe forced himself to speak up. "These people aren't hurting anyone. Why are you bothering them?"

"I've got a warrant, wiseass." The man thrust an open, meaty hand at Moe. "Let's see some ID."

"Let's see the warrant," Moe said, shocking himself with his aggressive tone.

"Unless you're the owner, I don't have to show you jack shit."

Moe could sense the anxious stares from people across the room. That was all right. Moe Rosen would show them that an American citizen had rights. Telling himself that he wasn't afraid of this guy, Moe nonetheless flinched as the INS man reached into his jacket. But the hand came out with a paper, not a gun.

"Here's the warrant," the man said, fixing Moe with a menacing glare. "Now I'll ask you one more time. Who the hell are you?"

"He owns the place next door," Detective Beck offered, coming over to join the INS man. Beck looked down at Moe. "I thought you didn't know Ms. Arcenciel."

"Detective Beck," Moe said, sliding his chair back and standing. "Would you mind telling me what this is all about?"

"Sit down," the INS man said, his body tensing.

Moe had the strange feeling that he was about to be hit. But before that could happen, Beck leaned over and whispered something in the INS man's ear.

"All right," the man muttered, unclenching his fist and walking off.

"Mr. Rosen," Beck said, motioning Moe closer.

Reluctantly, Moe complied. The restaurant had gotten very quiet.

"Listen," the detective said, taking Moe's elbow and guiding him away from Miz Ark, "I tried to warn you about these people."

"Warn me what?"

"This restaurant is a front," Beck said, sounding earnest. "Did you see how she orchestrated that riot? What do you think that was about?"

Moe shrugged. He didn't like being seen conferring with a white policeman while dozens of black people were having their papers checked. The scene smacked of apartheid.

"Mama-san," Beck said with a tilt of his head toward Miz Ark. "The INS is convinced that she's the ringleader."

"Really?" Moe asked, intrigued in spite of himself. "What's her crime?"

"She smuggles aliens, Mr. Rosen. Illegal aliens. West Indians, mostly, but who the hell knows. Asians. Africans. Anybody who can pay the freight."

"Why should I believe you?" Moe asked, reflexively checking his pocket for the Piaget.

"I don't give a rat's ass what you believe. But I thought you were a straight guy. You don't have a clue what you're getting into."

"She seems like such a nice woman."

"That's what they all said about Jim Jones. While he was passing out the Kool-Aid."

The INS man was waving for Beck. The detective nodded, then turned to Moe. "Ask your Haitian friend about what goes on down in her basement."

"Her basement? What—"

"Listen, Mr. Rosen, you want to take a walk on the wild side, you go ahead." Beck pointed a finger. "Forewarned," he said, backing away and nearly tripping over a broken plate.

Confused and conflicted, Moe went back to sit with Miz Ark. Her expression was blank. Her eyes were trained on something across the room.

"Say nothing," she advised Moe without looking at him. "They have failed. They are angry. Do not give them an excuse."

Moe picked up a menu and forced himself to start reading. He asked himself what a conch fritter could taste like.

A few minutes later it was all over. Beck and the INS agents left through the front door. The forty or so patrons dispersed slowly, talking among themselves, straightening up tables and chairs. Brooms and dustpans appeared. A busboy emerged from the kitchen pulling along a pail of sudsy water and a mop.

"Did they catch anyone?" Moe asked Miz Ark.

"No."

"How did they all get out?"

"Do not trouble yourself," Miz Ark said, giving hand directions to a boy with a broom. She turned back to Moe. "Anyone who has traveled thousands of miles to get here can manage a few more yards to stay."

"What goes on in the basement?"

Her eyes flashed for a moment. *"Bon.* So that's what the policeman was talking to you about. It's nothing very sinister, I'm afraid. We use the basement as a kind of community center. Space is so dear in New York. I make it available for civic meetings, dance recitals, any worthwhile cause. What does the policeman say, that I am a Communist?"

"He says you're a smuggler. Illegal aliens."

"Oh, my." She laughed. "What will they think of next?"

"Where is Marlene from?"

"She'll be along soon. You can ask her yourself. Oh, do you still want me to send the girl about that job?"

"Sure. Of course. And thank you for the recommendation."

"I'm sorry you won't be able to finish your meal. Promise me you'll come back and let me make it up to you."

"Sure. That was quite a scream." Moe stood and brushed himself off. "It reminded me of, you know, that horror movie."

"Which one?" Miz Ark asked, struggling to her feet with her cane.

Moe's mind went blank. A stunning woman was approaching. She was tall, with dark skin, great eyes, a short Afro, tight jeans, and an oversize leather jacket.

"Mr. Rosen says I scream like a horror movie," Miz Ark told her.

"Wish one?" the woman asked him.

It was Marlene!

"The one with the plant people," Moe said, speaking fast to mask his surprise. "The original was black-and-white, but they remade it in color a few years ago. It has these pods that turn into humans. With Donald Sutherland and—"

"Invasion of the Body Snatchers," Marlene said.

"That's it!" Moe exclaimed, amazed that she knew it.

"Quite appropriate, under the circumstances," Miz Ark observed wryly, looking around at the mess. "Good night, you two."

"But I haven't paid for the soup," Moe told Miz Ark, shocked by her assumption that he and Marlene were leaving together.

"Good night," Miz Ark said, dismissing them.

"Less go," Marlene said, confounding him further. When had all this been decided? And by whom?

Obediently, Moe followed Marlene out. It was chilly. The street was dark. Everything felt different. He glanced down the block, looked for his shop, felt his pocket for the Piaget.

In the dark, without an audience, Moe's confidence evaporated. Even without her hair, Marlene was nearly as tall as he was. Strange things were happening to his insides. It had been years since he'd been this close to a gorgeous woman. He wondered if people were staring at them, a mixed couple in an all-black neighborhood. He wondered if there would be trouble. He took his father's silence as disapproval.

"Do you have a car?" Marlene asked.

"No," Moe said, surprised to discover that he had no idea where he'd been walking. "God, I'm dumb," he apologized.

"No, you're not. You're a sweet man with big soft eyes. Come on." She gave his arm a little tug. "My car's about two blocks over."

It was weird being alone with her, walking next to her. His legs were numb but his clothes had developed nerve endings. He could feel her through the fabric of his jacket.

"We turn here," she said, leading him. "One more block. So, what do I call you?"

"Moe is fine. Everybody— Wait a minute!" he cried, stopping short. "What happened to your accent?"

"I was starting to wonder about you," she chuckled, tugging his arm and getting them moving again. "I leave the accent at work, along with the wig and the uniform."

"But I don't understand," Moe said, thoroughly befuddled. "You mean you're not West Indian?"

"I was born in Queens. Kew Gardens. But I like pretending to be West Indian. I do the accent pretty well, though, don't you think?"

"You do it great," he told her, feeling dazed. "Marlene. But—"

"I got tired of worrying about having dark skin and nappy hair. West Indians actually like themselves. By the way, what does Moe stand for?"

"Moses. It's a biblical name."

"No kidding," she teased, squeezing his arm and sending sensations of pleasure straight to his brain. "Moses. That's a good name, a serious name. Here's my car."

"Nice car," he said, though he had no idea what kind it was. He had no idea what anything was anymore. It was as if he were living someone else's life. *Big soft eyes*—what exactly did that mean?

She opened the passenger door. A light came on. Moving like a robot, Moe slid in and pulled the door closed. The light went out. He reached over and fumbled around until he got her door open. The light came on again. He watched her get in. She seemed to get more beautiful each time he looked at her. Her eyes flashed toward him and he felt his insides turn to Jell-O. It got dark.

She started the car. He tried to sit up straight. He could hear her breathing. *You don't have a clue what you're getting yourself into*, Beck had warned him.

The car started to move. To Moe, the slow-rolling tires sounded like nylons swishing against thighs.

TWELVE

The sergeant hustled her in and pushed her into the wooden armchair in front of the desk. She was hanging her head, but the colonel could see that she had been crying. Tears had streaked her cheeks and spotted her white dress. Patches of the cheap fabric were sticking to her skin. Despite his displeasure with her pressed hair and wrinkled clothes, the colonel felt himself tingling with anticipation. After more than forty-eight hours of dead ends and lame excuses, here, finally, was their first real lead.

The sergeant came to attention and saluted. Ferray ended his answering salute with a twist, indicating that he wished the door locked on the sergeant's way out. The sergeant stared back in confusion. Ferray repeated the gesture, making it even more blatant, and waited while the idea slowly worked its way into the man's consciousness.

The colonel drummed his fingers on the desk, impatient for the sergeant to leave. He was curious to see the face that had taken his men nearly two days to find.

"Young lady," he said the moment he heard the door click.

She looked up. Her eyes were large, wet, and wonderfully mournful. Save for a small scar on one cheek, her dark skin appeared smooth and unblemished. With her lips pressed together it was difficult to judge the shape of her mouth, but her cheekbones had character and her neck was uncommonly graceful. A country girl, to be sure, but strangely appealing.

His eyes were drawn to her chest where her fretful, irregular breathing was making her dress jiggle. She wasn't wearing a bra. Savoring the moment, the colonel held his gaze steady while his imagination slowly dissolved the cloth and exposed her breasts: succulent little fruits, each tipped with a large, wafer-thin nipple, dark and delicate as carbonized tissue paper.

Ferray shifted in his chair and felt his network of pleasure coming alive, sending a stream of electrical impulses tingling through his body. She would tell him everything. Everything.

The colonel drew in a sharp breath. Her cheap white dress reappeared. He looked down. Her ankles were crossed. Ugly rubber flip-flops clung to mud-stained feet. She would need a bath.

He cleared his throat. "With your permission, Mademoiselle Voisin," he said in formal French, "I would like to begin."

She glanced up and mumbled something in Creole. Her face was wet. Her nose was running.

"Forgive me," he said in her language. "Where are my manners?" He rose. "Please excuse me for a moment."

He went into his bathroom and returned with a damp towel for her face. She rubbed hard, in the manner of country children. When she was done, she glanced up. He tapped his chin, showing her a spot she had missed. She hurriedly rubbed it clean.

He took the towel and seated himself behind his desk.

"Miss Voisin, may I call you Antoinette?"

"That is my name, sir."

She still looked frightened, but she was no longer trembling. With her face scrubbed she was actually quite attractive.

"Antoinette is a lovely name," he said affably, folding the towel carefully and putting it aside. "My name is Colonel Hugo Ferray. Would you like to call me Hugo?"

"No, sir. Not at all, sir."

"As you wish." He was pleased by her inability to look at him directly, even for a moment. "Now, Antoinette," he said, adopting the tone of an indulgent teacher, "do you know why you have been brought here today?"

"No, sir."

"Antoinette," he teased, leaning back and swiveling, "is that really the truth?"

The clasped hands in her lap began wrestling with each other.

"Antoinette," he said, bringing his chair upright and staring at her, "I want to ask you about a friend of yours."

"A friend, sir?"

"Fabrice Lacroix."

"Oh." Her head slumped. She seemed crestfallen.

"Fabrice Lacroix *is* a friend of yours, is he not?"

Her head remained down. "Yes, sir," she whispered.

"A *good* friend."

"Yes, sir."

"Your good friend Fabrice worked for the Jouvier family, Antoinette. You knew that."

"Yes, sir." With each response her voice grew a little more faint.

"You also knew that there was a fire at the Jouvier home the other night."

"I heard so, sir."

"How did you 'heard so,' Antoinette?"

"From people, sir," she mumbled into her chest.

"Which people? Speak up."

"Everyone hear about the fire, sir."

"*What* did everyone hear about the fire, Antoinette?"

She shrugged. "Fire was big-big, sir."

"What else?"

"Fire burn up the whole Jouvier house, sir."

"Did you hear how the fire started?"

She shook her head. The colonel suppressed a smile. Her first lie.

"Antoinette, your good friend Fabrice Lacroix started that fire."

Her body contracted. "No, sir," she whispered.

Defiance. How nice. "Look at me, Antoinette."

She tried, but failed.

"Fabrice Lacroix started that fire."

"No, sir."

"How do you know that, Antoinette?"

"Fabrice would not do such a thing." Her voice was little more than air.

"But he ran away. Did you know that?"

"I heard so," she mumbled, shifting her hips uneasily.

The colonel felt a pulse of excitement. "Why would Fabrice run away, Antoinette?"

"I do not know, sir."

"But you know that he did not start the fire."

"Yes, sir." She sounded miserable.

"Who *did* start the fire, Antoinette?"

She paused and nibbled her lip. "I do not know, sir."

"Who could it have been, Antoinette, if not Fabrice?"

She mumbled something. The cadence was familiar. He asked her to repeat it.

She crossed herself. "Tonton Macoutes, sir."

His burst of laughter startled her. "There are no more Tonton Macoutes."

"So they say," she whispered, crossing herself again.

The colonel smiled. The Tonton Macoutes, Papa Doc's secret police, had been disbanded years ago. The people in the bush still feared them. Ferray had always considered them undisciplined rabble.

He spoke softly. "Have you seen Fabrice Lacroix since the fire, Antoinette?"

"No, sir."

"Are you sure, Antoinette?"

"Yes, sir."

"Look at me!"

Her head snapped up. She glanced at him, looked away, and started trembling again.

He spoke slowly. "Have you seen Fabrice since the fire, Antoinette?"

"No, sir."

"Don't look down. I want to see your face. Now tell me: Have you seen Fabrice Lacroix since the fire?"

She strained to keep her chin up. "No, sir."

"Do you know where Fabrice is, Antoinette?"

She buried her face in her hands. "Yes, sir," she cried.

The colonel nearly came out of his chair. "Where? Where is he?"

Her head drooped. She was sobbing. Ugly gasping sounds were coming from her throat.

Unwilling to lose the moment, Ferray asked her again. She tried to speak, but nothing emerged but blubbering.

He slapped the desktop. The noise startled her into momentary silence. He asked her again.

She managed to get some words out. "Fabrice is . . . the Island . . . Beneath . . . the Sea, sir."

The Island Beneath the Sea. The place the country people believed all dead souls went.

"Is Fabrice dead, Antoinette?" he asked urgently.

She was weeping silently. Tears were running through her fingers.

"Are you telling me that Fabrice Lacroix is dead?" he demanded.

She continued crying. Her head went up and down.

Ferray grasped a pencil and began tapping its eraser against the desktop. This was not what he wanted to hear. Was it possible that she was lying? Of course it was possible! He counseled himself to remain calm.

"Where did Fabrice die?" he asked her, tapping the eraser. "Where is his body?"

She sniffled. "At the Island Be—"

"How do you know?"

"He . . . took the raft, sir."

The colonel stopped tapping. "What raft?"

"Agwe's raft, sir. For the festival."

He wished he could see her face. "Fabrice Lacroix took it? You are absolutely sure of this?"

"Yes, sir." She sniffled hard.

"How? How do you know this?"

"The raft . . . is gone, sir."

"So what?" he roared. "A raft disappears. Anyone could have taken it. How do you know it was Fabrice Lacroix?"

"The raft is gone, sir," she repeated stupidly, and immediately began sobbing again.

His fury lifted him from his chair. He was clutching the pencil in his fist. "Did Fabrice tell you he was taking it? Is that it? Did he come to you and tell you he was taking the raft?"

"No, sir!"

"You're lying!"

"No, sir."

"Are you lying to me, Antoinette?"

"No, sir."

"Because if you are—"

The pencil snapped in two. He threw it at her. The pieces struck her. She shrank back in the chair, hunched her shoulders, and began to wail.

He banged the desk with his fist. "Silence!"

She pulled her legs up and curled into a ball. The sight of her exposed thighs made him want to rush over, throw her to the floor, and fuck her right there.

He took a furious swipe at the air and sat back down. He leaned back, took a deep breath, stared up at the sluggish ceiling fan, and tried to reason with himself. This poor, stupid girl wasn't the problem. The incompetence of his men was the problem. The botched operation at the Jouviers' was the problem. Fabrice Lacroix's escape was the problem.

He swung his chair around to face Antoinette. "Sit up properly," he told her in a calm voice. "And stop your blubbering. Look here." He tossed her the towel. "Clean your face. Quickly now."

His intuition told him that the girl was telling the truth. Her story made sense. Lacroix stole the raft and put out to sea. Yes, that would explain why none of their informers had been able to find him and claim the reward. The night Fabrice had escaped, Ferray had been too enraged to sleep: his first escape! And that damnable houseboy had seen his face, knew his name. Ferray recalled lying in his bed and listening to the swirling wind and worrying that the rain would wash away the fugitive's tracks. Yes, the sea that night must have been treacherous, deadly. He would have the girl make a crude drawing, but unless this raft differed radically from the traditional design, her simpleminded analysis was almost certainly correct: Fabrice Lacroix, while trying to escape his fate, had set out to sea in a flimsy bamboo raft—a craft literally designed to disintegrate—and had almost certainly drowned.

Drowned. Almost certainly . . .

Absently, the colonel went over to retrieve the pieces of the broken pencil. "Almost certainly" was not good enough, not nearly good enough. Anything could have happened. The raft could have been washed back to shore. Lacroix could be anywhere. Anywhere!

She was still weeping. He stood looking down at the bare nape of her neck and felt the anger welling up in him. That a stupid country girl like this should cause him—

Her whimpering suddenly became too much to bear. He grabbed a fistful of her hair and wrenched her head back. She cried out in fright, her body shrank, and her arms came up to cover her face. His nostrils filled with her female smells of sweat and fear.

The colonel held her head over the chair back and cocked his other fist, trying to decide where to strike her. He began shaking with fury. He didn't want the word of some houseboy's teenage whore; he wanted proof! Proof that Fabrice Lacroix was really dead. Incontrovertible proof!

He yanked her head back farther. She screamed in pain and he felt an erection starting. Look what she was doing to him now! His fist shook. He wanted to smash it into her face, to hear her shriek, to see her blood spurt. But hitting her wouldn't— What if Lacroix wasn't dead?

His rage bubbled over. Without thinking, he reached down and ripped open the front of her dress, revealing her breasts. She cried out. He got a better grip on her hair and jerked her head back even farther. She moaned in pain, her hips lifted, and her hands reached up and struggled to loosen his hold. Yes, her body would amuse him, he thought furiously, using his weight to hold her down, but this wasn't the body he wanted. He wanted Fabrice Lacroix's body! He wanted to see it with his own eyes, feel its death with his own hands!

He pulled her head back until her body arched like a bow. Holding her like that, ignoring her tortured screams and her flailing arms, he slapped her hard across the face. When her arms flew up for protection, he drove his hand down between her thighs. She was doing everything in her power to fight him off, but her exertions only excited him further. In a frenzy now, he grasped her throat and squeezed until her screams stopped and her body shuddered and went slack.

She lay there with only the whites of her eyes showing, her face wet, her mouth open and bloody, her arms hanging loose at her sides.

He relaxed his grip enough to ease her pain, but not enough for her to alter her posture. She began gasping. Her stomach muscles were twitching. Between sobs, she began mumbling for mercy. He bent over and brought his mouth to her ear. Her skin was wet and glistening. Her smell was intoxicating.

"Can you hear me, Antoinette?"

"Yes, sir," she croaked, trying not to move.

"Fabrice is dead."

"Yes, sir," she whimpered.

"This," he said, squeezing his hand between her thighs, "now belongs to me."

"Yes, sir," she squeaked, arching her back but trying not to resist.

"What did you say?" he demanded, releasing her only long enough to get a better grip.

Her arms came up reflexively, but immediately dropped back down.

"Yes, sir," she squealed in something approaching a wail.

"Good."

A sound. Alien. Loud. Shaking the charged air. The colonel paused and turned his head, searching for its source. The sound came again, but this time as his intercom. He freed his hands and stumbled to his desk. He was dizzy. His face was burning. The girl was some sort of witch.

"Here," he snapped at her, tossing her the towel. "Clean yourself up."

He leaned on the desk and pressed the intercom. His hand shook. "Yes?"

"Mr. Townley is on the telephone, sir," the sergeant said. "I told him you were busy, but he says it is very important."

"All right."

Ferray was having trouble catching his breath. He felt feverish. The phone was slippery.

"Ferray here," he said between gasps, then quickly covered the mouthpiece.

"Bob Townley, Hugo. Hope I'm not disturbing you."

The colonel dropped into his chair and took a deep, trembling breath. "Not at all, Bob . . . always a pleasure. . . . What can I do for you?" He glanced over. Her face was scrubbed, her dress was more or less back in place, and she was fumbling in her pocket for something, probably a comb, he thought absently. Look at that hair.

"Something has come up, Hugo," Townley said. "I'm still in the area. I wonder, could you spare a few minutes if I came right over?"

"Sounds important." Ferray's breathing was nearly normal.

"It's not something I can discuss over the phone."

"I see. All right, then. When can you be here?"

"Fifteen, twenty minutes?"

"I'll look forward to it."

Ferray replaced the receiver, wondering if Townley had somehow learned about Fabrice Lacroix's escape. It was unlikely, but everything in this country was for sale. Then again, if not Lacroix, what else—?

A movement caught Ferray's eye. She was holding something up with both hands, displaying it to him. It looked like—yes, it was—an American dollar bill.

"What are you doing?"

She hurriedly stuffed the bill into her pocket. "Nothing," she said, turning her face away and pulling the dress together.

"Look this way. You missed something. Here." He walked over and took her chin in his hand.

She winced but did not resist. He lifted her chin, licked his fore-finger, and wiped a small blood smear from the corner of her mouth.

"There. That's better." Shocked by a sudden urge to have her breast in his hand, he released her and backed away. She was a sorceress.

"Did Fabrice give you that money?"

"No, sir," she mumbled.

"You are a very poor liar."

She stared at the floor. The hands holding her dress together were trembling. He walked over, squatted down in front of her, and rested his fore-arms on her covered knees. She was drawing him to herself like a magnet.

"You can keep the money."

She peeked at him. "Truly?"

"Yes. But only if you tell me what you were doing with it."

"Nothing, sir."

"Now, Antoinette," he teased, "you don't want to make me angry again, do you?"

He felt her knees press together. She clutched the fabric to her chest. "No, sir. Not at all, sir."

"Then tell me. Why did you show me the American money?"

"I was . . . not showing you, sir," she said haltingly.

"Oh?"

"I was showing *them,* sir."

"Them."

"The l'wah presidents, sir. The ones in the tomb. They wish to see everything."

He shook his head. More Voodoo bullshit. "Who are these l'wah presidents?"

Holding her dress together with one hand, she took out the dollar and showed him the brick tomb and the big eye and explained about the l'wah presidents.

"I see," he said, pretending to be impressed. "Thank you for that explanation."

"You are welcome, sir."

"Tell me, Antoinette," he asked mildly, "do you think these l'wah presidents can help you?"

She seemed to shrink. "I do not know, sir."

"Well, I know, Antoinette. The only one who can help you now is me."

"Yes, sir."

"So you must do your very best to please me."

"Yes, sir," she whispered.

"All the time."

"Yes, sir."

"No matter what I ask."

"Yes, sir." She sniffled. "But I am a good girl, sir," she pleaded.

"I'll be the judge of that."

He tickled her knee, but she didn't laugh. Her eyes never left the floor. Feeling like a lion toying with a gazelle, the colonel smiled, placed his hands on her knees, and used them to help him rise. He went and stood behind the desk to hide his new erection, then pressed the intercom to summon the sergeant. He glanced at his watch. Townley would be arriving shortly. There were things to do.

The sergeant knocked, entered, saluted.

Ferray leaned forward to flatten his stubborn erection against the desk. "Escort Miss Voisin to my quarters," he ordered the sergeant. "And, uh, show her how to use the television."

"Yes, sir."

Ferray gave the sergeant a knowing look. "See that she is not disturbed."

"Yes, sir."

"Miss Voisin," Ferray said, "watch some TV. Have something to eat. Get some rest. I will be along a bit later."

"Yes, sir." She stood and smoothed her dress.

He had forgotten how tall she was.

After they left, the colonel hurried into his bathroom and removed his shirt. He stood at the sink sniffing his hand obsessively, inhaling all he could of her raw, pungent scent before having to wash it away with soap and water.

He dried himself, sprayed with deodorant, and then went over and selected a fresh shirt from his closet. He checked his hand. Though faint, she was still there.

Townley arrived. They shook hands. The CIA man was chewing a toothpick. He seemed distracted.

"This Jouvier business," he said, dropping into the same chair Antoinette had occupied.

Ferray tensed. "Are you referring to that unfortunate fire?" he asked warily.

"I'm afraid so. The old man's death is generating a lot of heat."

"Fires will do that," Ferray quipped, relieved that this was about Jouvier and not about his missing houseboy.

"Newspaper guys," Townley grumbled, thinking out loud. "Freedom of the press. All that crap. Bad timing. Questions."

"There are always questions."

"Yeah, but this time the wrong people are asking them."

"And how can I help?" Ferray inquired, his mind drifting, offering snapshots: Antoinette moving about his apartment wearing only her panties, playing with his TV, opening his refrigerator, testing his bed . . .

"Look," Townley said, clearly uncomfortable, "things are happening."

"What sort of things?"

"The fact is, Hugo, our days here are numbered."

"Are you people leaving?" Ferray asked, trying to appear disappointed.

"*Our* days, Hugo. Yours and mine."

"This is my country," Ferray reminded him.

"Not for much longer, Hugo. There's a new government coming in."

The colonel shrugged. "There have been new governments before."

"This one has Washington's full backing, Hugo. That's the word I get."

"All right," Ferray sighed, absently reaching for a pencil only to remember what he'd done with the last one. He clasped his hands instead. "I appreciate the information, Bob. But what has any of this to do with me?"

"The word we get is that this new group is going to be cracking down, coming down hard on anyone they can blame for corruption and— pardon the expression—brutality. They're talking arrests, show trials, the whole nine yards."

"Are you saying . . . ?"

"No one knows for sure, Hugo, not at this point. But we wouldn't want to see you hurt."

"Then see to it that I'm not," Ferray snapped.

But that was simply reflex. The colonel knew that the Americans cared no more about his safety than he cared about theirs. Their only concern was that their involvement remain secret. Whereas his concern was . . . what?

"We'll do everything we can to protect you," Townley continued. "But our influence with these new boys is . . . well, let's just say, Hugo, that we'd prefer not to leave anything to chance."

Act grateful, Ferray counseled himself. He had always known this day had to come. He had just not expected it today. Or anytime soon. At least they were offering him a chance to get out. In their place, he realized, he would not have been so generous.

"When?" he asked, interrupting something Townley was saying.

"Excuse me?"

"How much time do I have? I'll need to tie up some loose ends."

"A week. Things are starting to snowball, Hugo. We wouldn't want you to wait any longer than that."

"A week."

"Maximum. Five days would be better."

"Five days, then."

Townley stood up. "I know this goes without saying, Hugo, but anything we can do . . . We need to keep a low profile right now, but . . ."

"Thank you, Bob." Ferray rose and offered his hand.

Townley grasped it firmly. "Where do you think you'll be going?" he asked, trying to sound casual.

"I'll let you know as soon as I decide."

The colonel escorted Townley to the door and stood there watching him walk to his car. The CIA man never looked back.

"Sir," the sergeant said when Ferray finally turned around.

"What is it?"

"Sir, my orders are not to disturb you when you are meeting with the American."

"Yes. And?" Ferray was weary.

"You had a call, sir. From Captain Ghede, sir."

"Yes. And?"

"He will be arriving tomorrow, sir, on the first New York flight."

"Good. Anything else?"

The sergeant consulted a note. "The captain's flight lands in the capital at eleven hundred hours, sir. He expects to arrive here before nineteen hundred hours, sir."

"Fine. Good work. Anything else?"

"The captain sends his regards to the colonel, sir."

"Fine." Ferray allowed himself a smile. "I'll be going to my quarters now. I will not want to be disturbed." He brushed the front of his trousers. "By the way," he said, recalling how fiercely she had struggled, "how many men did you station there?"

The sergeant stiffened. "Station, sir? I didn't—I mean, you didn't—"

But Ferray was already out the door.

THIRTEEN

The storm was over. Up on the bridge Tomás Cruz let his body sag against the wheel while his mind floated through the soft, seaweed fringes of sleep. His senses, sputtering like *Esperanza's* ruined engine, continued to deliver flickering impressions: the gentle rocking of the hull, the slurp of water against wood, the sweet, after-storm smell of fresh vegetation.

A cool gust tickled open an eyelash, revealing a mercury-colored sea. Reluctantly, Tomás pushed himself upright and opened the other eye. The sky was a hovering carpet of thick gray cloud. Just below it, the sea's smoothly undulating surface was spotted with flotsam: twigs and branches, ravaged palm fronds, shards of bone-white Styrofoam, a coconut husk bobbing darkly.

"*Enfermo!*" cried a voice from the deck, the shrill female sound boring into Tomás's skull like a toothache.

He gathered himself, moved to the rail, looked down.

"*Enfermo!*" the woman barked again—Sick!—jerking a little girl's arm and pulling her away from the dark-skinned stranger who lay unconscious on the tarp.

Tomás shook his head in disgust. Women! As if there had been a choice. As if Tomás Cruz, or any sailor—any man!—could have left the boy drifting out there like that, with only his head and one shoulder above water and his rigid fingers clinging to those few scraps of water-logged bamboo.

The nearest thing to a miracle Tomás had ever seen, and these women had wanted him to—

"*Enfermo!*" the woman scolded, angrily shaking the little girl's wrist. The child began to cry.

Tomás stepped back from the rail and squeezed the wheel with both hands. *Enfermo!* Why did these women keep insisting that the boy was sick? The boy was not sick! Exhausted, yes. Half-dead from exposure, without a doubt. But sick? Truly sick? Sick with something to infect others? No!

Tomás had spotted the boy floating off the port bow just after first light and, with the help of two men, had hauled him aboard. After prying his fingers from the sodden wood and laying him out on the tarp, Tomás had held the boy's head, washed his face, and coaxed him to gag down some fresh water. Checking him over carefully, Tomás had found no sores, no rashes, no open wounds—nothing that could possibly endanger anyone on board. Yet these Christian women—so devout they seemed unable to stop crossing themselves—were behaving as if the stranger carried plague. It shamed the memory of his Maria for her to share the title of *woman* with such creatures.

He corrected *Esperanza*'s heading, holding her bow into the wind to keep the stream of black smoke pluming out behind them. The horizon remained blank, but Tomás sensed land nearby. The Americans were said to guard their borders jealously; one of their airplanes or patrol boats would see the smoke soon. Absently, Tomás fingered the old coin on the silver chain around his neck. He tried to take a deep breath, but his chest was too tight. Weariness weighed on his shoulders like heavy rope. He wanted a cold beer, some soft music, a long sleep. Soon, he told himself, rubbing his lucky coin, soon.

He leaned forward and looked down to the deck. The boy was still sleeping. Watching him breathe, Tomás wondered idly what he had been doing out there, who his people were, where his home was. His pockets had revealed nothing: no wallet, no papers, no money, not even a photograph. He could have been from any island in the Caribbean's looping, thousand-mile chain, but something told Tomás that this boy was not Cuban. A sailor's nationality was of no importance to Tomás Cruz, but he understood that to the Americans it meant everything. Even in Tomás's small village it was known that any Cuban—even a thief or a murderer—was welcome in America, while a refugee from any other island was treated as a criminal. America's policies made no more sense to Tomás than Cuba's. Which was one reason he had always been content to be a fisherman: fish have no politics. How many times had he said that to his mate Ernesto? To his wife, Maria? To the loud-mouths in the cantina? He reached up and rubbed the hollowed coin. How many times?

For years the medallion around Tomás's neck had carried a photo of Maria. Fashioned from a seventeenth-century Spanish "pillar dollar," the first coin used in the New World, the silver medallion had been presented to Tomás on March 5, 1961, for hitting a home run under the lights at the Estadio Julio Catorce in Cienfuegos before a crowd of seventy-four hundred people. Fidel Castro had been the pitcher. The count had been three and one. Tomás still smiled whenever he remembered the delicious shock in his arms as his bat connected with Castro's fastball, and that look in El Comandante's eyes—a mixture of fury, disgust and grudging admiration—as he raised that famous beard to follow the arc of Tomás's ball into the center-field stands.

The first thing Tomás had placed in the coin was a photo of Maria's face that he had cut without her knowledge from one of their wedding pictures. But in time the salt air had ruined it, spotting Maria's clear skin, blurring her sweet features, clouding those wide, trusting eyes, and finally Tomás had scraped away the crumbling paper and replaced it with a single coiled strand of her long black hair, which he had found on his pillow one morning after they had made love. Then, last month, he had discovered that somehow that too was gone, and now the coin contained only money: three carefully folded American $100 bills, the tourists' down payment for this voyage.

Tomás turned and watched the thick smoke rising behind *Espe-ranza*'s stern. It spun up into the sea breeze, thinning as it rose, fading from black to gray and then to nothing. For some reason the sight made him sad. He wondered what Ernesto was doing right now. He tried to estimate how far the smoke would be visible, but he lacked the skill to make the calculation. Far enough, he told himself, pushing up on his toes and feeling his calf muscles stretch. He reached up and pressed the worn, old coin between his fingers. He and *Esperanza* had made it through the storm. All their passengers were safe. They had even res-cued a castaway from God only knew where. The sea was so peaceful. Ernesto was probably out fishing; the fishing was sometimes good after a storm. The Americans would be here soon. Tonight the tourists would eat their supper in Florida.

He felt a prickliness along his arms, which he feared might be pride. *Cuidado*—take care—old fool, he warned himself, you are not there yet. God can always change His mind.

"Political refugees," he said out loud, practicing his English.

"Captain," a man called up to the bridge.

Tomás kept his eyes trained on the horizon. "Yes?"

"How much longer, Captain?"

Tomás sighed. A foolish question required no response. A new, unpleasant grating sound was coming from the engine: probably a burnt-out bearing.

"The Americans," the man below persisted. "How much longer, Captain, until the Americans find us?"

"Twenty-five minutes," Tomás called out, and was pleased to hear his ridiculous prediction ignite a commotion down on deck.

Tourists! How in God's name could he know how much longer it would be? *Esperanza* was doing her best, but no engine, not even a Cummins, could last much longer. He looked over the rail and saw a woman fussing with something directly below him.

"*Señora,*" he called, "be a good Christian and give our guest some water."

The woman pulled her shawl around her shoulders. "*Enfermo,*" she muttered, crossing herself and backing from view.

Tomás considered asking one of the men, but decided to wait. Why involve the tourists at all? The stranger was his responsibility. For a moment he saw the boy floundering in heavy, wind-whipped seas, clinging for dear life to those broken bamboo sticks. And then, as the image faded, Tomás was struck by a curious thought: Was it possible, he wondered, rubbing a stubbly cheek, that God had spared Tomás Cruz and *Esperanza* not to save these useless tourists but to rescue this mysterious dark-skinned boy?

—⁓—

Twenty minutes later *Esperanza* was still belching black smoke. The horizon remained bare, but the land had begun sending emissaries: seabirds in increasing numbers were swooping down in search of scraps, inspecting *Esperanza* closely and then flying off screeching their displeasure. Down on deck the tourists were chattering worse than the gulls. On the crumpled tarp, the stranger slept on undisturbed, the edges of his T-shirt rippling in the freshening breeze, his broad chest rising and falling, his mouth open as if awaiting a Communion wafer. Five more minutes, Tomás decided, and he would ask one of the men to give the boy some water.

And then, without warning, at a distant spot where a moment ago there had been nothing—Tomás raised a hand to shade his eyes, squinted—there was . . .

Something.

Yes, but what? Tomás wished for binoculars, but— Yes, it was a boat. But whose boat? The distant silhouette seemed stark, military. The hull appeared to be white with, yes, an angled stripe. Red? Was that red? Russians were red. From this distance it was—yes, a damned red stripe, and, Christ, it was so difficult to see!

Tomás felt a faint shudder before he heard the rising whine of twin diesels. The boat was moving fast now, turning this way, growing. But was it . . . ?

He snapped his head and blinked, trying to clear his vision. If those damned tourists would just stop their yelling . . .

Then he saw it, fluttering from the stern: the three colors. Americans!

—⁓—

Tomás shut down the engine and descended the swaying ladder. Ignoring the barrage of questions from the delirious tourists, he walked over, closed the engine cover, and climbed up on it.

"My friends!" he cried, flapping his arms to quiet them.

It took several tries, but eventually they gave him their attention. When the Americans arrive, he told them, we must be calm, polite, resolute. We must act like the Cubans we all are. He reminded them to control their children. And, he warned them, they must say nothing to the Americans about the stranger; as captain, he would deal with that.

Then, perhaps responding to their bubbling excitement, he decided to rehearse them one last time.

"Why did we leave Cuba?" he asked them.

"Communism!" they cried out in unison.

"And why do we go to America?"

"Democracy!"

"Do not forget," Tomás murmured, resting a hand on a man's shoulder and easing himself down to the deck.

The tourists rushed forward and mobbed him, grabbing his hands, pumping his arms, slapping his back. Embarrassed by their foolishness, Tomás retreated toward the ladder, but their unwelcome touching continued even as he climbed.

Alone on *Esperanza*'s bridge, Tomás watched the approach of the sleek American boat. It was big, at least eighty feet, and all steel. When it drew close, it cut its throttles and began rocking in its own wake. Through a loudspeaker, it identified itself in English and Spanish, announced that these were U.S. territorial waters, and declared its intention to board. The tourists cheered and waved their arms. Tomás, imagining the American captain as a younger, clean-shaven version of himself, faced their bridge, squared his shoulders, and saluted.

Churning the water like a bull pawing the ground, the American vessel closed to within a few feet, its wake sending the suddenly puny *Esperanza* rocking crazily. Uniformed sailors appeared along the American's rail and deployed onion-shaped bumpers. Political refugees, Tomás reminded himself, and went down to greet the world's most powerful nation.

The chubby junior officer who stumbled aboard had the crisp white uniform Tomás had expected, but he was impossibly young, with red pimples on his chin and white salve slathered on his nose.

"No ob-lay Span-yole," the American declared, nearly losing his balance as he offered a soft hand.

"I have much English," Tomás assured him, using the handshake to help steady the boy.

"Cuban?" the American asked, setting his feet wide and pulling a clipboard from under his arm.

"Cuban," Tomás confirmed, waving the tourists back.

"Everybody? *Todo?*"

"Political refugees," Tomás declared solemnly.

The American glanced around. "Jeez, it looks like you people have been to hell and back."

"Is true. Seas very bad."

The young officer looked up at the bridge, then over at the mangled cabin. "Wow," he said, shaking his head sympathetically, "will you look at this old tub."

"Please," Tomás asked with a confused smile, "what is *tub?*"

"Tub," the American said, twirling a hand. "You know. Scow. Junk bucket. Beat-up old wreck."

"*Esperanza* is wreck?" Tomás asked incredulously, suddenly noticing that this American had hard little eyes, like a pig's.

"Okay, back to business." The American lowered his eyes and read from his clipboard, "Is this vessel carrying any contraband?"

Tomás did not understand the word. He turned and shooed the tourists back. The Coast Guard boat loomed above *Esperanza* like an iceberg.

"Contraband. Illegal," the American explained, raising his voice. "Do you have any drugs on board? Any guns? Any Cuban cigars?"

"Political refugees," Tomás repeated uncertainly. Had he heard correctly? *Esperanza,* a wreck? The wind had shifted. The American smelled like a cheap woman.

The young officer, looking away, was using his pen to make a head count. "I get sixteen. Is that right?"

Tomás did the math: fourteen tourists, himself, the boy. "Yes," he said, staring at the white splotch on the American's nose. "Sixteen."

"And your name, skip?" the American asked, his pen poised.

"Tomás Cruz."

The little pig eyes swung up, twinkling. "Any relation?"

"Relation?"

"To the real one."

Tomás squinted. What did this mean, *the real one?*

"Tom Cruise," the American declared, smiling. "You know, pops, the big star."

Pops the big star? Tomás looked around helplessly.

"Tom Cruise," the American teased. "Nicole Kidman?"

Tomás shrugged, mystified.

"*Rain Man?*"

"Rain?" Tomás replied doubtfully, glancing at the clouds.

"*Top Gun? Risky Business? Mission Impossible?*"

"Films? Hollywood films?"

"We've got liftoff," the American cried, staring skyward as if searching for the bird that had splattered his nose.

Tomás turned and angrily shooed the tourists back. This was difficult enough without them crowding around.

Consulting his clipboard, the American said, "Next, is there anyone on board this vessel who requires immediate medical attention?"

"Again, please?"

"Med-i-cal a-ten-tion. You know, pops, is anybody here, uh—what's that word?—*malade?* Sick?"

"*Enfermo,*" Tomás offered.

"What was that?"

"En-fermo."

"That's the guy over there?" The officer indicated the crumpled tarp.

"Yes," Tomás agreed warily. This was it.

"You have his papers?"

"No papers."

"No papers?"

Tomás shook his head. He felt his heart beating as he fingered his lucky coin. Now what?

"Do you know where he's from?" the American asked. "His hometown."

"Cienfuegos."

"Can you spell that?"

"Yes. Absolutely."

Tomás spelled, the American wrote.

"He's the only one?" the American asked.

"Only one?"

"Fermo," the officer said impatiently, jabbing his pen toward the tarp. "The snoozer. He's the only one sick?"

"I think yes," Tomás replied cautiously, not sure he was following.

The American started writing again. "Fermo," he said. Is that spelled *F-e?*"

"Yes. Absolutely."

"Okay," the American said, writing. "Fermo. Now we're getting somewhere." His pen did not seem to be working properly. "But," he said, shaking it, "I'll need more than his initial."

"Yes?" Tomás asked, once again confused. *"Enfermo,"* he repeated, hoping for another clue.

"Work with me on this, pops. N. Fermo. Fine. I've got that. Now what does the *N* stand for?"

Tomás cocked his head, trying to understand. The *en?*

The American looked about in exasperation, took a deep breath, and then, as if speaking to a fool, asked, "What . . . is . . . Fermo's . . . first . . . name?"

"Navidad." Maria's favorite brother was named Navidad.

"Can you spell that?"

Tomás spelled it.

"Excelente." The American beamed. "Navidad Fermo. See, that wasn't so hard, was it, pops?"

"Not so hard." Tomás glanced toward the bridge, hoping *Esperanza* realized that, in addition to his little pig eyes and the bird droppings on his nose, this American had the brain of a chicken.

The youngster unhooked a large walkie-talkie from his belt, brought it to his mouth, and began to mumble. He paused from time to time and listened to the device make squawking noises.

Finally he turned back to Tomás. "They're sending a chopper for Fermo. A medevac." The American held one hand above his head and made a childish twirling motion with his index finger. "You know," he said, continuing to spin his finger, "a helicopter?"

Tomás smiled but said nothing. A helicopter! Before this American was even born, Cuba had used helicopters to crush the invasion at Bahía de Cochinos, the Bay of Pigs.

When the American lurched off to get the tourists' names, Tomás went over and knelt on the tarp. A musty odor heavy with decades of dead fish rose from the deck, reminding Tomás that he and *Esperanza* were getting old.

The boy was sleeping fitfully now. His facial muscles were twitching, as if in his dreams he was engaged in some terrible struggle. Tomás raised the sleeping head, dampened a cloth, and wiped the boy's face, then squeezed some water on his dry lips. How curious, Tomás thought, that he felt closer to this boy than to anyone else on board. He thought about the boy's waking up in America among strangers, with nothing of his own. It did not seem right.

Tomás laid the boy's head back down and tried to arrange his limbs to make him more comfortable. From somewhere beyond the clouds came a faint rumble of thunder. Reflexively, Tomás reached up and grasped his old coin. Perhaps the American had been right about the rain.

FOURTEEN

Moe swept the sharp, hissing tongue of flame back and forth across the small, elevated crucible, waiting for the misshapen chunk of gold inside to react. The heat from the torch warmed his skin and soothed his nerves. Working with gold had always been a kind of therapy for Moe. He still couldn't understand what had possessed Marlene to arrange this date tonight, unless she simply felt sorry for him. After the raid at Wedo's, he had behaved like a complete schmuck with her, first by suggesting a ratty diner and then by sitting there like a zombie and watching the light play over the planes of her face.

He glanced down and checked the time; he still had half an hour. Bending closer, he trained the tip of the blue—the hottest part of the flame—on the crucible's rounded base. The latest in his long line of design failures was taking its sweet time getting to its melting point. Moe jiggled the torch, urging it on; he'd promised Marlene he'd be waiting outside when she finished work. After his bumbling performance the other night, it seemed the least he could do.

Inside the crucible the edges of his last disaster began softening like sagging shoulders. Moe adjusted his goggles and inched closer, holding the torch steady. As the gold started to melt, its impurities began rising to the surface and burning off in the air—*ffft, ffft, ffft*—showering him with sparks. A magical transformation was taking place right before his eyes: a failed design was becoming a bubbly puddle of sunlight, brimming with promise, fresh as renewed hope.

When the gold was fully molten, Moe reached over, switched off the gas, and picked up the long-handled mold that since childhood he had called "the candle snuffer." Proceeding with great care, he tipped the crucible until a thin, sizzling stream came cascading from its lip, forming a short-lived but glorious golden rainbow that emptied into the cone-shaped mold. When the mold had cooled enough, Moe turned it upside down and, with a few practiced taps, sent a newborn gold ingot sliding out into the world.

He stared at the lopsided little cone. Its radiant heat was distorting the surrounding air, making the ingot shimmer like a mirage. Locked somewhere inside it was the design he was looking for: Moe Rosen's signature shape, something as distinctive as the Nike swoosh. With gold, Moe believed, anything was possible. In an earlier incarnation, this very gold could have adorned an Egyptian pharaoh or a Scythian prince or—God help him—an African queen.

Moe brought his goggled eyes to within a few inches of the still-warm surface and began searching for its elusive secret.

—◈—

A harsh sound wrenched him back.

The doorbell!

He leaped up from the bench—what time was it?—and saw Marlene standing outside in the street. He buzzed her in and rushed through the store, accidentally bumping a showcase and toppling all the carefully arranged hands inside.

"You stood me up," Marlene declared, glaring at him.

"No, I—"

"Had me standing out in the rain like some—"

"Come inside. Please. You're wet."

She shook the water from her oversize jacket but made no move to come in. Raindrops glistened on her face like tinsel. Even angry, she was beautiful. Moe couldn't believe he'd done this.

"Let me show you what I've been doing," he pleaded, stepping aside to encourage her advance. "In the back."

"Man's tryin' to get me in the back," she muttered, angrily pulling the bottom of her jacket down below her hips.

"I'm not," he insisted, unsure of what he was disclaiming. "Look. This is all my fault, I know. But I'm really glad you're here. I was working and got carried away. Don't be mad. Please?"

She studied him with narrowed eyes.

"Please?" he said, gesturing her inside.

She shrugged and entered. He locked the door. Even in the dark she was stunning.

"Come on, I'll show you what I've been doing." He reached out to take her arm, but something stopped him.

She noted his frozen hand. "Are you afraid of women?" she asked warily.

"No," he insisted, stuffing the cowardly hand into his pocket.

"Black women?"

"Not at all. Absolutely not. No."

"So it's just me," she said, moving closer, crowding him.

They were the same height. Her eyes seemed to glow in the dark, like a leopard's. He backed away and lowered his gaze. He'd forgotten the question.

"Being with me makes you uncomfortable."

"A little," he admitted, fidgeting.

"That's okay," she sighed. "I understand."

"You do?"

"Sure. After all, I'm only a waitress."

"That's not it."

"Yes, it is."

"No. It's just . . ."

"What?" she demanded, jarring him.

"You're just so beautiful," he said before he could stop himself.

The silence tingled. She looked at him uncertainly.

"Well," she said, fiddling with the zipper on her jacket, "I wasn't expecting that."

He led her to the workroom.

"Have you ever felt pure gold?" He picked up the precious little cone.

"I don't know."

"Here." He turned her wrist and dropped the cone into her palm.

"Wow," she exclaimed, hefting it. "Why is it so heavy?"

"Pure gold weighs twice as much as lead." He was thrilled to have her in here, sharing the space with his dreams.

"I have gold jewelry," she said, rolling the cone in her palm, "but it doesn't feel like this."

"Most jewelry is fourteen karat, which is only fifty-eight percent gold."

"What's the rest?"

"Stuff. Copper, silver, base metals—all of it much lighter than gold. That little piece you're holding weighs six troy ounces, half a pound. That's what I was working on when, you know, I should have been meeting you."

"It looks like a miniature ice cream cone." She handed it back. "What were you doing with it?"

"Looking for a design," he said, tossing it up and catching it.

"You're a designer?"

"Well," he said, flattered, "that's what I did in California."

"When were you in California?"

"I lived there five years."

"Whereabouts?"

He slipped the cone into a leather pouch and pulled the drawstring. "Hollywood."

She seemed intrigued. "You designed jewelry for the movies?"

"No. Costumes." He hadn't exactly designed costumes either, but he'd always planned—

"Oh, wow," Marlene gushed. "That's incredible."

"Not really. Actually—"

"Hey," she said, pointing at the clock, "we should go."

"Okay. Sure. Whatever you say. Where are we going?"

"Some of the guys from Wedo's are getting together at a club. Does that sound okay?"

"Fine. Give me thirty seconds."

He fixed his tie, locked the leather pouch in the small safe, double-checked the big safe, slipped on his raincoat, and flipped off the lights. Walking her through the store, he felt buoyant. The evening was yet young. She was gorgeous. That Hollywood line had been inspired. He'd straighten it out later. Who could blame him for stretching the truth? And how much of a stretch was it? Before being called home, Moe had been costume manager for the Sony Studios in Burbank. He hadn't done any actual designing, but if he'd been able to stay there—

Something poked him in the side.

"You're drifting," Marlene told him.

Outside, she waited under the awning while he locked the outer door and secured the grate. The rain was coming down in a fine, supermarket-produce mist.

"Here," he said to her, "take my coat. Your hair will get wet."

"It's only a wig." She took his arm instead. "Come on, the car's this way."

The street was deserted. The sidewalk glistened as if someone had sprinkled it with gold dust. For a moment it felt like the old neighborhood.

"This club we're going to," he said. "What kind of place is it?"

"It's owned by Trinnies. P.O.S. stands for Port of Spain. It's a dance club."

"Okay, but I don't dance."

"There's an old African proverb: 'If you can walk, you can dance.'"

"Nice," Moe replied, skirting a puddle. "But whoever said it never met me."

—◦◦◦—

A scowling black man built like a Lincoln Navigator was standing by the side entrance of an ordinary-looking apartment building.

Moe hung back. "This is the club?"

"They don't have a permit," Marlene explained, whisking him inside.

The door closed behind them. They were in a shabby hallway. Straight ahead, a long set of narrow stairs led downward to darkness. Something didn't seem right; the music coming from the stairway was faint, but the entire building was shaking.

An enormous, light-skinned black woman appeared above a Dutch door. "Check yuh cose?"

She had red hair and a faded yellow gown that revealed far more of her loose, freckled bosom than Moe cared to see. Lowering his eyes, he slipped off his raincoat and draped it over the door. Marlene tossed her jacket on top of it.

"Boat tuhgedda?" the woman asked.

Moe looked up. "Excuse me?"

"Yes," Marlene said, reaching past him, taking the numbered cardboard square and sliding it into his jacket pocket.

He turned to say something clever, but her outfit stopped him cold. It wasn't just the clinging pink sweater or the tight white slacks, it was the shock of bare midriff in between.

"What?" she asked, anxiously examining herself.

She twisted around. The back view was even more outrageous than the front.

"What? Tell me."

"You look great."

"That's it?"

"That's enough."

"Stop making jokes," she said, picking something from her sweater. "You scared me."

Moe grasped the metal railing and led the way down. The poorly lit stairway was steep and creaky. The music still seemed far away, but the vibrations increased as they descended.

Moe waited nervously at the bottom while Marlene clicked down the last few steps. In the jewelry trade, where people often carried fortunes in diamonds, remaining inconspicuous was a virtue. Marlene's outfit could have stopped traffic in Malibu. There was no telling what effect it might have in Brooklyn.

He gritted his teeth and pulled open the door. The sound hit him like the heat from a blast furnace. He was staring into a maelstrom.

Marlene walked right into it. He followed her. The door closed behind him. His eardrums trembled. His senses were under assault. The huge room seemed crowded, but flashing lights rendered his eyes nearly useless. He knew he was moving, but he could no longer feel his body except as a baffle for the music.

A long table had apparently been reserved for Wedo's employees and their dates. Moe thought he recognized several of the faces, though the flashing lights made positive ID impossible. Two more bridge chairs were pulled over, and Moe and Marlene joined the group. There was a lot of handshaking and smiling, but the volume of the music precluded speech. Moe noted that more than half the chairs were empty and assumed that their occupants were part of the undulating mass that covered the nearby dance floor.

The music stopped abruptly. The clotted dancers trembled to a halt. Couples drifted off. Gradually, Moe's senses returned to normal. It was warm. The air was laced with sweat and perfume, rum and beer. Shifting beams of colored light were reflecting off a large mirrored ball that reminded Moe of the prom scene in *Carrie*.

The room was packed. Moe estimated the crowd at two hundred and assumed that nearly all of them were black, though the slowly spinning ball colored them red one moment, green the next, yellow a moment later. Moe glanced down at his hands. They were the color of talcum powder.

"Drink?" Marlene asked.

"Sure," Moe replied gamely. "Why don't you order for me?"

He looked around. The room tingled with a sense of carefree, almost reckless abandon. He watched Marlene talking to people. She was so intense, so alive. Her couldn't get over how exciting it was just being near her.

The waiter returned with a small tray crammed with drinks. Moe was passed a touristy-looking plastic coconut with a long straw, a fruited skewer, and a paper parasol. He would have said something, but Marlene was turned away, busily talking.

When everyone had a drink, one of the men stood up and proposed a toast to someone or something called the floop. Glasses were clinked, the floop was invoked, and everyone took a drink. Not wanting to appear a wimp, Moe hoisted his coconut and boldly swallowed a mouthful, instantly scorching his throat. The air exploded with raucous sound.

Couples began deserting the table for the dance floor. Moe felt his skull pulsing in time with the jackhammer beat. Marlene was engrossed in an animated conversation with a good-looking young man across the table. Feeling abandoned, Moe raised his drink and carefully took a sip. When it didn't burn as badly as before, he took another, and then one more after that. Marlene kept jabbering away. Moe took another drink, a big one, then removed the skewer and wolfed down the pineapple chunks and the maraschino cherry. When he lifted the coconut again, he discovered it was empty.

Moe closed his eyes. The music was crashing against his head like angry surf. He wasn't used to drinking. Something started pulling his hand. He looked up. It was Marlene. He took a deep breath and struggled to his feet. He felt a little dizzy.

Taking both Moe's hands, Marlene began snaking backward, drawing him away from the safety of the table and into the dark, throbbing jungle of dancers. The music blared. The floor shook. Colored lights flashed. Deeper and deeper they went, picking their way through a thicket of moving bodies.

They arrived at a tiny clearing. Marlene released his hands and, still facing him, began clapping in time with the music. He did the same; with the beat pounding through every fiber of his body, it was easy. It was also fun. Next, while continuing to clap, she began shifting her weight from side to side. He followed suit, his confidence rising; this wasn't much harder than a bar mitzvah fox trot.

But then, as he watched, she gradually extended her movements until her body was moving with a sensuous fluidity. Moe tried it, but where her body was loose and graceful, his felt stiff and clunky. Marveling at Marlene's effortless, animal grace, Moe struggled to awaken genes dormant for millennia, trying to reach back to a time when their common ancestors danced around campfires in Africa's Great Rift Valley. Despite his determined efforts, Moe's ancient dancing genes refused to kick in.

Afraid of making a spectacle of himself, Moe reverted to the basic step-clap, step-clap, rationalizing that there was almost no room to maneuver anyway. Lights flashed, colors shifted. The air was heavy with the odor of fresh sweat. The music was brutal, the beat relentless. Moe soldiered on gamely, clapping and stepping, occasionally hopping this way or that to avoid one of his more reckless neighbors. The song was endless. The air grew closer, hotter, heavier. Moe began to perspire. Marlene was gorgeous. He couldn't take his eyes off her. Being with her, looking at her, watching her move—all were easing his discomfort at being in an alien place.

The song ended. There were cheers and crackles of applause. Gratefully, Moe dropped his hands and stopped shuffling in place. He was overheated, but reasonably sober. The air tingled with a welcome quiet. Marlene approached and rested a weary forearm on his shoulder. She was wet and glowing and breathing hard. Beads of sweat covered her nose and upper lip. Her eyes shone.

She leaned closer and brought her hot cheek next to his. "Tell the truth. Wasn't that fun?"

"Watching you was fun. But I felt—"

His breath caught as she draped her other arm around his neck, stepped in, and pressed her belly against his. A new song had started up, a slow one. Apparently she wanted to dance some more. Everyone around them was dancing. He had to do something.

With neither of her hands available, he had no choice but to place both of his on her back. His left hand touched down in a safe, sweatered area between her shoulder blades, but his right hand landed with a squish. He hadn't meant to touch her bare skin, but when she trembled and nestled closer, he left it there. She tightened her grip around his neck and began moving her hips in time to the music. He tried to follow along. The tips of her breasts brushed his chest, retreated, brushed again. She rested her cheek against his. It was hot and damp, like her back. Her breasts located the spots they wanted and settled in, pressing against his heart.

Suddenly Moe felt himself stir and he tried to back away, but a hand slid down his back and pulled him in tight. Her thigh insinuated itself between his legs and stayed there, delivering an erotic massage. Moe glanced around anxiously. On all sides, couples were fused together, swaying like tendrils of some huge, underwater life-form. The music rose and fell like a tide. He and Marlene swayed together. Moe felt helpless and exposed. In almost no time his erection had stretched out to its full length along her thigh and was straining for more. Moe tried picturing the ugliest blind date he'd ever had, to no avail. Her leg was relentless.

Something banged on Moe's shoulder. Marlene released him. He turned to find himself facing a tall, thirtyish black man in a loose-fitting, dark suit. The man smelled of rum.

"Get loss," he said to Moe. "Ah wanzuh."

Moe's brain struggled to switch gears. The man wasn't speaking Swahili; he wanted Marlene. A quick glance revealed that the interest was not mutual.

"We're together," Moe told him.

"You was." The man looked past Moe to Marlene. "I like dark meat," he assured her with a feral grin.

Moe didn't move. People all around them continued to dance. The man was slightly drunk, but he had a good four inches on Moe. The light made the pockmarks on his cheeks look like craters.

"C'mon, Midnight," the man said to Marlene, reaching for her.

"Take a hike," Marlene told him, backing out of reach.

"You best hush up," the man warned her.

Moe centered himself between them. Up close, the man's eyes looked watery but mean.

"Listen here," Moe said, trying for firm but friendly. "I really think—"

"Shut up," the man growled, staring down at Moe and shifting his weight menacingly. "You white motherfuckers all the same. Think you can come fuck with our women."

"I'm not your women," Marlene told the man.

He pointed a finger. "I tole you, shut the fuck up."

"Back at you," she said.

Moe raised open hands as a sign of appeasement. This was getting ugly.

The man talked over him. "You think your big black ass too good for me?" he challenged Marlene. Then his features softened. "Shee-it," he chuckled. "C'mon, Lick-rish," he said, reaching out for her. "Less dance."

She backed away and made that chirping sound with her teeth.

"C'mere, you black bitch," the man snarled, lunging for her.

Moe slid over and, with his hands still raised, blocked him with his chest. The contact ratcheted the tension up a notch. The man stared down at Moe, his body rigid, his eyes brimming with hate. The music kept playing. The lights kept blinking. Everyone kept dancing.

"Let's go," Marlene said to Moe, tugging the back of his jacket. "I want another drink."

Moe's eyes remained locked with the man's. "Okay," he said, and, keeping his hands raised and open, took a tentative step back.

The man didn't move. Marlene tugged again. One of Moe's calf muscles started trembling. He retreated another step. A couple bumped against him but kept dancing.

The man still hadn't moved, but he looked ready to explode. He was breathing through his nose. Marlene tugged harder. Moe took another step back and then, out of range of the man's fists, lowered his hands and turned to follow her. His heart was thumping. His back tingled. He tried to take a deep breath.

Before he could exhale, the man had flashed past him, spun Marlene around, and grabbed her hair with one hand and a breast with the other. She pushed at him and cried out. Without thinking, Moe rushed up and punched the man in the ribs, a glancing blow, but enough to spin him back toward Moe in a murderous rage, his teeth bared and his arm drawn back to strike. Moe ducked way down to avoid the wild punch and then came up fast, pushing off with the full strength of his legs and aiming a furious blow that missed the man's face but by some miracle landed flush on his throat, sending him tumbling backward, gagging and clutching at himself with both hands.

Moe was on him before he hit the floor, flailing away with both fists. The next thing he knew, people were holding him, everything was confusion, women were screaming.

Moe felt himself being pulled backward. He tried to stand, but his legs were tangled. His arms were pinned back. He couldn't seem to catch his breath. But then he saw less than ten feet away the bastard who'd put his filthy hands on Marlene. The world went red and Moe tried to attack him again but was unable to break free. The other guy was being held too. He was twisting and kicking, screaming that Moe was a white devil, a white motherfucker, a white everything. More men joined in and helped drag him away.

Moe stopped struggling and started saying "Okay" over and over again. The men holding him relaxed their grip. When he began brushing himself off, he discovered that his hands were shaking badly. He tasted bile at the back of his throat.

"Come on, Rocky," Marlene said, taking his arm.

For a moment, he hadn't recognized her without the wig. Her sweater was torn.

"Are you okay?" he asked.

"I'm fine," she said, leading him away.

People made a path for them. Someone had turned off the music. His hands were still trembling, but not as much.

Back at the table, everyone was standing.

"You guys take care of him," Marlene said, then went off with some of the women.

Moe was happy to sit down. The Wedo's men all crowded around, patting his shoulders and making jokes. But they seemed tense, nervous, apprehensive, almost like penned cattle spooked by the scent of a wolf. They kept pressing Moe to have another drink.

"I had that thing in the coconut," he told them, not wanting to mix.

An older man Moe recognized as the Wedo's cashier bent close to tell him something. The man seemed jittery. He smelled of Old Spice.

"You muss leave fwom here," the man whispered in a silky Haitian accent.

"Excuse me?"

"Zat man you fight wiss. Twuss me, Missa Rosen, zat is a dangerous man: a bad man."

"Bad how?" Moe asked, choking back a bubble of fear.

"Miz Ark tell you. Miz Ark, she know to fix evwy sing."

"Bad how?" Moe demanded, squeezing the man's arm.

"'Is name Michel Pioline," the cashier whispered. "'Is fazza was close fwom Duvalier."

"Okay," Moe said, tensing for the rest.

"'Is fazza," the man repeated, enunciating each word, "was close fwom Duvalier. Duvalier is Papa Doc."

Moe released him. "And?"

"Missa Rosen, you's an Amewican man. You dozen know 'bou Papa Doc an 'is Tonton Macoutes."

Moe sensed the man's fear, but couldn't understand it. Hadn't Papa Doc died thirty years ago?

"Bess to leave here now," the man advised urgently, straightening up. "Where Marlene is?"

"The ladies' room, I think."

"I twy fine her." The man hurried off.

Moe took a deep breath. The Wedo's men were all still milling about nervously, their eyes darting around the room as if on the lookout for ghosts. Moe found it disconcerting. Why would Haitians here in America still be worried about Papa Doc and his Tonton Macoutes? Moe read *Time* and *Newsweek;* he knew Haiti's history. François Duvalier had been a physician. He had exploited his people's belief in Voodoo by calling himself Papa Doc, claiming that he had occult powers and setting up a Gestapo-like secret police called the Tonton Macoutes that had terrorized the nation. But Papa Doc, evil bastard that he was, had died thirty years ago. Why, Moe wondered uncomfortably, would anyone be afraid of him now? This was America, for God's sake. America! There were no Voodoo doctors in America. There were no Tonton Macoutes in America. Were there?

They brought another coconut with a parasol and a fruit stick. Moe tossed the plastic straw under the table and took a quick gulp. It didn't seem as strong as the first one. He tried to think nice thoughts. He'd won the fight. Marlene had called him Rocky. The music started up again, a number that sounded like a car crash. Moe desperately wanted to get out of here and go home. He didn't like the idea of secret police. What was keeping Marlene? What if this Michel Pioline bastard was waiting for them outside right now? With reinforcements.

Moe shook his head and took another gulp. The liquor was taking the harsh edge off the music, but it couldn't seem to wash away the awful taste in his mouth. What could be keeping Marlene?

She came back to the table as the song ended. She was wearing her wig. They had pinned her sweater back together. Three Wedo's guys insisted on escorting them out to the car.

"Are these our bodyguards?" Marlene asked, taking Moe's arm.

"No, no," he scoffed. "They're more like chaperones. You know, guarding your honor."

She gave an insouciant chirp. "They're a little late."

—⨇⨇—

"What's a floop?" he asked as they were driving home.

"Say what?" She hadn't been paying attention. Neither of them had mentioned the fight.

"A floop. You know, what everyone was toasting back there."

She stopped for a red light. "You really don't know?"

He glanced at the side-view mirror—no one appeared to be following them—then looked down at his hands. His knuckles were all scraped. They didn't hurt. Had she asked him a question? The light changed.

"A floupe is a combination float and troupe," she said. "The float rides up ahead on the flatbed truck. With the band."

"The band," Moe said, keeping an eye on the mirror.

"Right. And the troupe marches directly behind the float. In matching costumes." She paused. "Which is what makes the float and the troupe a single unit. Which is why it's called a floupe."

"This floupe is for what? Some kind of festival?"

"The West Indian Day parade," she said, braking for a stray cat. "Come on, Rocky, don't tell me you never heard of the West Indian Day parade."

"Sure I have. I read the papers. They hold it every year on Labor Day. On Eastern Parkway. It's the biggest parade in the city."

"There you go." She smiled.

He loved it when she smiled. Her whole face lit up. "So let me see if I've got this straight," he said, shifting around to see her better. "Wedo's is going to have a floupe in this year's parade."

"Uh-huh." She wriggled in her seat. "You like staring at me, don't you, Rocky?"

"Does it bother you?"

She shook her head. Moe couldn't tell if she was smiling. The car got very quiet.

"I embarrassed you," she said in a flat voice, continuing to stare straight ahead. "Dancing with you like that."

"Not at all."

"You're a lousy liar, Rocky."

"I'm a worse dancer."

"I had to find out. Time, you know. There's only so much of it."

"Find out what?"

She glanced over. "Don't take it the wrong way."

It took a moment to sink in. "You thought I was gay?" he asked incredulously.

"Hey." She shrugged. "Guy your age. Tall. Nice-looking. Single. Owns his own business. You know . . ."

"You're single too. You go to college at night."

"Yeah, but—"

"And you're a lot better looking than I am."

She sucked her teeth. "So you say."

"You're beautiful."

"Most guys think I'm too dark."

"Too dark for what?"

She made that funny chirping sound again. Apparently that was all the answer he was going to get.

"How do you feel?" he asked. "I mean, where he, you know . . ."

"Sore," she said, making a turn. "But I'll be fine by Thursday."

"What's Thursday?"

"Our next date."

"Okay. I mean, *good.*"

"How about right after work?"

"I'll wait for you outside."

"No, I'll come to the store," Marlene said. "Same as tonight."

"Fine."

She stopped for a light. It made her face red. She was smiling again. "That way you'll have more time to work—"

"That was all my fault."

"—on the costumes."

"Excuse me?"

"For the floupe. That's what I was telling everybody at the club tonight, that you're going to be our designer."

"I am?"

Her face turned green. "Oh, yeah," she said, hitting the gas. "We're all in your hands, Rocky."

His mind was racing. All in his hands? Designer? How . . . ? "How many people in the troupe?"

"About a hundred. I'll tell you all about it on Thursday. Here's your building." She pulled up by a hydrant.

A hundred! Plus he'd have to design the float and—what a night.

She turned off the engine, but kept her hands on the wheel. She was staring straight ahead. "Do you want to kiss me, Rocky?"

"What? Of course. Sure. Absolutely."

He put his arm around her and she slid toward him. He was aiming for her lips but at the last moment he veered off and kissed her forehead instead.

"I have this weird taste in my mouth," he explained, wondering what he was afraid of.

"That's okay."

"Our first kiss. That should be . . . I don't know . . . You know what I mean?"

She kissed her index finger and touched it to his lips. "Thursday."

FIFTEEN

Antoinette huddled in the darkness. The air was heavy with spice, sweat, dried blood, and rum. It was warm, but she could not stop shivering. She shut her eyes, hugged herself, and retreated into the past.

She was with Fabrice. He was walking her home. They stopped by some bushes to kiss, and soon they were on the ground and kissing harder. Then she felt his hand go up under her skirt and touch her in a way no boy had ever touched her before. As she squirmed free, she started shaking all over, her heart beating so fast she thought it would burst. Fabrice took her in his arms and rocked her back and forth, back and forth, back and forth. She wanted Fabrice here right now, holding her like that again.

A sob escaped her throat, frightening her. She heard voices across the room and held her breath. It was too dark to see, but she could tell they were talking about her. She did not want to think about what they were saying, she wanted to think about Fabrice. But it was bad to think about Fabrice. Fabrice could not help her now. Fabrice was not coming back to her, not this time. Because this time Fabrice was not up swimming with some rich white woman at some grand house, he was down with his ancestors on the Island Beneath the Sea. Fabrice was gone. Nothing would bring him back. Antoinette grabbed the flesh of an arm and pinched herself hard, the way her mother used to do when she'd done something bad. She should not be thinking about Fabrice.

The voices across the room sounded angry. She could not hear their words, but she was sure they were talking about her. She rubbed her arms up and down. The shivering was terrible. Even her teeth were shaking. She had been afraid before, but never like this, not even that time at Ville Bonheur, when her mother had carried her to Saut d'Eau, the sacred waterfall. She had been nine years old. A luck bath, her mother had called it, making it sound like fun. And at first it had been exciting; Antoinette had never seen such a waterfall, had never seen so many people in one place before. But then her mother had undressed her in front of all those people and forced her into the angry, rushing water. The rocks had been nasty and the water had been jump-up cold. Hugging herself now, Antoinette remembered how her mother had held her under, the icy water pounding so hard she could hardly breathe and roaring so loud it swallowed her screams.

She snapped back to the present. It was dark. The candles and their moving shadows only made it worse. Antoinette bit her knuckle. The vague shapes on the other side of the room were talking louder. She strained to hear the words.

". . . not have come back here," a woman hissed.

"Where then?" a man asked. The houngan! He was back!

"Anywhere," the woman said, her voice rising. "This is the first place they will look."

"And so?" The priest did not sound angry.

"Soldiers will come." The woman's voice was tough as coconut skin. "Many of them. With guns."

"And so? The l'wahs do not fear the devil himself. Do you think they will run from a handful of soldiers?"

"It is not the l'wahs I am worried about."

"Then you are worried about the wrong thing."

"She should not have come," the woman insisted.

"She is a member of our society."

"Yes, but—"

"The l'wahs do not abandon their children," the houngan declared, "and we will not abandon one of ours."

"Yes, but—"

"Go now," he said impatiently. "Help with the preparations. Your skills are needed there."

"As you wish."

Antoinette heard feet scraping, the creaking of the screen door. Her shivering was coming in bursts now, like waves. She shut her eyes and for a brief moment saw Fabrice huddled on Agwe's raft, far from shore, tossed by angry waves. She wanted him here, holding her. She wanted—

"Child!"

She had not even heard the houngan approach. He was squatting down in front of her. The cuffs of his white pants wanted washing. His shirt was crowded with little pineapples. Antoinette had known the houngan her whole life. His presence warmed her insides. His eyes saw right down to her *gros-bon-ange*, her soul.

"So, child," he asked with his familiar, funny-tooth smile, "do you know me?"

She sniffled hard. "Yes, houngan."

"Are you able to listen to me?"

"Yes, father." She gathered up her skirt and knelt down. The earth was cool against her knees.

"Do you believe?" the houngan asked her.

"Yes, papa." His voice passed through her as smoothly as a hot comb through oiled hair. Her shivering had stopped.

She heard a sound like fingernails on a dry washboard. She looked down. The asson, the houngan's sacred rattle, was shaking in his hand as if alive.

"I am calling to the l'wahs," the houngan told her as the bones inside his magic gourd began scratching out a gravelly, rhythmic song.

"Yes, papa," she whispered, watching sparks of candlelight dancing on the asson's ornamental beads.

"First I pay my respects," the houngan said, speaking in the same halting rhythm as the bones, "then I remind the l'wahs . . . that

Antoinette Voisin . . . is a loyal *serviteur* . . . who feeds them well . . . and honors their ceremonies."

"Thank you, papa," she whispered, listening to the asson's beat, feeling its power reaching deep inside her.

"I will tell the l'wahs . . . that Sister Antoinette . . . has undergone the rituals . . . to become a hounsi . . . in this parish."

"Yes, houngan."

He continued chanting in time with the dry, rhythmic rattling of the asson. Candles flickered. The air filled with the sharp smell of spices. Antoinette felt parts of herself going numb.

"I will remind the l'wahs," his chant continued, "how soldiers came . . . and dragged Sister Antoinette . . . from our village . . . and delivered her . . . to their bokor."

"Yes, papa."

"How their bokor . . . tore her clothing . . . and put his . . . rough hands on her."

She bit her lower lip, pressed her knees together, and shuddered.

The houngan began rocking slowly back and forth, adding his body's motion to the joined rhythm of the asson and his voice.

"I will remind . . . the l'wahs," he chanted, "how Sister Antoinette . . . escaped from that bokor . . . and came here . . . to us . . . I will—"

His body continued rocking, the asson continued beating, but his mouth fell open and his eyes rolled up until they showed only white. Antoinette crossed herself four times in rapid succession, twice to the left and twice to the right. The houngan, she knew, had entered the spirit world. Without taking her eyes from him, she reached into her dress, took out Fabrice's gift, and placed it on the ground so that the l'wah presidents could see what was happening. That done, she closed her eyes, sat back on her ankles, and gave herself over to the steady rhythm of the asson.

After a time she heard a far-off voice calling to her. She opened her eyes. The asson was silent. The houngan was smiling at her. She hurriedly took up the l'wah presidents and stuffed them back inside her dress.

"You are fortunate, child."

"Yes, papa?"

"The l'wahs know this wicked bokor. The l'wahs say that if you had not run, he would have filled your belly with his evil seed."

"Ay!"

"Listen to me, child. The l'wahs know everything. It was the l'wahs who gave you the courage to climb through that window and escape. It was the l'wahs who made you invisible during your long journey here. I have seen the l'wahs, child. I have spoken with them. The l'wahs are pleased with Sister Antoinette."

"Is true?" she asked in thrilled amazement.

"Yes, child." He brought his face close to hers. She smelled the spirit world on him. It was old and strange and sweet. "The l'wahs have spoken to me. They have explained to me what must be done. Can you guess who among them wishes to protect Antoinette Voisin?"

"No, master," she replied, wondering which l'wah would care enough about her. She remembered her granmama Sophie, who had given her sweets when she was little, and her great-aunt Mathilde, who had sewn her First Communion dress.

"Stay, child," the houngan said, rising to his feet. "I will show you."

He returned with a leather pouch and squatted down in front of her.

"Tell me what you see, child." He held out his arm and released a thin, steady stream of cornmeal from his fist.

Antoinette watched as a large white *V* appeared on the ground. The houngan reached into the pouch, refilled his hand, and created a second *V,* this one overlapping the first but pointed in the opposite direction. The area where the two *V*'s overlapped formed a giant diamond.

"What do you see?"

"The two worlds," Antoinette murmured.

"Yes, child." The houngan paused to refill his hand. "Our world and the world of the spirits. Look, child." He added to the design. "See how each world is a part of the other. We serve the l'wahs out of love and respect, and the l'wahs serve us because we are their children's children, the newest links in the race chain stretching out across the abyssal waters, stretching back to far-off Ginnen, stretching all the way back to Damballah and Ayida Wedo, the serpent and the rainbow, who came together in love to make us all."

As he spoke, his hand moved back and forth over the large diamond formed by the crossed V's, first drawing a line straight down its middle and then adding a series of small diagonals to each of the halves, transforming the diamond into a shield patterned like a palm leaf.

"Ayizan!" Antoinette exclaimed.

"Yes, child." The houngan smiled, adding little cross-lined stars in each corner of the vevay. "Ayizan, the first priestess, the protector of the race, the great healer, the conqueror of evil."

"Ayizan," Antoinette murmured, overwhelmed. Dizzy with excitement, she felt weightless. If the great Ayizan was protecting her, no man—no army of men!—could harm her.

—⁂—

"She was right here in this office," Ferray said, banging his desk with his fist. He could feel his anger ricocheting off the walls, flying back to taunt him. "In that very chair," he said, staring at it.

And suddenly there she was, sitting there in that cheap white dress with those wide, frightened eyes and—

The memory overwhelmed him. He began experiencing it all again: the sound of ripping fabric, the sight of her bare, trembling breast. Her desperate writhing. Her moans. Her raw animal smell.

The vision melted under his fury. He stared at the floor, half-expecting it to crack. He noticed that one of his boots was dirty. This was intolerable! What sort of men was he cursed with? Too stupid even to see to the proper cleaning of his boots. What—?

Ferray heard a faint static of words. He grasped the edge of his desk, looked up, and saw the reassuring, obsidian bulk of Captain Ghede.

The colonel dropped into his chair. His head was throbbing. His throat was dry. Spots of light danced before his eyes. He raised a hand and forced himself to swallow .

"Repeat what you just said," he told the captain.

"I was asking, sir: When I find the Voisin girl, do I bring her back here to you?"

Ferray took a deep breath. It was good to have Ghede back. No one ever escaped Ghede. But even with his trusted Ghede it was necessary to be crystal clear. Crystal clear. There was so much to be done. So little time and so many loose ends. He had not even told Ghede that they would be leaving. First things first.

He shook all indecision from his head, looked steadily into Ghede's eyes, and spoke slowly and carefully. "These are your orders, Captain. Antoinette Voisin is not to be brought back here. She is to be eliminated. Is that understood?"

Ghede shifted his weight and suppressed a grin. "Yes, sir."

"She is to be eliminated today. She is to be eliminated by you. Personally. Is that understood?"

The captain's shoulders pulled back. His eyes took on their hunting glint. "Yes, Colonel!"

"Find her and take her someplace where her screams will not be heard. She is young and healthy. After you are done with her, François, the men will all want a chance. Let them draw lots, or however you wish to arrange it." Ferray pointed a warning finger. "But remember, this slippery bitch has already escaped once. You must not let her out of your sight. Not for a second."

"Understood, Colonel."

"Good." Ferray looked down and began scraping the dirty boot with the heel of the clean one.

"Will there be anything else, sir?"

"Yes!" It was maddening, the damned scuff wouldn't come off. Angrily, Ferray began rummaging through his desk for the macoute.

"Ah," he said, finally locating it. "Here." He handed the dark-stained, woven sack across the desk to Ghede. "Bring me her nipples."

—◈◈◈—

The houngan was gone. The women had her now. There were about ten of them, all wearing white dresses, with white wraps covering their hair. Two of them were sitting in a corner stripping palm leaves into fringe while two others were working beneath a central canopy of white mosquito netting, covering a raised wooden platform with mombin leaves.

An old woman took Antoinette's hand and led her to a metal folding chair. After she was seated, two large women struggled over with a basin filled with soapy water and maneuvered it onto a table behind her. Antoinette's hair was washed, dried, oiled, combed, and then wrapped with a long strip of white fabric.

The basin was removed and another, even larger one was brought in and placed on the dirt floor. Delivering bucket after bucket, four younger women filled it with water. When they finished, Marie-Josée approached with a wicker basket and poured perfume and sprinkled white hibiscus petals into the basin. The women who had delivered the water surrounded Antoinette, stood her up, and began unbuttoning her dress.

She stayed their hands and asked for a safety pin. When one was found, she reached in, removed the dollar bill from her bra, and pinned it to the lapel of her dress, making sure that the tomb was facing out. She then called over Marie-Josée, showed her the great eye, and asked her to arrange the dress so that it would have a good view of the ceremony.

Antoinette stood in the flowered water while they bathed her with big sponges lathered with white coconut soap. She was not embarrassed here the way she had been years ago at Saut d'Eau. For one thing, she was no longer a child; she was a woman of seventeen years. For another, there were no strangers here, as there had been that day at the waterfall.

Stream after stream of cool, sweet-smelling water coursed down her body. The women turned her this way and that. The petals tickled her calves. She felt as if the sponges were rubbing away all her earthly fears. Under the wrap her hair felt clean and soft and luxuriant. She looked across the room and saw her dress folded over a chair with the pinned bill clearly visible. She raised her arms straight above her head and turned a slow, full circle in the basin, showing her sleek, clean self to the l'wah presidents.

After the bath, they oiled her body, slipped a white cotton robe over her head, led her to a table at the center of the room, and formed a circle around her. On the table were two ceramic bowls, one empty and the other containing grain. When everyone was in place, a woman entered the circle carrying a noisily flapping, plump white hen. Antoinette took some grain from the bowl, placed it in her palm, and offered it to the bird. But the hen was too busy trying to escape to notice the food. The woman finally subdued the creature by stuffing it under her arm and pinning its wings. Antoinette approached and offered the grain again. The hen cocked its head, hesitated and then pecked at the corn, swallowed, squawked, pecked some more. Then, led by *la place*, Marie-Josée, the women in the circle began clapping their hands and chanting a prayer to Ayizan. The woman holding the bird stepped away from Antoinette and, grasping the hen by its neck, used her free hand to snap each of its legs and each of its wings. Then, with a firm grip on the neck of the frantically squawking bird, she raised it above her head and swung it around sharply, breaking its neck. The circle fell silent.

When the bird's spasms subsided, two women stepped forward. One cut the bird's throat while the other held up the empty ceramic bowl and caught the blood. The woman who had killed the bird laid it on the table and searched its body until she located a perfect white feather. She plucked it, held it aloft for all to see, and then placed it in the bowl of blood. Next, the hen's beak was broken off and added to the bowl. The carcass of the bird was then wrapped in a white cloth and taken away.

Marie-Josée now came forward with a pair of scissors. She said a prayer, reached under Antoinette's head wrap, and cut a lock of her hair. After displaying the hair to the entire circle, Marie-Josée added it to the blood, feather, and beak in the bowl. Using the same scissors, she then cut a curved sliver of nail from Antoinette's left index finger and, after showing it around, added that to the bowl. Then Marie-Josée lifted the bowl, recited a prayer, and holding the bowl out in front of her, walked around the inside of the circle three times. Then, walking backward this time, she made three more circuits for the benefit of "the invisibles," whose spirit world was a mirror image of the earthly one.

While the women chanted, Antoinette was escorted to the raised platform and laid out on the bed of mombin leaves. Grain from the same bowl that had fed the hen was placed on her forehead and in each of her upturned palms. Her face was covered with a mask of finely fringed palm leaf, the heavenly symbol of the priestess Ayizan. Finally, when Marie-Josée was satisfied that the *serviteur* was properly prepared, the white mosquito netting was lowered into place, the attending women retreated, and, looking like a dark angel in a white shroud, Antoinette Voisin was left to make her journey alone.

—◦◦◦—

Ghede jumped out as the Jeep slid to a stop. Jogging to regain his balance, he scanned the village across the way, alert for any sign of attempted escape. But the rows of ramshackle huts shimmered silently in the thick afternoon heat, and except for a scrawny, three-legged dog snuffling for scraps, the single, mud-filled street was deserted.

Without taking his eyes from the village, Ghede signaled his men to line up behind him. Nearby, a row of mismatched planks bridged the sewage ditch that ran parallel to the road, a standard feature of towns without plumbing. Ghede sniffed; for a hot day, the stink was not too bad. He looked down into the shallow ditch and noted the steady flow of muddy water. During the dry season, the night soil often remained in these ditches for weeks, filling the air with a stench that only flies, beetles, and dumb country peasants could tolerate. It was hard for Ghede to believe that he had lived in a place like this for the first fifteen years of his life.

Choosing the sturdiest plank, Ghede led his small company across the ditch and into the village. He walked briskly. Low, dark clouds were rolling in from the sea. Rain would be coming soon. If they hurried, maybe they could be gone from here before it arrived.

Making no attempt to hide his presence, Ghede walked down the center of the sloppy street, the thick red mud sucking at his boots. He chuckled as the crippled mutt, its tail tucked up between its legs, hopped off and hid between the cinder blocks holding up a dilapidated shack.

Stopping at the entrance to the poor excuse for a temple, Ghede called for whoever was inside to come out. After a moment he heard the shuffle of feet. The screen door creaked open. A thin, old man in worn white slacks and a tourist shirt covered with little pink pineapples stood in the doorway. What little hair he had was white. A red bandanna was tied around his scrawny neck.

"You are the houngan," Ghede declared.

"And so?" The man's few remaining, crooked teeth gave him a strange, almost mocking smile.

"We are here for Antoinette Voisin," Ghede told him, suppressing the impulse to grab the insolent old fool by the throat.

"And so?" the houngan responded, pushing his luck.

"She was being questioned on a matter of state security. She escaped."

"She is not here," the houngan said flatly.

Instinctively, Ghede adjusted the holster on his belt. "I do not believe you, old man."

"You are free to believe whatever you wish. Now, if you will excuse me . . ." He released the screen and backed into the darkness.

Ghede caught the door before it closed and followed the houngan inside. His men hurried in and clustered behind him. The air was laced with sharp, conflicting smells. Ghede stood blinking, waiting for his eyes to adjust to the dark. Flickering candles provided shifting glimpses of many small, crowded altars lining the walls. Overhead, dozens of glass bottles dangled from the ceiling beams. At six foot two, Ghede had to duck to avoid hitting them as he walked across the dirt floor.

The houngan was standing in a doorway leading to another, even darker room. Ghede approached him. Antoinette Voisin was close. Ghede could smell her fear. The air reeked of it: that and clarin, the raw rum used in Voodoo ceremonies.

"Stop," the houngan said, centering himself inside the doorway and holding up a hand.

"Why should I listen to you?" Ghede demanded, nonetheless obeying the old man's warning.

"Look here." The houngan pointed down at the ground between them. A line of grain extended from one edge of the doorway to the other. "None may cross this line."

Ghede laughed. "Why? Will you turn me into a zombie?"

"I am not a bokor. I do not traffic in zombies."

"What then?" Normally Ghede would simply have pushed the old man aside, but something was holding him back.

The houngan raised a sideways hand and made the sign of the cross twice, the first right to left and the second left to right.

"Speak up, old man," Ghede threatened, raising his voice to counter a new, unwelcome chill in his blood. He no longer believed in Voodoo, but he was still Haitian.

"Death," the old man intoned, again making the sign of the mirrored cross. "Any man who crosses this line will surely die."

"*You* crossed it." Then, in response to the nervous shuffling of his soldiers' feet, Ghede unsnapped his holster and aimed his .45 at the old man's head.

"Killing me would change nothing," the houngan assured him, looking calmly down the barrel of the gun.

"You think I fear a line of cornmeal drawn by a toothless old man?" Ghede reached across the line and pressed the gun barrel against the old man's forehead.

The houngan remained motionless, staring up at Ghede. His eyes were making the captain uncomfortable. It would be so easy to squeeze the trigger and blow the old fool's brains out. But the colonel would be angry; killing a houngan was not the same as avenging an attack on your sister or snatching a pretty girl off a country road. No, killing a houngan could stir up an entire district, force an investigation. Besides, Ghede reminded himself, Antoinette Voisin was almost certainly hiding somewhere in this dark room.

"Out of my way," he declared, shoving the gun against the old man's forehead hard enough to send him flying backward.

The houngan landed with a thud. Ghede stepped up, scattered the cornmeal thoroughly with his boot, and walked into the room.

"You see?" he said, turning to his men. "I am still alive. The old man has no powers. Look"—he gestured toward the doorway floor—"even his line has disappeared."

The houngan was struggling noisily to his feet. Ghede spun about and used his muddy boot to push him back down.

"What do you say now, old man?"

"Anyone who enters this room will die," the houngan cried out from the floor. "Ayizan has decreed it."

"Ayizan?" Ghede laughed. "You think I am afraid of an old woman?"

"Afraid or not," the old man declared, maneuvering to his knees, "you have crossed the line. You will die."

Ghede placed his boot on the old man's shoulder and pushed, harder this time. The houngan bounced backward across the dirt. He lay there groaning.

"Come," Ghede told his men, using his gun to wave them forward.

The men inched closer, but none entered. Ghede reached down and pulled back the slide on his automatic, chambering a round. The unmistakable sound echoed ominously in the darkness. Moving single file but quickly, the men hopped over the invisible line into the room.

"Spread out and find her," Ghede ordered them, planting himself squarely in the doorway and holstering his weapon. "Set something on fire," he suggested in a loud voice. "Let's have some light in here."

SIXTEEN

The deputy sheriff waved Parker in and locked the door. "Procedure."

"Sure," Parker replied, taking a look around the cramped hospital room. It reminded him of a seashell: smooth, clean, and white. Except for the guy asleep in the bed, who was the color of black bean soup.

"So what's his story?" Parker asked, noting the IV.

The deputy went to the night table and picked up a batch of papers. Both he and Parker were in uniform, though Parker's INS garb was snug and crisp while the deputy's outfit looked slept in. Both men were wearing side arms.

"Detainee is Navidad Fermo," the deputy explained. "An undocumented alien, age unknown but presumed to be late teens, early twenties.

Fermo was medevacked here by Coast Guard chopper. Transfer to County was completed at oh nine thirty today. The CG Interdiction Report states that Fermo was one of sixteen Cuban nationals crammed onto a shitbird fishing boat discovered violating U.S. waters." The deputy looked up smiling. "Stop me if you've heard this before."

Parker laughed. He was thirty-one. Boats full of Cuban defectors had been clogging the Gulf Stream since before he was born. Here in south Florida, Cubans now outnumbered Americans.

"What's wrong with him?" Parker asked.

"*Nada*. The doc says all that's wrong with *Señor* Fermo here is exposure: sunstroke, moonburn, shit like that. He says the IV is for 'hydration,' which, according to the floor nurse, is just a fancy way of saying 'water.'" The deputy rubbed his nose, smirking at some private joke.

"What?"

"That floor nurse?" The deputy hitched up his pants. "Word is, she's hot to trot. You like big tits?" He gave Parker a wink. "I think you are definitely her type."

"How about you?"

"Me? Shit. My wife, Luisa, finds one lipstick stain and I'm Bobbittized." The deputy put his hands behind his neck and twisted his torso. His gunbelt creaked.

"What happened to the TV?" Parker asked, noting the empty brackets hanging from the ceiling. He'd worked in a dockside warehouse one summer; the brackets reminded him of the business end of a forklift.

"TVs're extra." The deputy stifled a yawn. "Somebody's gotta order it. Then they charge you by the day. Another goddamn racket. Your name's Parker?"

"Bobby." He offered his hand.

"Joe Schultz. Tell you what, Bobby, I can hang in here a few more minutes. They got a gift shop downstairs. Go get yourself something to read. Without TV, it gets boring."

"Thanks. If you're sure . . ."

"You go ahead. I'll start on the papers. We got three sets, remember: Coast Guard, my office, and now yours." Schultz shook his head. "Lotta work for one dehydrated Cuban. Then again," he chuckled, "some hot-blooded *chica* is going to thank us."

"Why's that?"

"When they undressed him? Before they cleaned him up and put on the hospital gown? Sleeping Beauty here is hung like a fuckin' horse."

———✺———

Parker held the door open. The nurse did have big tits. Also big hair, a big beauty mark that looked a lot better on Cindy Crawford, and a big ass, which she managed to rub against him as she sashayed into the little room.

"You're a nice-lookin' fella."

"Thanks." He locked the door and returned to his chair and magazine.

"You married?"

"No," Parker said without looking up, hoping she hadn't misconstrued his locking the door. Christ, that was all he needed. He hid his face behind his *GQ*.

A few minutes later, sensing something, Parker lowered the magazine and found himself staring at her starched, double-wide rear end. His impulse was to get away from her, but she was bent over the bed doing something to the patient. If she was working with a needle or some sharp instrument, any sudden movement might spook her. These days, one pinprick was enough to get AIDS.

"You almost done?" he asked hopefully.

"Oh." She swiveled to face him. "I thought you were asleep."

"No, I didn't want to, you know, disturb you while . . ."

Her mouth opened expectantly. The sight of her fat, pink tongue made Parker vaguely nauseous.

"What are you so nervous about?" she asked, leaning back against the bed. "You locked the door." Bending a knee, she used the metal bed frame to pry off a ripple-soled shoe.

Parker looked over at the patient in the bed.

"He won't wake up," the nurse assured him, lifting her white-stockinged foot and setting it next to him on the chair.

Parker's thigh recoiled from her touch. He covered his crotch with the *GQ*.

"What are you hiding under there?" she teased, trying to work her toes beneath the magazine.

"Listen," he said, forcing himself to look at her.

She looked back at him coyly, her toes continuing to probe.

He released the magazine and grabbed her ankle with both hands. "Listen." He squeezed the ankle as if it were her neck. "You don't understand. I . . . I have herpes."

She froze. "Is it active?"

"I'm afraid so," he said earnestly.

Her foot slid from the chair and began fishing around the floor for her shoe.

"Jesus," she said, smoothing her skirt. "I'm glad you told me."

"Look, if it weren't for the blisters . . ."

"Sure," she said distractedly, limping around to the far side of the bed to put on the shoe. "I better, you know, be getting back."

"How about him? Don't you have to do anything?"

"All he needs is rest." She tightened the bed linen. "The IV is good for two more hours. He shouldn't wake up before then."

She started moving toward the door. Parker got up to unlock it.

"Thanks for being straight with me."

"Hey."

"You really are a good-looking guy," she said, shaking out her hair. "The uniform suits you."

"Thanks."

This time when he unlocked the door, she managed to slip past without touching him.

———✸———

Parker couldn't seem to concentrate. He'd been trying to read an interview with David Duchovny, but the boy in the bed kept intruding into his thoughts.

Things happened for a reason; Parker believed that. Getting assigned to this place, with these regs, with this particular detainee—any fool could see that none of that was accidental. But what Parker couldn't decide was whether he was being punished, rewarded, or merely tested. Waiting for a sign, he turned the page and began perusing an *X-Files* photo montage. Like Agent Mulder, Agent Parker believed that the truth was out there.

The first hint came a few minutes later, while Parker was admiring an ad for Gucci underwear. A moan, or what sounded like a moan, came from the bed. Parker closed the magazine, held his breath, and waited. A moment later the summons came again.

Parker rose and approached the bed. Fermo was having a bad dream. Beneath the sheet, his body was writhing about as if struggling to free itself from some unwelcome restraint. Impulsively, Parker reached out and gently pressed his palm against the boy's forehead.

The effect was startling. After an initial, violent tremble, Fermo relaxed. His breathing eased and became regular. Behind his closed lids, the rapid eye movement slowed, then stopped altogether. Parker kept his hand on the dark brow, urging the boy back into deep, untroubled sleep.

Parker stood there gazing down at the innocent face. The boy's skin was so warm, so smooth, so alive, that Parker's hand began first to tingle, then to tremble, then almost to burn. But when he withdrew it, he became light-headed. The strength drained from his legs, forcing him to his knees.

As his breathing returned to normal, Parker discovered that his head, as if by design, was now in line with the boy's waist. While his eyes monitored the sleeping face, his fingers, acting on their own, sought out the deep crease between the mattress and bedsprings and began loosening the sheet.

Fate could step in and stop him at any time, Parker told himself as his fingers slowly tugged the sheet free of its moorings. If the boy woke up or made a sudden move or cried out in his sleep, the game was over. Parker's fingers reached the end of the sheet and began crumpling it up. The better to lift it with, he told himself, feeling like the Big Bad Wolf. He stifled a nervous laugh. *Hung like a horse,* the deputy had said. Well, Parker would soon see what all the fuss was about. He reminded himself that a single knock on the door would be enough to end this: a nurse, a doctor, even a candy striper with cookies and milk. One little knock and Parker would drop the sheet, jump to his feet, and pretend that nothing had happened.

And even without the knock, he assured himself, nothing was going to happen. He was curious, that's all. Who wouldn't be curious after a remark like that? And why had Schultz said that? Parker hadn't asked him. And who had sent in that nurse to harass him? Was Parker supposed to believe all that was an accident? He hadn't been thinking about sex before he got here, not at all, not for a second. Agent Robert Parker was a careful man. Seven years on the job and not a single misstep, not a single blemish on his record. Not one. Despite all the swarthy young Latinos he'd picked up—"I'll do any-sing, *señor,*" the words delivered in such deliciously insinuating whispers, "Any-sing you weesh, *señor*"—with their hard little bodies and their dark, frightened eyes. Not once in all these years had Parker yielded to temptation on the job. He had been a rock. But now, alone in this locked room with this sleeping horse-boy, he felt his resolve starting to crumble. Suddenly, with a single reckless motion, he raised the sheet, ducked his head, and entered into its forbidden world.

Everything was different inside the translucent canopy. Parker could feel his heart thumping against his chest wall. He was enveloped by a heady, raw, musky odor. The pastel-green hospital gown extended two-thirds down the muscular thighs. The legs were slightly splayed, the far one showing a well-turned calf, the near one a smooth dark shin with a smattering of curly black hairs.

What, he asked himself, was the worst that could happen? The boy could wake up, but so what? Parker would invent some plausible excuse. Hadn't he come up with that inspired herpes line? Besides, Fermo was in his custody; the INS was responsible for him. Surely a federal officer had the right—the obligation, even—to make sure that everything was . . . in order. A nervous giggle escaped Parker's throat. His muscles tensed, but the horse-boy did not so much as stir. Parker took it as a sign for him to continue. What, after all, was the harm in looking? Nothing. Absolutely nothing.

And even if he did do something, what undocumented alien would be stupid enough to make trouble for an INS agent? In fact, now that Parker thought about it, what undocked alien wouldn't be flattered to have an American immigration officer showing such a personal interest in him?

Reaching down between the boy's knees, Parker grasped the hem of the hospital gown and with exquisite care—holding his breath now—raised it—careful, careful—yes, the boy was naked underneath—peeled it back—careful, care—oh my God!—and lowered it—oh, my sweet God!—into a gentle heap on the boy's belly.

Parker stared, dazed with delight, moving his head to view his subject from different angles. The thrill of this illicit act fueled his mounting excitement.

The little tentlike enclosure was overheating, and Parker reluctantly began backing out, startling himself when the sheet came down like a curtain.

The air felt different outside: not only cooler but far less charged, infinitely less dangerous. Pushing carefully to his feet, Parker walked around the bed to his chair, alternating small tentative steps with deep, oxygen-rich breaths. When he reached the chair, he was too wound up to stop, so he reversed course and headed back the other way.

As he traced out this little horseshoe circuit about the room, Parker found himself wondering how the boy's other side compared with what he had already seen. The temptation to find out grew more irresistible with each lap.

But turning the boy would require actual physical contact. Parker couldn't risk that. He'd been to enough parties to know what would happen once he started touching. Thinking about it both terrified and thrilled him. Meanwhile, his growing need for tactile activity was spreading over his body like a rash. Why should he stop? What was he afraid of? The door was locked. His relief man wasn't due for hours. The chances of discovery were practically nil. Even if the boy woke up—

No! He had to stop thinking like that. Parker glanced around feverishly for something to distract himself. The only window looked out on a dreary portion of roof: brick, asphalt, the vented metal housing of an air-conditioning unit. That wasn't going to do it. He looked around the room. No TV. Not even a radio.

Desperate for something to do with his hands, Parker went over to the night table and pulled on the top drawer. It opened with a loud, metallic scrape. He peeked over, but the horse-boy didn't move. Was that another sign? Parker, his mind whirling, no longer knew what to think.

He turned back to the night table and began rummaging through the drawer. He pushed aside some blue gauze packets and uncovered a giant jar of petroleum jelly and a round metal container with—yes, a full roll of strong white adhesive tape. Talk about signs!

Parker tried to close the drawer but his hand was shaking too badly. He was feeling feverish. With a shudder, he realized that he wasn't going to be able to stop himself.

He looked over at the boy sleeping peacefully in the bed. He could see where the gown remained bunched up beneath the sheet. Parker felt his face break into a grin. He had things to do, precautions to take. The IV presented a logistics problem. Parker wouldn't be able to turn him over without removing it. No, he decided, he'd be better off leaving him on his back, bending his knees and raising his hips up and—

At which point, of course, the horse-boy would turn into a bucking bronco. Parker would have his hands full. But as long as the horse-boy's wrists were secured to the bed frame—where was that tape? Ah, yes, there it was—and as long as the gag was firmly in place—

Parker patted his back pocket, felt his wallet. Okay, that was one less thing to worry about.

SEVENTEEN

"Here," Ferray said, tapping the map with his forefinger. "Do you know the area?"

"Yes, Colonel," Captain Ghede replied. "The mountain region up past Saint-Cyr de Bois. The road becomes quite narrow, as I recall."

"A problem for the truck?"

Ghede bent to the map and traced part of the route with his finger. "No, sir." He straightened up. "No problem at all."

Ferray checked his watch. This time tomorrow he would be in the capital, picking up his ticket for the evening flight to Miami. Courtesy of the CIA, two first-class seats had been reserved in the names of Ferray, H., and Ghede, F.

"Tonight will be our final mission here, François," Ferray said wistfully, sliding the map into its leather case. "Let us try to make it perfect."

"Yes, sir," Ghede replied sullenly, taking it as a rebuke.

"Get that out of your mind."

"I could have made that old bastard talk," Ghede grumbled.

"Of course, François. But you followed orders. That is what a good officer does: he follows orders."

"Begging the colonel's pardon," Ghede demurred, coming to attention, "a good officer completes his assignment."

Ferray shook his head in frustration. He should never have sent Ghede out after the little whore. In the scheme of things, Antoinette Voisin meant nothing. But Ghede was like a moray eel: once he got his teeth into something . . . like that damned business in New York with the mugger.

The colonel stared at the ceiling. He needed Ghede sharp and focused tonight. Sharp and focused.

"At ease," he ordered the captain.

Ghede's hands slapped together at the small of his back. His body remained tight as a drum.

Affecting a dour expression, Ferray began pacing behind his desk. "All right, François," he sighed, "explain it to me again."

The captain repeated his belief that the Voisin girl had been sent off somewhere, probably to participate in a long Voodoo ceremony.

Ferray pursed his lips. "How long?"

"Three days. The purification ceremony to the goddess Ayizan lasts for three days."

Ferray continued pacing.

"Yesterday would have been the third day. If I took the Jeep, sir, and left right now—"

"Now?" Ferray cried incredulously.

"Certainly not, Colonel. Tomorrow would be better. Much better. With the colonel's permission, I could leave at first light."

Ferray stopped pacing. "Would that give you enough time?"

"Absolutely, sir."

"Well, the girl *is* a loose end . . ."

"Look, sir." Ghede pulled something from his back pocket. "The colonel's macoute." He held up the empty sack and shook it hopefully.

"All right. But, only if tonight's mission is successful."

"I guarantee it."

—⟋⟍⟋⟍—

Ferray kept the Jeep in second gear as it climbed the dark, wet, mountain road. Rounding a bend, he swung the wheel sharply, barely avoiding the mess from yet another rock slide. The rains had played havoc with the narrow roadway, leaving it littered with everything from pebbly mud to man-size boulders. Ferray had negotiated the lower stretches without incident, but up here where the grade was steeper, the dangers seemed magnified. The harsh wind and chill mountain air added to his sense of dread.

This was a remote sector, far from any village, miles from the nearest electricity. Though little was visible beyond the headlight beams, Ferray was acutely aware that he was winding his way up a mountain, that there was nothing between the narrow shoulder and the hard, unforgiving ground below.

Only a few more miles, he counseled himself, steering carefully around a fallen branch. He felt a sharp, hard tap against his chest and thought how glad he would be when this whole ugly business was over. The night was clear, but each new turn revealed only another vista of bleak, jagged rock. Ferray had scouted this route two days ago in bright sunshine, but now, in the chilly blackness, nothing seemed familiar. The Jeep bounced across a deep fissure, and Ferray heard his rifle case clatter from the backseat to the floor. He squeezed the wheel and cursed. That kind of jolt could throw off the sights.

And then, just like that, Ferray was furious. The rubble-strewn road suddenly became a microcosm of this entire wretched nation. Haiti was cursed, its miserable history little more than a string of recurring disasters. The brightest jewel in France's colonial crown? The world's first black republic? What had it all meant? Three hundred years of slavery and squalor, hurricanes and corruption, Voodoo and poverty.

Taking advantage of a stretch of decent road, Ferray slid a Roy Orbison tape into the cassette deck and turned up the volume. As it often did these days, the first song, "Pretty Woman," got the colonel thinking about his mother. Marie-Denise Ferray, a good-hearted, illiterate country girl, had died when he was ten, leaving her only child to fend for himself in the capital's teeming streets. In the sixties of Ferray's youth, Haiti was so poor that its largest export was, literally, the blood of its people. Every day hundreds of poor Haitians would line up outside the clinic hoping for a chance to stretch out on a wooden plank and watch a pint of their life drain from their undernourished black arms into clear American jars. When their jars were full, the grateful donors would each receive a white Band-Aid and enough money to keep them in scraps until they were strong enough to come stand on the line again.

Roy Orbison's sweet, mournful voice droned on. The colonel discovered that he had taken a hand off the wheel and was rubbing the spot inside his elbow where the Band-Aid always went. He shook his head and sent a loud, bitter laugh into the chill tropical night.

The road became steeper, its surface worse. The colonel comforted himself with the thought that he would soon be past the summit and heading down to Pointe d'Amour, the spot those overpaid mulattoes in the tourist office liked to advertise as "Lovers' Leap."

The headlights revealed a broad, leafy branch blocking the road up ahead, but rather than risk stopping, Ferray downshifted to first, aimed for the narrowest section, gritted his teeth, and bounced over it. The gun case clattered. Ferray leaned forward, switched off the tape, and listened for a flat tire. After a few tense seconds, he allowed himself to exhale. He didn't want any more music. What had he been thinking about? Ah, yes, tourism. Tourism had been another cruel joke. Rather than boost the economy, as the politicians had promised, tourism had actually driven the children of the poor out into the streets to barter their hard little bodies for a few desperately needed American dollars. No one had suspected that along with their money the tourists were giving Haitians something called AIDS.

The colonel felt a burning behind his eyes as he recalled how those same American benefactors who had so generously fucked Haiti's children had then decreed that because of AIDS, America would no longer send tourists to Haiti or buy Haitian blood, thus managing to make "the black Bangladesh"—as one witty congressman had phrased it—even poorer.

And all that, Ferray reminded himself, steering carefully, was mere prologue for the next betrayal: America's unilateral decision, announced with typical Yankee arrogance, to return Haiti's former leader—that little gelding of a priest who had gotten himself expelled from both his country and his church—to the presidential palace. The festive, televised restoration was accomplished by a convoy of American helicopters landing on the palace lawn while squads of heavily armed American troops patrolled the streets and an armada of American warships clogged the harbor.

Yes, Ferray told himself, swerving to avoid a particularly ugly mudslide, it was a good time to be getting out.

Approaching the summit, the colonel reminded himself that Ghede would soon be coming up this same mountain, driving the big army truck—another gift from the endlessly generous Americans—negotiating these same perilous curves with the entire garrison seated on the planks in back in full battle dress, all of them staring at the dark tarpaulin that covered the truck's steel ribs like a shroud, all of them rocking and bouncing in sleepy unison, all of them looking forward to the coming mission, hoping for another exotic treat like Madame Jouvier or a brace of squealing, panicked teenage girls to pass around.

Ferray steered the Jeep around a gentle turn, downshifted into first, and headed slowly down the straightaway. After exactly three tenths of a mile he turned onto a side road that led up to Pointe d'Amour, a wide overhang of solid rock where tourists came to stretch their suntanned legs, admire the panorama, and pose for color photos.

The colonel pulled into the deserted parking area, yanked the emergency brake, killed the engine, and eased himself from the Jeep. He walked to the edge and stood peering down into a darkness as thick and impenetrable as tar. Far down the mountain, two tiny lights appeared and began twinkling intermittently. Ferray estimated it would be twenty minutes before the truck reached the summit.

He looked up into the clear, moonless night. The sky was like the inside of a huge, star-lined black bowl. Staring up into the vast, cold immensity of the universe, Ferray sensed the murmuring of the millions of troubled souls arrayed below him. What was this island, he reflected, but the tip of a dead volcano poking its nose just far enough above the water to sustain what passed for life here in the third world?

But this was not life. Life was in America: a real continent, not some geologic anomaly. And by this time tomorrow Hugo Ferray would be in Miami with his green card and his safe-deposit keys and all of America spread out before him like an accommodating whore.

He stared out into the darkness and tried to convince himself that he would not miss this land. Closing his eyes, he tried to summon up a loving image of his mother, but as always the picture he retrieved was of a scrawny woman in a faded green dress lying faceup on a dirt floor, her hair full of bright pink curlers, her eyes frozen open in terror, her mouth crawling with flies.

Ferray opened his eyes. Somewhere behind him he heard an army truck straining toward the summit. Come on, Hugo, he urged himself, stepping back from the precipice, it's time to go to work.

Returning to the Jeep, he slid the rifle from its case, checked the magazine, and with a firm, practiced motion, snapped it into place. He slipped his arm through the leather strap and slung the rifle over his shoulder. Taking the blanket from the backseat, he followed his flashlight beam out to the edge of the promontory. After spreading the blanket and dousing the light, he unslung the rifle and arranged himself in a fully prone position. Sighting through the rifle's green-tinted nightscope, he shifted around until his body was properly aligned and his weight evenly distributed. By habit, he licked a forefinger and gauged the wind, though at this distance—less than fifty meters—he knew the wind would not be a factor.

The truck was approaching the summit, its throaty rumble carrying easily through the thin, chill air. Ferray reached into his shirt pocket and removed the flat-nosed sniper round that had been tapping against his chest all through the long ride from camp. He took a moment to run his fingers along its hard, cool, beautifully tooled surfaces and let its compact, deadly weight rest in his hand. Then he set his elbows, opened the breech, and slid it home. With luck, he would not have to use it.

The truck came around the turn above him like some massive, growling beast, its outline dimly visible behind its glaring headlights. It was entering the straightaway that ended directly below Ferray's position.

The truck's engine skipped a beat, growled, and then resumed at a lower pitch. Ghede had shifted into second gear. If he was following his orders, the sergeant next to him in the cab was slumped over dead. The sound of the engine increased as the truck picked up speed. It was close enough now for Ferray to hear the rattling of its chassis and the slapping of its canvas.

Another shift of gears, this time into third, and the truck was nearly upon him, hurtling recklessly through the black night, the whine of its engine rising to a scream as it streaked past below him like an apparition and, failing to turn, simply sailed off into the void.

As Ferray watched, the truck seemed to hang out there for a moment, suspended, eerily silent. Slowly, its headlights swung over until they were pointed straight down, and then the truck fell from view, plummeting through empty space for what seemed like minutes, its flailing engine sounds and high-pitched human wails steadily diminishing until, without warning, they were stilled by a distant flash. After a moment of absolute silence, there were two explosions, the first the result of a fully loaded truck free-falling two thousand feet before striking solid rock, and the second, coming less than a heartbeat later, from the two extra fifty-gallon drums of gasoline igniting on impact.

Ferray glimpsed something moving on the road below. The glow from the distant fire backlit Ghede's distinctive silhouette as he dusted himself off and walked slowly toward the spot where the truck had gone over.

The sight of his second-in-command filled Ferray with a sudden, burning rage that rose in his throat and rushed out to encompass the whole world. He had been hoping that Ghede might fail to get out in time, might go over with the truck, might spare Ferray this moment. But Ghede had carried out his mission to perfection. How had Ghede turned out to be such a fool? Ferray had found him, trained him, taken him under his wing. For more than ten years Ferray had treated him like a son. Ferray had even named him, leaving the innocuous François but replacing Arcenciel—the French term for rainbow—with something more appropriate: Ghede, god of the dead.

Damn it! Ferray fumed. What had gone wrong? How could Ghede have done something so dangerously stupid? In New York, no less, the city with the largest police force in the world. And then to come back here and boast about it! By Ghede's own admission, his sister had not even been seriously hurt in the attack. Which made killing that mugger even worse. Which made it the act of a fool, the act of a man who could no longer be trusted. And to have gone and involved that Duvalierist bastard Pioline!

No, Ferray assured himself, adjusting his grip, this time Ghede had crossed the line.

Down below, Ghede turned away from the edge. Facing Ferray's promontory, he pumped a fist into the air and centered his broad chest in the crosshairs. The colonel hesitated. This bright green shape filling his telescopic sight was like a son to him.

EIGHTEEN

"Any press?" FBI agent Fox asked, keeping his voice low.

"Not yet," the Miami detective, Borinquen, replied, peering down the crowded corridor to make sure.

"Who discovered the body?" the FBI agent asked, squeezing against the wall to let an orderly pass with a cart.

"The nurse."

"I'll need to speak with her."

"No problem." Borinquen consulted his pad. "Name's Gloria Stennis."

"Sooner rather than later." Fox hated the smell of hospitals.

"I'll send someone right now."

"I'd appreciate that." The FBI agent studied the milling crowd. Their eyes had that same trancelike quality he'd seen in Oklahoma City after the bombing.

"You want the area cleared?"

The FBI agent smoothed his suit jacket, tugged at the cuffs of his white shirt. "I'd appreciate that."

"I'll get some uniforms right on it." Borinquen added, dropping his voice, "I'm assuming that the Bureau will be heading this up?"

"We'll try to coordinate things for you," Fox replied with a tight smile. Officially, the Bureau's role in homicides was restricted to "assisting local authorities." But as a practical matter, whenever a federal agent went down, the Bureau ran the show. Borinquen, Fox told himself, committing the name to memory. If things fell right, he'd get a mention in the report.

"Did the Cuban take Parker's gun?" Fox asked.

"No. The gun's still there. Looks like he went through the wallet, though. I figure that's why the pants. All the cash is gone."

Fox inclined his head toward the crowded hospital room. "Those all your people?"

"You mean Cubans?"

Fox gave him a look. "I mean Miami PD."

Borinquen forced a laugh. "I'm a little freaked." Clearing his throat, he said, "Yeah, those are some of our best guys." He took a step toward the half-open door. "Come on, I'll make the introductions."

"Don't trouble yourself. But I would like this corridor cleared. And I really do need that nurse."

"Right. I'll take care of it."

"I'd appreciate that. Oh, and I take it the faxes have gone out? Airports, bus terminals—"

"Everybody," Borinquen said. "Full statewide alert went out twenty minutes ago, as soon as I had a description to go with the name. We'll be concentrating on Little Havana—if necessary, going house to goddamn house."

"Sounds good."

"I'll go find that nurse."

"I'd appreciate that."

Fox walked over and rapped on the door with his knuckles. Hands stopped. Heads turned. Fox did the requisite gender check.

"Gentlemen," he announced, holding up his ID as he squeezed into the room. "My name is Schuyler Fox, special agent in charge of the FBI's Miami field office. Pursuant to requests from local and state authorities, the Bureau will be assisting in this investigation. We have a full team en route. In order to preserve the integrity of the crime scene, I would ask that you touch as little as possible and I would remind you that under no circumstances is anything—and that means anything—to be removed. Thank you for your cooperation.

"Now, I'll go wait out in the hall while you finish up." He glanced at his watch. "You've got two minutes."

Fox was checking the corridor for exits when Borinquen approached with a short, busty nurse. Fox allowed the detective to stay while he took her through her discovery of the body. He liked that she'd noted the exact time. Her anxiety was giving her skin a damp sensuality, but Fox found the mole by her lip a real turnoff.

"Nurse Stennis," he said.

"Gloria," she corrected, making eye contact.

"Gloria. Is there anything else you can remember? Anything at all." He didn't want to upset her by using the victim's name.

"He was reading *GQ.*"

"Very good." Her perfume was making Fox's nose itch. He tried to ignore it. "What else?"

She fidgeted for a few seconds, then mumbled, "Herpes."

"Excuse me?"

She looked away and gave a self-conscious shrug. "He sort of, I guess you could say, confided in me."

"I'm not surprised." Fox's intimate tone was intended to recapture her attention. It worked. "What about herpes?"

"He has it. Had it, I mean. He said it was a real bad case, blisters and everything."

"*He* being Agent Parker," Borinquen interjected. "The victim."

"Agent Parker," she said nervously. "Right."

"Please continue," Fox said to her, giving Borinquen a look.

"Am I in trouble here?" the nurse asked, crossing her arms, nibbling her lip, staring at the floor. "Because all I did—"

"Not at all," Fox assured her, glancing at her bust. "You're being enormously helpful. Please continue."

"I screamed. I feel so dumb. I've been a nurse for . . . quite some time. But I was so shocked." She looked up at Fox. "You can understand that."

"Indeed I can." He kept his eyes away from the mole and its single, hideous little hair.

"It wasn't the blood. It was . . ." The fingers of one hand did a little dance. "Actually," she said with sudden conviction, "I think it was the tattoo."

"Tattoo."

"On Agent Parker's left buttock," Borinquen explained.

"A snake," the nurse said.

"A cobra," Borinquen volunteered.

"I didn't know," she said.

"Know what?" Fox asked, giving Borinquen's ankle a quick kick.

"The kind of snake," she said. "I forgot the name. But he's right. Cobra. You know"—she raised her hands as if to choke herself—"it has that neck thing."

"A hood," Borinquen said.

Fox was about to kick him again when—

"Special Agent?"

Fox turned. It was one of the team from inside the room. He looked worried.

"There's something you ought to see," the man said under his breath.

"In a moment," Fox told him.

"It's really important."

"Nurse Stennis, please excuse me." Fox gave her one of his cards. "Thank you for your cooperation."

Fox followed the man into the hospital room. Somehow, with everyone else gone, it seemed even smaller.

"Shut the door," the man said, and when Fox did, added, "Lock it."

The man looked like a computer nerd: short and chubby, with thinning hair combed over a shiny bald spot. Thick glasses magnified watery eyes.

"Nat Brisnick. I'm with the ME's office."

"Special Agent Fox." He offered his hand, but Brisnick was wearing latex gloves.

"I thought you should see this." Brisnick hurried around to the far side of the bed.

Fox was getting his first clear look at the body. Agent Parker was sprawled out on his belly wearing only his short-sleeved INS shirt and calf-length black socks. There was something vaguely obscene about the bikini lines separating his deeply tanned thighs from his milk-white, tattooed ass.

The rearing cobra on his left cheek was nicely done. Its body was air force blue, its eyes and forked tongue red, but a shade of red much lighter than the pool of blood the top half of his body was lying in.

Though it was thick and sticky now, Fox imagined it gushing from the gaping wound on the side of Parker's neck.

As he stared at the body, three ideas struck Agent Fox in rapid succession: a little over an hour ago this lifeless lump of flesh had been a federal agent, there but for the grace of God, and hunting down this Fermo bastard was going to be a pleasure.

Brisnick was waving him over. Fox circled the bed and watched as the ME's man reached over and raised the dead agent's naked hip, exposing his groin.

Fox reacted as if he'd been slapped. Parker was wearing a condom.

"You saw?" the ME's man asked, lowering the hip.

Fox raised a fist and cleared his throat, buying himself a moment to think. Fate had sucker punched him. His mind flashed "Ruby Ridge," "Waco," "Ruby Ridge."

Fox stopped himself. He had to take this one step at a time. Maybe there was a better way.

"Who else knows?" he asked calmly.

"You were speaking with the nurse. Does she . . . ?"

"No. Did you . . . ?"

"No," Brisnick assured Fox. "I just—"

"All right," Fox said, raising a hand. He couldn't afford one false step. . . . Then again, maybe this didn't have to be as bad as it looked. Who was to say what had happened? After all, he was the agent in charge. What if the Cuban had slipped it on after Parker was dead, to send some kind of macho message—a "Fuck you, Yankee" kind of thing? That would be a lot more palatable than—

His mind was whirring much too fast. Get a grip, he ordered himself, carefully checking the knot in his tie. This is a career moment, he counseled himself. Do not fuck it up.

"Let's take this step by step," he said to Brisnick. "Who was here when you arrived?"

"The nurse."

"Who else?"

"Nobody else."

"You're sure?"

"Yes, sir."

"How about doctors?" Fox asked.

"I'm a doctor."

"Congratulations. I meant hospital staff."

"No. I was down the hall signing off on a DNR when I heard the nurse scream. I got here first. I've been here straight through. I'm the only one who's examined the body."

This was almost too good to be true. "You're sure?"

"Positive."

Fox liked positive.

Brisnick went to the bed. "See the tape?" He pointed to the bed frame.

"Shit," Fox muttered, reflexively rubbing his wrist. So much for the "macho message" scenario.

"Same on the other side," Brisnick said, his mouth making a guilty little twitch.

"This side looks torn." Fox bent closer.

"This side too. It took some real strength to do that. I'm thinking adrenaline."

"Swell," Fox muttered. "Give me a second."

He forced himself to take a long, slow look around the little room. All the sordid pieces were clicking into place: the cobra tattoo, the bare ass, the locked door, the condom, the tape on the bed frame, the neck wound, the bloodstained TV bracket dangling from the ceiling. God damn it to hell.

Fox looked from Brisnick to the damaged bracket and back again. "What do you figure? A kick?"

"That'd be my guess." Brisnick stepped up to the bed. "Fermo must have been on his back, right about here, with his knees bent all the way back. That way, see, he'd have had the bed as leverage when he straightened his legs and pushed Parker off him." Brisnick's hand moved in an arc from the bed up toward the TV bracket, tracing Parker's probable trajectory.

"Okay." Fox tried to visualize the scenario. "So Parker is on top of him, right? They're . . . well, let's just say a struggle develops. Fermo somehow gets his feet planted on Parker's chest and pushes him off with enough force to send him flying neck-first into the bracket."

"Right. But it had to be one hell of a kick," Brisnick marveled. "The Cuban must have woken up, either before or during."

"Which? It could be important."

Brisnick pulled a miniature flashlight from his pocket, went over and lifted the hip again.

"The condom looks clean." He peered closer. "And there doesn't appear to be any discharge. I'd say before."

"Before."

"Before. But I can't be definitive until I get the lab results."

"You won't be getting the lab results," Fox decided.

"But—"

"The FBI uses its own lab."

"Well, sure. But—"

"What didn't you understand?"

"Okay. Fine. No problem."

Fox was acting tough, but inside he was desolate. Five minutes ago he'd been all ready to charge out there and play Eliot Ness to the media, and now this . . . "career moment."

Fox stared at the body in the bed and cursed his fate. *The fickle finger,* his ex-wife used to call it. Well, he thought, fuck her too. The main thing now was to keep all his options open. As always, he reminded himself, his first responsibility was to the Bureau. Which meant preserving deniability for his superiors. Which meant he couldn't discuss this with anyone. Which meant he had to rely on this wimp Brisnick.

Which meant there was no way to really cover himself. Which meant that if the shit ever hit the fan, the Bureau would shred him faster than one of J. Edgar's love notes to Tolson.

"So," he said to Brisnick, taking a deep breath. "Let's get this show on the road. Are you taping?"

"Taping?"

"Do you use a tape recorder or do you write out your report?"

"Oh. Write. No tape."

"Good." Fox pointed to the dead man's groin. "You never saw that."

"Excuse me?"

"You heard me."

"But—"

"Not one goddamn word. Not a peep. Not to anyone. Ever."

Brisnick looked terrified. "Yes, sir," he gulped.

Fox reached into a jacket pocket and pulled out a small glassine envelope. "Now," he said to Brisnick, holding it out, "reach in there and get it for me."

"But—"

"It's evidence. I'll take full responsibility."

"But—"

Fox laced his voice with menace. "Do it."

"Yes, sir." Brisnick took the bag and slouched over to the bed.

When he was done, Fox took the foul little package and slipped it into his jacket pocket. He gave Brisnick a hard stare.

"Not a word," Brisnick promised. "To anyone. Ever."

"I'd appreciate that."

"You can rely on me."

"I'm glad to hear it." Fox reached into another pocket and pulled out a pad. "What's your full name?"

"Why?"

Fox put on his campus-recruiter smile. "The Bureau has a program. It awards plaques to people who've been especially helpful."

170

"Plaques?"

"Plus the framed commendation, of course. Signed by the director. It's a nice thing to list on a résumé."

"Nathan R. Brisnick." The ME's man spelled the last name and added an M.D.

"You like it that way? With the middle initial?"

"If it's not too much trouble."

"No trouble at all. Oh, and as long as I'm writing, you might as well give me your home address and phone number."

After providing the information, Brisnick asked what he should do about the press.

"No comment," Fox told him. "That's your answer to every question. Once you say that a dozen times, they'll leave you alone."

"They're probably outside with their cameras right now," Brisnick said, looking uncomfortable.

"I need you to stay here with the body. I'll deal with the press."

"This is going to be a big story, isn't it?" Brisnick asked anxiously.

"What can we do?" Fox shrugged. "The victim was a federal agent. His killer was an illegal alien."

"But if the poor guy was just . . ."

"Just what?"

"Nothing," Brisnick mumbled.

"The victim was a federal agent."

"Yes, sir."

"And his killer was a goddamn illegal alien."

"Yes, sir."

"An ingrate Cuban. Probably a career criminal, just like half the bastards Castro sent over back in eighty. You remember the Mariel boatlift?"

"Yes, sir."

"That's the story. The whole story."

"What do you think they'll do to him?" Brisnick asked.

"Who?"

"Fermo. The Cuban."

"Try him and fry him. Johnny Cochran and the whole goddamn Dream Team couldn't save this guy."

NINETEEN

Moe snapped awake. Sticky, clammy, and unsteady on his feet, he stumbled into the bathroom, anxious to distance himself from the demon that had been pursuing him in his nightmare.

He pulled off his damp pajamas, threw them in the hamper, and while waiting for the shower to warm, went to the sink and squooshed some Mentadent onto his toothbrush. The mixture came out light on the white, heavy on the blue. Everything felt lopsided this morning.

He stepped into the tub, turned his back to the water, and felt better instantly. The drumming spray sent pleasant little wake-up ripples radiating from the nape of his neck to the farthest reaches of his body. Cool, twisty rivulets snaked down his back, making his skin tingle. He closed his eyes and imagined that he was standing under a tropical waterfall in a lush jungle clearing. Shafts of sunlight pierced the distant canopy, glinting off wet, green leaves and smooth alluvial stones, surrounding him with miniature rainbows. While the waterfall continued its restful barrage, Moe's attention was drawn to a narrow path at the edge of the undergrowth. Leaves parted. Marlene emerged from the jungle, her head and shoulders bare, her torso sheathed in bright red cloth, her dark arms shimmering in the sunlight like polished mahogany.

Unaware of his presence, she walked to the water's edge and tested it with her toe. Something alerted her and she looked up and saw Moe standing in the waterfall. For a long moment, nothing happened. Then, staring at him, she reached up and slowly undid the knot holding her

dress. The water rushing over Moe seemed to sigh. The red fabric loosened, fell away, and—

A sudden flash of cold shocked Moe back to reality. He hopped clear
and opened his eyes. The water quickly turned warm again, but when
he reentered the stream and closed his eyes, Marlene had disappeared.
Instead, Moe saw the ugly, snarling face of Michel Pioline and, with a
shudder, recognized him as the demon from his dreams, the evil emis-
sary from another world.

The gun, his father reminded him. *Today.*

Moe nodded and began soaping. They had always kept a loaded automatic in the big safe, a .380 Colt. Moe still had a carry permit for it. He
didn't like guns, but Dad was right. He'd take it out and start carrying it.

Everywhere, his father said.

"Right," Moe agreed. "Everywhere."

—*∿∿*—

Moe saw it sitting there on the sidewalk and immediately looked away
in disgust. He would have to scoop it up and spray the area with Lysol
before he could open the store. What a way to start a day.

Usually it was just pee. Washing away dog pee was part of the morning regimen, something shop owners joked about among themselves.

Look again, his father told him.

Reluctantly, Moe turned and looked. His initial glance had suggested rottweiler, Doberman, or shepherd, but closer inspection now
revealed a pile of ordinary dirt. Moe should have been pleased that it
was only dirt, but he wasn't.

It reminds you of something, his father said.

"Yeah," Moe admitted.

Almost exactly the same place.

"I know," Moe muttered.

The memory surged back in. One morning, ten years ago, Moe and
his father had discovered a black swastika spray-painted on the side-

walk in front of the store. Ten years ago, but Moe remembered it as if it were yesterday.

The swastika had appeared on their doorstep in the midst of what had come to be known as the Korean Boycott, a months-long action that had started as a minor incident but had quickly escalated into a cause célèbre. A Korean grocer in the neighborhood had accused a Haitian woman of shoplifting. An argument had ensued. No one had been hurt, but afterward each party had accused the other of racial slurs and physical abuse. The city's media had pounced on the story, avidly playing up the racial angle.

Virtually overnight, the grocery became the target of angry, placard-waving black protesters. The store's owner and his family were cursed at and threatened. Potential customers were chased away. Anti-Asian flyers were distributed to passersby. The protesters' declared intention was to drive all Koreans out of "their" neighborhood. The grocer was equally determined to keep his store open. Uniformed police were stationed there, but their presence did nothing to relieve the tension. In fact, their determined passivity served only to encourage the protesters. An ugly scene grew progressively uglier. Violence was in the air.

To Moe and many others, the most disturbing aspect of the affair was that the boycott appeared to have the tacit approval of David Dinkins, the city's newly elected mayor. Dinkins, New York's first black mayor, shocked much of the city by refusing to enforce a court order requiring the police to keep protesters a prescribed distance from the grocery's entrance. Even some of the mayor's supporters viewed his decision as racially motivated. Slowly but surely, all the interracial goodwill generated by his election eroded, replaced by mutual fear and distrust. The city, cynics said, was reverting to its natural state.

Eli Rosen and his son watched the boycott with growing despair. As the dispute dragged on, Moe was sorely tempted to go over, walk through the gauntlet of protesters, and buy some groceries from the besieged store. But with both his parents ill and no one else available to care for them or to run the shop, Moe could not risk getting injured. Instead, he sent a series of checks to the Korean group that was helping to keep the store afloat. Eventually the protesters' ranks thinned and the boycott fizzled. The exhausted city welcomed a period of bruised, fragile peace. No one had won. No one was happy.

Two months later Eli Rosen was dead. The following month Hannah Rosen suffered a fatal stroke. A few months after that, Ziskin's Pharmacy, the last of the old-time stores on the block, closed its doors for good.

Now, ten years later, Moe gazed at this pile of dirt and saw it as the incarnation of that swastika. The sight stirred in Moe some ancient race consciousness, a disquieting combination of fear, guilt, anger, sadness, and resignation: the realization that—as his father had so often warned—even in America, Jews would always be outsiders.

Moe made sure the street was clear before he took out his keys and opened the locks. He went inside and grabbed the broom. It would take just a few seconds to—

Moses! his father growled.

Moe put down the broom and went into the office. He opened the safe, took out the loaded gun, checked the safety, and slipped it into his jacket pocket. It felt like an anchor in there.

The day went by like a blur, work interspersed with flashing images of Marlene, swastika, Marlene, dirt, Marlene, Michel Pioline, Marlene, Beck, Marlene, Marlene, Marlene.

Business was good. Chains, earrings, a baby bracelet—*Don't forget the safety clasp,* his father had to remind him—and a layaway on a diamond engagement ring: brilliant cut, sixty-four points, VVS with H color. Still, busy as he was, Moe managed to use the breaks between customers to finish resizing Miz Ark's Piaget. When he called her and offered to drop it off after six, she sounded thrilled.

"Oh," she said, "I nearly forgot. Do you still want that girl?"

"'Want that girl'?" Moe asked uncomfortably, imagining angry black demonstrators outside his shop—chanting slogans, waving placards, handing out leaflets—denouncing his lust for one of their women.

"Air. The girl for the sales job."

"Oh. Air. Yes, I still want her."

"*Bon*. I can send her around to you, shall we say, Friday afternoon?"

"Great. Sure. Friday afternoon. Thank you."

"You thought I was talking about Marlene," Miz Ark noted with a chuckle.

"Not at all."

He heard that same weird chirping sound Marlene made with her teeth.

—◦◦◦—

Moe arrived at Wedo's clutching a small black leather purse. The restaurant was only about half-full. A quick scan confirmed the absence of Michel Pioline. Marlene was nowhere in sight either, which provided a different kind of relief. The air was heavy with some exotic spice that Moe knew he'd be smelling all day tomorrow in his store. Miz Ark was sitting alone at a small table against the far wall. She waved him over.

Before joining her, Moe unzipped the purse and, reaching under the gun, carefully extracted a blue velvet gift box.

"Your wrist, please," he said, zipping the purse before resting it on the table.

The bracelet fit perfectly, with just the right amount of play. Its intricate gold links gleamed against Miz Ark's dark skin.

"Oh, my," she said, raising it to catch the light.

"I polished it. And I was able to take the scratches off the crystal."

"You must allow me to pay you."

"Fat chance." Moe laughed.

"You are an evil, wicked man. Now sit down, please. Would you care for some tea?"

"No, thank you," he said, taking the chair facing her.

"My little brother gave me this." She examined the watch with undisguised delight.

"Nice." Moe wondered what "little brother" did for a living.

"I must tell him about this when he calls tonight," she said, holding the Piaget to her ear and listening to it. "He calls every Tuesday."

"Sounds like a good brother."

"Oh, yes, François is a very good brother. And let me tell you, Moe Rosen, when François moves up here to the States, there will be no more trouble from *salauds* like Michel Pioline."

"So you heard about that," Moe said, embarrassed.

"I have been trying to contact Sebastian Pioline, the boy's father," she said, waving to someone across the room. "But Sebastian has been out. When he calls back, I will see what can be done."

"Thank you. I really . . . It was . . . This morning . . ." He caught himself.

"Something happen today?" Miz Ark asked, suddenly alert.

Moe took a deep breath and told her about the dirt. As she listened, her expression hardened. At one point, a waitress tried to approach, but Miz Ark waved her off.

"What did you do with it?" she asked Moe.

"The dirt?"

"Yes."

"I swept it into the gutter."

"Not with your hand," she said anxiously.

"No. A broom." He didn't like the way she was looking at him. "I keep a broom in the store."

"Think carefully," she said, reaching out and grasping his wrist. "Did any of it touch your skin?"

"No."

She squeezed. "You're sure?"

Even the fish above his head seemed to be tensing. "Absolutely sure."

She relaxed her grip. *"Bon."* Her features softened into a smile.

"Tell me," he said, rubbing his wrist, "do you think Michel Pioline is behind this?"

She began carefully aligning the salt and pepper shakers. "It would not surprise me."

"How about the dirt? What does it mean?"

"Perhaps nothing." She shrugged, straightening the plastic menu. "Some say that throwing dirt is a way of putting on a curse."

A curse. Moe didn't like the sound of that.

"But it is only a foolish superstition. Besides," she said, stirring her tea, "it only works if the person touches it. And you did not touch it."

"I used the broom. I'm sure of it."

"*Bon.* I will speak with Sebastian Pioline. In the meantime"—she surprised him by reaching out and patting his purse—"better safe than sorry."

Moe heard something. "What's that noise?"

A rhythmic sound, like jungle drums, seemed to be coming from the basement.

"Some of the children have a folkloric group," Miz Ark said. "I allow them to practice here after school. They will be marching in the parade. Oh, that reminds me. Marlene says that you have offered to serve as our designer. Is that so?"

"Well," Moe said, feeling himself redden, "she said you needed help with the floupe and . . ."

"The young fellow who designed for us is no longer here, I'm afraid. Deported. He had a big talent, but he always waited until the last moment. And now here we are, with Labor Day less than five weeks away."

"Five weeks," Moe said, the enormity of the task hitting him for the first time.

The drums downstairs were getting louder. The floor was starting to vibrate. Moe could feel it through the soles of his feet. Miz Ark was speaking to him.

"Excuse me?"

"Is it true? What Marlene says: that you were a designer in Hollywood?"

Moe cleared his throat. "Marlene mentioned a float. My understand-ing is that a flatbed truck carries the band and rides ahead of the troupe."

"You have never seen the parade?" she asked, astonished.

"No, but I have a pretty good idea what it's like. I've seen *Black Orpheus*. Twice."

"Black who?"

"*Black Orpheus*. It's a movie about Carnival in Rio. Believe me, Sirene, I understand costumes."

Miz Ark looked dubious.

"I can do this," he assured her, hoping it was true.

The drums were beating faster. The table was starting to shake.

"The parade is about more than costumes. You are an American. Amer-icans do not understand the importance of this event to West Indians."

"But I want to understand." Moe was trying to ignore the drumbeats even as they were working their way up his legs.

Miz Ark glanced up at the gently swaying fish, as if asking them for strength. She clasped her hands on the table and leaned closer. "The parade is both a celebration and a competition. It has been going on for thirty years now, and it just keeps getting bigger—troupes and floupes and steel bands and floats and who knows what all—each trying to be more exciting, more flamboyant, than the rest, each trying to make a mark here. All the political bigwigs come out and march. They wouldn't miss it. No-neck Mayor Giuliani will be there at the head of the pack, you can be sure, grinning and waving his Yankee baseball cap. There will be more than a million people lining the parade route, Moe. Imagine—a million people. People come from the back of beyond for this. Every street will be hip to jowl with food stands and drink stands and souvenir stands and arts and crafts. And the colors, Moe, the dancing, the music . . ."

Moe's whole body was pulsing to the drumbeat from below. "I'll do it," he declared, energized by her description, anxious to be part of it. "I'll get preliminary drawings done over the weekend."

"For the float too?"

"Yes."

"My, my, you are ambitious. But wait a moment. Did Marlene tell you our floupe's theme?"

The drumming stopped suddenly. "Theme? No. I—"

"How could the girl forget such a thing? We already sent in the entry. It's too late to change. Your designs, Moe, must match our theme."

"Okay. But—"

"Our theme is 'the golden door.' From the poem by Emma Lazarus on the Statue of Liberty."

"'I lift my lamp beside the golden door,'" Moe recited, recalling the line from elementary school.

"Emma Lazarus was a Jew."

Moe's mind was elsewhere. Hokey as it was, he found the idea of The Golden Door captivating. This was his big chance. This was the kind of opportunity he had always dreamed about, all those days at the Sony Studios working with other people's costumes. The Golden Door. His imagination soared, and for one glorious moment—a flashbulb's flash of time—his mind's eye was filled with a riot of color and shape, motion and noise. Red, white, and blue. Gold everywhere: glittering, shining, reflecting, gleaming. The Golden Door. A million people.

Yes, Moe told himself, he could do this. He absolutely could.

TWENTY

Fabrice could see by the sun that it was late afternoon. He picked up his pace. He had no idea where he was, but his stomach wanted food and he would need a place to pass the night.

The truck parked by the side of the road up ahead appeared to be a kind of clothing store. Brightly colored shirts and long-legged blue jeans waved invitingly from a clothesline strung across its open rear doors. Fabrice glanced down at his faded T-shirt, his threadbare jeans, his ragged sneakers, and told himself to keep walking; this was probably just another trick.

A chubby black man appeared at the back of the truck. He was wearing a fancy white shirt with frills down the front. "Come see the latest fashions," he called out as Fabrice approached. "Best prices in town."

Fabrice hunched his shoulders and kept walking. He could not risk speaking with anyone in this wicked place. His feet were sore, his head ached, and his belly was empty, but at least he was standing on solid ground, which was far better than being tied down to a bed or thrown about by an angry sea.

"Check it out, check it out," the man by the truck cried, waving to Fabrice like a street vendor back home.

But Fabrice was not fooled. This man, this truck, these fine clothes, were probably all tricks. Whatever this place was, Fabrice suspected it was filled with evil l'wahs. Just then, as if to punish him for the thought, one of them stirred the air and sent sandy grit flying up into his face.

Fabrice stopped to rub his eyes. The sand might change what he could see, but it could not change what he knew. And he knew that on his way to the Island Beneath the Sea he had been snatched up and brought here—wherever "here" was. Waking up with his arms pinned and his mouth taped and that red-faced man's finger up inside him had been horrible, but somehow Fabrice had escaped. Now, wandering alone in this alien place, Fabrice knew that the most important thing was to prevent some evil l'wah from sneaking up and stealing his soul: the absolute worst thing that could happen to anyone. Without a soul, Fabrice would become that most accursed of all creatures, a mindless slave for some evil l'wah: one of the living dead, a zombie.

A fresh breeze brought cooler air and the smell of the sea. Fabrice looked around. There was no sea: only the road and the cars, the man and the colorful truck, the empty sky, the sun, and acres and acres of movay grass, the kind that grew back no matter how many times you killed it.

Fabrice was close enough now to hear the clothing flapping in the late-afternoon breeze. The man was urging Fabrice to come over, but Fabrice stared at the ground, pretending not to hear. As he walked alongside the truck, Fabrice heard the man mutter, "That *zozo* don't have no money."

At the sound of Creole, Fabrice spun around. "Who are you calling *zozo?*"

"You are Haitian!" the man exclaimed delightedly, hopping down and rushing over. He threw an arm around Fabrice's shoulder. "Tell me your name, brother," he said, turning Fabrice around and pulling him toward the back of the truck.

Too tired to resist, Fabrice gave the man his name. "And what do they call you?" Fabrice asked, as politeness required.

"Jean Monette. This is my truck." He patted it as if it were a horse.

His head was round as a breadfruit, with the same rough skin. His grin revealed a gold front tooth.

Fabrice glanced nervously at the road. Cars were passing in both directions. He could feel their eyes on him. He should not have stopped. But as long as he had . . .

"Tell me, please, what place is this?"

"What you mean, 'what place'?" Monette narrowed his eyes. Then he spread his arms, taking in the road, the movay grass, the distant, scattered buildings. "Everything you see, brother, all of this is Miami."

Miami? Fabrice took an awkward step backward. Did this Jean Monette take him for a fool? How could this be Miami? This had to be . . . someplace else.

Fabrice suddenly felt weak as a leaf. His head was spinning. For an awful moment, he was back on the sea.

When he recovered, he saw that Monette was studying him hard and frowning.

"Look at you, brother," Monette scolded. "You look like some beggar from Cité Soleil."

"I am no beggar."

"A Haitian cannot go around Miami dressed like that. You will make the Americans think bad of us."

"But I, I—" Fabrice stammered, and forgot what he was about to say. His belly wanted food.

"Look here, my brother." Monette pulled a bright red T-shirt from the truck, shaking it open and holding it up.

The beach scene caught Fabrice's eye. A small black dog was pulling down the bottom of a little girl's bathing suit, embarrassing her and exposing her milk-white bum. There were many big letters.

"What it says?"

"'Florida. The Sunshine State.'"

Florida? Fabrice looked around suspiciously. First Monette says Miami, now his shirt says Florida. No, Fabrice decided, the shirt was just another trick. If this was Florida, where was the sea?

The man who called himself Jean Monette came over and held the shirt up against Fabrice's shoulders, checking the size.

"Because you are my brother, I will make you a special price."

"No," Fabrice said, stepping back, "I do not like this shirt." He did not want a little girl's naked bum next to him.

Monette tossed the shirt aside and grabbed another. "How about boats?"

"Boats?" Fabrice looked around. All he saw were cars: big shiny cars.

"Hey, my brother, look here."

Monette was holding up a blue T-shirt with three white sailboats. In the water below the boats, there were big pink letters.

"What it says?"

"'I love Miami Beach.' It's nice, yes?"

"Yes. I like that."

"You have money?"

"Of course." Fabrice reached into his jeans for the bunch of bills he had taken from the dead man's wallet.

Something came out with the bills and clattered to the ground. Fabrice bent and snatched it up. It was a big old coin on a metal chain. Fabrice stared at it lying in his hand, wondering how it got into his pocket. It must have happened while his clothes were hanging in the white room's closet.

"That is yours?"

"What do you think?" Fabrice challenged, quickly slipping the chain over his head and dropping the coin down inside his shirt. It was heavy, like the Jouviers' special silverware.

Monette stared at the money in Fabrice's hand. "You need some new jeans. What is your size?"

Fabrice stuffed the bills back into his pocket. When he said he didn't know his size, Monette reached out and lifted his T-shirt. Reflexively, Fabrice jumped back and slapped Monette's hand.

The big man started laughing. "You think I want to play with your *zozo?*" he teased. "Do I look like a *masissi?*"

"Not at all," Fabrice mumbled, deeply embarrassed. "I meant no disrespect."

"No problem, brother." Monette held out the sailboat T-shirt and a pair of new jeans. "Go up into the truck and put these on. It is dark in there. No one will see you."

Fabrice took a deep breath, grasped the truck's bumper, and swung himself up. He bent down, took the shirt and the jeans from Monette, and went inside, picking his way past piles of T-shirts, stacks of shoeboxes, giant cardboard cartons.

Fabrice liked it in the truck's belly: it was cool and dark. Perhaps this Jean Monette would let him stay here and work, perhaps he would even teach him to drive this truck. Fabrice grasped the mysterious coin and squeezed it. Could this land really be America? Why not? The l'wahs could do anything they wished. And all these clothes, he marveled, looking around. What other nation except America could have so many fine new clothes?

Monette called to him from outside, "You best give me those sneakers too. I have the newest-style Nikes. You know about Nikes?"

"Of course," Fabrice answered indignantly. "Michael Jordan."

Monette had the rough laugh of a man who drank a lot of rum. Fabrice no longer knew what to think. Monette seemed like a normal man. And out there on the horizon, past the buildings, was that not water?

Fabrice yanked off his sneakers and tossed them out. When he pulled his T-shirt up over his head, he felt the strange coin bounce against his chest. Which l'wah would have put this thing in his pocket, and why? And what did it mean? The world had gone crazy; that much was clear.

"How does the shirt fit?" Monette called to him.

"Not so bad," Fabrice conceded, hoping to keep the price down.

Fabrice understood that Jean Monette only wanted to sell things and make money. But this shirt with the sailboats was pretty. It felt soft against his skin. And he liked the words *I love Miami Beach*. The words made Fabrice feel happy inside. They—

A siren!

Fabrice dropped into a crouch and froze. A flashing police car pulled up behind the truck, blocking the only exit. Two white men in clean blue uniforms got out and stood by their doors adjusting their sunglasses and their guns. Fabrice's heart was racing. He had managed to escape from one bad man; now the evil l'wah was sending two.

Fabrice bit his lips and moved deeper into the truck. Near the back, he slipped in behind a big wooden crate, dropped to his knees, clasped his hands to his forehead, and begged Erzulie to protect him, to help him keep his soul.

When he opened his eyes and peeked out, the two policemen had moved closer to the truck and were speaking with Jean Monette. Fabrice strained to hear the words, but the flashing lights were confusing him. His heart was beating so loud he was sure the police would hear it.

". . . Cuban," one of the policemen said to Monette. "You see any Cuban guys today?"

"Who does not see Cubans in Miami?" Monette joked.

"Funny," a policeman said sourly, walking past Monette and peering into the back of the truck.

"A young guy," the other one said, bending to look under the truck. "Black. About six foot, hundred sixty pounds."

"You said a Cuban?" Monette asked, serious now.

"That's right. Goes by the name of Fermo. Navidad Fermo."

"No, I have not seen this man. What did he do?"

"Anyone in the truck?"

Fabrice hugged himself, hoping to become invisible.

"A customer. A boy, trying on clothes. But he is Haitian. The same as me."

Both policemen stepped back. Their eyes never left the truck as they reached down and drew their guns.

"This fellow is Haitian."

"You're sure of that, are you?" one of the policemen asked, aiming his gun at the open cargo bay.

"Of course I am sure," Monette told him, sounding nervous. "The boy's name is Fabrice. He speaks Creole."

"Hey, Fabrice!" the other policeman called out, raising his gun and pointing it in Fabrice's direction. "Put your hands in the air and come on out of the truck. Real slow."

Fabrice huddled behind the crate, too frightened to move. These policemen wanted to kill him, just like the *masissi* in the little white room. Erzulie, he prayed, help me!

"Fabrice," a policeman angrily demanded. "I want you out here. Now!"

"Come out, my friend," Monette called to him in Creole. "These men will not harm you."

Fabrice said nothing. His head ached. His heart was beating like a drum.

"They are looking for a Cuban man," Monette told him. "They want to see you. That is all. To be sure you are not this Cuban man they are looking for."

These police were lying. Fabrice knew it in his heart. They claimed to be looking for some Cuban man, but they were really looking for him.

"Do not be afraid, Fabrice. These police are good men. American men."

"They will shoot me," Fabrice said in Creole. "They will take my life."

"No harm will come to you. I give you my word. Come out now, before they lose patience and start to shoot up my truck."

Fabrice did not want to be responsible for that. This was not Monette's fault. There was nowhere left to run. "Okay," he called in English, "I come out now."

He pushed slowly to his feet and raised his hands. His knees were weak. His head felt as light as a dried sea urchin.

"Nice and slow," one of the policemen warned. "Keep those hands up where we can see them."

"Yes, yes, I am do it," Fabrice said, feeling with his toes before taking each small step. With his hands above his head, his palms were brushing against the metal ceiling. It occurred to him that he had never even gotten to try on the Nikes.

Both policemen were aiming their guns directly at him now. When he reached the line of flapping clothes, the sun cut him straight in his eyes. He wanted to shield his face with his hand, but he didn't dare. Instead, he stood there squinting against the piercing glare.

"What's your name?" a policeman demanded.

"Fabrice Lacroix."

With the sun in his eyes, Fabrice couldn't see much, but he could still feel the guns aimed at him. He begged Erzulie not to abandon him now. His legs felt weak.

"Keep those hands up!" a policeman barked at him.

"Yes, sir. Look, sir, I am do it, sir."

"Where are you from?" the other demanded.

Fabrice recited the Jouviers' address.

"That's in Haiti?"

"In Haiti, sir. Yes, sir. Very much in Haiti, sir."

"You speak English."

"Yes, sir. Madame Jouvier, sir, she teach me. Madame teach me." The sun was like fire in his eyes. His forehead was wet.

"Ahblay spanyole?"

Fabrice cocked his head and squinted. "What you say, sir?"

"You heard me," the policeman growled.

"He said, 'Ah blay ess pan yole,'" his partner said.

"I no understand, sir," Fabrice pleaded. The clothes on the line were slapping at him. The sun was making him crazy. Everything was a blazing white. His face felt as if it were burning.

"Soo nombray Fermo?"

Fabrice could not understand these words! These policemen were going to shoot him and steal his soul. He was lost. His arms started shaking.

"Soo nombray Fermo?"

Fabrice's heart was about to burst. He began to sob. What kind of words were these? What did they mean? Why didn't Jean Monette help him? Where was Erzulie?

"Answer the question!"

Wild with terror, Fabrice looked to the heavens and cried, "I love Miami Beach!"

TWENTY-ONE

"This way, if you please," said the bank officer, inviting his customer to precede him into the vault.

"Thank you," Ferray replied, feeling awkward in the stiff brown loafers and dark blue suit.

The unfamiliar surroundings only added to his anxiety. Ferray had never been here before. The lunacy of that circumstance had been gnawing at his insides since leaving Haiti. What had seemed a sensible precaution years ago now struck him as the rankest idiocy. Ferray had allowed Ghede to choose the bank, deliver the signature cards, make all the trips, fill all the safe-deposit boxes. Now, entering the vault for the very first time, Ferray was frantic to get his hands on those boxes and find out if his trust in Ghede had been justified. He switched the heavy briefcase to his left hand and flexed the fingers of his right, restoring their circulation. He would have his answer soon enough.

The air was ice-cold, adding to the room's sense of geometric perfection. All the walls were sheathed in stainless steel: row upon row of precisely aligned, discretely numbered, shiny blocks, each block protecting a safe-deposit box. Ferray had the keys to four of them. He looked around. Which four? And what would he find in them? He pushed out his chin. His necktie felt like a noose. The shoes were pinching his toes unmercifully. He didn't like being a civilian.

"This way, if you please," the bank officer said, his footsteps sharp against the marble floor.

Ferray followed along, putting his hand to his stomach to feel the keys tucked inside the waistband of his Jockey shorts. The long chain to which they were attached never left his neck. But chains could break; the shorts gave him a second level of protection. Ferray had worked too many years to risk losing these keys.

The flight from Port-au-Prince had been bumpy but otherwise uneventful. The rum he'd consumed had calmed his nerves but troubled his stomach. His discomfort had worsened at the U.S. Immigration booth where the female agent had subjected him to a long, distrustful glare before accepting his documents. He had stood there dreading her reaction to the contents of his briefcase. But then, after typing in his name and reading her computer's response, she had stamped his passport and waved him through without inspecting anything. Still, her suspicions had heightened his own. He had dropped his bags at the hotel, grabbed a taxi, and come straight to the bank. Finally, after the girl had located the file and checked his signature, he had been turned over to this gray-suited bureaucrat who moved as slowly as a beached sea turtle.

Using his master key in combination with one of Ferray's, the banker opened the door to the first box and stood back. It was one of the large boxes, down near the floor. Ferray squatted and tugged the handle. The box barely moved. Ferray's heart soared.

"Will you require assistance?" the banker asked.

Ferray bit his lip and nodded, too excited to risk speech.

"One moment, please." The banker walked off.

Ferray stood there staring down at the open door, the cool air from an overhead vent washing over him like a welcome rain.

The banker returned with a sturdy metal cart. Working together, the two men maneuvered the long, fabulously heavy metal box out of its cavity and onto the cart. To Ferray, the concentrated weight strongly suggested gold, but with the bank man right there, he suppressed the urge to lift the lid and find out.

"Perhaps you would prefer to take all four boxes with you now?" the banker asked hopefully.

"Yes," Ferray replied, pulling out his handkerchief. Despite the arctic cold, his face and neck were drenched.

Ferray managed to hoist the second box onto the cart without assistance. Though long and poorly balanced, it weighed far less than the first—no more than thirty or forty pounds. The third box proved lighter still, and the fourth, by comparison, felt positively empty.

Lined up side by side like miniature coffins, the four rectangular boxes covered the cart. Ferray laid his briefcase on top of them and, following the banker, rolled the cart into an adjacent corridor.

The banker opened the door to a small, windowless room whose dimensions suggested a cell. Ferray hesitated.

"Take as long as you like," the banker said. "When you are through, just press that button on the wall."

"Thank you." Ferray carefully maneuvered the cart through the narrow doorway.

"Will you require anything else at this time?"

"No, thank you."

"In that case . . ." The banker nodded politely, stepped back, and let the door swing shut.

Ferray was alone with his treasure. He sucked in a huge breath and let it out slowly. He loosened his tie, then reached out to the boxes and ran his hands over their smooth, cool metal. Everything he had worked for all these years . . .

He pulled the hinge on the first box, raised the lid, and gasped. A line from a book bubbled up from his memory: "And everywhere the glint of gold."

How had he amassed so much? Ferray wondered giddily, running his fingers over the neatly stacked gold bars, patting them, rubbing them, lifting them one after another, marveling at their deliciously sinful weight. He felt a twinge of sadness for Ghede, the loyal subordinate who had made all the trips and faithfully filled all these boxes with his own two hands.

But Ghede was dead. He had done his job and now he was dead. Another soldier lost in the line of duty; sad, perhaps, but necessary.

Ferray promised himself that he would at some point go to New York and pay his respects to Ghede's sister. Ghede had mentioned that she had a restaurant somewhere in Brooklyn. Impulsively, Ferray decided that he would surprise her with a small gift, a token of his esteem for her dear, departed brother. Yes, he thought, delighted by the idea; a gift would be just the thing.

Ferray stood there gazing at his lovely gold and allowed his joy to pour out and fill the little room, pressing itself against the wood-grain plastic walls, the acoustic ceiling tiles, the linoleum floor. He balled his fists to keep himself from shrieking out in glee. He'd done it! All the years, all the work, all the plans. But he was here. He was free. He was rich. He'd done it!

Feeling light as a feather, he removed his jacket and hung it on the back of the molded-plastic chair. He pulled off his shoes and tossed them in the corner. He unfurled his handkerchief and slowly, lovingly wiped his face. Then he opened the briefcase, took out a legal pad, went to the first box, and began his inventory.

The box contained several layers of gold bars of various sizes. He listed them individually, then double-checked the total weight. Including the four bars he added from the briefcase, the box now held a little more than sixty-eight kilos. Ferray did a quick calculation. Each kilo was worth roughly $10,000. Sixty-eight times ten thousand equaled . . .

He underlined the number and stared at it, his eyes tracing over its curves as if it were a woman. Six hundred eighty thousand: the number seemed so . . . so correct. So personal. So well deserved.

The first box contained nothing but gold bars. The second contained only coins, hundreds of them: gold Krugerrands, Canadian Maple Leafs, Chinese gold Pandas, new U.S. Gold Eagles and old U.S. $20 gold pieces, Spanish gold doubloons, and scores of ancient coins, some in custom holders, others in bags or envelopes or pouches. Ferray inventoried them as best he could. He calculated that the modern one-ounce gold coins were worth $72,000. For convenience's sake, he wrote

"320M?" at the bottom of the coin list. That way, the combination of bullion coins, rare coins, and bars totaled an even million dollars.

The third box contained a glittering jumble of jewelry and loose stones: watches, bracelets, necklaces, rings, chains, pins, and a collection of envelopes and bags and pouches with assorted diamonds, rubies, emeralds, sapphires, cameos, and carved jade. The jewelry inventory took well over an hour because, in addition to the complexity of the task, Ferray's mind kept wandering. He was surprised by how often he was able to connect an individual item with a specific mission. He would pick up a piece of jewelry and suddenly find himself recalling a face, a phrase, an expression—some little detail about an individual or a house. When he opened the briefcase, for instance, he was reminded of the graceful sway of the servant girl's hips, her healthy smell when she'd bent to deliver his coffee, the mournful look in her eyes as he was leaving. So many memories, he thought, absently grasping an edge of the briefcase between his thumb and forefinger and massaging the supple leather.

Still, something had been nagging at him throughout the jewelry inventory—a little thing, but persistent—and he suddenly realized what it was: a piece was missing. A watch. Yes. He remembered that one specific watch because the woman had refused to give it up and Ferray, upon leaving, had simply instructed Ghede to collect it for him during the next phase of the operation. It was a little gold watch with a matching gold bracelet. He even remembered the brand.

Ferray shook his head and smiled, rebuking himself for such pettiness. He would not allow one missing watch to cause even a tiny ripple on his deep sea of contentment. He would not begrudge his devoted Ghede a single wristwatch, no matter how fancy, especially now that the poor fellow was dead.

Ferray closed the box and secured the hinge. On his inventory, he estimated the jewelry's value at half a million dollars, though he suspected that the diamonds alone would prove to be worth at least twice that much. Ferray liked surprises.

Only one box remained, and there was no secret as to what it contained: cash. Smiling in anticipation, he reached over, loosened the hinge, and raised the lid.

The box was empty.

Ferray did not become upset. He simply assumed that he had made some foolish mistake. Somehow, in his excitement, he had overlooked the cash in one of the other boxes. It was an oversight easily corrected. Methodically, he reexamined the other boxes, shifting the stacks of gold bars, burrowing through the containers of coins, sifting through the piles of jewelry.

Nothing.

Like a slowly spreading stain, the realization sank in: The cash—his cash—was gone. All of it. Gone. The banded packs, the bulging envelopes, the shopworn stacks secured with rubber bands—most of the bills American, but also large-denomination French francs, German marks, even some Dutch guldens.

Stolen.

Every last one of them. Even his giant Swiss ten-thousand-franc note, a single bill worth more than six thousand U.S. dollars, which had emerged from the deepest recess of a sweaty German's safe.

His mood darkening like the sky before a tropical storm, Ferray anxiously ran his hands around the insides of the safe-deposit box. Its emptiness stoked his anger. He thought about Ghede, that villainous, thieving, ungrateful bastard. He only wished that Ghede were still alive so he could have the pleasure of killing him again. He would do it slowly this time, using the long steel needle he always carried in the seam of his trousers; he imagined inserting it into the soft flesh under Ghede's chin and driving it straight up into his treacherous brain.

His fury congealed into an icy calm. Moving like an automaton, Ferray selected six diamond rings from the jewelry box and placed them in the briefcase. He felt as if he were in a trance. His anger was so intense, so pure, so all-encompassing, that it transcended physical feeling.

After repacking and securing the boxes, he took out his handkerchief and carefully wiped his face. He slipped on the loafers, fixed his necktie, put on his suit jacket, and pressed the button to summon the bank's lackey.

Ferray assured himself that everything was going to be all right. If his military career proved anything, he told himself, it proved that Hugo Ferray was not a man to be trifled with, even from the grave.

Hearing the banker's footsteps on the stairs, Ferray reached out and patted the empty safe-deposit box. Nothing, he reminded himself, was really lost; not his money, not even his dainty little Piaget. Ferray knew where everything was. Everything. All he had to do was go to Brooklyn and retrieve it.

PART THREE

FAUCHON

TWENTY-TWO

To the west, a coppery orange the color of river mud was creeping up into the sky. Fabrice quickened his pace. The day was ending and he needed food and a place to pass the night. He had meant to ask Jean Monette for a job, but the police, with their guns and shouts, had chased the idea from his head. After the police had left, Fabrice had been so confused that the only thing he had asked Monette about was a place to eat. That had been foolish. He knew that now. He had to stop being foolish.

Fabrice began to walk faster. He wished that Antoinette could see him now. Dressed in his new Nikes, new socks, new jeans, new shirt, and new Florida Marlins baseball cap, Fabrice felt like Rico, the black detective on his favorite TV show, *Miami Vice.*

Fabrice stopped short and stared down at his feet. This, he told himself, tapping the ground with his toe, was the actual Miami of *Miami Vice.* The idea was as dazzling as if he had stepped into the TV show itself, with its pink birds and fast cars and jiggly women. He looked up the street, half-expecting to see Rico and Sonny come zooming around the corner, chasing after some bad guy.

Except, Fabrice realized with a sudden shiver, the bad guy they would be chasing after would be him. He glanced over at his spidery shadow, then reached up, pulled the peak of the baseball cap down over his eyes, and started walking.

He turned the corner and saw the low, boxy building Monette had described. Its many bright windows were full of people. A long cement walk led through a poorly tended lawn to a big glass door. Fabrice hesitated. His belly wanted food, but he had never been inside such a place. He had no papers. He had caused one of their police to get his neck torn open. Fabrice slid his hand into his jeans pocket, fingered what was left of the American money, closed his eyes, and begged the l'wahs to give him a sign.

His eyes popped open at the sound of a child's cry. The cry came again. It was coming from somewhere among those parked cars. He made his way over, slipping sideways between cars, and discovered a dark little girl, seven or eight years old, wearing a pink dress, with a head full of tight braids and a face stained by tears. Fabrice looked around. Who would leave a child where a car could crush her up? Where was the mother? Why had the l'wahs sent him a child?

The little girl was staring up at Fabrice, more curious than afraid. He walked over and offered his hand. She hid her arms behind her back like Antoinette.

"Good day to you, little miss," he said in his best English.

"You talk funny."

"I talk same like you."

"Do not."

"What do they call you?"

"Shaneekwa. What's *your* name?"

"I am called Fabrice."

"You have a fish on your head, Fabrice."

"Yes. It is baseball fish."

"Fish don't play baseball."

Fabrice smiled, wondering if all American children were this forward. "Shaneekwa," he asked, squatting down in front of her, "how many years have you?"

"Eight," she said, holding up fingers.

"Is not possible," he gasped, pretending to be shocked. "I had you for ten. Or twelve."

"I like you. You can be my friend."

"Tell me, *ti fam*," he said, gently cupping her chin and wiping her tear-streaked cheeks with the bottom of his shirt, "where are your people?"

"You mean grumps?" she asked, holding still for him.

"Who is 'grumps'?"

"Grumps is my grandma and grandpa, silly. But they were mean to me."

"Ah, so that is why you are here with the cars."

"Rocket scientiss."

"Please?"

"They're inside." She gestured with her chin.

He took her hand.

When he opened the glass door, the food smells started crickets jumping in his belly. He reached up and removed his cap as Shaneekwa pulled him along past tables full of people, blacks and whites all mixed together. There was talk and laughter and the rattle of plates.

Suddenly a big, old woman came rushing up and grabbed Shaneekwa away from him.

"You come with me," the old woman said, turning and dragging the child off.

From the back, the old woman was as wide as a milk cow. Fabrice followed her. He felt people staring at him. His heart was thumping. What if more police came? What if they demanded to see his papers?

The old woman sat herself at a table opposite an old man and pulled Shaneekwa down next to her. She and the old man began to talk. Fabrice stood nearby, trying to think of something clever.

"You found her?" the old man asked him.

"Yes, sir." Fabrice stepped closer.

"Where was she?" The old man had a patch of cottony white hair above each ear and a little green caiman on the pocket of his yellow shirt.

"She was with the cars, sir."

"That little devil," the old man muttered, shaking his head. "Are you here by yourself, young man?"

"Sir?" Fabrice leaned closer. There was so much noise.

"Are you alone?"

"Oh. Yes, sir. Much alone, sir."

"Well, sit yourself down." The old man patted his bench and slid over to make room.

A white lady in a shiny white dress came to the table. "I see you found her," she said to the old man.

"This nice fellow found her." He asked Fabrice, "Are you hungry?"

"Yes, yes." Fabrice nodded his head. "Very much hungry, sir."

"Get him a menu," the old man told the white lady as if he were her boss.

The white lady returned and put a sheet of plastic on the table in front of Fabrice. The plastic had writing on it. Across the way, Shaneekwa was bouncing up and down.

"Sit still," the old woman told her, then turned to the old man. "Aren't you going to make the introductions, Mr. Jackson?"

"Pardon me, young man. My name is Isaiah Jackson and this good woman is my wife, Mrs. Jackson. I believe you've already met our granddaughter Shaneekwa."

"Please to make your acquaintance, madame and sir. I am called Fabrice Lacroix."

"He—" Shaneekwa said.

"Hush up," her grandmother said, then turned to her husband. "I'm guessing he's from the islands. Am I right, young man?"

Fabrice did not know what "the islands" were. "I from Haiti," he told her, hoping it was all right.

"You see." The old woman smiled. "What did I tell you?"

"He's mine!" Shaneekwa cried in a sudden burst of fury, banging a tiny fist on the table and making the silverware bounce. "I found him first! He's mine!"

The old woman grasped her wrist and shushed her.

The white lady was back. "You folks ready to order?"

"Do you know what you want?" the old man asked Fabrice.

"Chicken?" he asked hopefully.

"How do you like it?" the white lady asked.

"Cooked. In a pan."

"He means fried," the old woman explained.

"One chicken in the basket," the white lady said, writing on a pad.

"Would you like a Coke?" Mrs. Jackson asked Fabrice.

"Yes, madame. Thank you, madame."

The old lady beamed. Fabrice resolved to "madame" her every chance he got.

"So," Mr. Jackson asked Fabrice after the white lady had gone, "where are you headed?"

Fabrice heard sirens. He looked out the window and saw two police cars race by, roof lights flashing. His heart started thumping again.

"Excuse, sir?" he said to Mr. Jackson.

"Are you staying here in Miami, or will you be traveling somewhere else?"

"Oh. I, uh, to New York, sir."

Fabrice knew that he could not stay here. After the police found that Cuban man, they would be coming after him.

"Ever been there before?" the old man asked.

"No, sir."

"You have family in New York?" the old woman asked.

"Cousins, madame," he lied. "Many cousins."

"He should come with us," Shaneekwa told her grandparents.

"We're not going to New York," her grandmother said.

"So what?" the child said. "He doesn't have to go to New York right away. It's only four days. I want him to come with us."

"Hush up," the old woman scolded. She exchanged glances with her husband, then turned to Fabrice and asked if he was a Christian.

"Of course, madame. Fabrice love Jesus very much."

"Is that a cross you're wearing?" she asked.

"Wearing, madame?" He followed her eyes down to his chest. "Oh." He pulled the coin from inside his shirt.

"Let me see," Shaneekwa cried excitedly.

Fabrice worked the medallion and chain over his head.

"May I?" the old man asked, putting out his hand.

"Of course, sir." Fabrice handed it to him.

"How much do you know about this coin?" Mr. Jackson asked Fabrice.

"Nothing, sir," Fabrice answered, unwilling to risk offending the l'wahs with a lie.

"I asked for it first," Shaneekwa reminded her grandfather, reaching for it.

"Hold on there," the old man said, blocking her. "This is made from a genuine piece of eight," he told his wife. "It's a Spanish treasure coin from—see the date here, Mrs. Jackson?—seventeen seventy-six. Isn't that something?" He turned to Fabrice. "Where did you get this, son?"

"A gift," Fabrice told him, wishing he had it back. The l'wahs might not like strangers touching it.

"A treasure coin," the old woman marveled, taking it from her husband and turning it over in her hand.

Shaneekwa made a grab for it, but the old woman held it out of her reach. "You can look, but you can't touch."

"You're touching," the child complained.

"I'm a grown-up. Look here," Mrs. Jackson told her husband, "I think it's a locket."

The old man took it back from her. "You mind if I open it?" he asked Fabrice.

"No, sir. Whatever you wish, sir."

The old man started playing with the catch. Fabrice had a bad feeling. For all he knew, the coin was a govi, a container for a dead person's spirit. Most govis were made from gourds or bottles, but—

The coin popped open. Shaneekwa screamed as green things jumped out onto the table. At first, Fabrice thought they were grasshoppers, but as they sat there and slowly spread themselves, he saw that they were folded American money. But why—?

Of course! He had given Antoinette one American money and now the l'wahs were rewarding him by giving him back three.

"Money," Shaneekwa cried, grabbing for it.

The old man beat her to it, covering the bills with his hands. She pulled at his fingers.

"Now you stop that," he told her sternly.

"I saw it first," she whined, sitting back, crossing her arms and pouting. "It's mine."

"It belongs to Fabrice," the old woman scolded. "You know that, child."

"I hate you," Shaneekwa told her.

The old woman's mouth fell open in shock.

"You take that back, young lady," the old man ordered. "Right now."

"Will not."

"I'll tan your hide," the old man warned her.

"Try it."

"Shaneekwa," Fabrice said, fearing the child could ruin everything. "What?"

"Say sorry to Granmamma."

"I will not."

"You must, or Fabrice is not your friend."

She searched his eyes and saw that he meant it. Staring down at the table, she mumbled that she was sorry.

Her grandparents exhanged looks.

The white lady returned and rested a big metal tray on a set of crossed sticks. Mr. Jackson refolded the bills, snapped the coin closed, and returned it to Fabrice.

"You were the chicken," the white lady said to Fabrice, placing a straw basket filled with food in front of him.

It smelled so good it made him dizzy, but he kept his hands in his lap while the white lady gave food to everyone else. He waited for the old woman to say grace and start eating before he picked up a chicken leg and carefully bit into it. The taste was so intense it made him shiver. No Haitian chicken ever had so much sweet, juicy meat on its leg. He ate as slowly and carefully as he could, wiping his mouth with the paper napkin after each bite. Several times, while he was eating, Fabrice noticed the old people talking to each other with their eyes. He begged the l'wahs to influence their thoughts.

TWENTY-THREE

Miz Ark swiveled her creaky office chair around toward the fish tank and was pleased to see that all her fish were healthy. Sighing, she tried to imagine how pleasant it would be to swim among friends all day in a clean, safe, gurgling world and to have food drop from the heavens. Chuckling at her own foolishness, she turned back to her desk.

For Sirene Arcenciel, it had been a typical day, filled with large problems and small satisfactions. Her brother had failed to call last night, which was both disappointing and worrisome. François was her baby brother, so it was only natural for her to worry about him. He was also an officer in the army, she had reminded herself, and was probably out in the bush, far from any telephone, on maneuvers or whatever it was that soldiers did. He would probably call tonight.

Even without François, Miz Ark had no shortage of things to worry about. Eurydice, her best cook, had called in sick again, the third time this month. Now Wedo's customers would have to go without their Wednesday bull-foot soup.

At ten o'clock a fax had come in from her Dominican suppliers in the Bronx informing her that the price of goat meat was going up another twenty cents a pound. At eleven, a call had come in from Mavis's

boyfriend, an Anguillan who worked for the Health Department, warning her of an inspection scheduled for next week. Sirene would have an
envelope ready, but there was always the danger they would send some
new choirboy inspector, in which case the fryer wanted a good cleaning
and Linston, the only one who could be trusted to do it properly, was off
visiting relatives in Toronto. Some l'wah was up to mischief today; that
was plain to see.

At eleven-thirty Jonquille had come running from the kitchen
screaming about seeing a rat the size of a bush pig. Sirene had called
the exterminator, who had promised to come immediately. That had
been five hours ago and no sign of him yet. Men!

She reached into the tickler file and pulled out the bills that had to
be paid today, a chore she'd been putting off since morning. There were
only three bills, but one of them was the damned electric, and with that
heat wave last month and that damned air conditioner . . .

"Ayida Wedo, give me strength," she pleaded, closing her eyes and
invoking her may-tet, the "master of her head." Ayida Wedo, the wife of
Damballah, was the spirit of the rainbow and the l'wah most responsible
for wealth, luck, and happiness.

Spending a moment with Ayida Wedo, whose Christian counterpart
was the Virgin Mary, lifted Sirene's spirits. She took out the checkbook,
gritted her teeth, and opened the electric bill. Nearly $2,000! How
could it be so high? Someone was piggybacking on her meter, she was
sure of it. Plus, she had a bad feeling about this nasty INS business in
Miami. When she had turned on the local Creole station this morning
and heard the news, her first reaction had been to thank God the killer
had not been a Haitian. But even so, the murder of an immigration officer was dangerous for everyone. That was something she tried to drum
into the young ones' heads, that when it came to violence, it was much
better to be the victim than the perpetrator. Look what had happened
after that crazy policeman had shoved a broomstick up Abner Louima's
behind. Yes, Louima had had to spend time in a hospital, but his one

busted bum had saved the bums of dozens of others. For months after that awful incident Immigration had stopped harassing Haitians, the city inspectors had settled for smaller bribes, the neighborhood police had become almost polite.

The phone rang. Sirene glanced down to see which light was blinking. It was her private line. She pressed the button, lifted the receiver, sighed. Now what?

Sebastian Pioline greeted her politely in Creole. Sirene responded in kind. They were not friends, but they managed to get along. Sirene considered Pioline a necessary evil: a cruel but practical man who got things done. She only half-believed the stories linking him to Duvalier.

"My dear Sebastian," she said, coming right to the point, "can we speak of the unpleasantness between your son Michel and my neighbor Rosen?"

"If you wish," he replied, sounding surprised.

"Rosen found graveyard dirt thrown against his store this morning."

"And you believe my Michel did this?" Piloine asked, but without the anger Sirene had expected.

"I believe it is possible," Sirene replied carefully. "Rosen is a popular man here in Brooklyn. His store is right next door to mine."

"This *blanc* insulted Michel in a public place, Sirene," Pioline said, his voice strangely subdued. "It is a question of honor. I cannot get involved."

"My people were there, Sebastian," Sirene said, unwilling to drop it. "Michel had too much to drink. He started the argument. Rosen was merely defending himself."

"We should speak of this another time."

"Something is wrong," Sirene said, wondering if one of his people was ill, or worse.

"Your brother and Michel had business together. Did you know that?"

"No. But why do you bring up François? What kind of business?"

"It was a few weeks ago. It is not important now. You have not heard, then?"

Reflexively, Sirene reached into her pocket and clutched her rosary. "Heard what?"

"About the accident."

Sirene froze. A spectral dagger had materialized in the air before her, its blade glinting with malice. It began to turn, as if searching for a target.

"Accident?" she heard herself whisper as she watched the long, cruel blade take aim at the center of her chest. "What accident?"

TWENTY-FOUR

Moe stopped pacing through the darkened store long enough to check his moon watch. Seven-thirty. Marlene was more than an hour late. He didn't like it; if she was going to be an hour late, she should have called.

He went to the front door and scanned the busy street. Nearly everyone out there was black. Most of them were women. None of them was Marlene.

He stood there watching the parade of strangers. People in uniforms: nurses and doormen and security guards. Thin, old men in cheap, gaudy clothes. Enormous women moving with unlikely grace. Packs of bright-eyed teenagers with boom boxes blaring, laughing, bumping one another, not a care in the world. Every second woman was pushing a baby carriage or had a young child in tow, or both: the population explosion, passing right before Moe's anxious eyes. Where the hell was Marlene? An hour late, people are supposed to call.

Some wanga, he thought sarcastically. A real wanga would have made Marlene appear; Moe couldn't even get her to call. He checked the time. Marlene was an hour and ten minutes late.

Okay, he decided, he would pace for a few more minutes, just to get it out of his system. Then he would call Peter Luger's and cancel their dinner reservation. After that he would close up and go get himself something to eat—some take-out Chinese, maybe, from that new Guyanese place around the corner—schlepp it home to gentrified Brooklyn Heights and get to work on the designs for their goddamn floupe. The Golden Door, he thought bitterly, looking out past the double-locked entrance to the crowded, bustling street. With all those people, he told himself, you'd think one of them could be Marlene.

He turned and headed back toward the office. Okay, okay, okay, chances were he'd been stood up. But so what? He didn't need Marlene. Pretty girls were a dime a dozen. Marlene wasn't even a real West Indian.

The bell rang. Moe spun around. Marlene!

She had on a new wig, but other than that she hadn't changed; she was still larger than life.

"I'm late," she said the moment he opened the door.

He reached out and took her arm, but the thrill of touching her was short-circuited by a noxious odor.

"It's bad, right?" she said, looking down and brushing her clothes with the back of her hand.

The smell was awful, but vaguely familiar.

"You don't have to say anything," she said, sounding miserable. "You have every right to be mad. I was supposed to be here an hour ago and now I show up smelling like a chicken farm."

Chicken! That was it!

Marlene was picking at her white V-neck sweater. Moe's fingers itched to help her. Despite the smell, he was starting to find her distress highly erotic.

"Listen," he said, thinking of how quickly a waterfall would wash away—

"You're right," she said, angrily brushing a breast. "I'd better go. I'll mess up the store. I just came by to apologize. Open the door and I'll—"

"It's still early."

She stopped fussing. "What?"

"I thought we had a date."

"Look at me."

"You're beautiful."

"Stop that. It's not funny. Besides, we can't go anywhere like this. I would have to go home and— Look, Miz Ark was all upset. She needed a rooster—a live black rooster—and I had to go all the way up to the Bronx to—"

"The Bronx!" Was she crazy? Michel Pioline was from the Bronx. "You shouldn't be—"

"What?"

"Nothing."

———

He sat in the front. She had all the windows open. He had the leather purse with the gun in his lap.

"Why," he asked, studying her lovely profile, "did Miz Ark need a live black rooster?"

"Miz Ark asks me to get her a rooster, Rocky, I get her a rooster. What she does with it is her business." She gave a chirp. "All I know is, she took it down to the basement."

Moe recalled Detective Beck's warning about Wedo's basement. An image, accompanied by the sound of drums, popped into his head: shadowy black dancers, a swaying crowd chanting in some unknown tongue, a black rooster rising up, flapping its wings, screeching. Moe's imagination supplied a single word: *Voodoo*.

———

Moe wandered through the one-bedroom apartment, examining things, touching things, lifting things, trying to distract himself from the sounds coming from the shower. Before going into the bathroom, Marlene had

lit candles and sticks of incense, turned off the lights. Every flat surface seemed to hold some exotic African object—a pair of brass finger
cymbals, small wooden sculptures: a warrior holding a spear, a kneeling pregnant woman, a highly stylized antelope. In one corner sat a
closed rolltop desk, incongruous among all the Africana. Behind it
stood a tall bookcase crowded with titles Moe couldn't make out in
the dark.

The small bedroom had squares of patterned fabric on the walls, a
dresser, night table, easy chair, four-poster bed. There was something
wonderfully perverse about roaming through Marlene's private space.
Moe approached the bed, reached down, and tested the mattress. The
air hummed as if electrically charged. Something on the night table
caught his eye. The candlelight was weak and erratic, but the object
appeared to be a small pendant attached to a loop of rawhide. He went
over and picked it up. The pendant—if that's what it was—was a
miniature leather box, hollow by the weight of it and stiff with age. The
little box was tightly crisscrossed with thin wire, which—Moe checked
with his fingernail—was almost certainly copper. Intrigued but stumped,
he replaced it carefully.

The shower stopped. Moe felt like a burglar caught in the act. He ran
to the corner and dropped into the easy chair.

The bathroom door opened. Framed by a rectangle of white light, she
looked like an alien emerging from a spaceship.

"Marlene," he called, letting her knew he was in the room.

"That you, Rocky?" She walked toward him. "I thought you'd be
inside watching TV."

"No, I—"

Her short, frizzy hair was glistening like tinsel. The candlelight was
creating a tiara of little water squiggles on her forehead. Lower down,
wet patches gleamed in the deep V of her terry-cloth robe. A tendon
behind Moe's knee began to vibrate uncontrollably.

She loomed above him. "Smell," she commanded, offering a forearm.

"Nice."

He sat back and clasped his hands in his lap, but he didn't know where to rest his eyes. She was probably naked under that robe.

"I still make you nervous," she teased, reaching out and tickling his ear with her finger.

"Not really," he lied, resisting the urge to brush it away, pleased she was doing it, wishing she would stop, thoroughly confused.

"We're studying symmetries. In my physics class at Brooklyn College."

"Physics?"

"Just a survey course. To satisfy my science requirement. But I like symmetries."

"Oh," Moe said dumbly.

"See," she said, gently mussing his hair, "I look at it this way. Miz Ark saved me. You saved Miz Ark. Now I can save you."

"Save me from what?"

She laughed. A whiff of floral sweetness floated by. Incense? Soap? Imagination? Who could tell?

"My stomach makes noises," she said. "After I eat."

"Well," he said, mystified, "that's, uh . . ."

Their table at Peter Luger's was gone. They'd have to go someplace else. He felt foolish sitting while she was standing. Her fragrance was affecting him like too much wine. She was so close. The urge to reach out and touch her was—

"We haven't eaten yet," she said. "Maybe that's better. If you know what I mean."

"Whatever you say." He pushed to his feet. She was hungry. That made sense. Now where—?

Suddenly they were kissing—he her, she him, Moe didn't know, but the shock made him stumble forward and send them toppling together onto the bed. Disoriented, off-balance, but kissing her as best he could, he groped about with his hand, trying to gain purchase on something, anything . . .

She was on top of him, their lips still locked, her body pressing heavily all along his, and his hand grasping, like a fleshy melon, a thrillingly bare, astonishingly firm buttock.

Confused but game, he sucked in air through his nose and kissed on. Her lips were softer and warmer than any he'd kissed before. The first brush of her tongue ignited a raw, unfamiliar hunger so powerful it made him want to swallow her whole.

When he regained his bearings, he saw that she was still on top of him but was now upright, her back straight, her knees straddling his. Her open robe was like stark white curtains framing a mysteriously dark stage. His hand was still clamped on her rump.

"So," she said, retying the sash and moving to make herself more comfortable. His handful of flesh changed shape as she shifted her weight. Embarrassed, he released her.

"It's too big," she said, sitting back on his legs.

"Too big for what?" he asked, feeling ridiculous lying beneath her in a suit and tie.

"It's hard to buy clothes," she said, absently fiddling with one of his shirt buttons.

Her body was giving off an aroma suffused with soap, flowers, and a deep undercurrent of woman. As she continued talking, wave after wave of it floated down, covering him like a net. His penis strained mightily against his slacks. He wondered if she saw it. Her fingernails, now inside his shirt, were gently scratching among the hairs on his stomach. He felt a shirt button open. He lay there, aroused but helpless.

"I need a shower."

"You'll be quick?" she asked, sliding both hands inside his shirt and lightly brushing the hairs on his chest.

"Very quick."

She removed her hands from his shirt and sat there staring down at him. Then, reaching down and casually gripping his rigid penis as if it were a saddle horn, she shifted her weight, lifted a leg, and stepped gracefully to the floor.

"I'll get you a towel," she said, walking off.

—*ᴧᴧᴧ*—

Moe clenched his teeth and kept lowering the water temperature until his stubborn erection finally began to droop, though each time he recalled how she had grabbed him, it bobbed up again. He soaped and tried to think. He knew that he was awake, but he seemed to have entered some strange sort of dream state combining anticipation, giddy disbelief, and anxiety. In California, Moe had slept with his share of attractive women, but this . . . No, something was wrong here. Marlene didn't belong with him; she belonged in a *Playboy* pictorial, "The Girls of Brooklyn."

—*ᴧᴧᴧ*—

Candlelight was slithering over everything in the room. She was waiting for him under the covers. The sight of her bare shoulders instantly reversed the effects of the cold shower. The rigid, heavy fullness in his groin seemed to ground him, give him confidence. He told himself that, against all logic, this was really going to happen. He went over to the chair and fished around in his jacket for the three foils of condoms he'd purchased out of wishful thinking. His towel unraveled. He let it fall to the floor. The cool, scented air tickled hairs all over his body.

"You have a choice," he declared, approaching the bed and reciting his selection for her.

"I haven't been with a man in a long time."

"Neither have I."

She laughed.

"No. What I meant was—"

"No kidding."

"So"—he held out the three packages like a card trick—"which, uh . . . ?"

"I'm allergic to latex. If you use one of those things, I'll break out in hives. You want that?"

"No, but—"

"I watch the calendar."

"Oh." He looked at the little foil packets in his hand and wondered what to do with them; now that he was here by the bed, he didn't want to go back to the chair.

"Are you worried about AIDS? Because—"

"No," he told her. "It's just, you know, with all the talk these days about safe sex . . ."

"No sex is safe." She pushed herself into a sitting position.

The sheet slipped down to her waist, exposing her breasts. He tossed the condoms over his shoulder and climbed into bed.

She nestled close and ran a hand along his flank. "How do you feel?"

He'd forgotten how to speak. His brain was experiencing sensory overload: her fingers, breasts, belly, thigh. When her toe stroked his ankle, he felt it along his spine. He needed to kiss her. To assure his aim, he held her chin with one hand and brought his lips to hers. Her mouth opened like a doorway to the unknown. Moe closed his eyes and plunged in.

Her skin was incredibly smooth. Her body was soft in some places, firm in others. He was trying to touch her everywhere at once. As his hands roamed over her, she became warm and damp and active. When his fingertips brushed between her legs, it was like touching live electric wires. The shock sent him into a kind of frenzy.

—————

"I don't know what happened," he said truthfully, staring up at a slowly spinning ceiling.

"Which part didn't you understand?" she teased, raising his head and sliding a pillow beneath it.

"Thanks."

"Likewise."

Shards of memory flashed through his mind: nails along his back, great tidal heaves, gasps and grunts, and . . . "Was that you?"

She stretched out next to him. "Was that me, what?" She brushed her bare hip against his.

He reached out, felt a leg, and then tentatively rested his hand on the inside of her thigh.

"Was that me, what?" she asked again, shifting to accommodate him.

"Making all that noise," he said, exploring her warm, impossibly smooth skin.

"The only noise I heard was coming from you."

"Me?" He lengthened his strokes. "I never make noise."

"Is that right?" She moved her hips. "Next time I'll have my friend Linda Tripp tape it."

He rolled toward her, propped himself up on an elbow, and caught sight of the pendant on the night table. "That's a strange-looking thing."

"What is?" She sat up and anxiously examined herself.

"This." He reached across her to pick up the little leather box. "What is it? A pendant?"

"Oh, that." She lay back, relieved. "That's called a *pacquet Congo.*"

"A which?"

"A *pacquet Congo.* It's African. Miz Ark says it's like a charm."

"A charm." Moe turned it over in his hand. "What's inside it?"

"Just some hair."

He raised it to his ear and shook it gently. There did seem to be something in there.

"What kind of hair?"

She hesitated, then said, "Yours."

He stared up at her, wondering if he'd heard right.

"That first day? When you saved Miz Ark and they helped you into the restaurant? You were woozy. I snipped off a little piece. Are you mad?"

He peeled back the sheet and ran his eyes over her naked torso. He'd been wrong about the *Playboy* pictorial. What he was looking at was nothing less than a centerfold.

TWENTY-FIVE

Grasping Shaneekwa's hand, Fabrice stopped in the middle of the big wooden bridge to get his bearings. People were streaming past them in both directions. He was still a little shaken from Space Mountain, but it was lunchtime and Mr. Jackson had said to meet them in a big glass building across from the castle. He scanned the area. Ah, there it was, exactly where Mr. Jackson had promised. He was a smart man.

The giant glass building was a restaurant, crowded with tables and people rushing about with trays of food. The cold air smelled of chicken and french fries. Mrs. Jackson saw them first and waved them over. She and her husband were sitting at a small white table with four white chairs.

Fabrice and Mr. Jackson stayed at the table while the women went for food.

"So," the old man said, "what do you think?"

"I say thank you, thank you a hundred times, but is not enough for how I feel inside."

The old man looked embarrassed. "Shaneekwa behaving herself?"

"Very much behaving. And full of laughing. Truly."

"That's great. This is working out real fine. Real fine. You like the shirt, right?"

Fabrice looked down at his new T-shirt. It was dark blue, with big white letters and a picture of the two smiling mice. Fabrice had lied and said that his suitcase had been stolen, so after they had got their rooms in the hotel, Mr. Jackson had taken him downstairs to the shops and bought him a big plastic bag full of things. The bill had been more than forty American dollars, but instead of paying, Mr. Jackson had handed the girl a plastic square from his wallet and then made a mark on the little paper she gave him. When Fabrice had objected to so many gifts, Mr. Jackson had said he would take the money from Fabrice's pay. Afterward, back in his room, Fabrice had used the pad and pencil by the telephone to do the math and discovered that even after buying all these things, he had still earned nearly ten American dollars for the day, and all he had done was ride in a big, beautiful car and carry a few luggages.

". . . there but for the grace of God," Mr. Jackson was saying.

"Excuse, sir?" The place was noisy. Fabrice pulled his chair closer.

"They better get that murdering son of a gun," the old man muttered.

"Sir?"

"That Cuban, the one who killed that immigration officer back in Miami."

"Oh."

"Makes you wonder, though." Mr. Jackson shooed someone reaching for one of their empty chairs. "I mean about the way of things." He shook his head. "I was a postal inspector for thirty-five years, Fabrice, did I tell you that?"

"No, sir."

"Yes, I was. Worked for the government until the service went private, got promoted to district supervisor, retired four years ago, and the missus and I moved down here and bought the place we have now."

"Yes, sir."

"Wasn't easy for a black man when I started out. Kids today don't understand that."

"Yes, sir."

"They're offering a half-million-dollar reward." Mr. Jackson placed his hand on one of the empty chairs and shook his head no as another hopeful approached.

"Reward, sir?" Fabrice dragged the other empty chair close and draped his arm over it.

"For whoever finds that Cuban. Can you imagine that, half a million dollars?"

"No, sir," Fabrice answered honestly.

"I'll tell you one thing. I wouldn't want to be in that Cuban's shoes."

Fabrice looked down at his Nikes. "No, sir."

Mr. Jackson bent closer. "Listen, Fabrice, before the women come back I want to clear something up. You don't have a passport, do you, son?"

"Everything stolen," Fabrice replied, staring at the floor. "Clothes. Papers. Everything."

"You never had a passport."

Fabrice rubbed a sneaker against the green carpet. He was tired of telling lies. Mr. Jackson was a good man.

"Isn't that right?"

"I run away from Haiti."

"That's what I figured from the get-go. Now, next question, how did you get here?"

"The sea." Fabrice met the old man's eyes. "I come by the sea."

"So did my grandfather," Mr. Jackson said with a smile. "Jumped ship in Brooklyn off a Trinidad freighter. No papers, no friends, no American money."

"I have American money," Fabrice reminded him, clutching his coin.

"You seem like a real nice fellow. Shaneekwa's really taken a shine to you. You just look after her and—"

"I do that."

"—and I'll do what I can for you. I have a buddy in New York. Maybe—"

A commotion began nearby. Fabrice twisted around, expecting to see police. People all around were on their feet, applauding and cheering. Fabrice stood up to see what all the excitement was about.

"What is it?" Mr. Jackson asked him.

"The boy mouse and the girl mouse. They are here."

"Swell." Mr. Jackson picked up his newspaper.

Fabrice watched as two people in mouse costumes danced from table to table waving their white-gloved hands. Children rushed over to hug them and have their pictures taken. Even grown-ups were pushing and shoving to get close to them.

As the girl mouse approached their table, Fabrice turned excitedly to Mr. Jackson. "Antoinette should be here."

"Who?"

"Shaneekwa," Fabrice corrected himself. "Shaneekwa should be here to see the big mouse."

TWENTY-SIX

The buzzer startled Moe out of his reverie. He had been daydreaming about Marlene again. He found himself standing in the middle of the store. A girl was outside waiting to be let in.

Walking to the door, he had the feeling that something bad had happened this morning, but he couldn't remember what.

"Good afternoon," he said to the striking young woman. "Please come in."

Eighteen, nineteen at the most, Moe thought as she floated past him into the store. Her light complexion suggested mixed parentage. She had everything needed to be a top model—the angular face, the slender figure, the poise—everything except the height. Even with heels, she stood no more than five three. Her outfit of black silk blouse, black skirt, and black pumps was becoming, if a bit dour.

"The Diana Vreeland look," he observed with a smile.

She stopped and turned. Her eyes widened. "Excuse me?"

"It's a compliment." Moe secured the door. "Diana Vreeland was the editor of *Vogue.*"

"I did not know that, sir."

"Before your time." He shrugged. "Anyway, for what it's worth, she was famous for wearing only black."

"I see. Diana Vreeland. I must try to remember that."

Her clipped English contained a hint of French, her *that* edging toward *zat*. Haitian, Moe decided, probably brought here as a small child. He liked the way her hair curved down and framed her face like cupped hands. She was lovely to look at, but Moe expected no more than a silver bangle or a pair of featherweight gold earrings.

"Well," Moe said, ushering her down the aisle, "how can I be of service?"

She stopped and stared at him oddly. "You are Mr. Rosen, yes?"

Her eyes reminded him of one of those rare, extravagantly beautiful creatures he'd seen on PBS, the kind that lived in sultry, exotic places like Madagascar or Sumatra. What were they called? Lemurs!

"You are Mr. Rosen?"

"Yes. Moe Rosen. I'm the owner."

"Well, then, am I not on time?"

On time? Moe was at a loss.

"Three o'clock?" she prompted him.

It didn't help.

"The sales position? I was told—"

"Air?" he asked tentatively.

"That is me. Yes, sir. Have I made some mistake?"

"No, no, no, no, no." He smiled. "I was just expecting someone . . ." His hand made circles, trying to conjure a word. "I don't know what I was expecting," he admitted with a shrug. "Come on, let's talk in the office."

Though he led the way with a smile, Moe was not really in the mood for a job interview. Something from this morning was still bothering him. He hadn't found any more dirt on the doorstep, but—

Wedo's! That was it.

Miz Ark had called and said that she had to go to Haiti. Her brother had died and she had to see to the funeral. Moe had responded like any good neighbor, by asking if he could do anything to help. Yes, actually, there was, she had said; she had people who could handle the restaurant, but she needed someone to handle her cash.

"Gladly," Moe had volunteered, assuming that she had some money she wanted stored in his safe.

But he had spoken too fast. It soon became clear that what she actually wanted was for Moe to collect all of Wedo's daily receipts.

"I'd really like to," he had responded, prepared to offer as many excuses as necessary, "but—"

"Oh," Sirene had interrupted, "where are my manners? I forgot to ask if you and Marlene had a pleasant evening."

And the next thing Moe knew, he had committed himself to collecting, nightly, all the table and take-out checks from their respective registers, running the corresponding register tapes, removing all but a $100 "bank" from each of the two registers, sealing everything in a manila envelope, and depositing the envelope in Wedo's safe, an old-fashioned left-right-left Mosler to which, much to Moe's dismay, he now possessed the combination.

"So, Air"—Moe took a deep breath and swiveled in his father's old chair—"tell me a little about yourself. How old are you?"

"Eighteen, sir."

"School?"

"St. Rose of Lima, sir. I graduated in June."

"How about college?"

"St. John's, sir. Beginning this fall."

"Both good Catholic schools."

"Thank you, sir. My mother."

"Your mother?"

"Believes in the Catholic schools, sir."

"I see. Well, Air, let me guess: You are hoping for full-time work through the summer and part-time work after school starts in the fall?"

She wriggled to the very edge of the chair. "That would be ideal, sir." Her whole face lit up. "Especially if I could get a position here."

"Why is that?" Moe asked, enjoying the way she talked.

She thought for a moment, making up her face in a delightful, child-like way. Where were the girls like this when I was in high school? Moe wondered, feeling ancient.

"The thing is," he said, thinking out loud, "we would have to have a system."

"Sir?" she asked, angling her head sharply, like a praying mantis.

"In terms of the customers. You'd be fine for the men, but I would have to handle all the women."

"Whatever you think is best, sir."

"Women would resent you. You're much too pretty."

"I see. Too pretty. Well."

They discussed when she could start, which turned out to be tomorrow. He talked about hours, wages. She agreed to everything. This was turning out to be a piece of cake.

"Do you always wear black?" he asked her, rummaging through the big desk drawer for a tax form.

"Only when I am in mourning, sir."

He stopped searching and looked up. "Oh, my," he said, genuinely distressed. "I didn't even think—I'm so sorry. I hope it wasn't someone close."

"My uncle, sir. I did not know him very well."

"Still," Moe said, commiserating. "Was he a young man?"

"Quite young, sir. Not yet forty."

"I'm thirty-nine." Moe tried to imagine himself dead.

"You look younger than that, sir."

Moe felt himself blush. "You're going to do just fine."

He located the withholding form and pulled it out. "I hope the government is still using these," he said, only half-joking.

"Yes, sir. Excuse me for asking, sir, but does this mean I have the position?"

"What? Yes. Of course. Didn't I—? I'm sorry. Excuse me. My head today is . . ." His hand began making circles again.

"In the clouds?"

"Close enough." He glanced at the form and realized that he had forgotten to ask about her papers. "I assume you have a social security number?" he asked carefully.

"Of course. I am a U.S. citizen, Mr. Rosen. I was born right here in Brooklyn."

"Me too," Moe told her with a relieved grin. "Which reminds me." He pointed to her neck. "I see you're wearing jewelry."

"Yes, sir." Her ringless fingers rose to caress a small gold cross on a thin gold chain. "Is this a problem, sir?"

"No, no, not at all. It's just that during your hours here in the store, I would prefer you to wear something we sell here. That way, if a customer admires it . . ."

"Oh, yes, sir," she said with a little bounce. "That is so clever, sir, if I may say so. I was afraid you had some objection to the sign of Jesus."

"You mean because I'm Jewish?"

"Yes, sir."

"Jesus was Jewish."

"You certainly know your Bible," she observed primly.

Moe chuckled. "We carry a large selection of crosses. You can wear one of them, or whatever else you like."

"Yes, sir."

"This seems to be a bad week for losing relatives."

"Why do you say that, Mr. Rosen?"

"I was thinking about the lady next door. You know Wedo's, the restaurant?"

"Of course I do."

"Well, I found out this morning that Miz Ark, the lady who owns it, just lost her brother. Kind of a sad coincidence, don't you think?"

She was looking at him with that wide-eyed, innocent, lemurlike expression again. "I do not understand."

"Her brother," he explained, wondering why it was so hard to communicate with these people. "Your uncle? Losing both of them."

"But Mr. Rosen," she said earnestly, "they are the same man."

"What?"

"The woman you call Miz Ark, she is my mother."

TWENTY-SEVEN

Sirene followed the two soldiers and the doctor down the long, sloping tunnel, their harsh, irregular footsteps echoing off the damp walls. With each few steps, the men drew farther ahead, but Sirene proceeded cautiously: the light was poor, the stones were wet, and her legs felt weak. The tunnel seemed strangely familiar to her—the low ceiling, the clammy walls, the wisps of chill, the puddles, the odor of lichens and moss—as if she had passed here in a bad dream.

She found the men waiting for her in front of an arched wooden door. As she approached, one of the soldiers inserted a key and pushed the door open. She felt the sudden rush of invisible spirits. They burst from the doorway and swarmed around her, terrified and lost, trying futilely to make contact with her earthly flesh.

"This way, madame," the doctor said, unaware of the ghostly presence.

Trying to ignore the frenzied swirling around her, Sirene hitched the straps of her bag higher on her shoulder and followed him inside. As she crossed the threshold, she felt the spirits peel off and leave her, unwilling even in their desperation to reenter the chamber.

Inside, the cool, stale air was heavy with the sickly sweet smell of formaldehyde. Weak yellow light buzzed from a single, naked overhead bulb. Sirene scanned the large room. Its walls were lined with stacks of wooden pallets, each bearing a number crudely painted in white. Even in the dim light she could see that many of the pallets were occupied. She shuddered, wondering which of these shrouded mounds was the *corps cadavre,* the mortal remains, of her baby brother, François.

One of the soldiers consulted a clipboard on the wall and called out a number. The other walked slowly to a pallet and pointed.

"We wish to examine the body," Sirene announced.

"Moving a body is much work, madame," the soldier at the clipboard informed her.

"I understand." Sirene reached into her bag.

She motioned the soldiers over and handed each an American $5 bill. Their eyes widened and their bodies bobbed with delight.

"Thank you, madame."

"Madame is very kind."

Moving quickly now, the soldiers first positioned a crude wooden table, then grasped the ends of the indicated pallet and pulled. The warped pallet slid out with an ugly rasping sound. With difficulty, the soldiers lifted it free and lowered it to the table.

"Would you be kind enough to move the table into the light?" the doctor asked them.

"Yes, sir. Immediately, sir."

The shrouded body bounced stiffly as the soldiers tugged and dragged the table across the uneven stone floor and positioned it under the single bulb. Sirene felt ill when she saw that the cloth covering the body was filthy.

She turned to the doctor, a thin, balding Haitian of perhaps thirty. "Please read the name."

He walked over and located a cardboard tag wired to a big toe. "Arcenciel," he read. "François. Captain."

She clasped her hands to her heart, then crossed herself four times.

"Does Madame require anything else?" one of the soldiers asked hopefully.

It took Sirene a moment to locate her voice. "A basin of water. Fresh, clean water."

"With pleasure, madame."

"Perhaps Madame would like a new sheet?" the other soldier suggested.

"Yes," she said, staring at the lifeless shape on the table. "A new sheet."

Neither soldier moved. Both were bent slightly forward from the waist, staring at her expectantly.

"There will be more money. Now please leave us."

"Yes, yes," the first soldier said, grabbing his partner's arm and backing toward the door. "We will return with—"

"Remain outside until I summon you."

"Of course, madame. Whatever Madame wishes."

"Now, madame," the doctor said when they were alone, "what is it you require of me?"

"I wish you to examine my brother's body."

"Certainly, madame. But for what purpose? You informed me yourself that your brother was killed in an automobile accident."

"I need you to assure me that he is truly dead."

"Madame?"

"I am a believer. A follower of Vodoun. Our rituals for the dead serve to separate the spirit from the body. This must not be done unless we are absolutely certain that the body is without life."

"I see," he murmured. "And what else, madame?"

"I must know if the body has been mutilated in any way; not by the accident, Doctor, but by humans. You must examine my brother and tell me if any of his flesh has been deliberately removed."

"As you wish. Will there be anything else, madame?"

"No."

"Perhaps you should wait outside, madame," he suggested, pulling on a pair of latex gloves.

"I will not faint." She walked to the end of the table opposite the tag.

She paused a moment to maneuver the soft flesh of her right cheek between her teeth. Then, as she raised the sheet, she bit down hard.

She looked down only long enough to be sure. The skull was horribly crushed, but it was François. Blinking away tears and tasting her own blood, she lowered the sheet and turned away.

"Shall I proceed?" the doctor asked.

"Yes," she managed to whisper.

As she crossed the room, her insides seized up and she swallowed the rising bile. Her mind was reeling. At the wall, she reached out and steadied herself against the ancient stone. Thus grounded, she closed her eyes and began to pray. Ever so slowly, the world settled back into itself. Standing by the table, she had felt François's *gros-bon-ange* hovering above his corpse. The anthropologists called it the soul, but the *gros-bon-ange* could not be explained with a single word. It was the consciousness of the entire race, the accumulated humanity of the bloodline reaching back through the generations and across the waters to ancient Guinée and beyond. Sirene knew that François's *gros-bon-ange* would remain with him for nine full days, watching his flesh for any signs of life, and only then, when it was sure he was truly dead, would it leave him and return to its ancestral home at the bottom of the sea.

Sirene knew that every individual had two distinct spirits within him, his *gros-bon-ange,* which connected him to every other member of the race, and his *ti-bon-ange,* which gave him his individuality. Sirene understood that the *gros-bon-ange* was self-sufficient; it was merely lent to an individual for use during his lifetime. But François's personal spirit, his *ti-bon-ange,* was now her responsibility, the most solemn responsibility she had ever had. Only she could prevent François's spirit from becoming like one of the pathetic things that had assailed her at the doorway: a spirit whose body had died but for whom the proper rituals had not been performed, a spirit condemned to wander aimlessly over this earthly world forever.

François had never been a believer, but Sirene knew that the l'wahs' existence did not depend on François or anyone else. For Sirene, their existence was no more in question than her own. She had spent her lifetime communicating with them, learning and practicing their rituals. Her task now was to convince the l'wahs to allow François's *ti-bon-ange* to join them in the spirit world: to give her brother's personal spirit, freed from its yoke of earthbound flesh, the opportunity to live in the sacred realm forever. While the doctor began his work, Sirene gathered herself, stepped away from the wall, and stood on her own two feet. In prayer after fervent prayer, she called on Legba, the guardian of the crossroads between the two worlds, to intercede with the other great l'wahs on François's behalf, to allow her brother's spirit to make the eternal journey. After a while she could feel him listening.

She heard a distant voice call, "Madame."

She shook herself, struggling to determine from which world it was coming. The voice drifted closer. She was floating.

"Madame." The voice was right beside her. "Madame!"

She landed with a start and opened her eyes. The room returned with all its cold stone ugliness.

"Yes, Doctor?"

"Please come here, Madame."

She approached the table. With the sheet removed, François looked so helpless, so sad. His skin, which had always been taut and darkly vibrant, was now slack and gray. Poor baby . . .

". . . shot," the doctor said, his gloved finger pointing to a small, crusty crater near the center of François's chest.

"Shot?" she repeated mechanically, not understanding.

"This man has been shot."

"Shot?"

"With a high-power rifle," the doctor said in the same clinical tone.

"Shot," Sirene repeated, then felt a sharp sting on her face, as if she had been slapped. Her vision cleared. She drew in a deep breath. "Shot?" she asked incredulously, the word's meaning registering at last.

"The bullet passed directly through the heart and exited the back."

"What are you telling me?" she asked, struggling to hold down—shot?—the fury she felt rising in her blood.

"I am assuring you that this man is dead."

Sirene scanned her baby brother's exposed and cruelly broken body. Deep inside her, she felt her formless sorrow congealing into hate. It gave her a strange pleasure. Hate was far more manageable than sorrow. Hate had form. Hate could be satisfied.

She felt an icy calm descend on her. "What of the other injuries?" she heard herself ask.

"All consistent with a fall from a great height."

"But the fall, you believe that it occurred after he was shot?"

"That is my opinion. Yes, madame."

"So," she thought out loud, trying to make sense of it, "someone shot my brother through the heart and then threw his body off a cliff."

"That is what the evidence suggests, madame. Yes."

"I see. Have you completed your examination?"

"Yes, madame."

"And did you discover any mutilation?"

"No, madame. I found no mutilation."

"Doctor, you have been of great service to me."

He bowed his head. "Madame, my sincerest sympathies for your loss."

"Thank you, Doctor. There is no need to keep you here any longer. If you would be so kind as to send in the soldiers on your way out . . ."

"I will stay and help you clean the body."

"Thank you, no. I must do that myself."

"In that case . . ." The doctor stripped off his rubber gloves and took her hand in both of his.

After he left, the soldiers hurried in with a basin of water and two clean sheets. Sirene gave them each another $5 bill and told them to wait outside and to keep the door closed. As soon as they were gone, she opened her bag and took out a large sponge and a bar of scented soap and laid them in the basin, then rummaged around until she found the scissors and the Ziploc bag with the needle and thread.

She walked to the end of the table. "My darling François," she whispered, and kissed his cold forehead five times, one for each point of Legba's cross and the last for the intersection at its center, symbolizing the crossroads of the two worlds, the earthly and the spiritual.

"My poor baby brother," she murmured, moving around the corner of the table and pushing up her sleeves. "First I will see to your spirit," she promised, threading the needle, laying it on the table next to his head and picking up the scissors.

She cut a lock of his hair and took fingernail parings from both hands and sealed it all in the plastic bag. Then, feeling the blood starting to pound through her veins, she carefully picked up the threaded needle.

"Hear me now," she whispered with quiet fury, raising her face and pointing the needle straight toward heaven. "As God is my witness, I declare before Damballah and Ayida Wedo, before Ayizan, before the holy twins Marassa, before Legba and all the other great l'wahs, that I will avenge the murder of François Arcenciel. Give me strength."

With that, she reached down, drove the needle through her baby brother's lips, and began to sew.

TWENTY-EIGHT

Moe heard a loud buzz, dashed over, and pressed the intercom. "Yes?"

"Mr. Rosen," the doorman announced, "there's a—what's your name again?—a Miss Williams down here for you."

It took a second for Marlene's last name to register.

"Okay," Moe said. "Fine."

There was a moment of silence.

Moe pressed the button. "Is there a problem?"

"Will you be coming down? Or should I send her up?"

"Send her up."

Moe could see he was in trouble the moment she stepped off the elevator. Without a word, she marched right past him into the apartment. He hurriedly locked the door and fastened the chain.

"Son of a bitch," she said, throwing her handbag and overnight case on the sofa.

She had her back turned. Moe went to touch her but couldn't. She seemed radioactive. Something must have happened at school.

"What? Tell me."

"'Will you be coming down?'" she said bitterly, mimicking the doorman. "'Or should I send her up?'"

"He doesn't know you."

"Right. He sees a black woman asking for Mr. Rosen and he stands there trying to decide whether I'm a maid or a whore."

"Now come on," Moe soothed, placing a tentative hand on her shoulder.

She shrugged it off and moved away. Moe didn't know what to do or say. She was right. Even through the intercom Moe had heard the snide inflection in the doorman's voice—had heard it and had let it pass. Why? He should have been outraged. "Hey, Manuel," he should have barked, loud enough for Marlene to have heard, "Miss Williams is my . . ."

He stared at her back. My what? he wondered.

His whatever, he told himself. Anything would have been better than his cowardly silence.

"Let me take your coat," he offered.

She wrenched the bottom of the oversize jacket down below her hips. She was right. He was a bastard. He didn't deserve to see any part of her.

"How was physics?" he asked, to show he remembered what course she was taking.

Silence.

"You're late. I was worried."

A slight, ambiguous movement of one shoulder.

"I missed you." He wished she would turn around.

A small, self-conscious shrug. Progress.

"How about something to eat?"

"Right," she grumbled, still turned away. "You'd like that, wouldn't you? So my stomach can start making noises."

"Let me hold you. Please?"

She spun around. Their embrace was awkward because of her jacket. He held her tight. Even through the thick padding he could feel her trembling. At least he hoped it was her.

"I'm so glad you're here," he whispered, nuzzling her fragrant neck.

She squirmed free and turned away. "So," she said, sniffling hard as she unzipped her jacket, "did that guy ever get in touch with you?"

"Which guy?"

"Some Haitian." She tossed her jacket on the sofa, revealing a blue T-shirt. "He came into Wedo's this afternoon looking for Miz Ark." She turned to him.

"God, you're beautiful."

"That's not funny," she snapped, wiping mascara from under her eyes. "I know I'm a mess. Where's the bathroom?"

"This way. You want your case? What about this guy?"

"Oh, nothing. I need my bag too. . . . Thanks. This place is nice, Rocky; it looks like you. Oh, that Haitian guy? He asked if I knew any place he could sell some jewelry. I told him he could go next door and check with you. Was that okay?"

He loved having her here in his apartment. He leaned over to kiss her cheek.

"I need a shower," she said, ducking away. "So, this guy, he never showed up?"

"No. Why, was there something special about him?"

"He gave me the creeps."

"Nice of you to send him to me," Moe teased.

"I didn't like the way he was looking at me. He had these weird eyes. You're staring."

"I know. I can't help it."

"This is one of those new miracle bras." She modeled it for him. "What do you think?"

"Miraculous."

"Very funny. Are there any clean towels in this joint?"

"I hung some behind the door for you."

She stepped into the bathroom and checked. "Sure of yourself, aren't you?"

"No. Just—"

The door slammed.

"—hoping."

TWENTY-NINE

The red Chevrolet raised a cloud of dust as it pulled off the blacktop and bounced to a halt. Up ahead, half a dozen women began sprucing up their roadside stands. The taxi driver, hired for the day, ran around to open the door for his passenger.

Sirene stepped from the air-conditioned car into the thick midday heat of the Haitian countryside. She brushed away the dust and fluffed out her black dress. She had stopped the car impulsively; the sight of the Madame Saras and their upturned crates had made her feel like a child again. Despite the ache in her soul, her body was pleased to be home.

As Sirene approached, the women stood fussing behind their stands, smoothing their faded cotton shifts, adjusting their head scarves, arranging their wares. They all appeared to be about Sirene's age, though with country people it was difficult to tell.

Moving slowly down the line, Sirene stopped before each crude stand to exchange soft Creole words with the vendor and to examine her wares. The first woman had constructed a little pyramid with her stunted tomatoes, the second had fitted her misshapen yams together like pieces of a puzzle, the third had made a sort of graduated necklace from her dozen or so undernourished onions. The next had enclosed her few small, mottled eggs within a raised circle of dirt, which she had decorated with a sprig of wildflower. The fifth woman had created a delicate standing structure with her emaciated carrots. The last was using an ancient paper fan with Baby Doc's faded portrait to shoo iridescent horseflies from her bunch of overripe plantains.

As Sirene had expected, the women were shy, courteous, dignified, happy for the company and the chance to do a bit of business out here in the bush. Though this was a main road, no other vehicle had come past since Sirene's had stopped. The heat shimmered beneath a cloudless sky. There was no breeze, no sense of time. Five minutes outside the car and Sirene's clothes were hanging on her like hot, damp laundry. She looked around. The land had not changed. It seemed as if the very air had not changed since she had left here as a young girl.

"Now, if you please," she told the women, gathering them around her, "let us conduct our business."

Sandals scraped the dry ground as the women edged closer. Sirene felt the sun pressing down on her. Though the other women's skin remained dry as salt, Sirene was forced to mop her face with a handkerchief.

"I live in America."

This announcement set them all giggling, though they were careful to cover their mouths.

"Are you rich then?" the carrot woman asked impulsively, and immediately looked ashamed.

"The l'wahs have been generous to me."

"How many children have they given you?" a different woman asked.

"Only one. A daughter of eighteen years."

"Is she an obedient child?"

"An angel. Truly."

"How is she called?"

"Her name is Erzulie."

"Ah," they exclaimed in unison.

"Is she very beautiful?" the plantain woman asked.

"I am told so."

"And her skin, is it very pale?" another asked.

"Yes. Very pale."

"How can you keep the men away?" a third inquired.

"I send her to a school with only girls. It is run by the church."

"Ah!" Heads nodded approvingly.

"And is it Madame's husband who has died?" the carrot woman asked, noting Sirene's black dress.

"No. My brother. I have no husband. My precious daughter is all I have left in this world."

They all crossed themselves and then took turns solemnly shaking her hand. Their sympathy was so heartfelt that Sirene found herself close to tears.

"I wish to buy all your goods."

They looked at her in wide-eyed astonishment.

"I have plenty of gourdes." She pulled a sheaf of bills from her wallet.

The women huddled anxiously, all talking at once. Sirene was confused until it dawned on her that she had been thinking like an American.

"Excuse me," she said, interrupting their conference, "I have changed my mind. I do not need so much. I wish to buy only half."

She saw their faces brighten. With no goods to sell, the women would have no market. They would lose each other's company. They would have to go home.

"How much will you pay?" the carrot woman asked.

Sirene proceeded to give each woman an equal amount of money. The women stared down at the bills in their dry, leathery hands.

"This is too much," the onion woman said.

"With respect, I ask each of you to accept a gift in honor of my dear brother's spirit."

The women looked at each other uncertainly. Sirene knew that country people would never take charity, but she did not think they would refuse this.

One of them whispered something to the carrot woman.

"Tell us his name," the carrot woman said to Sirene, "so that we may pray for him."

—◦∿∿◦—

Sirene sat in the car waiting for the dust to settle. The village on the far side of the ditch looked and smelled like all the others they had stopped at today: dirt streets, a stray dog, shacks of weathered board and tar paper and corrugated tin, cement blocks, oil drums, rusty pieces of metal that had once belonged to something, the stink of human waste. Haiti seemed even poorer than she remembered it.

She stepped from the car and shook out her dress. There was still no breeze, but the air was cooler. She would have to be careful crossing the ditch—those mismatched planks looked even shakier than the last ones—but the temple could not be far.

The old man who answered her knock had a sympathetic smile but few teeth. The red bandanna around his neck indicated that he was a houngan.

"For the l'wahs," Sirene said, handing him a bag containing what was left of the produce.

He accepted it graciously.

"And this is for you, papa." She handed him a bottle of rum.

The old man took the bottle, brushed it against the little pineapples on his shirt, and studied the label.

"Barbancourt five star. Madame is too generous."

"Not at all. It is my pleasure."

"Madame requires my services?"

"Yes, if you please."

He led her inside, lit a candle at a small table, and invited her to sit. The dim room, crowded with sacred objects, smelled as distant and as familiar as her youth.

—◦◦◦—

"So," the houngan said after they had spoken for a while, "it would seem that the angry soldier who came here was your brother."

"From everything you have said, I am now sure of it. I apologize for the way you were treated."

"No matter. I am well now, as you see. Besides, dear madame, it was not this old man but the l'wahs who were offended."

"Yes, papa, but it was not the l'wahs who shot a bullet through my brother's heart."

"However it occurs," he told her, reaching out and patting her hand, "it is always hard to lose a loved one. Your brother's spirit must be our concern."

"The arrangements have already been made. All the rites are being observed."

The old man seemed surprised. "Then of what service can I be to you, madame?"

Sirene chose her words carefully. "I thank the houngan for his understanding and his wisdom. I have learned that my brother did bad things, papa, to you and to others. But I knew my brother. We shared the same blood. François was not a believer, but his spirit was good. He could only have done these evil things while under another's spell. I ask you to help me find that man, the man he was working for."

"I am not the one to help you." The houngan slid his chair back and pushed slowly to his feet.

Sirene was desolate. She hung her head. This had been her best lead.

"Rest here for a moment." The houngan patted her hand. "I cannot help you, but I will fetch you someone who can."

———

She was a handsome girl, tall and straight, with lustrous hair, delicate features, and smooth skin marred only by a small scar high on one cheek.

"How old are you, child?" Sirene asked, inviting her to sit.

"I made seventeen years last month, madame." She took the seat but kept her eyes downcast.

"I have a daughter about your age," Sirene said, hoping to put her at ease.

The girl nodded but said nothing. She stared down at her hands, which now lay knotted in her lap.

"The houngan tells me your name is Antoinette. Is that correct?"

"Yes, madame."

"And what do your friends call you?"

"Some call me Twah," the girl said with a shy little shrug.

"And your boyfriend?" Sirene teased. "What does he call you?"

The girl's head remained down while her right hand rose and brushed her dress, as if feeling for something. Then her shoulders trembled, and to Sirene's dismay, a single tear ran down her cheek.

"What have I said?" Sirene asked, resisting the urge to take the child in her arms. "I am a friend. I mean you no harm. Did not your houngan tell you that?"

"Yes, madame," the girl whispered.

"Then why do you cry?"

"I cry for a boy, madame. A lost boy. I am a foolish girl." She reached up and wiped away the tear. "I ask Madame to forgive me."

"There is nothing to forgive, little one. I too have lost a boy."

Antoinette's eyes appeared for the first time. "Is true?"

"My brother. I have lost my little brother."

"I have lost my heart," Antoinette said simply.

"And what was your heart's name?"

"His name was Fabrice, madame. Fabrice Lacroix."

"And what happened to him?"

The story poured out of Antoinette in a torrent: the fire at the Jouvier house, the disappearance of Agwe's raft, her arrest by soldiers a few days later, her miraculous escape, her protection by Ayizan, her continued longing for Fabrice even though she knew he could never return.

"Listen, child," Sirene said gently. "I have a car and a driver outside. Have you seen them?"

"Yes, madame. Everyone in the village has seen them."

"Have you ever been in a car like that, Antoinette?"

"Only the tap-taps, madame. Never a car such as that."

"Would you like to go in the car with me, Antoinette? You must be hungry. We could drive to a town and find some food. Would you like that?"

"Thank you, madame, but I can not."

"And why?"

"I am in hiding, madame. The army is hunting for me. They have already sent soldiers here. Did you not hear? One of them beat the houngan."

"Yes, I did hear about that. It was awful." Sirene clasped her hands on the table and leaned toward the girl. "But who sent these men, Antoinette? Do you know the man who sent them?"

"Oh, yes, madame." Antoinette's eyes were suddenly flashing. "That is the man who hurt me and wanted to do worse. He is a monster, madame. A devil."

Sirene's body tensed. Her lower back was seized by a sharp, throbbing pain. "His name," she whispered. "Do you know his name?"

"His men call him colonel, madame," Antoinette said, hunching forward, her hands in her lap becoming fists. "But he calls himself Hugo.
Hugo Ferray."

THIRTY

Fabrice felt crickets jumping in his belly. People were rushing everywhere. Corridors led off in all directions, like spokes of a wheel.

"This way," Shaneekwa cried, pulling him by the hand.

"Gate twenty-nine," Mr. Jackson reminded her.

"Where's the fire?" Mrs. Jackson pleaded from somewhere behind
them in the crowd. "Fabrice," she called, "you make that child slow
down, you hear me?"

"Yes, madame," he answered, using his weight as a brake.

"Everyone's getting ahead of us," Shaneekwa complained.

Her grandfather came alongside. "It's not a race. We have plenty of
time."

"We do not," the child insisted, tugging on Fabrice's arm.

Fabrice could see that Shaneekwa was upset that he was leaving. He
was upset too, but not about that. Everywhere he looked there were
police, their hard eyes searching the crowd. He squeezed Shaneekwa's
hand and slowed her enough to allow Mr. and Mrs. Jackson to catch up.
The police might not notice a man with a family.

With a little hop, Shaneekwa led them onto a giant moving rubber
strip that was wide enough for three people. Remembering the one at
Sea World, Fabrice looked up, half-expecting to see sharks swimming by
overhead. But nothing was above them here but a shiny white ceiling.

They were carried past shops and restaurants and areas with brightly
colored seats. Every few seconds they passed another color television

set hanging from the ceiling or poking out from a wall, as if TVs were some giant American fruit. Fabrice had been in this country almost five days now, but he still couldn't believe it. America was so rich it made even the Jouviers seem poor.

He looked down and saw that Shaneekwa was resting her head against his side. He reached down and stroked her hair. She was a strange child, serious one moment, laughing and full of wonder the next. These four days had been like a dream. Mr. and Mrs. Jackson were honorable people. Fabrice was grateful that the l'wahs had put them all together. He was sorry to be leaving, but perhaps one day the l'wahs would bring them all together again.

—⁓—

The lady behind the counter took the papers and studied them. Fabrice felt himself going numb.

"Will you be traveling alone, Mr. Lacroix?" she asked without looking up.

"Yes," Mr. Jackson answered for him.

"And would you prefer an aisle or a window?"

"Window," Mr. Jackson told her.

"Twenty-three A," the woman said, then wrote something on a piece of cardboard, tore it off, and slipped it into a pocket in the paper and handed the whole thing to Fabrice.

"Come on," Mr. Jackson said, leading him away. "And put that ticket in your bag so you don't lose it."

"Yes, sir."

"Hey," Shaneekwa called, "where are you guys going?"

"We'll be right back," Mr. Jackson assured her.

"I'm coming too," she announced.

"We're going to the boys' room," Mr. Jackson told her. "You stay here with your grandma."

"Swell," she grumbled. "Be quick," she called to Fabrice.

Fabrice waited at the tiny round table, pretending not to notice the two police, a man and a woman, standing right outside. Finally, Mr. Jackson returned with two paper cups and a paper plate with food.

"Okay, my friend," the old man said, putting everything down and then rubbing his hands together, "let's go over this one more time."

Fabrice listened as best he could, nodding whenever it seemed called for, but all he heard was a rush of sound like the sea made when Agwe was very angry. In a few minutes—unless the police grabbed him up first—he would be getting on an airplane and flying to New York. Even with the ticket in his bag it still seemed impossible. An airplane. New York. Impossible.

Mr. Jackson's mouth continued to move, sending words shooting past Fabrice's ears. He assumed Mr. Jackson was explaining again about the man he had worked with in the postal service, the man who knew everyone in New York, the man who could—

". . . eat," Mr. Jackson said.

Fabrice lifted a cookie, took a bite, told his mouth to chew. An airplane. New York. Impossible.

"Hey," Mr. Jackson said, reaching out and shaking Fabrice's shoulder, "did you understand everything I said?"

"No, sir," Fabrice admitted, patting his own chest. "My heart is . . ."

"I'm excited too, Fabrice. But this is important. You have to listen. Drink some milk."

Fabrice lifted the paper cup and drank. It was cold but it had no taste. He had to concentrate on what Mr. Jackson was saying.

". . . like the underground railway," the old man said with a grin. "And I'm the conductor."

"Sir?"

"Where is your ticket? You have your ticket?"

"Yes, sir. In the bag, sir."

"And your money?"

"Yes, sir. Here and here, sir." Felice tapped first his hollow coin and then the pocket of his jeans. "Thank you, sir."

"Stop thanking me and listen. What is my friend's name?"

"Please, sir?"

"My friend. The man who will be meeting your plane in New York. What is his name?"

"Henri Soldat, sir. A Haitian man, sir. Tall like me. With white hair like you."

"He will be holding a sign that says what?"

"Fabrice, sir. The sign will say Fabrice. My name, sir."

"Good. Henri will take care of you. You listen to him, do you hear?"

"Oh, yes, sir. Fabrice do everything Henri Soldat say. Everything. Exact."

"Good. You have the paper I gave you?"

"Yes, sir. Paper right here, sir." Fabrice pointed to the Sea World satchel between his feet.

"If you run into a problem, you call me on the telephone. The number is on the paper. This is exciting for me too, you know."

"Is wonderful, sir. Fabrice very happy."

Mr. Jackson pushed Fabrice's outstretched hand away. "Now, is there anything else you need? Think."

Fabrice thought. "Sir." He bent over and reached into his satchel. "There is this, sir."

"A postcard?"

Fabrice placed it on the table. "Yes, sir. I buy at Sea World. Is possible Mr. Jackson can send to Antoinette?"

"Who is Antoinette?"

"A friend, sir. In Haiti, sir."

"You better not tell Shaneekwa," Mr. Jackson said with a wink.

"No, sir. Not tell Shaneekwa at all, sir. You can write for Fabrice?"

"Glad to."

Mr. Jackson took out a pen. "What's this Antoinette's last name?"

Fabrice knew the name, but not the letters. Mr. Jackson said he had taken a little French in high school.

"Antoinette is easy," he said, writing it. "But Vwa-zan," he said, making a face. "Well, best I can figure, that should be V-o-i-s-i-n. That sound right?"

"If Mr. Jackson say," Fabrice replied uncertainly. "I write my name."

"Fine. That will be fine. Now, where does she live?"

Fabrice said the name of the village and Mr. Jackson wrote it out.

"That was easy. Now, what all did you want to say?"

Fabrice's mind went blank. He couldn't think of anything but her name.

"Anytime you're ready."

"What to write?"

"This Antoinette, she's your girlfriend?"

"Yes, sir. Very much, sir."

"Does she know where you are?"

"No, sir. Not at all, sir."

"Then maybe you could say, 'Regards from America. Thinking of you. Love, Fabrice.'"

"That is wonderful, sir. You can write all that?"

"All except the 'Fabrice.' You said you would do that."

"Yes, sir. With pleasure I do that, sir. You believe Antoinette will like picture?"

"Yes. Of course she will. Everybody likes Shamu."

THIRTY-ONE

Moe was in the office rechecking the seams on the sample costume. Air was up front working with a customer. Moe was worried. Tonight the whole troupe would be seeing his designs for the first time, and he still couldn't decide how to begin his presentation. He was tempted to start by explaining how his vision of The Golden Door had developed, taking them through the process step by step, laying the conceptual groundwork before unveiling the large color rendering of the float. But there were dangers to that approach. What if they had trouble understanding his accent? What if he talked too much? What if they weren't interested in his ideas, only his designs? What if they didn't like those either? He wished Air would hurry up and sell this man something so he could ask her advice. The girl had a real head on her shoulders. Why was the guy hovering over her like that? It was creepy.

He turned the costume over and checked the elastics by the thighs. When Air had first volunteered to model it for the troupe, Moe had been absolutely thrilled, but now he found himself riddled with doubts. He shivered at the sudden image of an ocean of black faces—more than a hundred of them would be out there tonight—staring at him, judging him. Who was to say they would like his work? He stared despondently at the flimsy little costume. Who was to say anything?

He smoothed out the costume on the desktop and took a few steps backward, trying to view it objectively. Yesterday he had been so sure, but now . . .

No, his mind was made up. This was final. He would not start his presentation with a long talk. That would be the kiss of death. No, what he would do first was unveil the rendering of the float, hopefully to some oohs and aahs, even—dare he hope?—a smattering of applause. He would point out the float's features and—why did Marlene have to have class tonight?—and call for questions and pray he could understand what they were saying. While this was going on, Air would be hidden somewhere in the wings, and then, when the moment seemed right— they'd have to set up a signal, a secret signal, so that—

There was a knock at the door. Air poked her head in.

"This gentleman, sir, he wishes to speak with you."

"Discount?" Moe asked under his breath.

"No, sir. He says that a waitress at Wedo's suggested that he come here."

"Waitress at—? Oh, wait a minute, I think—okay, fine, I'll just—" He started to come out. "No, I better . . ." He hurried back in, folded the costume, wrapped it in tissue paper, and placed it on top of the safe.

"Did he give his name?" he asked Air, slipping into his jacket.

"Yes, sir. A Mr. Fauchon. He is Haitian."

"Okay. Foe-shon. I've got it." He buttoned his jacket and walked briskly down the aisle.

"Monsieur Rosen?" the man inquired, coming to attention.

"Yes. Moe Rosen." Moe extended his hand. The man's bearing was almost military. "Mr. Fauchon?"

"Honoré Fauchon." The man added a small bow to his formal handshake. "A great pleasure, sir."

"Likewise."

Sure, Moe told himself, this had to be the same guy, the one who'd told Marlene he wanted to sell some jewelry. Moe saw what she meant about his eyes; they were small, hard, and yes, creepy. Moe suspected he was a fence.

"May we speak in private?" Fauchon inquired.

"Certainly. Let's go into my office."

"You are so kind."

Moe swiveled his desk chair to face this Mr. Foe-shon, who sat with his hands clasped on the briefcase on his lap and a gold Rolex President— genuine but probably stolen—peeking out from beneath a starched white cuff. Both safes were locked. Moe had the gun in the desk. It was loaded. When he'd sat down, he had opened the drawer a crack.

"I know your time is valuable, Mr. Rosen," Fauchon began pleasantly, "so I shall, as you Americans say, come straight to the point."

"Please."

"I came to Brooklyn to see Madame Arcenciel, the owner of the establishment next door, but I was told that she has gone away."

"She went to Haiti. Her brother died."

"Yes, I know. A terrible tragedy. Her brother François and I were business partners."

"I see. Well, she should be back any day now."

"Yes, so I have been told. This is a sad time. I was in New York for a family funeral as well. Naturally I will remain here until Madame Arcenciel returns, to pay my condolences, as you say, in person."

Moe nodded sympathetically. He didn't believe this guy for a second.

"François and I were very close," Fauchon declared solemnly. "The least I can do is pay my respects to his sister."

"I'm sure Miz Ark—that's what she's called around here, Miz Ark—will appreciate the gesture."

"I sincerely hope so. But in the meantime, Mr. Rosen, one of her workers suggested that you might be able to assist me in disposing of some jewelry."

"Really? Which worker was that, may I ask?"

"A dark, handsome, strong-featured girl. A waitress. Rather tall, rather—how shall I say this?—bountiful? I believe her name is Marlene."

"Oh, yes," Moe replied evenly. "Marlene."

"You know her, then?"

"Indeed. And what sort of jewelry are you interested in selling, Mr. Fauchon?"

"I have a few pieces with me." He snapped open the briefcase. "If I may show you?"

"Please."

Fauchon handed Moe a large diamond solitaire in an old-fashioned platinum setting. Moe put his loupe to his eye and brought the stone into focus.

"Nice cut," he remarked, turning it slowly in the light. "I would estimate two hundred twenty-five points, VVS, and probably G or H."

"My apologies, but could you please translate that for me?"

"I'm sorry." Moe put down the loupe. "I thought you were in the trade."

"No, no," Fauchon replied with a little chuckle. "François and I dealt in estates, liquidations mostly. He was the expert on jewelry. I am merely an administrator."

"I see," Moe replied warily.

"Some time ago, for example," Fauchon said casually, "François made his sister—the lady you call Miz Ark—a gift of a—how do you say?—a wristwatch. Gold, with many little diamonds. As I recall, it was a Piaget."

"Yes, I sized it for her."

"How very nice. At the time, François said it was quite a good wristwatch. Would you agree?"

"Absolutely," Moe gushed, feeling guilty for his former suspicions. Despite his creepy eyes and stilted manners, this Fauchon was clearly on the level. Who else would have known about the Piaget? Also, it made sense that it had come from an estate. Moe chastised himself for judging people too harshly. He hoped he hadn't been too obvious.

"So, would you be so kind as to explain to me what you said about this ring?"

"My pleasure." Moe was anxious to make amends. "I'm no expert, Mr. Fauchon, but to my eye this is an excellent stone. Diamonds are judged by what are referred to as the four C's: carat, cut, color, and clarity. Carat refers to weight. A carat is one fifth of a gram and contains a hundred points. So this stone which I estimate at two hundred twenty-five points would be two and a quarter carats, quite a good size for a diamond. Further, the cut, the way it has been faceted, seems excellent. VVS stands for 'very very slight,' referring to its clarity, the degree of occlusion or imperfection within the stone. The best stones, of course, are IF, or 'internally flawless.' But the next best grade is VVS. The imperfections in a VVS stone cannot be seen with the naked eye. Finally, diamonds are graded by color. The absolute best color is designated by the letter *D*, which actually means that the stone has no color whatsoever. Stones graded E and F are nearly colorless, with only a negligible yellow tint. G, H, and I are also considered gem quality, though they will have a bit more yellow. The better its color and the better its cut—and, as I've said, Mr. Fauchon, your stone appears to be well cut—the better the stone will refract light: the more 'life' or 'fire' or 'brilliance' the stone will have."

"That is all fascinating," Fauchon declared, busily taking notes. "Absolutely fascinating. So a diamond—excuse me, a stone—like this one, Mr. Rosen, the one you have just examined, could one estimate its value?"

"One certainly could. Diamond dealers have price charts that are updated weekly."

"So would you venture an estimate of this ring's worth?"

"Oh, I'd venture," Moe said laughing, "but I'd only be guessing."

"Please. I am very curious."

"No, no. I'd really rather not. I'm not current on the prices for loose stones."

"But you believe the stone is valuable?"

"I *know* the stone is valuable."

"Ten thousand American dollars?"

"More. Probably twice that much. Now, did you say you had other pieces to show me?"

"Yes, I have five more, if you do not mind spending the time."

"To me, Mr. Fauchon, looking at fine jewelry is like looking at beautiful women: one can always find the time."

"In that case . . ." Fauchon brought out the next piece.

"What I can do, if you wish, Mr. Fauchon," Moe said after he had examined them all, "is to refer you to a major diamond merchant, a man who regularly buys and sells quality stones like yours."

"You know this man? Personally?"

"Yes. He has an excellent reputation. If you like, I can call him for you. His office is in Manhattan, in the Empire State Building. Of course, you will be under absolutely no obligation to accept his offer."

"That would be most kind of you, Mr. Rosen. Most kind. I would like to see him today, if that could be arranged."

Moe made the call and set up an appointment for four o'clock. He wrote out the name and address on a piece of Eli Rosen & Son stationery.

"I must return to Wedo's and thank Marlene for sending me here," Fauchon said, slipping the paper into his briefcase.

"No need."

"Seeing her again would not be a burden," Fauchon said with a little smirk.

"I'll be seeing her later myself."

"Ah," Fauchon replied with a smile that was meant to be friendly but didn't quite make it.

"Marlene and I are, uh, seeing each other."

"My congratulations, Mr. Rosen." Fauchon glanced out into the store to where Air was dusting a showcase. "I see you surround yourself with . . . lovely jewels."

"My salesgirl is Miz Ark's daughter," Moe explained, hoping to prevent any misunderstanding.

Fauchon's head snapped around. "Excuse me?"

"Miz Ark's daughter."

"How interesting." Fauchon studied Air with a strange intensity.

Moe experienced an unpleasant little tremor. Fauchon's eyes were more than creepy, they were . . . mean. Moe felt the need to pry them away from Air.

"Mr. Fauchon."

"Ah, Mr. Rosen." The Haitian turned back to Moe. "Excuse me, I was . . . I am . . . well, I must admit, a bit shocked. François, you see, never told me he had a niece."

"She's a lovely girl. I'm lucky to have her here."

"Yes, yes," Fauchon said distractedly. "And François's sister," he asked suddenly, "this Miz Ark, has she other children?"

"No. I believe Air is her only child."

"Air?"

"It's short for Erzulie."

"Of course." Fauchon smiled. "Erzulie the temptress. I should have known."

THIRTY-TWO

Fabrice was pleased to have Mr. Jackson's friend Henri Soldat as his guide in New York. A clever, sharp-tongued, white-haired old man who walked with a cane, Henri Soldat looked like the great l'wah Legba, the keeper of the gate, the guardian of the crossroads between the two worlds.

When Henri Soldat first asked him about a job, Fabrice explained his dream of driving a taxicab. No good, Soldat replied. The problem was papers. To drive a taxi here, Fabrice would require a New York driver's license. To apply for a license, he would need immigration papers. Soldat knew people who could provide such papers, but those people charged more than the few hundred dollars Fabrice had arrived in New York with. The taxi would have to wait. What other kind of work could Fabrice do?

Gardening? No, gardening was no good either. Here in New York, Soldat explained, groups of men went around in trucks caring for people's lawns, and though most of these workers were illegals like Fabrice, nearly all of them spoke Spanish. Did Fabrice speak Spanish? Ah, well.

Fabrice described the other things he did for the Jouviers. Soldat shook his head and said that Fabrice was twenty years too late. These days, he explained, the rich people in America did not want servants with black skin; they wanted Latins or, better yet, Asians. Black servants, Soldat explained, were no longer "politically correct."

"What means *politically correct?*" Fabrice asked.

"Do not try to understand the Americans," Soldat advised. "It will only make your head hurt."

"Yes, sir."

"Forget about driving a taxi, Fabrice. Forget about gardening. Forget about working as a servant in some rich person's house. Come, let's go for a walk. I have some ideas."

Fabrice's blood began to race the moment he stepped from the dark calm of Henri Soldat's apartment building into the sunlit confusion of Brooklyn. The sidewalk was crowded with noisy children. The street was clogged with cars and vans and angry trucks. It felt like Port-au-Prince, but without the dust and the bad smells.

Soldat moved with surprising speed, snaking between people and making it hard to keep up. As Fabrice hurried along, he caught strange, random glimpses: ladies' wigs on faceless heads, big luggages strung together and hung from overhead ropes, cutoff hands holding gold jewelry, loaves of bread stacked like bricks, metal sticks full of cooked chickens, rows of women sitting with the tops of their heads inside big plastic beehives. Some shops had so much to sell that their goods were spilling out onto the street: baby carriages and children's bicycles, plastic toys that barked and bounced or swam in pans of water, big wooden tables stacked with ripe fruit and healthy vegetables, giant speakers blasting music so loud it made the air shake.

Soldat went into shop after shop to speak with the boss, each time making Fabrice wait outside in the street. After several hours and more than two dozen shops, the old man was starting to look worried. Fabrice, however, remained confident. The l'wahs had carried him across a raging sea and given him the magic coin, which was still around his neck. They had sent him to the kindly Mr. Jackson, who had in turn sent him to a friend who looked and acted like Legba. Henri Soldat might doubt the power of the l'wahs, but Fabrice Lacroix did not.

"Here," Soldat said, holding open a door.

"I go inside?" Fabrice asked uncertainly.

"I'm hungry," the old man grumbled, shaking the door impatiently. "And my feet hurt. Now come on."

The rush of food smells made Fabrice's stomach growl. They had not eaten since leaving the house, and the sun had moved halfway across the sky since then. Soldat threaded his way through the many crowded tables, pausing often to smile and pat shoulders and shake hands. Finally, near the back of the large room, Soldat found them a small, empty table. He put down his newspaper and picked up a menu while Fabrice looked around. The air was cold, but the people looked happy, talking loudly and laughing while they drank sodas and beer and ate from plates heaped with food. A few of the women were young and shapely, but many more were middle-aged and fat. In a back corner, old men bent over tables playing dominoes, smacking the pieces down just as they did at home. The music was bouncy and nice. The fish overhead were only painted wood, but Fabrice liked the way they danced on their strings. He liked the bathing-girl posters even more.

Soldat put down the menu. "I want you to practice your English."

"Yes, sir."

"The name of this restaurant is Wedo's," he said, speaking each word carefully. "Wedo's is the neighborhood's most popular restaurant."

"Yes, sir."

"You understand *pop-u-lar?*"

"No, sir."

"Pop-u-lar means that many people like it."

"Pop-u-lar."

Soldat picked up his newspaper. The sight of the Haitian flag near the top of the page started Fabrice thinking about home. He wondered what day it was there and who would go out and clean the pool and what Antoinette was doing right now.

"Fabrice," Soldat said, lowering his paper, "what was the name of that family you worked for?"

"The Jacksons, sir."

"No, no, boy. The family in Haiti."

"Excuse me. That is the Jouviers, sir."

"The Jouviers. Right. What kind of work did he do, this Monsieur Jouvier?"

"Monsieur Jouvier has a newspaper, sir. Like the one in your hand, sir, but a different one."

Henri Soldat had an unhappy expression on his face.

"What I do, sir?"

"Look here." Soldat folded the paper, holding it out and pointing to a part of it.

Fabrice leaned forward and looked where the old man was pointing. There were no pictures, only long neat rows of letters.

"What it means, sir?"

Soldat pulled the paper back as if hiding something. "Nothing. There was a bad storm at home, that's all."

"A bad storm, sir? But you made talk of Monsieur Jouvier."

"No, no," Soldat replied gruffly, shaking the paper and folding it a new way. "Just a bad storm, that's all." He waved at someone. "I'm hungry. We should order."

The waitress was a big, dark-skinned woman with long, straight hair. She wore a shiny white dress and white shoes and spoke English with a strange accent. Soldat called her Marlene. He told her some things and she wrote on a paper.

"Miz Ark in the back?" Soldat asked her.

"No'zuh, Mr. Soul-Dot. Miz Ark gone to Haiti. She be back in two, tree day."

Soldat motioned her closer and whispered something to her.

"Lemme go see if Maxim in de back dem." She walked off toward the kitchen.

"What do you think of her?" Soldat asked, following her departure with greedy eyes.

"I think the hair is not truly hers."

The old man leaned closer. "How about the rest?"

"She looks strong, sir. Big and strong."

"I wouldn't mind finding out," Soldat snickered, tapping his cane against the floor like Legba when he gets excited.

The food arrived in big steaming bowls: fish smothered in spicy red sauce and surrounded by dumplings smooth and heavy as river stones. It was delicious, fresh and flaky. Even the coffee was good, thick and dark and full of flavor. Fabrice understood why this place was—what was that word?—pop-u-lar, though he was amazed that so many black people who did not look rich could afford to eat here.

The waitress came over and whispered something in Henri Soldat's ear, then gave him a paper.

"I have money," Fabrice protested when Soldat handed her a plastic square.

"Hush up."

"Yes, sir. Sorry, sir."

After Marlene returned his plastic and took the paper, Soldat turned in his chair and watched her walk off. "Big gorgeous woman like that," he sighed, shaking his head. "You want some advice, Fabrice?"

"Yes, sir."

"Don't get old."

"Yes, sir. Thank you, sir."

"Marlene says they don't need any new workers right now."

"That is sad."

"But she gave me a good lead." The old man tucked his newspaper under his arm and used both hands to help push himself to his feet.

—⟋⟍⟋⟍—

Next, Henri Soldat took Fabrice to another restaurant, two blocks down the same busy street, but this one was squeezed between other stores and had only one window. Inside the window was a ledge covered with a red-and-white checkered cloth. On the cloth was a big iron kettle, and leaning against the kettle was a little blackboard like the one the ti-Jouviers had in their playroom. Fabrice assumed the words and numbers written on it told people what food there was inside and the price for it. The front door had a bell like a goat wore that rang every time someone went in or out.

Fabrice put his hand to the window and peered inside. The room was long and narrow. There were many tables and chairs, but most of them were empty. On one side in front was a counter where some people were standing.

A curtain all the way in the back parted and Henri Soldat came limping through with his cane.

"The boss wants to meet you," he announced when he came back outside.

"That is good."

"Listen to me. The name of this place is May's Pepper Pot."

"See the pot there." Fabrice pointed to the window.

"Hush up and listen." Soldat grabbed Fabrice's arm and shook it. "The owner is Mrs. Masson. Say it."

"Mrs. Masson."

He poked Fabrice in the belly. "Tuck in that shirt. Stand up straight. Speak only English. Only English. You understand?"

"Yes, sir."

The place was not nearly as grand as Wedo's. The walls wanted painting. There was no music and no wooden fish. There were beach posters, but none with girls. Some of the linoleum squares in the long room were curling up at the edges. They entered a dim, narrow hallway with closed doors and cartons stacked high on either side. It was warmer back here. At the end of the hallway was a curtain of wooden beads, and through that was a big kitchen crowded with cooking equipment. This room was hot. A thick white mist hung in the air by the ceiling. A man and a woman in T-shirts and stained aprons were working at a stove. In one corner was a long metal table with some kind of water machine and bins full of dirty dishes.

"This way," Soldat said.

The office was much nicer than the kitchen. It had a desk and chairs and an air conditioner with flapping red ribbons. On the wall was a big color photograph of President Aristide in a neat blue suit. The lady at the desk was dark and bony, with hard eyes, a mean mouth, and a head crowded with curls the color of rust. Her loose blue dress had no sleeves. She had a burn scar on her upper arm the size and shape of a squashed mahogany bug.

"Mrs. Masson," Henri Soldat said, "may I present Fabrice Lacroix."

"Please to meet you, madame," Fabrice said, adding a little bow.

The woman angled her head, did something with her mouth, and eyed Fabrice suspiciously. "How old are you?"

"I have nineteen years, madame," he answered, holding himself very straight.

She asked him questions about his work with the Jouviers. Her voice was hard like gravel. She talked fast.

"Are you married?"

"No, madame. Not at all."

"Do you have any children?"

"No, madame."

"Do you have family here?"

"No, madame."

"How long have you been in New York?"

"Three days, madame."

"You want to stay in America?"

"Yes, madame."

"Are you willing to work hard?"

"Yes, madame."

"I need a dishwasher. The job pays five dollars an hour plus meals. Eight-hour day, six-day week. Interested?"

She was speaking much too fast. "Please, madame, how much dollars each day?"

"Forty."

"In Florida I get fifty."

"Go back to Florida."

"But I am here," Fabrice said, confused.

"Forty dollars a day. Yes or no?"

"Yes," Henri Soldat said.

"Have him here at ten-thirty tomorrow morning."

"Fine," Soldat said.

She turned to Fabrice. "Don't be late."

"No, madame."

"When you come in, ask for Danielle."

"Yes, madame."

"Danielle is my daughter."

"Yes, madame."

"She also is not married."

"Yes, madame."

"She is an American citizen."

"Yes, madame."

Mrs. Masson turned to Henri Soldat. "Nice-looking boy."

THIRTY-THREE

The only thing that broke Ferray's concentration during the long, stressful, nighttime drive from Brooklyn was the surprise sight of Yankee Stadium looming off to his right and all lit up like some huge confection. Ferray had never been to the Bronx and he did not like driving through New York at night, but his first concern was security, and making the trip after dark in a rental car reduced the chances of being seen to almost zero. He watched the steady parade of headlights along the Cross-Bronx Expressway and imagined they were the handheld torches his ancestors had carried into Bois-Caiman in August of 1791, the night their leader Boukman had sacrificed a black pig and started the slave rebellion against the whites, a battle that lasted thirteen brutal years and resulted in the world's first black republic. Ferray watched the procession of torchlights passing by him and thought, oh, to have been alive then! To have been a part of that!

But, he told himself with a sigh, who can choose the times into which he is born or the missions life will give him?

In truth, things were going well for him in New York. An FBI agent had met his plane at Kennedy Airport, delivered the new documents and credit cards, explained the monthly stipend, and taken him to the neatly furnished apartment in downtown Brooklyn that would be his rent-free for one year, to help him—in the FBI man's quaint phrase—get on his feet.

Ferray exited the expressway, made the prescribed turns, and parked in the recommended underground garage. The office was on the second floor of a large but otherwise undistinguished office building. He was buzzed into an empty reception room whose walls featured Haitian paintings. All these idyllic island scenes looked the same to him. Painted in bright tropical colors and filled with carefree, frolicking natives, they depicted the sort of delightful if patently false vision of Haitian life that made tourists happy.

He crossed the room and entered the open office. A tall, slim, well-dressed man of about thirty rose from behind the desk to welcome him.

"Sebastian?" Ferray asked.

"Sebastian is my father. I am Michel Pioline."

"A pleasure." Ferray offered his hand. "I am Honoré Fauchon. But I was expecting—"

"My father is a cautious man, especially over the telephone. Everything is in order, I assure you. As you requested, no one else is here. Please, have a seat."

"Thank you."

Ferray liked what he saw. Pioline kept himself lean and hard. His eyes were intelligent. His deeply pitted face suggested a natural cruelty.

Pioline sat at his desk. "You introduced yourself to my father as an associate of François Arcenciel."

"Yes. François told me that he had 'worked with Monsieur Pioline,' and I simply assumed . . ."

"I worked with François. My father's reputation is still strong. Unfortunately, his body is not. As we speak, he is having one of his twice weekly dialysis treatments."

"I did not know," Ferray said sympathetically.

"My father should live for many more years," Pioline assured his visitor, eyeing him warily. "Unlike François Arcenciel, who, we have learned, has met an untimely death."

"Yes," Ferray sighed. "I heard the same. A great pity."

"I liked the man." Pioline absently fingered a square-cut diamond pinkie ring. "When he came to us, he knew precisely what he wanted. We worked well together. There were no problems. He gave his word and he kept it."

"Qualities much to be admired."

"Do you share them, Monsieur Fauchon?"

"You will have to be the judge of that," Ferray replied with an easy smile.

"Arcenciel was in the military," Pioline remarked, slowly rotating the ring. "A major, I believe."

"A captain."

"Of course," Pioline said, rubbing the ring meditatively. "Now I remember. He worked for a major."

"He worked for a colonel."

"Yes, yes, yes. I believe the colonel's name was Fontaine."

"Ferray," his guest corrected. "Colonel Hugo Ferray. I never met the man, but François always spoke highly of him."

Pioline studied his guest for a long moment. "Tell me, Mr. Fauchon," he said, clasping his hands on the desk, "why is it that no one in Haiti has ever heard of you?"

"Like the Piolines," Ferray replied evenly, "I am a cautious man."

"A wise policy. But assuming that this is more than a social call, how can you expect me to do business with a man about whom I know nothing?"

"Cautiously."

"*D'accord.* And how can I be convinced that you are not working with the police?"

"The police would never ask you to do what I need done. Nor would they pay nearly as well."

Pioline smiled. "May I offer you a drink, Monsieur Fauchon? A small rum perhaps?"

"Only if you will join me, Monsieur Pioline."

"Michel."

"Ray."

As they sipped their drinks, Ferray outlined what he wanted done.

"Since this concerns Miz Ark," Michel said when Ferray had finished, "I must tell you something before we proceed any further."

"As you wish."

"A few weeks back I was involved in some minor unpleasantness with one of her employees. An argument at a dance club. I was offended at the sight of an attractive black woman throwing herself at a white man."

"Naturally."

"I had too much rum. The woman had too much mouth. The white man struck me from behind. People rushed in to break it up."

"Were the police involved?"

"No."

"Then the incident is of no importance," Ferray assured Pioline.

"I learned afterward that the woman's name is Marlene Williams. She is a waitress at Wedo's. The white man is a jeweler named Rosen."

"I know them both."

"Is he still fucking her?"

"Yes."

"I wanted revenge, but my father urged me to let the matter drop."

"A wise man."

"Tell me," Pioline asked, "this job of yours, how many men will it require?"

"Yourself and one other. Someone who will follow your orders precisely."

"And when would this have to be done?"

"A week from now. Perhaps two. We must wait for the conditions to be exactly right. You will have to be prepared for my call."

"Understood." Michel once again turned his ring. "And assuming I agree to help you, Ray, what would be my compensation?"

"*Cent cinquante mille.* One hundred fifty thousand American dollars."

"And the terms?"

"One third in advance. The balance on completion. If we are agreed, Michel, I'll call next week to arrange a meeting."

"Would you like another drink?" Pioline held out the bottle.

"No, no." Ferray covered his glass with his hand. "I have to drive. And Michel," he added, rising to leave, "when you do this, please do not wear that ring. You don't want to leave a mark."

THIRTY-FOUR

Moe felt weird. He hadn't been down in this basement in more than thirty years. He'd been a little kid then, and visiting their neighbor's basement with his dad had been an adventure: the two Rosen men on a secret mission. Peering through the darkness now, Moe recalled seeing giant wooden crates and imagining that they contained live wild animals from Africa, angry rhinos and snarling lions and saber-toothed tigers that might break free at any moment and eat him and his dad alive.

Eat him alive. Right. The phrase brought Moe right back to tonight's presentation. He felt along the wall and flipped on the lights. The room looked completely different: cleaner, neater, much larger. The walls were freshly painted. The sloping linoleum floor was polished. Scores of bridge chairs were set out in concentric circles around—

Wait a minute. That big pole in the center of the room. Moe didn't remember that at all.

He walked over and examined it. Both the pole and its round, foot-high base had been meticulously and rather wonderfully painted. The colors were vibrant and the style was what smug Manhattan galleries termed naïf. The pole showed a gigantic snake of some kind, its power-ful body rendered in iridescent greens and golds. The snake was entwined around the pole, as if climbing it. Moe stared up at its impos-ing head; the forked red tongue and piercing blue eye made it seem at once fearsome and intelligent.

Stepping back to get a better perspective, Moe saw that both the round, wooden base and the background on the pole had been painted so cleverly that the snake appeared to be ascending a rainbow that began on the earth and rose into the clouds.

Ask her what they do down there in the basement, he remembered Detective Beck suggesting.

Jesus Christ, Moe shuddered, I'm making a presentation to a roomful of snake worshipers.

Music, Moe thought suddenly, we have to have music. He turned and hurried back upstairs.

The manager—the thin, well-spoken one with the Haitian accent—was working the cash register. As always, his white shirt, red bow tie, and black slacks were immaculate.

"Max," Moe said, extending his hand.

"Mr. Rosen, sir."

"Music," Moe said anxiously. "What can we do about that?"

"Sir?"

"For tonight's presentation. While people are getting seated, and then after, when we unveil the costume. Music. What do you think?"

"Music is an excellent idea, sir."

"Is there, like, a sound system down there or—"

"I will arrange it, sir. What sort of music did Mr. Rosen have in mind?"

"What sort? Oh, I hadn't really—I don't know. What do people—?"

"We received the new Wyclef Jean CD today."

"Oh. Well, that's good, I guess. What do you think?"

"An excellent choice, sir. I will see to it."

"Great, Max. Thanks. And then, when Air makes her entrance, we should have something . . . I don't know. What do you think?"

"I will speak with young Miss Ark when she arrives, sir. Have no fear, together we shall devise something appropriate to the occasion."

"That's great." Moe grasped Max's hand again and pumped it gratefully. "I knew I could count on you." Moe released the hand and began looking around in a panic. "The rendering," he cried, absurdly patting all his pockets. "Where is it? Max, where did I put it? My drawing. I had it."

"I believe you left a large item in Miz Ark's office, sir. Could that—?"

"Yes, yes, yes. Look, I better get it and— So you'll take care of the music?"

"Yes, sir. I will see to the music, sir. Mr. Rosen must try to relax."

"Steady as a rock."

—⌖—

Moe stood with his back to the wall. The room was filling fast, faster than he'd expected: too fast. He'd been standing here trying to collect his thoughts, but all the lights were on and people kept nodding to him and saying hello, and between responding and smiling and trying to remember names, he hadn't been able to keep anything in his head.

He tried to calm himself by listening to the music. Wyclef Jean had a pleasant enough voice. But the lyrics . . . It sounded like French, but it wasn't; the same way Portuguese always tricked him into thinking it was Spanish. Why did languages do things like that? Didn't they realize how irritating it was? And Wyclef. What kind of name was Wyclef? Moses had always been a tough cross to bear, but Wyclef? It sounded like one of those spaced-out sixties names, like Moon Unit or Dweezil or that skier—what was her name?—Peek-a-boo. How could anybody call their kid Peek-a-boo?

Moe caught himself. Why was he thinking about names? Who cared about names? He had to figure out what to say to all these people. Why were there so many of them? The room was packed, nearly every seat was taken, and more of them kept pouring in. It was as if they were all gathering to witness an execution. Air was hidden away over there in one of those closets. He'd checked the costume and he thought she looked fine. But what did he know? He wasn't a West Indian. He could barely understand these people when they spoke. How could he possibly know what they would like?

Moe wished Marlene were here, or at least he thought he did. He wasn't sure of anything anymore. For a while there he'd been so sure of things. Like that evening he'd gone out alone and walked the three-mile parade route, trying to visualize the street filled with floats and bands and exotic costumes, the sidewalks lined with a million cheering people. He'd thought about The Golden Door and what it might mean to the crowd, many of whom would be recent immigrants themselves. And then, about two miles along, the evening light had suddenly changed. The street had been bathed in a warm golden glow, and in a single thrilling flash Moe had seen it all: the newcomers struggling up the ramp—drab, poor, weary from their journey—passing through the golden door and emerging transformed, energized, dancing—their lives not just changed . . . not just changed . . . but reversed. Reversed! Yes, that was the key: lives turned around, fortune turned inside out. Yes!

Moe had stood transfixed in the last shimmering rays of summer light, the busy street had melted away, and suddenly he'd seen it all—every-thing!—the float, the costumes, all of it. In a swoon, he'd rushed home and started sketching feverishly, desperate to get it all down on paper before the vision faded. And he'd done it. He'd done it. He'd been so sure! So sure! But now . . .

Somebody was waving. Moe waved back, forced a smile. It was sti-fling down here. Too many people. Moe loosened his collar. The man was still waving. What—? It was Max. He was waving for Moe to get started. Get started? Moe hadn't even composed his first sentence. No, a few more minutes and—

The music stopped. Something happened with the lights. Everything went dark except for a bright circle of light down around the snake pole. The audience was chattering excitedly. Max entered the circle, and to Moe's amazement, the audience became hushed.

"Mr. Rosen," Max announced, and slipped back into the darkness.

The audience twisted in their chairs. Moe could feel eyes searching the room for him. He fixed his tie, clutched his rendering, took a deep breath, crossed his fingers, and headed down the aisle. The room had become deathly still.

He stepped into the circle of light and tried to decide what to do with the rendering. He could keep it tucked under his arm or rest it against the pole. But what if he'd been right and the snake was some sort of reli-gious thing? Then touching anything connected with it might be an insult. Why the hell hadn't he asked someone?

He bent over and rested the rendering against his leg. The hot lights made him feel as if he were inside a sauna.

"Ladies and gentlemen," he announced, looking out into the dark-ness and clasping his hands at his chest. "Many of you know me. I'm Moe Rosen from Eli Rosen and Son, the jewelry store right over"—he started to point, got confused, pulled his arm back—"right next door."

"We knows you," a voice called out from the darkness.

"Good." Moe smiled. "I—"

"But Marlene knows you better," the voice proclaimed.

Laughter all around. Catcalls. Whistles.

"Look, he blushin'," a woman cried out, generating hoots and hollers all around.

Moe reached into his pocket for his handkerchief and the rendering slid to the floor. He bent over and returned it to an upright position. When he straightened up, it fell again. This time when he bent to pick it up, he raised it to his chest and held it there, securing its protective overlay with his thumbs so no one could peek at it.

"This," he announced over the continuing chatter, "this is the design for your float."

He began slowly circling the pole, the three-foot-wide rendering across his chest. The audience gradually settled down.

"As you know, your theme this year is The Golden Door. The float and the costumes have been designed with that in mind. This drawing will show you what the float will look like from the side, from the front, and from the back.

"Where the costumes?" someone called out.

"First the float. Then the costumes."

He stopped circling and, holding the artboard with one hand, used the other to peel up and fold back the protective cover. Then, holding it with both hands as if it were a stone tablet, he raised it in front of his face and, holding his breath, walked in a slow circle around the pole, giving everyone a chance to see it.

His ears tingled, straining to hear reactions from his audience. But all he heard was the nervous scraping of his own sideways footsteps. Maybe they can't see it, he thought desperately, raising it above his head as he started his second circuit.

Nothing. Whichever direction he faced, the awful silence went on and on. He shuffled along miserably. Maybe the perspective drawings are confusing them, he thought. Maybe they're not used to seeing the same thing from three different angles. Maybe he should have explained it first: the ramps, the slide, the stage, the torch. Maybe—

The sight of the snake's head over his shoulder surprised him. He stopped, lowered the drawing to waist level, and looked around. All was darkness. The room was quiet. He decided that there was nothing to do but ask for questions and comments.

He took a deep breath, opened his mouth, and heard the drums. Real drums, not a recording, coming from somewhere in the back of the room: heavy, throbbing, offbeat rhythms, like two or three drums talking to each other. All around him Moe could feel the audience stirring. The sound was moving the air, ricocheting off walls, producing currents and countercurrents. People began to clap and move to the rhythm. Clutching his rendering, he edged from the circle of light into the darkness.

His eye caught something off to one side, near the back of the room: a dark, triangular shape moving, turning, spinning down a far aisle in time with the steady, complex rhythm of the drums. The audience, sensing the presence, turned, murmured, increased the volume of its hypnotic clapping. As Moe watched from the shadows, the dancing haystack shape—which he now realized was Air twirling barefoot in her black, ankle-length cape and matching pointed cap—moved gracefully, steadily down the aisle toward the light.

By the time she entered the bright circle, every eye in the room was on her. Keeping her arms inside the cape to hold it closed, she dipped and spun her way around the pole, giving every part of the audience a chance to see her.

Moe was thrilled. He couldn't take his eyes off her. Her entrance was inspired. The drums were perfect. Despite her constant motion she was managing to keep the hat on and the cape closed.

With a sudden thud, the drums stopped. Air was hunched over, frozen in place. The room trembled. The audience held its collective breath.

And then *boom!* The drums began again, louder and faster, and Air leapt to one side, spun around once, twice, three times, this last time releasing one end of the cape and reversing it in midair, unleashing an explosion of color that made the audience gasp. As she continued spinning, the reversed cape revealed itself as a dazzling, red, white, and blue complement to her brightly sequined leotard, the sudden sight of which—with its pattern of red and white swirls, its free-form gold stars, along with the shock of her bare legs flecked with golden glitter— brought the audience to its feet, whistling and cheering and roaring its approval.

The drums continued their dense, insistent, sensuous rhythm. Air continued to dance and spin, circling the pole again and again. Her skin began to shine with perspiration. In a single motion, she hooked the flag-cape around her neck, reached up, pulled off the cap, shook it inside out, and replaced it on her head so that its sequins gleamed and, as she spun, its long Mylar strips fanned out around her like a maypole. Then, just as they had practiced, she spread her arms beneath the cape and started it turning like a pinwheel. Without breaking her rhythm, she reached into its hidden pockets and pulled out handfuls of golden glitter with which she showered the jubilant audience. Moe, standing in the back, felt redeemed.

—*ev/v*—

"Now, my friends," Air said when she had finally calmed everyone down, "shall we tell Mr. Rosen what we think of his work?"

Moe was both thrilled and embarrassed by the ovation. He reentered the light, stood beside Air, and waved for quiet. When he got it, he began by thanking Air for doing such a wonderful job, then joined the audience in applauding her. He next thanked Max for whoever was handling the lights, thanked the audience for being so receptive.

"If I knew its name," he said impulsively, gesturing toward the pole, "I would even thank the snake."

"Damballah!" someone called out.

"Thank you, Damballah," Moe said, bowing to the pole.

The audience was delighted.

"Now," Moe said, uncovering his rendering, holding it at his chest and showing it around, "let me explain how the float will work."

When he finished, he asked for questions and comments.

A man in front jumped to his feet. "First prize!" he cried, thrusting a fist into the air. "First prize! First prize!"

The audience cheered lustily.

With Air's help, Moe explained each element of the costume.

A hefty woman up front raised her hand.

"Yes, ma'am," Moe said, nodding to her.

"Pardon me, but evwysing look vewwy spenseeve."

"Okay, okay," Moe called, raising his arms to quiet the cries of "What she say?" "The lady has asked an excellent question: What will all this cost?"

The audience calmed down.

"Each costume," Moe announced, "will cost about sixty dollars."

There were groans all around. Moe was shocked.

"Listen," he told them. "Please. That sixty dollars covers everything: the leotard, the cloak and hat, the sequins, the Mylar, the glitter, everything. That's a great price. A terrific price. I'm getting everything in wholesale lots."

"An' how mush for the float?" a man called out.

Voices all around seconded the question.

"I'm not a carpenter," Moe responded. "I don't know exactly how much the float will cost." More groans. "But Miz Ark told me that you folks have been collecting funds all year. Listen," he said, raising his voice against the loud grumbling, "most of this is just plywood and paint and—"

"One moment!" a voice called out from the back.

Moe shaded his eyes and peered. A hand was waving from the far darkness.

"Yes?" Moe said, pointing to it.

A man stood up. "May I speak?"

Moe couldn't see the face, but the voice sounded vaguely familiar. "Of course," Moe told him. "Please."

"Thank you." To Moe's surprise, the man started walking down the aisle.

Moe recognized the gold Rolex the second the light hit it. Fauchon was wearing a white, short-sleeved, intricately embroidered guayabera shirt over dark slacks. He stepped right up, squeezed in between Moe and his brightly costumed model, and introduced himself to the audience.

"Ladies and gentlemen," he announced, "I was a business associate of Miz Ark's brother François, who, as many of you know, was recently killed in a tragic accident."

He paused for a moment and looked down, as if moved by the memory.

His head came up. "Though I am a stranger here," he went on in a louder voice, "I ask you to allow me—in memory of my dear friend and in honor and respect for your community—to contribute the money to pay for all your beautiful costumes."

In response to the wild cheering that engulfed him, Fauchon bowed modestly. Air, still glistening with perspiration and glitter, took his arm, rose on her toes, and planted a kiss on his cheek. When Fauchon turned and offered his hand, Moe reached for it. But instead of merely shaking, Fauchon grasped Moe's hand and raised it high above their heads. Holding it there, he quickly did the same with Air on his other side. Then, holding their joined hands aloft, Fauchon paraded them around the pole like trophies.

THIRTY-FIVE

The sign wanted painting, Sirene decided, studying Wedo's facade from beneath the awning of the Queen of Sheba Styling Salon across the street. As she watched her workers moving about soundlessly

behind Wedo's plate-glass windows, setting up for a new day, Sirene felt
her strength returning. Her journey to Haiti had been sad and exhaust-
ing. Her search for the elusive Colonel Ferray had been futile. She was
glad to be home.

You see, little brother, she told the spirit hovering above her shoulder, that restaurant is all ours, yours and mine, built with your money
and my sweat. Look over there, brother. We are in America. That is our
business. It is a beautiful thing, is it not?

She shifted her glance. Next door to Wedo's, Eli Rosen & Son was
still locked up tight. She thought about Marlene and Moe, then about all
the money sitting in her safe and all the things she would have to do
today.

Time for us to go to work, she told her brother's spirit, stepping out
into the sunlight and heading across the street.

Even the fish dangling overhead seemed excited by her return.

"Yes, yes, yes," she said, trying to deflect her workers' effusive greet-
ings. "Fine, fine, fine," she assured them, hurrying across the dining
room and pushing through the kitchen door only to find herself
engulfed by a second wave of well-wishers. Embarrassed by all the
attention—"Yes, yes, yes, fine, fine, fine"—she headed for the sanctuary of her office.

"Max!" she cried just before closing the door.

She was seated at her desk wiping her eyes with a tissue when he
entered.

"Something fly into my eye," she explained, motioning for him to
shut the door.

She turned to her gently gurgling fish tank. All her fish were still
alive, darting happily about the tank. Life goes on, she told herself,
watching their agile, carefree movements. Life goes on.

She sniffled hard, swiveled back to Max, and asked after his wife and
children. He assured her everyone was fine. His grin was embarrassing
them both.

"Back to work," she declared, arranging the mound of mail on her desk into neat stacks. "First, have there been any raids by Immigration?"

"No, boss."

She crossed herself both ways. "Surprise inspections by the Health Department?"

"No, boss."

She crossed herself twice more. "And how was business?"

"You have the receipts, but I would say good."

Sirene swiveled, listening to her chair creak. The office felt as comfortable as an old housedress. It was nice to see Max smiling, though she had never liked that gold tooth.

"What else?"

"Sophie's boyfriend ran off again, this time with an Anguillan."

"What else?"

"We had to start using that canned akee from Thailand. They're out of stock on the Jamaican."

"Our customers will survive. Tell me about Labor Day. How are the preparations coming along?"

"You heard about Mr. Fauchon?"

"Yes. My daughter could not wait to tell me about our mysterious benefactor. You have met him?"

"Yes. He speaks highly of your brother. It seems they were quite close."

Sirene felt a stirring in the air behind her, but when she turned, she saw nothing.

"And how do the costumes look?" she asked, changing the subject.

"Wonderful," Max declared, brightening. "Mr. Rosen has a gift. Young Miz Ark did an estimable job as his model. The float promises to be spectacular."

"That is lovely news. Now about the booth. Is everything organized?"

"I placed the orders for the food and paper goods last week."

"Excellent. And have we secured the same location?"

"Yes, but only after I spoke with Dolores privately."

"How much?"

"A hundred dollars. I took it from petty cash and left a chit."

"Very good. How much is the rent this year?"

"Fifty more than last year."

"Those scamps," she cried, slapping the desk. "Three hundred dollars for one day's rental."

"You should tell them to go to blazes."

This exchange was almost as much a tradition as the parade itself. Even with the increase and the bribe, the rent was cheap and they both knew it. The booth was a gold mine. Last year it had taken in over $6,000, more than half of it profit.

"Have we paid the committee yet?"

"No. I explained that you were away."

"Another bill for this afternoon," she sighed, making a note. "Three hundred, you said?"

"Yes, boss."

"Is Marlene in yet?"

"No, boss."

"All right. I need you to call the security people. I will want two armed men to escort you to the bank. No uniforms."

"What time do you want them here?"

She consulted her watch. The sight of the Piaget's tiny hands sent her tumbling back to when François was a baby. He had been so small, so beautiful. She remembered the first time their mother had let her hold him and—

"Sirene," Max said sharply.

"Eleven o'clock," she told him, snapping out of it. "I'll need that long to check everything and make out the deposit slips."

After he left, she locked the door, opened the safe, and went to work. With only minor discrepancies, all the envelopes checked out, confirming that her choice of Moe Rosen had been inspired. Between the cash and the charges, today's deposits totaled close to $50,000. Perhaps, as some of the girls insisted, the handsome jeweler really was charmed.

She unlocked the door, poked her head out, and called for Max.

"I should go away more often," she told him, displaying a thick brown envelope.

"The guards have arrived," he told her, taking it. "This should not take long. Oh. Mr. Fauchon is waiting for you in the dining room."

—⟨∾∾⟩—

"Honoré Fauchon," the imposing stranger declared with a bow. "At your service."

"I am Sirene Arcenciel."

His hand was warm, his grip compassionate. Sirene felt a strange turbulence in the air.

"My dear Madame Arcenciel," he murmured, "please accept my deepest condolences."

"Thank you."

"Madame, your dear brother spoke of you so often and with such affection that I feel I have known you for years."

"In that case, Mr. Fauchon, you must call me Sirene."

"How very kind." He came around to hold her chair. "And you must call me Ray."

"Ray," she said, considering it.

"A ray is a very small part of the sun," he pointed out playfully.

"Or a fish with a nasty sting."

He smiled. "François warned me about his sister's sharp tongue."

"Did he?" she asked wistfully.

"Yes, but he never revealed that she was such a handsome woman."

"Once perhaps," Sirene replied with a wry smile. "Before she took on the shape of a molasses barrel."

"Only dogs like bones."

She smiled at the old Haitian proverb. The sparkle in his eyes reminded her of François, but this man was far more quick-witted. She was curious to learn how they had become friends.

"You know," he said, pointing to her wrist, "I remember the day we decided to give you that lovely watch."

"We?"

"The impulse was entirely François's, of course. My contribution was merely to applaud his choice."

"Regarding your relationship with my brother—"

"And how perfectly it fits," he remarked, still admiring the Piaget.

"I have my neighbor to thank for that. Have you met Mr. Rosen?"

"Indeed I have. Mr. Rosen seems to be a man of many talents."

She signaled for the waiter. "What may I offer you, Ray?"

"Tea would be lovely."

"Two teas," Sirene told the waiter. "And a plate of Marcie's butter cookies." She turned to her guest. "But you must promise to allow me no more than two."

"Four."

"Three, then."

"You see, François was right. He always said we would get along."

This time, the mention of her brother's name wrenched a sob from her throat.

Her guest lowered his eyes. "Such a terrible loss." He shook his head. "But at least you still have your daughter."

"Yes," Sirene said solemnly, crossing herself both ways.

"I have met her. A lovely child."

"Thank you. And where is your wife?"

"I have never married."

"You are still a young man."

"You are too kind." He smiled. "And in truth, I have not abandoned all hope for a family."

Sirene felt François's spirit rustling the air behind her. "Ray," she said, forcing herself back to the present, "please tell me how you knew my brother."

"Of course," he replied, forcing a smile. "But before I begin, Sirene, I must beg you to tell me about your trip." He clasped his hands at the edge of the table. "I was here in the States when . . . when it happened and . . . well, the reports I received were . . . To be honest, I am still not even sure how . . . This whole thing has been so . . . My dear Sirene, if you would not mind too very much . . ."

"No, no," she assured him soothingly.

She proceeded to recount her sad adventure, which, though it had ended only yesterday, seemed to have occurred half a lifetime ago and in another world. She detailed the difficulties of locating her brother's body, described the dungeon-like room with its damp stone walls, bone-chilling cold, stacks of filthy pallets . . .

Her guest listened with rapt attention, recoiling at the wretched conditions of the morgue and then covering his face at the news of François's murder.

When he regained his composure, she asked him if he knew a Colonel Hugo Ferray.

"Who?"

"My brother's commanding officer. Colonel Hugo Ferray."

"The name is familiar to me," he said, knitting his brow. "François must have mentioned him. But, no, I have never met this man. Why do you ask?"

"He is the man responsible for my brother's death."

"Sirene," he asked, looking at her oddly, "how do you know this?"

"I know it," she said with conviction. "And wherever he is, I will find him."

He reached out and covered her hand with his. "We will find him together."

THIRTY-SIX

A busboy set down a clattering bin of dirty dishes. Fabrice glanced down to make sure his coin was tucked safely inside his T-shirt, then picked up his scraper, pulled over an empty dish rack, and went to work. Before he was halfway through the bin, a second one arrived, and then, less than a minute later, a third. Someone in the kitchen turned off the radio. The lunch rush was starting.

Fabrice began increasing his pace until the four parts of his routine—grab, scrape, rinse, stack—fused into a single continuous movement, a kind of dance. After a few minutes he achieved the ideal rhythm, a rhythm that drew him in like the hypnotic beating of the drums.

The bins were arriving fast now, crowding his stainless steel table. Deep into his work, Fabrice imagined that he was building a bridge, a bridge of floating plastic bins laid end to end, a bridge that would one day stretch unbroken all the way from Brooklyn to Haiti, a bridge that would allow Antoinette to walk to America without even getting her feet wet.

As dishes and silver passed swiftly through his hands, Fabrice thought about Antoinette's soft skin and sweet smile and how the sea breeze lifted her hair. He imagined her gathering up her skirt so she could hop from bin to bin without tripping. He wondered if she still had the dollar bill he had given her for her birthday. He wondered if she still kept it in the same place. He wondered if she had received the picture of the leaping whale. He wondered if she ever thought about him.

The bins were coming very fast now, but Fabrice was keeping up. He liked it when it got busy like this. He liked the deep, steady, fevered rhythm of the work. He liked the heat and the noise of the kitchen, the crackling of the fryer, the hissing of the grill, the cries of the cooks, the food smells in the air. He liked the feel of the l'wahs' coin tapping against his chest as he worked. He liked having his own station, his own little corner of New York. He liked the idea that each emptied bin was bringing Antoinette a little bit closer.

———⌇⌇⌇———

When the wall clock read seven, Fabrice pulled off his gloves and apron, hung them on the stick to dry, and took his washrag and clean T-shirt into the tiny bathroom.

After drying off with paper towels and wriggling into the clean shirt, he hurried out to the dining room. As usual, Danielle Masson was waiting at a corner table.

"Where's your notebook?" she asked when he arrived.

"I big dope." He slapped his forehead and trotted back toward the kitchen.

"You are not," Danielle called after him.

When he returned a few moments later, she asked him to sit.

"Yes, miss."

"Call me Danny."

"Excuse. Yes, Danny."

He sat down and saw a plate of food on the table.

"I fixed it for you," she explained, smiling at him with a face that knew it was not pretty but wished it were.

"There is time?"

"Yes. Go ahead. I ate before."

He placed his notebook safely out of reach and took up his fork. "Thank you, miss."

"Danny."

"Excuse. Thank you, Danny."

He ate carefully, feeling her eyes on him. The food was good: oxtail in a spicy sauce with rice and beans and fried plantain.

"You want a Coke?"

"I will go," he said, starting to rise.

"Sit." She bounced up and headed toward the cooler in the front.

Fabrice sighed as he watched her waddle off. Danielle Masson was a nice girl, but she had the shape of a *zabocah:* small on top and big and round at the bottom.

Before his first day here Henri Soldat had told him that people were talking behind their hands about Mrs. Masson, saying that she had her eye out for a boy without papers who would marry her daughter for the green card.

"I have girlfriend," Fabrice had pointed out.

Soldat had looked at him and raised his finger to his lips.

So Fabrice had not told Danielle Masson about Antoinette. One day Danielle had stopped by his station and told him that free classes for reading and writing English were being held in Wedo's basement. When he had asked if he could go, Danielle had surprised him by saying that she would go too. She had accompanied him to every class for the last three weeks.

Danielle returned with a can of Coke, wiped the top with a napkin, popped it open, slid in the straw, and put it down in front of him.

"Thank you, Danny."

"You're welcome." She returned to the seat directly opposite him, smiling at him.

"I hope I do good in class tonight," he told her, looking down at his food.

"I'm sure you will. Just remember, if we're ever stopped in the street by a policeman, you let me do all the talking."

"Yes, Danny."

"Tell me the truth, Fabrice," she asked in a new voice, "do you think Air is beautiful?"

"You mean teacher?" he asked, gathering his remaining rice into a neat little pile.

"Yes. Do you find her attractive?"

"Miss Ark is girl." Fabrice shrugged, pretending indifference.

"You think she's too skinny?" Danielle asked hopefully.

"She is skinny, yes."

"I'm asking because some men—well, I don't know about you, Fabrice, we don't know each other all that well yet—but some men prefer women with a little more"—she wiggled her fingers—"what would you call it?"

"How is time?" he asked, not wanting to call it anything.

—⟨◊⟩—

"Fabrice, please come up here to the blackboard."

"Yes, Miss Ark."

"Good luck," Danielle whispered from the next desk.

He slid from his chair, touched his coin for luck, and went forward and stood by the blackboard. The class of about forty, most of them women, was arrayed before him in a half circle of plastic desk chairs. He felt their eyes on him. Miss Ark handed him a piece of the white chalk and told him not to be nervous.

"Fabrice, do you know your alphabet?"

"Yes, miss."

"Good, because now you are going to spell a word for us."

He clutched the stick of chalk and gulped. "Yes, miss."

"Write the word *go*. As in 'I go to class.'"

"How I do that?"

She had him sound out the word, one sound at a time. He did as she instructed and told her the first sound was a *G*. She had him write a *G* on the blackboard. Then she asked him what the next sound was, and he told her *O*, and she had him write that letter after the *G* on the blackboard.

"Congratulations, you have written the word *go.*"

He looked at the two letters together on the blackboard and said the word to himself, and then he heard the noise and saw that everyone was smiling at him and clapping hands. Embarrassed, he put the chalk in the wooden groove and hurried back to his seat.

After class, Fabrice stayed to straighten the chairs while Danielle went upstairs with Miss Ark. The girls were friends. Danielle was older, but they had both grown up in the neighborhood.

He flipped off the lights and started walking across the room toward the staircase. He stopped before the poteau mitan, grasped his coin, closed his eyes, and said a prayer to Damballah and Ayida Wedo, thanking them and the other great l'wahs for everything they had done for him, asking them to bless Antoinette and the Jouviers and the Jacksons, thanking them for giving him Miss Ark as a teacher and asking them to please—please!—send a nice boy for Danielle Masson.

THIRTY-SEVEN

Once, when he was ten, Moe had accompanied his father on a business trip to Switzerland. They had arrived late at night and gone straight to their room. Moe remembered slipping out of the big, fluffy, unfamiliar bed the next morning, tiptoeing to the window, and gazing out in wide-eyed stupefaction at massive, snowcapped mountains. Now, nearly thirty years later, Moe woke up, looked across the bed, and experienced that same, childlike sense of alpine wonder. Everything about Marlene was extravagant, from the sheeted outlines of her body to the boldness of her features to the darkness of her skin; her vitality, her appetites, her endless reservoirs of energy, her curiosity, her drive, her earthy humor, her vulnerability, the way her eyes flashed when she was angry, the way her tender looks melted his insides, the fierce intensity with which she made love. He thought about all those fruitless hours spent searching for perfection in the workroom, when Marlene had been right next door the whole time . . .

Moe raised the sheet, ran his eyes down Marlene's lovely back and over her shapely flanks, and shook his head in awe. He was in another world. One simple act—jumping in to aid a neighbor in distress—had changed his whole life. In little more than a month he had gone from a loser to a winner. More than a winner: a wanga. Moe had never felt so alive. Marlene was the best thing that had ever happened to him. Business was terrific. He was a working designer. The troupe was happy with their costumes. The float was nearly finished. Air was a treasure.

And there was more. The word about Eli Rosen & Son was starting to get out to the industry. Firms Moe hadn't heard from in years were calling for appointments to present their latest designs. Last week old man Slovitch had sent Shlomo to the store with a preview of the new F&S fall line and an offer of a three-day, all-expenses-paid junket for two to Las Vegas. Moe took a rain check, saying that he was simply too busy right now. There was no point trying to explain to Shlomo about Marlene's physics course or the West Indian Day parade or that he felt a stronger kinship to Wedo's West Indian Kitchen than to Fishbein and Slovitch.

"So what do you think?" Marlene asked sleepily, rolling over and propping herself up on an elbow.

"About what?" he asked, admiring her torso and trying to imagine what Gauguin could have done with a model like this.

"You just looking," she asked, rubbing an eye, "or should I go brush my teeth?"

"Brush, by all means."

"I should shower." She covered her mouth as she yawned.

"We could shower together," he said impulsively.

She gave him one of those looks that melted his insides. "Give me two minutes."

She rolled off the bed and stood stretching.

"You're staring," she grumbled.

"You're beautiful."

She made that chirping sound as she walked past him, then gave him an insouciant wiggle of her behind.

He watched her go. He'd caught himself this time, but sometime soon, he knew, he would simply blurt out that he loved her. What would happen after that, he didn't know.

———〜〜〜———

Air was working with a customer, a young man of about twenty in baggy jeans and a Tommy Hilfiger shirt who seemed far more interested in her than in the oversize gold medallions arrayed on the counter between them. Moe was puttering around in the office and keeping a paternal eye on her when he noticed Ray Fauchon standing outside in the street.

Fauchon's presence was becoming an irritant. In the last few weeks the Haitian had become almost proprietary about Air, stopping to wave whenever he passed the store, waiting outside for her every day after work, presumably to escort her wherever she was going. Though both Air and her mother seemed delighted by the attention, Moe was troubled by it, suspecting that Ray's interest in the teenager was not entirely healthy.

Moe felt responsible for the child, and not only because she was working for him. He genuinely liked her. In addition to being attractive, Air was bright and charming, honest and hardworking. Her mother was Moe's neighbor and friend. Also, Air's success at selling jewelry was a testament to Moe's good judgment in hiring her.

Moe checked his watch. It was nearly closing time. Rather than leave Fauchon standing out in the street, Moe walked through the store, opened the front door, and invited the Wedo troupe's benefactor in.

"You are too kind," the Haitian said, casting a sideways glance at Air and the boy.

"Let's go to the office," Moe suggested, allowing Ray to precede him up the aisle.

Air's customer was bent forward with his elbows resting on a showcase and his baggy-jeaned rump extending out into the aisle. Though there was plenty of room to pass, Fauchon went out of his way to bump him as he went by.

"Hey," the boy said, turning on Fauchon, "you watch yourself."

Fauchon stopped and looked directly into the boy's eyes. "I am so sorry," he said, turning the apology into an insult.

Bristling, the boy drew himself up to his full height. Fauchon tensed.

"Ray," Moe said, shepherding him toward the office.

Fauchon nodded to Air before accompanying Moe inside.

"You're not used to these kids," Moe said, pulling the guest chair over next to his desk.

"That was my fault." The Haitian turned the chair to give himself a view back into the store. "I should not have pushed the boy."

"No harm done."

"Back home we treat people with respect," Fauchon explained, keeping his eye on Air. "We do not leer at decent women as if they were *platonnades.*"

"As if they were . . . ?"

"Sluts."

"Kids," Moe said, trying to lighten the mood. "Around here, Ray, most of them are okay. Honestly. They dress a little weird, but they go to school, go to church, hold down part-time jobs. The problem is that awful rap music and the violence on TV and in the movies and—"

"I disapprove of all that." Fauchon scowled as the boy resumed flirting with Air.

"The hostility is just a pose."

"You don't say," Fauchon replied distractedly, staring daggers at the boy.

"Ray . . ."

Fauchon did not respond. The boy had reached out and was now fondling the medallion Air was modeling for him.

To Moe, Fauchon's stare was more threatening than anything the boy was doing.

"Ray," Moe said again, rapping the desk with his knuckles.

"Excuse me," Fauchon said, turning to the noise.

"You're new here, Ray. Believe me, that kid out there means no harm. Air knows how to handle guys like that."

"Perhaps." Fauchon adjusted his gold Rolex. "But she should not have to."

"It's all part of growing up."

Fauchon gave him a funny look.

"Air's only eighteen, Ray. She just graduated from high school."

"Eighteen is not a child," Fauchon said stiffly.

"No, but it is a little young for guys like you and me."

Fauchon reacted as if he'd been slapped.

Reflexively, Moe rolled his chair back a few inches and tried to shift the conversation. "Air will be starting college in a few weeks."

"I am aware of that," Fauchon replied coldly.

"Marlene will be getting her degree next spring. She takes night courses at Brooklyn College."

"How nice." Fauchon's attention had returned to the boy in the store.

"The two girls get along really well."

Fauchon did not respond. The boy was leaning across the showcase, fingering one of Air's earrings.

"Yes," Moe continued, troubled by the menace in Fauchon's eyes, "Air will be going to Marlene's physics class tomorrow."

Fauchon's head swung toward Moe slowly, like a turret. "Excuse me?"

"Tomorrow night," Moe said, pleased to have captured Fauchon's attention. "The girls are going to Marlene's physics class."

"At Brooklyn College? Tomorrow?"

"After work. It's a night class. Seven-thirty to nine. Air wants to see what a college course is like."

"Air should not be taking the subway at night."

"Marlene has a car. She drives to class."

"Well, that is a relief, I must say."

"How come?"

"I will be flying to Miami tomorrow. I will not be here when Air finishes work. I know it must appear foolish, but after what happened to her uncle . . ."

"I understand. What's in Miami?" Moe asked.

"Business."

"What time is your—? Oh, excuse me."

Moe met Air at the office door, took the sales slip and the cash, went to his drawer, and made change.

"I'll be done soon," Air said to Fauchon.

"Take your time," he told her.

Moe waited until she closed the office door. "Listen, Ray. About before. If I said anything to offend you . . ."

"No, no, no," Fauchon insisted, dismissing the idea with a wave of his hand.

Both men watched as the boy exchanged a few final words with Air and ambled out of the store. Fauchon stood and smoothed his white shirt.

"Will you be back from Miami in time for the parade?" Moe asked, holding the office door for Fauchon.

"You may rely on it," Fauchon assured Moe with his most pleasant smile of the day.

PART FOUR

WHITE
DARKNESS

THIRTY-EIGHT

"It wasn't a great class," Marlene said as they joined a group of students walking down the broad stone staircase.

"I liked it," Air insisted, and went bounding off down the steps like a frisky colt.

"Don't get lost," Marlene called after her. "I'm responsible for you."

Air was waiting at the bottom of the steps. "Thanks for letting me tag along tonight," she said when Marlene arrived.

"No problem. Dr. Jaslow is a little dry, but he really knows his stuff. At least you got a taste of what a college course is like. That was the idea, right?"

"Frankly, I just wanted an excuse to get out of the house. My mom has been driving me crazy."

People were coming out of buildings all around the quadrangle. Marlene got her bearings and, with Air in tow, started walking along a crowded path toward the Bedford Avenue gate.

"Smell," Marlene said, inhaling theatrically through her nose.

Something sweet was in bloom. The air tingled with it. The night was warm and breezy and not too humid. Marlene breathed in the lovely floral scent, telling herself that when these flowers came out next year, she would be getting her degree.

"One more week of class," she announced to no one in particular, taking Air's arm and joining a knot of students crossing Bedford Avenue against the light.

"Are you worried about the final?" Air asked when they reached the other side.

"This is my only course this session. I aced the midterm and I haven't missed a single class. Girl, with a decent final I might get myself an A."

"That's great." Air spread her arms and twirled. "I never realized so many people took night courses."

Marlene knew that Air was still a little giddy from all the attention she'd received from the men in class. The stares and nods and sideways glances had never stopped, even though Air's outfit tonight consisted of nothing more than an oversize St. John's sweatshirt and a pair of stonewashed jeans. Marlene looked over at the irrepressible teenager; the kid sure had something. Walking next to her like this, Marlene felt like her big sister.

They walked to the corner, turned off the well-lit avenue, and entered a darker side street. The only thing Marlene didn't like about night classes was the night. When they had parked here two hours ago, it had still been light. Now, as if triggered by the dark, Marlene's right hand went into her bag, dug beneath the notebook, and grasped the small canister of Mace. The college was surrounded by an upper-middle-class neighborhood of private homes on quiet, tree-lined streets, but Marlene didn't believe in taking any chances. This might be a low crime area, but it was still New York.

"Your mother really has been wired since she got back from Haiti," she remarked to Air, making sure the nozzle was aimed correctly.

"She sure has." Air girlishly took Marlene's arm. "She's got Mr. Fauchon acting like my bodyguard lately. I mean, I guess I can understand it, what with my uncle and all, but it's not like I'm a baby. I wish she'd just chill."

Even with heels, Air was at least six inches shorter than Marlene. That sweet scent was still in the air, but it was fading. The shade trees lining their side of the street were absorbing the light from the street-lamps. Marlene thought about crossing over, but the street was empty and she'd been parking in this neighborhood without incident for more than five years now.

"I like Mr. Rosen," Air declared suddenly. "I like him a lot."

"Me too." Marlene peered ahead and tried to remember which tree she'd parked her Corolla under.

"Do you love him?"

"We've only been together a month."

Air bumped her playfully with her hip. "But you're sleeping with him, right?"

"God, you're a nosy child."

"I am not," Air protested, tugging Marlene's arm. "I just want to know."

"Here's the car." Air had nearly made Marlene walk right past it. Releasing the Mace, Marlene began rummaging for the keys.

"So?" Air asked, drifting around to the passenger side.

"So yourself," Marlene teased, unlocking the door, sliding in, reaching over, and opening the passenger door.

Air got in, pulled her door closed, started feeling around for her seat belt. "So, come on," she teased, "tell me."

"Lock your door." Marlene locked hers with an elbow while fiddling with the Toyota's ignition key.

"What's that smell?"

Marlene stopped and sniffed. The odor was faint but sharp, vaguely pharmaceutical. It seemed to be coming from—

She sensed the movement—a swiftly moving shadow—a fraction of a second before something flashed past her eyes, clamped itself hard over her nose and mouth, and wrenched her head back against the seat. At almost the same moment, before she could even cry out, someone or something from the back seat reached over and pinned her arms to her sides.

Reacting with a desperate and terrified fury, Marlene struggled mightily to free herself, stamping the floor, arching her back, and wrenching her head from side to side. When she tried to scream, she felt a sharp pain in her nose and throat. Holding her breath, she began bucking wildly with her hips, pushing down against the floor with all her strength, twisting her shoulders. She fought to free an arm, reach the Mace, hit the horn, smash some glass—something!

Nothing worked. She was running out of breath. The bastard holding her was as strong as an ox. Her hands were free, but with her arms trapped, there was nothing close enough to grasp or scratch. She felt the car rocking. She heard muffled cries. Her heart was racing, but no matter what she did, she couldn't free her face from the awful cloth. She needed to breathe! In a frenzied burst of panic, she marshaled whatever strength remained and pushed against the floor with both feet. Her mouth came free, but before she could even scream, it was covered again. Writhing helplessly now, she took a breath, whimpered, shuddered, took another. Her throat burned. Her muscles started trembling. The hand pressed mercilessly against her face. She felt herself fading, becoming weightless, floating, drifting away. She grunted weakly and stopped struggling.

THIRTY-NINE

Moe forced himself to wait until the third ring. He didn't want Marlene to know how anxious he became whenever she was late. Dr. Laura had done a whole thing on smothering the other day on the radio. Moe knew it was something he had to guard against.

The third ring. He snatched the receiver. "Hello," he said, trying to sound nonchalant.

"Mr. Rosen?"

"Yes. Who—?"

"This is Max, sir."

"Of course. I'm—"

"Mr. Rosen, excuse me, sir, Miz Ark wonders if you could come here directly. To the restaurant, sir."

"What's wrong?"

"It is an emergency, sir. May I tell Miz Ark you are on your way?"

"Of course, Max. I'll just— Sure, I'll be down as fast as I—"

The phone went dead. Moe stood there waiting for his brain to catch up.

Emergency, Max had said. What kind of emergency? A robbery? An immigration raid? Why did they need him?

Wait a minute! Maybe the emergency wasn't at Wedo's; maybe it was at his store. A break-in. No, the alarm would have gone off, the security company would have called. Unless—

Moe asked himself why he was still standing around. Whatever it was, he'd better get going. He started for the bedroom.

Wait! What about Marlene? Christ, he had almost forgotten about Marlene. How was he going to handle this? He turned in place, looking, thinking.

Okay, he decided, trotting to the bedroom. He would leave a set of keys for Marlene with the doorman. That was good: he had to go by the doorman to get out anyway. This way she'd let herself in and be here when he got back. He pulled on his sports jacket, went to the dresser, and started stuffing things into his pockets: wallet, change, keys, extra keys, pen, Tic Tacs, gun. Was that everything? Extra keys for Marlene? Yes.

He turned for the door, stopped. How was he going to get there? Subway? No. Too late, too dangerous. Cab? No. Might take forever to find one. Car service? Car service! What was the number? He spun around. Where was that phone book?

He dashed into the kitchen, found the book, dialed the number, and stood tapping his foot while it rang. What the hell could the emergency be? Why hadn't Max told him? It was almost certainly not the girls. If it was the girls, Max would have told him. If it was the girls, he'd be going to a hospital or—

Could something have happened to the float? A fire! That place they were building it in was a firetrap. He knew it! Christ, the parade was in three days. They'd never—

"Hello? This is an emergency. I need a car. . . . Immediately! . . . What? . . . Yes, I have a goddamn account."

———❦———

Max hurriedly unlocked the door. His red bow tie was drooping. He looked haggard.

"Tell me," Moe said.

"Quickly, sir." Max led the way through the deserted dining room and pushed through the kitchen doors.

Moe had to jog to keep up. He glanced around. The restaurant seemed okay. That wasn't it. It had to be the float or—

Max opened the door to Sirene's private office and motioned Moe in. The room was small, constricted, with a low ceiling. An old wooden desk, one guest chair, and opposite them, a brightly lit rectangular fish tank on a wrought-iron stand. Strange, elaborately sequined pictures covered the walls: a mermaid, a snake, a woman with a spear, an embroidered map of Haiti. Sirene, wearing her same black dress, was sitting at the desk. Her face was blank. She appeared to have been crying.

"They took my baby," she said, her voice oddly emotionless, as if she couldn't believe it. "And they took Marlene."

"*Who* took them?" Moe asked, taking a step toward her and nearly tripping over an oval throw rug in bright African colors. "Sirene, what are you saying? Have the girls been arrested?"

"My baby," Sirene said again, getting up, moving past Moe and going to the softly gurgling fish tank. At her approach, several small, iridescent fish darted away.

Neon tetras, Moe thought. "Sirene," he asked, resisting the urge to grab her shoulders and spin her around to him, "who took the girls? Where are they?"

Ignoring him, she picked up a yellow tin and sprinkled some fish food into the tank.

Moe watched the flakes sink and drift. "Max," he demanded, turning to the manager in the doorway, "what the hell is going on?"

"Miz Ark received a telephone call," Max said calmly. "Young Miss Ark and Miss Marlene have been kidnapped."

"When?" Moe asked mechanically, feeling numb.

Max told him what time the call had come. Moe checked his watch, trying to think. The second hand was moving so slowly. His mind started racing. Kidnapped! Marlene. Air. Why? Who? He asked himself what time the girls had left for school, how long it normally took, when the class let out. The police would need to know all that.

He glanced over at Sirene. She was still turned away. He suspected she was in shock. Somehow, he was going to have to handle this. Starting right now.

"Do we have any sherry?" he asked Max.

"No, sir. We have rum."

"Get it, please. And three glasses."

Moe reached down and felt the gun in his pocket. Some bastard had kidnapped Marlene. If anything happened to her . . .

He turned for the door, remembering that he had Detective Beck's card back at the shop. He could go— No, he decided, it was better to simply dial 911 from here, get the ball rolling. He could call Beck later.

"Sirene," he asked, reaching out and touching her shoulder, "have the police been notified?"

She wheeled to face him. "No police," she pleaded, gripping his arm. Tears were coursing down her cheeks. "The man said if we call the police, they will kill them both."

"But—"

Moe saw the terror in her eyes. "Okay," he promised, peeling her hand off and holding it in both of his, "no police."

Now what the hell was he supposed to do? He didn't know anything about this world, these people. "Talk to me, Sirene," he pleaded.

She looked down and straightened the throw rug with her shoe, then went and sat at her desk. "The man said they will contact us," she said softly.

"When? How?" If Moe was going to act, he had to have facts, information.

She shook her head, sending new tears down the wet channels on her cheeks.

"What else did he say?" Moe asked, handing her his handkerchief.

She took it but didn't use it. "The girls are safe." She turned her head and stared at the picture of the smiling mermaid. "'Safe for now.' That's what the man said: 'for now.'"

"Okay." Moe wished the office had room to pace. "At least we know they're safe. That's good. That's very good." He turned in place. "That's a start."

Max returned with a bottle and glasses. Moe poured a shot of rum for each of them. He drank his in a single gulp, shuddering as it burned its way down. Sirene finished her drink, took the bottle, poured herself another.

"Pioline!" Moe exclaimed, furious with himself for not thinking of it before. "Of course! That bastard—"

"No," Sirene said, sounding tired.

"Yes," Moe insisted, shaking a fist. "It's got to be him. He—"

"I called his father," Sirene said, sounding tired. "Michel is in Atlantic City with some friends."

"I don't believe it." Moe stamped his foot. "Who else could it be? Who else would take Marlene?"

Sirene was staring across at her fish tank. "These people were after my child, not Marlene."

"You don't know that."

"I do. The man said so."

"Did they mention ransom?" Moe asked Max.

"Yes," he replied, "but they did not give a number."

Moe nearly cried out with joy. Why hadn't they told him this first? Money was something they could deal with. Sirene had money. He had money. They could both get more money. He rubbed his hands together. Now he could put together a plan. They would pay the ransom and get the girls back safe and sound. Safe and sound. *Then* they would tell the police. The police would—

A horrible thought intruded, piercing Moe with an icy fear. What if they hurt Marlene? What if—? He felt so helpless. He looked around. None of this seemed real. How could something like this happen? What was he supposed to do? Those bastards could be . . . doing anything. What was there to stop them?

"Money," Moe said out loud. "We've got to get money."

FORTY

Marlene awoke with a start. In rapid succession, she realized that she was alive, she didn't know where she was, she couldn't see, she was lying on her side, she was dressed.

Her head hurt. Something was covering her eyes. When she pressed her face against the coarse blanket, the stuff on her eyes felt like bread dough, mushy but not wet, secured with what felt like an elasticized headband. Her wrists were tied behind her with some sort of plastic strips, which her fingers told her were too strong for her nails to cut through.

She rocked from side to side and felt around with her legs, hoping to discover Air right next to her. No such luck. When she moved, she heard the creak of bedsprings. She seemed to be on one of those cheap, metal-framed fold-ups that people with too many kids kept hidden during the day. Still, she had the sense that Air was nearby. She thought about calling out to her, but decided against it. They were probably better off if the guys thought they were asleep. Guys, she thought, shuddering at the memory of her near suffocation.

It wasn't hot in here and it wasn't cold, but it felt strange not knowing what time it was, how long she'd been out, or whether it was night or day. Not that it mattered: once Rocky and Miz Ark realized they'd been kidnapped, they'd move heaven and earth to get them back.

Her mouth was dry and the arm she was lying on was going numb. She licked her lips and cautiously shifted her weight, trying to make as little noise as possible while taking care not to roll off and hit the floor. It took time, but she maneuvered herself onto her other side.

She lay there trying to breathe normally, telling herself that things weren't so bad. This stuff on her eyes, the things on her hands—these guys were pros. Pros didn't kill their hostages, usually didn't even rough them up. Hostages were their meal tickets. This whole thing was about money, not sex. Look, she reasoned with herself, they could have done whatever they wanted when she was out cold. And they hadn't done a thing. No, this was a straight business deal. These guys were interested in money and nothing else. Which was okay. Miz Ark had money. Rocky had money. Rocky had probably already called the cops. The cops probably had special kidnap squads out searching for them right now, contacting sources, running down leads. Damn, it felt weird not being able to see. And her shoulders were sore from being pulled back for so long. Still, no matter how you sliced it, these guys were making a huge mistake messing with Miz Ark's daughter. Miz Ark was the Mother Teresa of that whole damned neighborhood. The West Indians would go ballistic when they found out Air had been kidnapped. These guys would be sorry they ever messed with—

Sounds!

Marlene tensed, drawing up her knees, listening hard, trying to control the sudden rush of fear.

Footsteps, coming from another room. A door opening, ten, fifteen feet away. A change in the air pressure. The smell of food. Tomato sauce? Pizza?

More footsteps, slow, coming closer, coming right up to her.

She was holding her breath when someone grabbed her upper arm, made her squeal with fright, pulled her to her feet, and then let go of her. Bent over, she wobbled, spread her legs to get her balance, laced her fingers together, and straightened up slowly, tentatively. It felt weird to be standing. She heard a rasping sound, then realized it was her own breathing.

Someone began unbuttoning her blouse.

"Hey," she said, stepping back and trying to shrug him off.

The slap caught her flush on the cheek and sent her down on the bed. Before she could set herself to kick, both her arms were grabbed—there were two of them! At least!—and she was pulled roughly back up to her feet. Her cheek was numb where she'd been slapped. She couldn't see a thing! The fear began pulsing through her with such force that she started to shake. Hands were at her blouse again. Other hands began undoing her pants. She bent over, tried to squirm free. This wasn't sup-posed to be happening.

"Come on, guys," she pleaded.

This time it was a punch, catching the side of her mouth and sending her spinning. The next thing she knew she was on the floor. She tasted blood in her mouth. The hands came back and dragged her to her feet. Her blouse was ripped open. Someone behind her began pulling down her pants. She tried to get away and tripped over them, falling heavily on her side. She felt hands grabbing her pants and panties together, wrenching her hips into the air and shaking her from side to side. She tried to kick at them, but her pants were already down at her ankles, and she couldn't stop them from pulling them off along with her flats. They dragged her up again and she tried to get away, but one guy held her arms from behind while the other one pulled up her bra, squeezed her breasts, and then pinched her nipples so hard she began jumping up and down, moaning in pain, twisting from side to side. The one hold-ing her arms tightened his grip while the other released her breasts and started slapping her face. She ducked her head, but the guy behind her hooked an arm through her elbows and used his free hand to tear off her wig, grasp her hair, and pull her head up.

The slaps were hard. They were coming fast. She felt herself bleeding. No matter how she turned, what she did, she couldn't make it stop. When her mouth opened to scream, someone stuffed a rag in it and then went back to hitting her.

FORTY-ONE

Moe checked his watch: seven-fifteen. What the hell was he doing in the store at seven-fifteen in the morning? Why he was opening the safe? He wasn't going to be able to play wanga today: draping bracelets, selling charms, measuring fingers for rings. Today was for waiting. Waiting for word. Waiting to find out. Waiting to learn what was happening.

But he couldn't just wait. It was too nerve-racking. He was desperate for something to do. At least if he could talk to the police. Detective Beck was no Sherlock Holmes, but he'd been around for a while, he figured to know something about police work, or at the very least know someone who did. New York had forty thousand cops. They had specialists in these things.

Without bothering to turn on the lights, Moe wandered up and down the aisle, feeling the fear seeping into his pores, weighing him down like waterlogged boots. He looked into the showcases and saw all the black hands. Every hand was Marlene's, dark and soft, graceful and elegant, reaching out to him for help. He went behind a showcase and took a hand out and held it against his chest, pressing its rigid fingers into his flesh, letting it feel the beating of his heart. The hand felt so helpless, like a wounded bird. He brought it up to his face and kissed the soft velvet skin of its palm, kissed each of its fingers, turned it over, and kissed the hard nubs of its knuckles.

Trembling, he returned the hand to its showcase, then went back to the office, checked his gun, and slipped it into his pants pocket. He wanted it there as a counterweight to the fear. He wanted someone to use it on. He wanted to find out who was responsible for this and pistol-whip him and then shoot him, first in the knees, then in the groin, then in the elbows. How many was that? Five? Fine, then he'd use both hands to steady the gun, take aim nice and slow—let him see it coming—and then shoot the last bullet straight through his eye into his brain, like they did to that guy in *The Godfather*.

Moe walked to the front window and looked up and down the street. A few early risers out for a stroll, a few cars passing by. He wondered what the girls were doing right now, hoped they were . . . Were what? He didn't even know if they were alive.

He went back into the office, plugged in the Mr. Coffee, thought about those old commercials, and remembered that Joe DiMaggio was dead. Hell of a thing to be thinking now. But at least DiMaggio, his father's favorite player, had been in his eighties. Eighties, for chrissake. Marlene wasn't even thirty. Air wasn't even twenty.

He checked the phone again, making sure it had a dial tone, making sure it was set right in the cradle so when it rang . . . when it rang . . . It occurred to him that he hadn't spoken with his father in more than a month, ever since he and Marlene—

The phone!

"Yes?"

"I have a collect call for anyone from a Cray Faw-Chone in Miami. Will you accept the charges?"

"What?" Moe said, confused. "I think you—"

"Moe?" A man's voice, but not Max's.

"Yes." Suddenly wary. "Who is this?"

"It's Ray. Ray Fauchon.

"Ray?"

"Will you accept the charges?" the woman demanded.

"Yes. Absolutely."

"Thank you. Go ahead please."

"Moe, tell me, is it true?"

"Is what true?"

"The kidnapping. The girls. I just heard."

"Yes, it's true." Moe lowered himself into his chair. "Where are you, Ray?"

"I'm in Miami. What happened, Moe? Are the girls all right? What's going on?"

"Nothing is going on, Ray. Not a damn thing. Sirene received a call . . ."

Moe told Fauchon everything he knew, which wasn't much. There was nothing Fauchon could do from Miami, but it was a relief to have someone to talk to. While he spoke, Moe kept watching to see if one of the other lines lit up. Speaking with Fauchon was bringing on pangs of guilt: if Moe had shown half as much interest in Marlene's safety as Fauchon had in Air's. . . .

"Any ideas?" Moe asked when he'd finished.

"How firm is Sirene about not calling the police?"

"Like a rock."

"Are you sure? If it could be done quietly . . ."

"No chance. Sirene is a basket case, Ray. She just sits there staring off into space. This guy who called really scared her."

"And no other leads? No clues at all?"

"Nothing."

"In that case, I suppose all we can do is wait for the next call."

"Right," Moe said glumly.

"Look, I'm going to throw my things together and get a taxi out to the airport. I'll catch the first available flight back."

"Good," Moe said gratefully.

"I don't know what I can do . . ."

"It'll be good having you here."

"Thank you. Oh, would you be so kind as to inform Sirene that I am en route?"

"I'll do it right now. I know she'll appreciate it."

"Let us hope that all these people want is money."

"From your mouth to God's ear," Moe murmured.

FORTY-TWO

Marlene awoke shaking. Everything came back to her at once. It hadn't been a nightmare; this was really happening. She was lying naked under a ratty blanket on a creaky metal bed. Her breasts were sore. Her face was sore. She was still blindfolded. Her wrists—

Her wrists were free! They must have untied them after— She must have passed out.

Wait! She was breathing through her mouth! She must have passed out and they must have untied her wrists and taken the rag out of her mouth and put her in bed and covered her with the blanket. Her heart leaped: maybe they weren't going to kill her after all.

She tried to lift her head but discovered that her cheek was stuck to the mattress: probably blood. Now that she was fully awake, her lips, her gums, her cheeks, everything felt swollen. Her nose hurt. She needed to pee. She needed to think. Air was still here somewhere. They had not been rescued. Rocky would be trying. Miz Ark would be trying. The police—

Sounds were coming through the wall. She strained to hear. A TV. Men's voices, faint. She pressed her thighs together, flexed her stomach muscles. It didn't feel as if she'd been raped.

She reached up and touched the blindfold. Having the use of her hands was like a miracle. It gave her a weird kind of confidence. And she'd been right: the blindfold was one of those sports headbands. It was covering a wrapping of gauze that was holding—she probed its edges with her fingertips—yes, some kind of Silly Putty, clay, dough. Pizza dough? She remembered smelling pizza.

She was about to peel off the headband when something made her stop. She drew up her knees, clasped her hands to her chin, and thought for a minute. If she took this stuff off her eyes, what was she going to see? A dingy room, this crappy bed, four blank walls? Then, when the kidnappers came back in, she would see their faces. And, it occurred to her that if she saw their faces, they might kill her. Whereas, she reasoned, her best chance of staying alive was to be a good hostage, a perfect hostage: not to make any trouble for them, not give them any excuse to kill her, or even give them cause to hit her again. They'd started taking her clothes off and she'd made a fuss and they'd gone off on her. She shuddered violently. No matter what, she couldn't go through that again. What had she been thinking about? Right. The blindfold. No, she wouldn't touch the blindfold. Because if she didn't know where she was or who they were, there was no reason for them to kill her. Even after the ransom was paid or she was found or whatever way she was freed, she wouldn't be able to tell the police much of anything. She hadn't even heard them speak. And they knew that. They had to know that. As long as she kept this blindfold on, they had no reason to kill her. None at all.

She needed to pee really badly. Maybe there was a bathroom. If she could get her cheek unstuck, she could get up quietly and feel her way along the wall. If she peed in the wrong place, it might give them an excuse to start beating on her again. Whatever happened, she didn't want that. Rocky and Miz Ark's people could break in here any second. Her job, Marlene reminded herself, was to stay alive until they got here. That's what it all came down to. Just. Stay. Alive.

It occurred to her that she didn't even know what day it was. She could have been asleep for one hour or twenty-four. Her mouth felt more like twenty-four. If there was a toilet, maybe there was a sink.

With the help of her fingers she freed her cheek from the mattress and began slowly, quietly, cautiously, to work herself out of the bed. For some reason, the TV suddenly seemed louder.

———❧———

Fauchon walked over and turned up the TV before joining Michel and his associate at the small dining table. Loup, as he called himself, was a shorter, more muscular version of Michel. Fauchon was meeting him for the first time. They exchanged pleasantries. If all went well, less than two days from now Fauchon would be killing them both.

"Any trouble?" he asked Michel.

"None at all."

"Tell me."

"As far as anyone knows, Loup and I are in Atlantic City. The snatch went perfectly. No one saw a thing."

"How can you be sure?"

"The street was dark. It was over very quickly. There was no noise. Loup did well."

"My compliments," Fauchon said to the new man.

Loup's smile exaggerated the long, crescent-shaped scar running down one cheek: an old knife wound, Fauchon suspected.

"Please continue."

Michel took a swig from a green bottle of Surge. "We parked in the basement and carried them as if they were drunk. No one saw us."

"Excellent. And since then?"

"We have not left the apartment."

"And the girls?"

"Separate rooms. Blindfolded. We slapped the big one around a bit."

"But not the young one," Fauchon said.

"Not a hair." Michel held up open hands.

"Sit here a moment." Fauchon started to rise.

"The big one isn't cuffed."

Fauchon sat back down. "Why?"

"Loup felt sorry for her. I don't think she'll cause any trouble. She's been asleep more than twelve hours."

"With her blindfold?"

"Of course."

"But you say her hands are free. What if she has removed it?"

"Loup," Michel said, sending him in to check.

"If she sees Loup's face . . ."

"She dies," Michel said. "Tell me, how are things on your end?"

"Everything is proceeding according to plan."

"Let me guess," Michel said with a smirk. "You will offer yourself as the courier for the ransom."

"Shhh," Fauchon teased, indicating the returning Loup.

"The big one found the pissoir," he reported. "She's in there now. The blindfold is still on."

"Go check the other one," Michel told him.

"I'll do that," Fauchon said, getting to his feet.

"I want some of the big one," Loup declared.

"You'll wait your turn," Michel told him.

When Fauchon opened the door, he saw Air curled up at the edge of the bed. She appeared unharmed, though a bit disheveled and more than a little frightened. He walked over and stood above her, admiring her fragile beauty. He would have to see how he felt about things after he had his money back, but at the moment the idea of marrying this girl was appealing. That was why he had been so adamant that she not be touched, and why it was fortunate they had Marlene to play with. He'd known Michel would like that.

The childish motion of Air's knees suggested that she needed to use the toilet. She recoiled at his touch, but he held her arm gently until she got used to it and then helped her to her feet and walked her across the room. Her trembling sent ripples of excitement through him. He was sorely tempted to fuck her right now, to spend the whole day fucking

her. But then she would be damaged goods, and it pleased him more—
at the moment, at least—to imagine Ghede's secret niece as his dutiful
wife. Plus, he reminded himself, this child would be inheriting a thriv-
ing business, one built with his money.

Once inside the tiny bathroom he turned her so her hands could feel
the sink and her legs the toilet. Her tension eased a bit until she felt
his hands unsnapping her jeans, unzipping the fly. He watched her
face as he tugged them down below her knees. She was pressing her
lips together so tightly they turned white. Her terror was absolutely
delicious.

When he looked down, the sight of her bright red panties shocked
him for a moment. Then he remembered that her superstitious cow of a
mother would have insisted on red panties to ward off the spirits of the
recently deceased. Voodooists believed that the dead shunned red, the
color of blood, because it reminded them of their former life. It was an
old Haitian notion that bright red panties could preserve a young virgin's purity.

A young virgin, he thought, kneeling down before Air, pulling down
the panties and staring at her taut, pale stomach trembling inches
before his eyes. She had a strong female scent. The pulsing of his blood
was making him dizzy.

He stood up and seated her on the toilet, pushing the panties and
jeans down around her ankles. Then he backed out of the room, shut the
door, and closed his eyes, resting his burning forehead against the wall
and bringing himself back under control. He thought about her blood-
red panties, shook his head, smiled. After their marriage he would take
pleasure in beating all that Voodoo nonsense out of her.

When he heard that she was finished, he reentered the room and,
though she tried to stand, kept her sitting while he gently dried her with
toilet paper. After washing his hands, he stood her up and slowly turned
her around, allowing himself one good long look before pulling up her
panties and fastening her jeans. He fed her cool water from a paper cup,

then returned her to the bed and checked to see that her wrists were not bound too tightly.

—◈—

Marlene heard the door open and close. Someone was in here with her. She curled up on her side and tried to stay calm. She had felt her way around the room, found the bathroom, the toilet, the sink. She had rinsed out her mouth, dabbed her tender and swollen face with fingertips of cool water, found her way back into bed, and covered herself with the blanket.

Her job was to stay alive, she reminded herself, tensing as she heard footsteps approaching. Whatever it took, she was going to stay alive.

The footsteps stopped. She sensed someone standing over her, thought she could hear him breathing. When the blanket started to move, she didn't try to hold it, just stayed there curled up, not moving a muscle except for her stomach, which began spasming in fear. She felt the air on her bare skin.

She sensed him standing over her, staring down at her like an animal licking its chops. When she felt his hand on her shoulder, a cry escaped her throat, but she cut it short. She was fighting to keep herself from covering her face with her hands, afraid that would encourage him to tie her wrists behind her and start slapping her again. Whatever happened, she didn't want that.

She allowed herself to be rolled onto her stomach, felt the air on her bare behind, felt his eyes appraising her. Maybe if she—

Oh, no! He was pulling her hands behind her and tying her wrists with those plastic things again. She choked back a sob. If she cried out, he'd stuff that rag in her mouth again and she'd feel as if she were suffocating. Oh, Christ, she was cooperating, why did he have to go tie her damn hands?

At least he wasn't being rough with her, she told herself, desperate to keep herself from panicking. Maybe he wasn't being rough because she wasn't resisting. She swore to herself that whatever he wanted, she wasn't going to resist. Her rump was now up in the air, exactly the way he had positioned it, and if that was the way he wanted it, fine.

She heard a zipper, heard him breathing, heard the sounds of a man undressing. When she felt his hand in her hair, rolling her over, she thought he was pleased with her, so she ventured a little smile. The hand left her hair, and the next moment her cheek exploded in pain and made her gasp. With the next blow she saw flashes of light and her back arched as the pain ricocheted inside her head and she felt her eyes squirting tears. She tried to stop herself, but she started squirming and moaning, trying to get away. The terror was like a screaming animal inside her brain, and she couldn't make it stop. She felt his weight pressing down on her chest. She tried to brace herself but there was nothing she could do. Nothing! Nothing! Oh, God!

But then she felt his hand slide under her head and she felt his body shift, and she knew that maybe he wouldn't hit her again and that just letting him do whatever he wanted wasn't enough, and she knew what she had to do and she was willing, she was willing, all she wanted was a chance, just one chance, and finally, after she licked her lips and opened her mouth and reached up again and again, offering herself, straining desperately to reach him, he gave it to her.

—⟳—

The door closed. He was gone. Marlene let out a sigh and felt tears wetting her eyes. Her body was slick with sweat, and itchy strands of fabric were sticking to her. She felt soiled and dirty and elated all at the same time. She was alive. She'd gotten through it. He hadn't beaten her again. She was alive! She was going to make it.

Now she could just lie here in her own sweat and let her breathing come back to normal and—

The door opened. Marlene felt an icy chill. She had forgotten there was more than one.

FORTY-THREE

When Fabrice came into the dining room after working his half shift, he was surprised to find Danielle waiting for him. Today was Saturday. There was no class today.

"Sit."

"Yes, Danny."

"I need to tell you something, Fabrice. Put your hands on the table."

"I do something wrong?" he asked, holding them out to show her they were clean.

"No." She took his hands, but not like girl to boy.

"What is wrong?" he asked, trying to read her face. "What I do?"

"You didn't do anything, Fabrice. Listen to me." She had his hands hard. "This family you worked for in Haiti, you said their name was Jouvier."

"I say that. Yes."

"And you said Monsieur Jouvier owned a newspaper."

"Yes?"

"Well, the other day I heard something about a family in Haiti named Jouvier."

"Something bad?"

"Yes." Danielle put his hands together and covered them with hers. "I went to the library today and checked the newspapers, just to be sure."

"Yes?"

"There was a fire, Fabrice. Last month. The Jouviers' house was destroyed."

"People are hurt?"

"Everyone was killed."

"Is not possible," Fabrice whispered, feeling a sudden emptiness in his head, a burning in his eyes.

"It's true. It was a terrible fire. Everyone was killed."

"Even children? Children are so . . ." He didn't have the word, even in Creole. He remembered Ogoun's eyes laughing at him after he'd dropped the knife.

"I know it's wrong," Danielle said, patting his clasped hands, "but I just keep thinking how lucky that you weren't there."

Fabrice felt something in his chest go hard. He remembered the soldiers, the sound of their boots, the clicking of their guns. He remembered how scared he was rolling down the hill and—

"Fabrice?"

"All Jouviers dead," he murmured, imagining them laid out in a row of white coffins, wearing white gowns, their eyes closed, their hands crossed at their chests.

There was noise down by the office. Fabrice looked up and saw Mrs. Masson running toward them. He freed his hands and stood up.

"Danny!" Mrs. Masson cried, rushing over and hugging her daughter. "Thank God!"

"Mom," Danielle said, struggling to free herself. "What is it?"

Mrs. Masson squeezed her daughter's head to her chest and held it there, kissing her hair.

"What, Mom?" Danielle pleaded.

"Miz Ark's daughter." Mrs. Masson stepped away and grasped the back of a chair. "Your friend Air."

"What?"

"She's been kidnapped. Along with one of their waitresses."

"When?"

"Last night. They were out somewhere together in a car. I don't know the details. But Martine just called me and my first thought was 'Oh my God, where is Danny?' and thank God you're here and you're safe." Mrs. Masson hugged her, stroked her hair. "Now come on, we must get over there and see if we can help. Air kidnapped. Can you believe it? Oh, God, Danny. Two days before the parade. The neighborhood is going to go crazy."

FORTY-FOUR

Moe heard the buzzer, hurried out to open the door for Fauchon, and then surprised himself by wrapping the Haitian in a heartfelt bear hug the moment he stepped inside. Fauchon was gracious about it, patting Moe comfortingly on the back while allowing himself to be hugged.

They went into the office, where Moe, ashamed of his outburst, busied himself by putting on some fresh coffee.

"We are all feeling the pressure," Fauchon offered.

"Have you seen Sirene?"

"Yes. A few minutes ago. The poor woman is in a terrible state. I pray she hears something soon."

"I wish to hell there was something we could do. This waiting is . . ."

"I know."

"I almost said 'the worst thing.'" Moe shook his head. "But that's just dumb. Whatever we're feeling is nothing compared to— Forgive me, Ray, I'm tired and I'm frightened and . . . Those poor girls!"

"I understand completely."

"Did you get your business done down in Florida?" Moe wondered why the coffee was dripping so slowly, why the phone refused to ring.

"That is of no importance."

They sat facing each other, sipping their coffee in silence, each lost in his own thoughts. Moe stared out through the darkened store to the busy street, watching people passing by as if nothing were wrong. The little patch of sky visible between buildings was turning a soft rose color. It would be dusk soon. And then night. Fatigue settled in behind Moe's eyes. The huge knot in his stomach tightened. He should have told Marlene that he loved her when he'd had the chance. He couldn't shake the idea that somehow that failure was responsible for this, that if he had just . . .

The coffee was giving him a terrible headache. It occurred to him that he hadn't eaten anything all day. Maybe he ought to go next door with Ray and try to down a few mouthfuls of soup. He needed to keep up his strength. How long could it be before they heard something? The girls were alive; he could feel it. They would hear something soon. Very soon. In the next hour or two. He was sure of it. It wasn't fair to keep Ray cooped up in here with him. He suggested that Ray might wish to go over and check on the float. They were supposed to have a full crew working tonight. At least it would give Ray something to do. His presence would cheer people up. There was a phone there if anything happened. Moe had the number.

"Fine," Fauchon replied. "Whatever you say. But you'll call me . . . ?"

"The second I hear anything," Moe promised.

———

The cavernous warehouse echoed with an eerie silence. The radio that was normally blasting the local Creole station had been turned off. Clearly, from the looks on their faces, the twenty or so workers present had all heard about the kidnapping. The float lay in more than a dozen pieces spread out across the floor, awaiting assembly. The huge flatbed truck that would carry it was parked in the center of the cement floor. Three people were working on Liberty's torch, still only half-covered in gold foil.

The foreman saw Ferray, rolled up the blueprint he'd been studying, and went over to greet him. They shook hands. The foreman dropped his voice. Had Monsieur Fauchon heard any news?

No, he hadn't, but they knew where he was. If a call came, he would pass along any information he received. In the meantime, he would just walk around and say a few words to the people here, if that was all right.

He went from man to man shaking hands, praising what he saw, asking questions about it, squeezing arms, murmuring words of encouragement, assuring each man that "things" would work out. He made a thorough inspection tour, pretending to be interested in every aspect of the work, poking his nose into every nook and cranny. In a far corner of the warehouse he discovered a tiny utility closet hidden away beneath a staircase. More bored than curious, he squatted down and worked open the oddly shaped wooden door. The inside gave off a strong musty odor of old paint and oily rags. He reached in and pushed away some cobwebs and pulled the string for the naked bulb. To his surprise, it worked. The floor of the tiny space was littered with dead roaches and old beer cans and warped girlie magazines, which, upon closer inspection, dated back more than a decade. He backed out, turned off the light, closed the door, and smiled to himself, thinking of those long-ago workers taking a break, crawling in there to guzzle a beer and peek at some naked women before returning to some low-paying, backbreaking job.

He straightened up, brushed off his hands, and looked around at all the men who had worked all week and were now volunteering their time and labor for some meaningless parade. He looked at the pieces of Liberty strewn about the floor, checked the keys in his waistband, and chuckled to himself.

FORTY-FIVE

Sirene checked her watch. Ten P.M. The girls had been gone twenty-four hours: a lifetime. She looked up at the sequined portrait of the mermaid Sirene, the wife of Agwe, which hung on the wall above her desk.

Help me, Sirene begged the smiling figure, help me get my precious daughter back.

The phone rang. Sirene's breath caught. She gripped the arms of her desk chair, stared at the blinking light, and told herself that this had to be the one.

It rang again. Her hand itched to grab it, but she held herself in check. Max would speak with them first. That was the plan. Then—

The blinking stopped, but the light stayed on. Max was speaking with them. Sirene counted to ten. The plan was for Max to buzz her and then listen in to their instructions. That way—

The little square of light went out. Another false alarm.

Sirene had started the day going through the motions—greeting people, making small talk, sipping tea—but she had begun to feel like a zombie, that most accursed of creatures, able to perform simple tasks but without consciousness, without will.

By lunchtime she had abandoned all pretense and retreated here to her office to sit and stare at her fish tank, to jump each time the phone rang and hold her breath for the buzz of the intercom. She had spent much of the time praying, for she knew that she would never get her daughter back without the help of the l'wahs.

Her thoughts kept returning to Moses, both the one next door and his ancient namesake. Her neighbor Moses had saved her once already; perhaps, with her prayers and Damballah's help, he could do so again. Moses, she thought, invoking the name like a prayer.

Moses was a powerful figure to the followers of Vodoun, not only because he had led his people out of bondage—an act that had a special resonance to the descendants of slaves—but because of his mystical connection with the serpent, the representation of the great l'wah Damballah. The Old Testament tells that when Moses went to the Egyptian pharaoh and demanded, "Let my people go," he demonstrated his holy power by throwing down his staff and turning it into a serpent. Thus, Moses and the serpent became entwined: one helping the other, one serving the other, one drawing on the magic powers of the other. The Bible says that Moses parted the Red Sea by stretching his long staff over it. And what was his staff but a serpent in a different form?

The phone rang again. Sirene clasped her hands, brought her rosary to her lips and kissed it, praying for help from both Mary and Ayida Wedo. But the intercom remained cruelly silent, and soon the light went off.

Moe had stopped in this morning. No words had been necessary. She had seen in his bloodshot eyes that he was as helpless and desolate as she was. After a few minutes he had taken his aching heart back to his own shop. And now each of them had spent an agonizing day waiting for the other's call.

There was a knock on the door.

"Come," she cried.

Max slipped in and closed the door. He looked drained.

"News?" she asked anxiously.

"They have returned Marlene. They threw her in the alley out back. She is unconscious."

Sirene exploded from her desk as if shot from a cannon. Max caught her in his arms and stopped her.

"I have called for an ambulance," he said gently. "Two of the women are with her now. There is nothing you can do."

"Release me," Sirene demanded. "I must see her."

"You must not see her." Max held her tight. "Sit down and let me tell you the rest."

She froze. "The rest? You spoke with them?"

"Yes. They told me where Marlene was."

He helped her into her chair, then bent to retrieve the red bow tie that had fallen from his shirt pocket.

Sirene was trembling. "How badly is she hurt?" She clutched her beads. "What did they say about Air?"

"Marlene has been beaten. Her face looks very bad." He reached into his back pocket and held out a stained envelope. "They left this note."

Sirene took it with her fingertips.

"It was pinned to Marlene's breast. With a safety pin. That is her blood."

Sirene crossed herself three times. Then, remembering what she held in her hand, she tore open the envelope, pulled out a paper, and read rapidly and silently, moving her lips.

"They say Air has not been harmed." She dropped the hand with the note to her lap. "They say Marlene is a warning of what will happen if I do not pay their ransom."

"How much do they want?"

"Seven hundred fifty thousand dollars."

"When do they want it?"

"Monday night, after the parade. That gives me two days. Max, tell me, will Marlene live?"

"We must pray for her and for Erzulie. We must have a full service. Everyone must attend."

"When?" she pleaded.

"Tomorrow night. I will make the arrangements."

"Tomorrow night," Sirene repeated, thinking about another whole day without her child.

Her thoughts were interrupted by the harsh wail of a siren.

"Hear the ambulance," Max said. "I must go with Marlene. Call Mr. Rosen and tell him she is alive. Tell him to stay in his shop and wait for my call."

Sirene was unable to move. She was numb.

"Sirene," Max barked. "Call Mr. Rosen now. Tell him Marlene is alive. Do as I say!"

"Yes, houngan," she answered meekly, reaching for the phone.

FORTY-SIX

"Come on," Danielle said, taking Fabrice's hand and leading him through the large crowd milling about outside Wedo's.

"What is happening, Danny? All these people are here for young Miss Ark?"

"I'll explain later," she said, pulling him along.

The door was locked, but Danielle knocked on the glass until one of the women inside let them in.

"I'm here to work," Danielle told the woman.

"Over there." The woman pointed to a long table set up against a far wall.

"I was hoping this would happen," Danielle whispered excitedly, squeezing Fabrice's hand and leading him across the empty dining room.

"Miss Ark is okay?" he asked hopefully.

"Not yet. But all these people are here to give money. To help pay the ransom."

"After money, then Miss Ark is okay?"

"We hope so. Meanwhile, her mother will only accept the money as a loan. That's why I'm here, to help them keep records. I do Mom's accounting."

A tall, thin man wearing the red kerchief of a houngan emerged from the kitchen leading a group of about ten people. Moving quickly, he assigned each of them a place behind the table. Someone else began handing out notebooks and pencils, the same kind Fabrice used in class.

"Where is Danielle Masson?" the houngan called.

"Here."

"Good. You will sit here, next to Miz Ark. I didn't want her here, but she insists. Who is this?" he asked, noticing Fabrice.

"He's in Air's class. He's with me."

"I wish to help Miss Ark," Fabrice told the houngan.

"Fine. You can go stand at the door. As soon as a space opens up at the table, you let someone else in."

"Yes, papa," Fabrice said. "I will do it."

"Good. Okay, people, here's Miz Ark now. Let's get started."

—◦◦◦—

Fabrice poked his head out the door. The line snaked down the block and all the way around the corner. More people were waiting now than when they had begun six hours ago.

There had been no problems at all, at least with the people on line. Policemen in blue uniforms and wearing guns had come at around eleven, demanding to know what was going on. Fabrice had run for the houngan, who had come out and explained to them that Wedo's was collecting funds for a Haitian charity. The big parade was tomorrow, he reminded them, and the West Indian community was in a generous mood. When the police asked if there was anything they could do to help, the houngan, whose name was Max, asked if they could please try to contact the banks in the area because all their cash machines were out of money and people were being forced to take vans to other parts of Brooklyn.

Danielle and the others at the long table never stopped working. Fabrice watched them counting out bills, writing in their books, and then turning and stacking the money in the same big plastic bins the Pepper Pot used for dirty dishes. When a bin became full, someone would carry it into the kitchen and return with an empty one. Waiters kept a nearby table filled with pitchers of iced tea, lemonade, cans of soft drinks, plates of cookies, and platters of little sandwiches, but few people took anything. It was clear to Fabrice that the lady in the mourning dress, Miss Ark's mother, was tired, but she sat at the center of the table and exchanged words and shook hands with every person who came by.

—✺—

Ferray saw the mob around Wedo's, crossed the street, and approached a white policeman who was standing in the shade of an awning twirling his nightstick.

"What's going on?" Ferray asked.

"The word I get is some charity drive. I hear they've emptied every ATM in Flatbush."

"How long has this been going on?"

"I've been here since two." The cop shrugged. "It's been pretty much like this since then."

"Amazing. I wonder which charity it is."

"Ask 'em," the cop suggested.

Ferray smiled and walked off, telling himself he should have asked for more.

———⟋⟍⟍⟋⟍⟍⟍⟍=———

When the line was gone and the last of the people had finished, Fabrice walked over to Danielle and, speaking softly so as not to disturb Miss Ark's mother, told her that he too wished to give money.

"That is so sweet," Danielle said with a tired smile, "but we have enough money."

"You have no money like this." He reached into his T-shirt and showed her his magic coin. "This money is from the l'wahs. See it here." He pried open the coin and showed her the three bills.

"Where did you get that?" Danielle asked him, amazed.

"I tell you before," Fabrice said, unfolding one of them carefully. "From the l'wahs."

"Seriously. Where did you get it?"

"The l'wahs give me this money."

"Young man," Miss Ark's mother said, motioning him closer.

"Sorry for loud talk, madame," he apologized, adding a little bow.

"You say that money is from the l'wahs?"

"Yes, madame."

"Then it must be magic."

"Of course, madame. Magic."

"And you wish to give your magic money to help my daughter?"

"Yes, madame. Miss Ark teach me to spell words. She is good friend to Danny. She must be free."

"Are you coming to the services tonight?"

"I would like."

"Please come. And please bring your magic money."

"But I give money now, madame."

"Please keep it. Come to the services."

"As Madame wish."

"Sirene," the houngan said to her, "we should go."

"In a moment." She looked too tired to stand. "How long have you been in America?" she asked Fabrice.

"More than one month, madame," he declared proudly.

"And how did you get here?"

"The sea, madame. I come with the sea."

"What is your name?"

"Fabrice Lacroix, madame."

She seemed startled. "You worked for the Jouviers?"

Now *he* was startled. "How Madame know this?"

"I was told that Fabrice Lacroix was dead."

"Is not true, madame." He patted his chest. "As Madame sees, I am well."

"Max," she cried, her eyes suddenly shining, "the l'wahs have sent us a sign!"

FORTY-SEVEN

Moe sat next to the hospital bed holding Marlene's hand and willing her to wake up. Her face was a gauze mask with dark splotches where blood had seeped through. Her nose looked like a stubby chimney poking from a stained, snow-covered roof. A green plastic tube taped to one nostril hissed softly, feeding her oxygen. An IV line taped to the inside of her elbow went up to a pair of squarish plastic bags hanging upside down on a metal rack.

Moe had been trying for the longest while to synchronize his breathing with hers, hoping to use his strength to help pull her along. It was a foolish idea, but he didn't know what else to do. He'd become obsessed with her breathing, convincing himself that as long as she kept breathing, everything would be all right.

"Mr. Rosen?"

He eased his hand from hers and stood up cautiously, making sure she could keep breathing on her own.

The doctor was a slim black man, younger than Marlene. He wore rimless glasses over dark, intelligent eyes. Moe followed him out into the hall.

The doctor spoke in a soft, calm voice. Moe nodded often, understanding little but trying to get the gist. Apparently, the cuts and bruises were not what the doctor was worried about. There were a lot of them, but they were superficial. Also, the soft-tissue trauma was not severe, and the collateral damage was manageable, which, whatever it meant, didn't sound bad. At this stage, Moe was just grateful that she was alive and that he could be with her. That other stuff . . . well, that was other stuff.

Right now, the doctor said, the most serious problem was the concussion. They were continuing to monitor her brain. A certain amount of swelling was normal, but if it got much worse, they might be forced to relieve the pressure by opening the skull. The doctor was hopeful that would not be necessary, but recovery from head injuries was notoriously hard to predict. They would simply have to wait and see. The best thing now would be for the swelling to abate and for Marlene to regain consciousness, even for a moment: a word, a conscious gesture, something. Once they had that, they could all breathe easier. In the meantime, the doctor remained cautiously optimistic. She was young. She was strong. It was too bad about the baby.

"Excuse me?" Moe said, certain he had misheard.

"She couldn't have been much more than a month along," the doctor explained in the same dispassionate voice. "Frankly, given the extent of the trauma, it would have been a miracle if she hadn't lost it."

"Lost it," Moe repeated, trying to absorb this. "Are you saying that Marlene was pregnant?"

The doctor glanced up at the ceiling and sighed. "Excuse me. I've been on for thirty-two hours straight and—"

"No, no, no, it's okay. It's a shock, you know, but, you know, a good shock, a nice shock. I mean, it would have been, if she hadn't, you know . . ." Something occurred to him. "Does this mean that whoever beat her up killed the baby?"

"Well, we can't be certain she would have carried to term—"

Moe shuddered as the enormity of it finally hit him. Marlene had been pregnant. The bastards had killed their baby.

"It's probably not something you should tell her right away," the doctor suggested. "When she's stronger . . ."

"No, no," Moe assured him absently. "I won't say a thing." His mind was firing questions, none of which it could answer. All he knew for sure was that he loved her.

"Other than that," the doctor said, checking his gold Seiko, "I want you to go home and get some sleep."

"I'm fine," Moe insisted, snapping back.

"Go home, Mr. Rosen. That's an order. You look like hell."

"Someone has to be with her. All the time. Especially since . . . you know . . ."

"Patient Services will be happy to arrange for a private duty nurse. Their office is downstairs off the lobby. I've made a note on the chart to have you called the moment there's any change. Now if that's all . . ."

"There's blood on the gauze. In several places."

"That's perfectly normal."

"Can I stay with her a few more minutes?"

"Only long enough to say good-bye."

"Thank you, Doctor." Moe groped for his hand. "Thanks for everything."

Moe went in and stood at her bedside. She hadn't moved. Her breathing seemed about the same. He checked the gauze. There appeared to be a little more blood in a few spots, but he couldn't really tell. He wished there were a clear space where he could kiss her. He didn't want to kiss her nose because of the oxygen thing. When he lifted her hand, it just lay there, but when he bent to her ear and whispered that he loved her, he thought he felt her squeeze. Afraid it had been his imagination, he took a deep breath, set his hand carefully, bent over, and said it again.

He waited, holding his breath. Nothing. He promised himself he was going to kill those guys, whoever they were.

FORTY-EIGHT

Fabrice felt the excitement the moment they walked in. It seemed impossible that this huge room throbbing with the energy of the drums was the same place he and Danny took their quiet little English classes. Hundreds of people were here now, more people than Fabrice had ever seen gathered for a service back home. He felt sure that the l'wahs would listen to the prayers of this many people and come and save young Miss Ark.

It was dark here in the back, but down at the center of the gently sloping floor the poteau mitan was surrounded by a circle of light. The light was making the painted figures of Damballah and Ayida Wedo sparkle, filling the air with their spirit.

Danielle took Fabrice's hand and led him into the mass of *serviteurs*, stopping often to introduce him to people she knew. Fabrice shook hands and spoke with them, sometimes in English, more often in Creole. Everyone was kind. Everyone was dressed in ceremonial white. Fabrice knew he was in America, but he felt as if he were at home.

⟿⟿

Moe felt a tug on his arm.

"Look there," a voice whispered, pointing across the crowded room. "Now it begins."

All Moe's senses kicked in at once. It was warm. It was dark. The air was heavy with sweat and perfume and the incessant beating of drums.

He was in Wedo's basement, standing next to Ray Fauchon. That swaying mass that filled the room was all people. Moe patted his pockets:
gun, phone, wallet. If anything happened with Marlene, they would call
him. If anything happened . . .

Bolts of fury crackled through Moe's brain, making his muscles
tense, his teeth clench, and his eyes burn. The idea that Marlene lay
fighting for her life in a hospital bed while the bastards who had put her
there were still free and still had Air was making his blood boil. Moe
had never before experienced this corrosive kind of hatred: his system
couldn't deal with it. It was giving him a headache. The nonstop drumming was only making it worse.

On a more rational level he understood how lucky he was: Marlene
was alive and safe, and God willing, she was going to be all right. But
each time he thought of all those tubes and wires and that bloody
gauze . . .

Fauchon leaned close and shook Moe's arm. "See the flags." He
pointed.

Moe looked. He couldn't believe he was actually attending a Voodoo
ceremony. He felt as if he were back in Hollywood, on the set of *Shaka
Zulu* or *Roots*.

Trying to ignore the drums, Moe watched the crowd rising, dipping,
moving like the surface of a rolling sea. He recalled how thrilled he'd
been the first time he'd seen Marlene dance . . . that outfit she'd been
wearing . . . the way she'd moved . . .

The police had come to the hospital and asked some questions. Moe
hadn't given them much. Brooklyn College, he'd told them, a course in
physics. No, he didn't know the professor's name. Yes, she had a car,
one of those little Japanese things. Blue. No, he didn't know the year.
Yes, they'd been going together six weeks or so. No, they hadn't had an
argument. Yes, he was sure. He'd been at home. The doorman's name
was Manuel. No, he didn't think Marlene had any enemies.

"See them there?" Fauchon pointed.

Moe saw a line of flag bearers making their way toward the clearing around the brightly lit pole. None of this seemed real. It seemed medieval, ancient, pagan.

"Every flag," Fauchon explained, speaking over the drums, "represents a different l'wah, or Voodoo spirit. Each has its own songs, its own rhythm."

Fauchon had made it clear that he did not believe in any of this "Voodoo nonsense," yet tonight he seemed uncommonly anxious to talk about it. Moe thought he understood why. Air was still a prisoner somewhere. Sirene was dancing around a painted pole asking for God's help, Moe was fingering his gun, Ray was rubbing his stomach and giving a crash course in Voodoo. Everyone was coping in his own way.

"How many l'wahs are there?" Moe asked, trying to sound interested.

"More than four hundred. But only a few are really important. That first flag, for instance, the one with the cross, that belongs to Legba the gatekeeper. Legba guards the sacred crossroads, the intersection between the world of the living and the world of the spirits."

"Is there such a place?"

"Right there." Fauchon pointed to the pole. "In Voodoo it is called the Po-to Mee-tan. The idea is that once Legba opens the gates, the l'wahs can travel from their world into ours through that pole."

Moe nodded. He'd thought the cross was a crucifix, but now he saw that it was even all around, like a plus sign. The crossroads, he told himself: Legba. As if there were going to be a quiz on it later.

Down at the center of the room, the flags were now arrayed around the perimeter of the bright circle. The drumming changed as other objects were carried into the clearing, each held high above the bearer's head: a long sword, what looked like a conch shell, other things Moe could not identify from this far away. His thoughts drifted back to Marlene, to the green tube taped to her nose, the soft hiss of the oxygen. He wished he were there helping her breathe. He closed his eyes and tried to do it from here.

Fauchon grabbed Moe's arm and squeezed. "Now comes the sacrifice," he whispered.

Moe nodded. In a weird sort of way, Fauchon seemed to be enjoying this.

———⟪⟫———

Sirene stayed near the poteau mitan, swaying with the drumbeats and awaiting the arrival of the *manjay l'wah,* the food for the spirits. Max had promised her a pure white billy goat, something the l'wahs would savor. Sirene was bone-tired, but she had been moved by the outpouring of support this afternoon, and she was heartened by the turnout tonight. The sickening fear that had been poisoning her spirit for two days was now infused with hope, and that hope was keeping her going. She moved around the clearing as if in a trance, letting the drums control her movements, showing her which way to go, which hands to clutch, which cheeks to kiss. The l'wahs were not here yet, but she knew in her heart they would come. With all these good people calling them, they had to come. The l'wahs loved her Erzulie almost as much as she did. That was the meaning of Fabrice Lacroix: he was a sign that the l'wahs would not abandon her. They would come here tonight and use their powers to save her precious daughter. She knew it. She knew it. She knew it.

Max had been right: the buck was a magnificent animal, young and strong and full of spirit, with bright ribbons decorating its horns. When Sirene offered it grain, it dug its muzzle into her cupped hand and ate greedily, delighting the crowd. Then, when the men raised it up and carried it around the circle and showed it to the four cardinal points, it bucked and bleated as if calling the l'wahs to witness, and when Max took the knife and severed its beard and castrated it and then slit its throat, its blood gushed out eagerly into the big earthen bowl.

After the goat had been carried away, Sirene circled the poteau mitan with the bowl, moving with the drumbeats, feeling all eyes on her. When the drums went silent, she stopped, closed her eyes, said a prayer, raised the bowl to her lips and took a long drink, feeling the shock and light-headedness that always accompanied direct contact with the spirit world.

The drumming resumed with a new urgency. After Max had set the bowl on a nearby table, Sirene dipped her index finger in the thick, warm blood and painted a cross on her forehead, then stood aside while all the officials of the congregation came forward and did the same.

Moving to the steady rhythm of the drums, the audience streamed forward and one by one dipped their fingers and anointed their foreheads with Legba's cross.

—◦◊◦—

Danielle Masson stood next to Fabrice and felt the rhythms of the drums working their way deeper and deeper into her being. Miz Ark had said that Fabrice was an omen, a sign from the l'wahs. Danielle had felt from the first that there was something special about him. She knew Fabrice did not find her beautiful. She knew she was not beautiful. But now, at this moment, feeling the slow but steady approach of the spirits, Danielle felt more than beautiful; she felt part of something timeless and profound. She sang the songs and prayed for her friend Air as people went to the poteau mitan with bowls of *farine*, cornmeal, and began drawing on the floor the spidery vevays, the complex diagrams of lines and curves and stars that were the mystical calling cards of the l'wahs.

The rhythm changed and people began a new dance: simple steps, unhurried, calm, and graceful. Soon the entire audience was on the move, slowly circling the room counterclockwise, the mirror direction of the spirit world. Perhaps it was having Fabrice at her side, perhaps it was the urgency of the service, the cross on her forehead, the size of the crowd—but Danielle felt different tonight: strange, blessed, outside of herself somehow. Her body, which had always felt misshapen and awkward, now felt as graceful and buoyant as a balloon. It felt so nice, so right, this lightness, this warmth and motion, this drifting toward a darkness strange and remote and calling to her, a darkness somehow without dark.

—*∾*—

"Now the nonsense starts," Ferray said with distaste.

"What do you mean?" Moe asked, turning to him.

"Just watch."

The drumming never let up, but now the steady movement of the dancers was occasionally broken by shouts and cries, which, Ferray explained to Moe, signaled that some fool had managed to hypnotize himself into the trance state called mounting. The idea was that the Voodoo spirit, having slid down the magic pole like some heavenly fireman, was now taking over the body of a supplicant, riding him like a horse.

Ferray had seen it all so many times before: the ranting and raving, the feats of strength, the whole litany of tricks that kept the tourists clicking away with their Kodaks. He tapped Rosen on the arm and pointed to a madman across the room who had torn open his shirt and grabbed a bottle of clarin. As Rosen watched, the man guzzled the raw rum, sprayed it into the air, and set it aflame. Then he bit off the neck of the bottle and began chewing the broken glass.

—*∾*—

Danielle had always felt the drums, felt their rhythm and their power, but they had never gotten inside her like this, prying her cells apart and making her whole body vibrate like some glorious instrument. The drums had her completely now. Her mind popped free and suddenly she was looking down on herself. She watched herself dancing, watched her round ungainly body moving so beautifully, so effortlessly, so sensuously. Things were beginning to blur, to run into one another: colors and shapes mixing like a child's watercolor. Her senses were starting to separate. She could no longer hear the drums, only feel them. She sensed different parts of herself floating off to different parts of the room. She understood that if she let herself go, she would be gone, would disappear, would—

Her foot caught on the floor and she pitched forward, flailing for balance. She felt steadying hands holding her up. She freed her foot and began dancing again. That had been so weird: one moment she had been gliding along, and the next her foot was stuck to the floor. Her mind shivered and relaxed and she soon felt herself dissolving again. She was both frightened and unafraid. There was no time and no space, only this huge empty chasm that she felt coming up behind her.

Without warning, her leg caught again. She stumbled heavily forward, straining mightily to free it. This time it was harder, as if she were pulling it from thick tar. The drums kept calling to her. As she resumed her dancing, the air around her became a sparkling fog, enveloping her in a soft, warm mist. Her mind lifted and began tumbling backward toward that immense chasm. She was trying to slow herself but she was speeding up instead. She couldn't hear. She couldn't see. This was so strange. It felt so good. It felt so scary. An emptiness was flying toward her. She felt a horrible pain and a rush of terror, and then in a panic she just let herself go and the white darkness swallowed her up.

—ᴧᴧᴧ—

Fabrice caught her as she fell. He had stayed close, waiting for the l'wah to finish working its way inside her. Danielle had not understood what was happening to her, but Fabrice had. He and several others were holding her gently now, letting her body jerk about as the spirit began to work her muscles. Fabrice watched her closely, anxious to discover which l'wah had mounted her.

—ᴧᴧᴧ—

Cries went up near the center of the room. Moe rose up on his toes for a better view. A chubby young woman had collapsed. People were helping her to her feet. As soon as she was upright, she took the arm of a nearby man, drew him close, and began brazenly rubbing herself against him.

"What's going on?" Moe asked Fauchon.

"Erzulie has appeared."

"Erzulie?" Moe exclaimed. "You mean—?"

"No, no. The l'wah Erzulie, Air's namesake. The goddess of love," he said sarcastically. "Everyone's favorite l'wah."

Some older women had taken hold of the chubby woman and were leading her off. She seemed unsteady on her feet.

"Where are they taking her?" Moe asked.

"She has to get into her costume. Then she will return and put on her show. The goddess could have picked someone a little better looking," Ferray remarked sourly.

Moe glanced around. On all sides the previously strict order of the proceedings appeared to be breaking down. Most people were still dancing to the relentless drumming, but more and more often there were cries and shouts as here and there individuals began acting crazy: fainting dead away or whirling like dervishes or shaking uncontrollably. Little clearings were forming all around the room to accommodate their bizarre behavior.

"What's all this?" Moe asked.

"Geddies. People who have been mounted by lesser spirits of the dead: relatives, ancestors, friends of the family. Anyone at all. They need space."

"Some of them are wearing sunglasses."

"The spirit world is dark. Their eyes are sensitive to light. Pardon me, Moe, but it is all such childish nonsense."

Ferray hated this freak-show aspect of Voodoo ceremonies. He turned away and rubbed his stomach, checking for his safe-deposit keys. He'd worked much too hard to take a chance of losing them now. As he caressed them, he thought about the newest member of his little treasure family.

Once the kidnappers had rejected Max, it had not been difficult for Ferray to get himself appointed official courier. Then, late this afternoon, he had called Sirene and told her that the kidnappers had contacted him and offered to make the exchange that night, a day ahead of schedule. An hour later, Max and two armed guards had arrived at Ferray's apartment with a duffel bag containing three quarters of a million dollars in unmarked bills. After showing Max out, Ferray had gleefully transferred the money to a pair of carry-on satchels. After a decent interval he had called Sirene and informed her that the kidnappers had changed their minds and that the exchange would take place as originally planned: Monday, after the parade. But the good news, Ferray had told the distraught Sirene, was that he had heard's Air's voice.

"How did she sound?" Sirene had asked anxiously.

"Tired. A bit frightened. She said she was unharmed."

"Thank God," Sirene had sighed. "But, Ray, what do we do about the money?"

"It is safe here. But, if you wish, you can have it picked up and stored somewhere else and then delivered to me again after the parade."

"The more times we move it, the more risk we take. If you do not mind, Ray, I think we best leave it where it is."

"As you wish."

"What would we do without you, Ray?"

"Please, Sirene, I do this for your brother."

Ferray had waited half an hour before driving to the shuttle terminal at La Guardia Airport, sliding the money-filled satchels into a rental locker, and driving back to Brooklyn.

Thus far, his plan was working perfectly. Tomorrow, after the parade, he would drive himself to the hideout and plant the emptied duffel in the basement. Then he would go upstairs and use his nine millimeter Glock semiautomatic to dispose of Michel Pioline and his muscular friend. He would rescue Air, deliver her back to her grateful mother, and explain to the police that in the confusion of the battle a third kidnapper—a white man he'd glimpsed only from the back—had escaped with the ransom money. All his energies, he would explain, had been directed toward saving the girl. Regarding the Glock, he would simply refer the NYPD to the FBI, which had provided it. The two dead kidnappers would make the local police happy. The loss of the money would be little enough for Sirene to pay for her daughter's life and her brother's treachery.

Reviewing the plan reconfirmed for Ferray its basic soundness. He would have his money back, with a bit extra for his trouble. Michel and Loup would be dead. Air would be eternally grateful. His resulting celebrity would serve him well after he and Air were married and Sirene suffered her fatal accident. Which reminded him: Rosen's shop. He still couldn't decide whether that space would work better as a sports bar or a room for private parties. Rosen didn't belong around here anyhow. It should not prove too difficult to drive him out. But Ferray would not be vindictive; if Rosen's whore managed to recover, she could go with him.

He reached over, patted Moe on the shoulder and, speaking over the drums, asked if there had been any change in Marlene's condition.

—◈—

The drumbeat changed, the two petro drums fading out and the three gentler rada drums taking over. Fabrice joined the others in the yanvalou, the water dance, bending his knees and rolling his shoulders and moving like the sea itself.

Fabrice had never been mounted, but he was happy for Danielle: it was a great honor to be mounted by Erzulie, who, like all great l'wahs, never appeared more than once at each ceremony. Erzulie was now Danny's *may-tet*, the master of her head. Danny would not be mounted at every ceremony, but when she was, it would always be by Erzulie.

Fabrice turned as an angry voice nearby began crying out words in *langay*, the ancient language of Guinée. A path opened and Fabrice saw a young man walking all stooped over with a cane. Legba was making his appearance. Fabrice suspected that all the great l'wahs would be here tonight.

A few moments later a cry went up nearby as a man collapsed to the floor and, refusing all aid, began to slither like a snake. Damballah, the only mute l'wah, had arrived.

The room was alive with spirits. Fabrice reached up and clutched his magic coin, wondering which of them had given it to him.

—ᴔᴂᴖ—

Sirene wiped the perspiration from her face with a handkerchief as she moved among her guests. Each time she came to a geddy she offered her left hand and felt a shock when their hands touched. Geddies seemed to be appearing everywhere. The forces of the spirit world were pouring into the overheated room. Sirene took heart; the power of the l'wahs was being marshalled for the safe return of her daughter. Now, with the help of the l'wahs, Ray would make the exchange tomorrow and she would have her daughter back home safe.

"Sirene!" a hoarse voice cried.

It was Legba, dressed in rags and sucking on a pipe, inching forward with the help of his cane. He had mounted a young man who owned a fruit-and-vegetable store two blocks away.

"Sirene," he called again.

"I am here," she declared in Creole.

Others crowded around to listen.

Legba fixed her with a penetrating stare. "The answer is in this room," he told her with a wicked chuckle. "But Sirene is blind. She does not see it."

"Papa Legba," she replied, staring into his glazed eyes. "Please tell me, what answer?"

"What answer do you think, foolish woman?"

"Tell me," Sirene beseeched him.

"Let someone else. I am too old," he grumbled, turning his bent back and shuffling off.

Sirene was not discouraged. L'wahs often spoke in riddles. The important thing was that Legba was here, walking among them, lending his divine presence to the proceedings.

—◦⁄◦⁄◦—

Moe scanned the room. The scene was like something out of an old Fellini movie. Nearly twenty people who had been "mounted" were now holding court in various parts of the room. Others seemed determined to work themselves into a frenzy. The drumming had been going on for so long that Moe couldn't imagine a world without it. The air was so heavy it felt as if it were hanging from the ceiling. The combination of body odor and perfume was overwhelming. And still they danced.

The spectacle reminded Moe of a line from W. B. Yeats that he'd once had to write a paper on in school: "How can we know the dancer from the dance?" Now, after all these years, Moe thought he understood what the poet meant.

"Look over there," Fauchon snickered. "The goddess of love reappears."

—◦⁄◦⁄◦—

Her body covered by a loose, flowing pink dress, her face hidden by a white veil, her arms cradling a bouquet of pink roses, Danielle Masson moved with the self-assured grace of a great beauty. Fabrice smelled her perfume and powder as she swept across the floor. He watched as she unfurled a white silk fan and went up to a man and handed him a rose, then began stroking his arm, whispering intimacies, touching his face with her fingers, lavishing the man with so much flattery and affection that he became embarrassed. After a few minutes, she left him and chose another, and then another after that, each time behaving as if he were the only man in the world. Fabrice followed her at a distance, staying at the fringes of her perfumed cloud.

After bestowing her attentions on more than a dozen men, the l'wah began to grow weary. Her flowers were all gone, her shoulders began to sag, her fanning became more anxious. She turned slowly in place, teetering, as if unsure of what to do next. All around her the dancing continued, the bodies of the believers rhythmically rising and falling, swooping and swaying, moving in a slow circle, carried forward by the steady current of the drums.

Afraid she was about to fall, Fabrice entered Erzulie's magic cloud and stood behind her. This close to her the air was so sweet it made him dizzy. When she turned and took his arm, the shock of her touch made him jump.

"Are you afraid of me?" she teased in softest Creole, stroking his arm.

"No, *maîtresse,*" he whispered, feeling himself tremble.

"Have you been true to me?" she asked him in a voice like smoothest silk.

"Yes, *maîtresse*. Always."

"Have you so much love?" she asked him in the same sweet, teasing Creole, rubbing herself against him like a cat. "Enough for Erzulie *and* for Antoinette?"

"Yes, *maîtresse,*" he whispered, his skin tingling.

Even through the veil he could feel her eyes caressing him. The Creole phrases poured from her mouth like gentle kisses. Fabrice felt as if he were being touched by a dream. This was truly the goddess Erzulie. Danielle Masson did not know of Antoinette. Danielle Masson did not speak Creole.

"Champagne for Erzulie," a woman offered, holding out a glass.

It was Miz Ark, the lady who had called this service, the mother of his missing teacher, the woman who had met with Antoinette in her village.

Erzulie reached out for the glass, raised her veil, and took a dainty sip. The softer rada drums had taken over from the petro, making it easier to hear.

"I have been betrayed," Erzulie lamented to Miz Ark.

"Everyone loves you, *maîtresse,*" Miz Ark assured her.

"Not everyone," Erzulie said, her voice filling with pain. "I have been betrayed." She started to weep.

Fabrice was not surprised by the change in Erzulie. Her appearances always began in great joy and ended in bitter sadness. Erzulie, who shared her love with so many, always ended by weeping openly, insisting that her love had been betrayed.

"Surely no one here has betrayed you, *maîtresse,*" Miz Ark suggested gently.

"You are wrong," the l'wah sobbed as tears rolled down her powdered cheeks and spotted her veil. "The betrayer is here. The betrayer is here among us."

Fabrice was startled by her words. In all the ceremonies where Erzulie had appeared, he had never heard her speak this way. Erzulie had always blamed all of mankind for her betrayal. No individual was ever accused. What could this mean?

"No one here would betray Erzulie," Miz Ark soothed.

"The betrayer is here," Erzulie insisted, then drank off the rest of her champagne and threw the glass to the floor, smashing it.

She turned to Fabrice and clutched his arm. He felt a bolt of electricity shoot through him.

"Find him for me," she whispered urgently. "Find the betrayer."

"How can I do this?"

"Find the betrayer."

"How, *maîtresse?*" he asked fearfully.

"You must," she growled.

"But how, *maîtresse?*"

"You must."

The stooped young man with the cane collapsed in a heap no more than ten feet from where Moe was standing. People crowded around to help revive him. The drums never faltered.

"Now he'll wake up and be himself again," Fauchon explained. "That's the way these so-called mountings work. They generally last from fifteen to thirty minutes."

Moe moved for a better look and struck something with his foot. He bent down and picked up Legba's bamboo cane, which must have slid across the floor when the man fell.

"What do I do with this?" he asked, showing it to Fauchon.

"Keep it. A souvenir."

Moe shrugged and hooked it over his wrist.

———⁊⁊⁊———

"Look at them," Ferray sighed, surveying the room. "You would think they would get tired, but, no, they have not stopped for a second. That damned drumming hypnotizes them."

He shook his head in disgust, took a step back, and turned his thoughts inward. Had he been dealing with professionals, his little ruse with the locker key would have been foolhardy. But his adversaries were people who danced in circles and painted crosses on their foreheads with goat's blood. They deserved to be treated like fools.

Driving back from La Guardia earlier, Ferray had been euphoric. Seven hundred fifty thousand dollars in unmarked bills—his money!—was now resting snugly in an airport locker. He could feel the fat little key inside the waistband of his shorts, alongside the four thin safe-deposit keys. He couldn't get over how easy it had all been, how masterfully he had planned it, how brilliantly he had carried it out. He had won! He was rich! He had beaten them all!

His exuberance had lasted all the way into Brooklyn. Then something had changed. Beating Sirene and Rosen and the rest of them felt good, but somehow it wasn't enough; suddenly he felt the need to rub their noses in it, to grind them down into the dirt.

And then, stopped at a red light, he had been seized by a terrifying thought: he could lose everything! Something might happen—a mugging, an accident, the chain could break—and then what? He had two separate treasures now. Keeping this new key with the ones from Florida was reckless. Prudence dictated that the new one be kept apart.

But where? He had driven on, considering his options. Hiding it here in the car made no sense: this was New York; the car might be stolen. Then, like a lightning bolt, the answer had come to him, the boldness of it taking his breath away, the delicious perversity of it thrilling him.

With mounting excitement, like a man possessed, he had driven to the warehouse. The street outside had been deserted. Inside, an elderly watchman had been fast asleep before a flickering black and white TV. Everyone was off preparing for tonight's Voodoo ceremony. Ferray had tiptoed between the unassembled pieces of the float to the secret little storeroom, had silently worked open the door, had reached in and felt around, and—almost as if fate was directing his hand—had discovered a nail in the ideal spot, on the wall above the doorway, where it would be invisible from the outside.

Now, as Ferray looked around the crowd and saw their stupid Voodoo antics, the idea that he had hidden the key right under their noses filled him with delight.

"Look," he said, tugging Rosen's arm, "Erzulie and her entourage are coming this way. Perhaps she will favor us with a smile."

—◦◦◦—

They were circling the room in a counterclockwise spiral, moving farther from the center with each circuit. Fabrice trailed along beside Erzulie, who continued to weep bitterly, insisting over and over that she had been betrayed. Many tried, but no one was able to console her. Several times she had to stop and wait while her body was racked by sobs. Each time she stopped she looked at Fabrice and declared that the betrayer was among them. Fabrice felt her pain in his heart and wished there were some way for him to relieve it.

She stopped again. Fabrice looked up and saw that she was standing before a white man who was for some reason holding Legba's cane.

"This man is a friend," Miz Ark assured Erzulie in Creole. "Let us keep going."

"The betrayer is near," Erzulie informed Fabrice, scanning nearby faces before moving on.

As Fabrice turned to follow her, he glimpsed something from the corner of his eye: something he recognized, something that chilled his soul and rooted his feet to the floor.

No, he thought wildly, it could not be!

He forced himself to look back.

It was!

"Ogoun," he growled, staring into the eyes he had recognized even in the dark, the eyes he had seen in the Jouviers' dining room. He could never forget those eyes!

"What?" Miss Ark's mother asked him.

The evil eyes started to move away.

"There is Ogoun!" Fabrice cried, pointing excitedly.

"Where?"

"There, madame! See, he wants to run."

"Who? But that—"

"Betrayer," Erzulie hissed.

"I will stop him," Fabrice cried, lurching forward.

"Ray?" Miz Ark exclaimed. "But—"

"Betrayer!" Erzulie shrieked.

Fabrice leaped for Ogoun's throat, but Ogoun threw him to the floor. Fabrice rolled over and grabbed, but he was too late. Ogoun was far ahead, shoving people aside, fighting his way to the staircase. People scattered and screamed.

"Stop him!" Fabrice cried, stumbling as he tried to get up.

"Betrayer!" shrieked Erzulie.

—⧸𝜄𝜄⧹—

Moe saw Ray's mouth fall open and his eyes go wide with terror. There was no other way to say it: he looked as if he'd seen a ghost. Then a boy started pointing at him and yelling things. It was clear they knew each other. Ray started to slink away, and Moe found himself moving along with him. Then the girl in the veil screamed out and the boy went for Ray's throat. Before Moe knew what was happening, Ray had knocked the boy down and was making a mad dash for the stairs, wildly pushing people out of his way. He had made it into the stairwell and was scrambling up the stairs when Moe, who had not even realized he had been chasing him, reached out with the cane, hooked Ray's ankle, and brought him down hard. Before Ray could recover, men had streamed past Moe and were dragging Ray back down into the basement. Once there, they wrestled him to the floor, spread-eagled him on his back, and struggled to hold him down. Other men were restraining the boy who had started it all. Moe was caught in a crush of bodies as people surged forward to see what was happening. It was madness.

—⟨⟨⟨—

Order was restored. Sirene and the boy exchanged feverish whispers. Moe couldn't understand a word. Obviously, something extraordinary had taken place, but Moe could only guess what it was. The look in Ray's eyes had made Moe's blood run cold. Perhaps Ray had done something terrible to this boy back in Haiti.

Moe stopped and looked around, sensing that something was wrong. It took a moment for him to realize what it was; the drums had stopped.

Ray, flat on his back, was still trying furiously to escape. Moe barely recognized him. Ray's chest was heaving and his eyes were wild. In his fury, he reminded Moe of a captured tiger, snarling and indomitable, dangerous even in restraints.

"Keep him still," Sirene ordered the men who were holding him down.

Ray's torso lifted into the air and twisted. He stared up at her with eyes like burning embers.

"Someone get me a knife," Sirene said calmly. "From the kitchen. A butcher knife."

FORTY-NINE

Nine of them went in a taxi van: the driver, Moe, Ray, Fabrice, Max, and four Haitians who worked as armed security guards and happened to have their guns with them tonight. Moe had his gun. Max had the one from Wedo's safe. Fabrice had a machete. Moe was in the front seat, squeezed between the driver and Max. He could sense Ray, silent and brooding, directly behind him. Even with his hands tied and flanked by two security guards, Ray's presence made Moe uneasy.

Sirene had adamantly refused Moe's plea to let the police handle this. She did not trust the New York police to save her daughter; she trusted Max, she trusted Moe, she trusted her countrymen. Ray Fauchon was an impostor. He was really a colonel in the Haitian army. He had killed her brother in Haiti and had then come up here and set up the kidnapping of Marlene and Air. Sirene was not about to turn him over to anyone's police.

Moe looked out through the windshield. It was 1 A.M. Streetlights glowed. The asphalt was wet. Dark buildings slid by on either side. Moe's eyes hurt. He hadn't slept in two days. There was a plastic crown on the dashboard with liquid sloshing around in it. The van smelled of flowers. Moe still found what Sirene had told him hard to believe. But he didn't want to think about that now. First they would free Air. Then, if what Sirene said turned out to be true, Moe wanted to kill Ray himself. Ray had sworn on his life that Air had not been touched and that he had done everything he could to protect Marlene. But the way Sirene had been holding that knife, he would have said anything.

The van moved smoothly through the Brooklyn streets. There was little traffic. No one spoke. It was as if they were commandos on a dangerous raid. Moe understood that the trick was going to be getting into the apartment. For that they needed Ray. Once they were inside, subduing the two kidnappers should not prove difficult. Moe anticipated that the whole thing would be over in a few seconds. The plan was that Ray would go to the door alone while Moe and the others hid in the hall. The moment the door opened, they would burst in, pushing Ray ahead of them, using him as a shield. If the kidnappers resisted, they would be killed. If Ray tried anything cute, he would be killed. After they got Air, they would decide how to proceed with the police. Ray was cooperating because it was his only chance of saving his life. He had already given them a diagram of the apartment. With any luck, both kidnappers would be in the front room.

They parked the van around the corner and entered the building in twos and a three, spacing their arrival in case the kidnappers were watching the street. They met in the lobby and took the elevator up together. When they got to the floor, they drew their weapons and, following Max's hand signals, silently took up positions on either side of the door. The security guards would go in first, Moe and Fabrice last. Max and the van driver would stay and guard the hallway.

When everyone was in place, Max untied Ray's hands and gave him a push. Moe thought he saw the merest flicker of a smile, little more than a twitch, cross Ray's lips as he turned and walked to the door.

Ray knocked, waited, identified himself. Moe heard the turning of two locks and the scratch of a latch chain.

As the door creaked open, the first two security guards jumped up and, pushing Ray ahead of them, forced their way into the apartment. They were followed almost instantly by the second pair of guards.

Even before he got in there, Moe could hear that something had gone wrong. He found all four guards on the floor, wrestling with a muscular man in a white T-shirt. Moe raced past them toward a door that was closing. He lowered his shoulder and crashed through, hitting the floor hard, losing his gun and sliding on his side. Before he could right himself, someone had pounced on him. Moe heaved himself over onto his back and saw the hated face of Michel Pioline, and above it, a knife in a hand drawn back to strike. Moe crossed his arms to block the blow, but before it came, the hand and knife jumped from the wrist, replaced by a spurting fountain of blood. In the next surreal moment, as Michel's mouth opened and his eyes turned to his empty wrist, his head was severed at the neck, first popping upward, then tilting crazily, and finally, after a moment of the most profound silence, striking the floor next to Moe with a thud.

Fabrice kicked the body over, extended a hand, and pulled Moe to his feet. The strikes with the machete had been so fast that Moe had not even seen the blade. Michel Pioline lay in three pieces on the floor, the largest of them quivering like a boated fish. Blood was everywhere. Moe saw some on his shirt. Looking around for something to wipe it with, he noticed a small figure in jeans and a sweatshirt huddled on a metal cot against the far wall.

"Air," he cried. "We're here. You're safe!"

"Mr. Rosen?" came the weak reply.

She tried to rise but fell back down. Moe went to her and saw that her wrists were bound behind her back. His hands were shaking too badly to untie her, so he asked Fabrice to do it.

Fabrice handed him the machete. Moe stood there for a few seconds, gripping the wooden handle and staring at the long, bloodstained blade. Fabrice had saved his life with this thing. Then Moe remembered his gun and started looking around for it.

Miraculously, Air had not been hurt. She was shaky, but able to stand on her own. When she saw Max, she ran over, buried her head against his chest, and began to sob. Michel Pioline's partner was on the kitchen floor, badly bloodied and tied hand and foot. Other than a few bruises, none of the raiding party had been injured.

Moe stood in the bedroom staring at a pair of fluttering curtains by an open window. Air was safe, but the victory was bittersweet. Moe's gun was missing. Ray Fauchon had escaped.

FIFTY

Antoinette was knee-deep in the river when a boy came with the message that the houngan needed to see her. Ignoring the nosy stares of the other women, she hauled her wash basket onto the bank and followed the boy up the hill.

"Here, child," the houngan called, hurrying out to her with a small paper in his hand. "See what has come for you."

"What is it, papa?" she asked, wiping her hands on her skirt.

"Look for yourself."

She held the card by its edges and turned her back to the sun. What she saw startled her. It was a picture of a gigantic fish leaping straight up out of the water, a huge black monster with angry white patches on its fearsome head.

She looked closer. The creature was about to gobble up a yellow-haired girl in a red bathing suit. The girl was flying through the air with her arms outstretched for help. But her tiny feet were only inches ahead of the creature's gaping mouth. Clearly, she was doomed.

Antoinette's hands trembled as she studied the photo and wondered who would send her such a thing.

It came to her with a shudder. That man from the army! He was sending her a warning! He was threatening to feed her to the fishes!

"See the other side," the houngan suggested.

Antoinette turned the card over. The back side was covered with writing, except for one corner with two little American flags. None of this made sense. What did all these words mean? And why would the army man use American flags? Were the Americans going to help him? Why would they? She had never done anything to them. This was all a terrible mistake.

"Houngan," she pleaded, "why do you say this was meant for me?"

"Look here." He brought it close to her and pointed. "See what it says. 'Antoinette Voisin.' Is that not you?"

She had to admit that it was. Turning the card over, she stared again at the monster fish. She had never seen so many teeth. That poor girl!

"And see here," the houngan said, turning the card back and guiding her finger down near the bottom. "What is that?"

Her mouth came open. Her knees went weak.

The old priest reached out and steadied her. "So, you recognize the mark."

"That is Fabrice's mark," she whispered, bending close and brushing it with her fingertips.

"Yes, that is Fabrice's mark. This card comes all the way from America."

He grasped her wrist and shook it gently. He was smiling. "Do you know what this means, child?"

Antoinette's mind was reeling. "Oh, papa," she cried, pressing the card to her breast.

"Yes, child?"

But Antoinette covered her mouth with her hand, afraid that if she said another word, her heart would burst.

FIFTY-ONE

Moe splashed his face with cold water, looked in the mirror, and saw a stranger, an older guy with the sunken, ravaged eyes of a battle-weary GI. It had been a tough couple of days. He rinsed his mouth and spit into the sink, remembering Michel Pioline and that knife, the sick gleam in his eye as he was about to strike, and then—

Moe grasped the sides of the sink and held on tight until the nausea passed. Then, still shaky, he went and got his cell phone, propped it on the sink, and stepped into the shower. The water washed the clamminess from his skin and helped clear his head. He'd slept for three hours. The hospital hadn't called, which meant there had been no change. Air was safe at home with Sirene. Michel Pioline was in hell. Ray Fauchon had escaped and the ransom money was missing, but those were police matters now. Regardless of what Sirene wanted, Moe knew that they were all better off letting the authorities handle it. He suspected that when they found Fauchon, they'd find the money.

The only thing Moe really cared about now was Marlene. Today was Monday. Visiting hours wouldn't start until ten. Moe had more than two hours to kill. He probably ought to eat something or—

My God, the parade! He had to go down and check the float and make sure the costumes were all right and—

—◦∿◦—

Ferray awoke with a start, instantly alert. He sat up and braced his back against the wall. It was cramped in here, and musty. Slivers of morning light were filtering through the cracks, allowing him to see snippets of the room outside.

Fitful as it had been, the sleep had done him a world of good. Staying here last night had been—there was no other word for it—inspired. He had been exhausted after his escape. It would have been folly to have headed directly to the airport. He might have taken a cab out there only to have discovered the shuttle terminal closed for the night. Worse, he might have arrived there and found the police waiting for him. Despite the services he had rendered them over the years, he had no illusions that the American authorities would protect him. In their place, he would have had himself killed; it was the only sensible thing to do.

Noises! Ferray froze. Voices, the clanking of a chain, the rumbling of a motor. The big metal door was coming up. Fresh light poured in through the cracks, covering Ferray with a weird design, almost like some intricate vevay. He stifled a laugh; the Voodoo bullshit never ended.

Still, the more he reflected on last night's proceedings, the more impressive his performance became. Held down by half a dozen goons, threatened by a crazed woman wielding a butcher knife, how many men would have had the presence of mind to do what Hugo Ferray had done: prepare his own escape by offering to lead them to the kidnappers' lair, and then, when they demanded the return of their money, directing them to a nonexistent hiding place in his apartment?

The noise was getting louder. At least a dozen people were out there now, perhaps two dozen. He could see their shadows flitting across the narrow bands of light slicing through the wall.

Suddenly he was seized by a burning fury for that wretched houseboy Fabrice Lacroix. How had his men allowed him to escape? The house had been surrounded. Twenty armed men. A routine mission. Ferray thought about the girl, Antoinette Voisin. A houseboy's whore, but also a sorceress. He recalled her smell, her trembling breasts, the texture of her hair, the way she had moaned and begged for mercy . . .

But he couldn't waste his energy thinking about that now. Those were things he could think about later, when he was far away from here, when he could look back on all this and laugh.

He reached down and rested his hand on the small bulge beneath his waistband, the one beside the gun. When they'd held him down on the floor, they had emptied his pockets, taking his wallet, his car keys, his apartment keys. But fools that they were, they had missed the only keys that really mattered. And now the key to the airport locker—the one he had hidden here—was back on the chain with its brothers.

Outside, the big diesel engine roared to life, making the thin wall tremble. Ferray fingered his keys. It wouldn't be long now.

The best revenge was living well, Ferray reminded himself, and he intended to do exactly that. Sirene could keep her precious little virgin for a while, but the Arcenciel women had not seen the last of Hugo Ferray. Neither had Fabrice Lacroix. Ferray looked forward to coming back and exacting his revenge on all of them: the houseboy first, then Sirene, and then those bright red panties . . .

He chuckled to himself, clutching his keys to keep them from rattling. Everything was straightforward now. He would wait in here until the float and all the workers left for the parade. When the coast was clear, he would slip out and catch a taxi to La Guardia. He would have the cab wait while he retrieved the satchels from the locker. After paying the taxi he would find a gift shop and buy himself some sunglasses, one of those stupid Yankee baseball caps, and perhaps even a matching satin jacket. He would dispose of Rosen's gun before walking through the metal detector and boarding the next available shuttle flight— Boston or Washington, it didn't matter. He would be at risk before he got on the plane, but the police presence figured to be light today because of the parade. On board, he would pay the fare in cash. Once he landed, getting to Miami should not prove difficult. In Miami, he would obtain new papers, grow a beard, sit in a beach chair, sip a banana daiquiri, and plot his revenge.

The noise outside his cramped quarters was picking up. People were shouting above the revving of the engine. He heard the gearbox grinding, smelled the diesel fumes. It wouldn't be long now. The truck was out on the street. He decided to wait two more minutes before opening the door and making sure everyone had gone. He reached down to the cuff of his trousers and slid out the steel needle hidden in the seam. If they had left a guard, it would be better to dispose of him silently.

———⌘———

Moe checked the time. It was 8 A.M. As people scurried about putting on finishing touches, he made a slow circuit of the float, shaking hands, offering congratulations. He stopped to watch as someone opened the golden door and checked its hinges. God, how he wished Marlene could be here to share this with him: to see that door open, to watch the sunlight reflecting off the gold foil, to feel the swoop and curve of the ramps, to see the red, white, and blue bunting flapping in the morning breeze—to feel the spirit of the thing, the way it all tied together into a single powerful statement.

They'd had to move the float halfway out into the street to attach Liberty's massive green arm. The tip of her golden torch now soared nearly twenty feet above the bed of the truck. A person unfamiliar with the Statue of Liberty might have thought the truck was carrying a fanciful lighthouse.

"A glorious day, Mr. Rosen," Max said, coming up beside him. "You should be proud of all you have done."

"I had a lot of help. Do you think the spiral staircase will be strong enough?"

"It is made of wrought iron."

"No, I meant the way it's anchored inside the arm. I'm worried the motion of the truck could shake it loose."

"I will speak to the foreman and ask that the bolts be tightened every . . . what would you suggest?"

"Half hour?"

"Every half hour," Max said. "A wise precaution."

"I wish we'd been a little more cautious with Ray," Moe said before remembering that Max had been in charge. "I'm tired," he explained, wishing he hadn't said it.

"Things work out for the best, Mr. Rosen. I believe that." Max smiled. "By the way, thank you for what you did for Fabrice."

"Fabrice saved my life."

"And your statement to the police has probably saved his. Fabrice has no papers, Mr Rosen. If the police knew that he killed Pioline, he would almost certainly be deported."

"Well"—Moe shrugged—"my fingerprints were the only ones on the machete."

"Yes, when I saw you wiping the handle, I wondered what you were doing."

"I thought the police were going to keep me there all night. But then some FBI agents showed up, and fifteen minutes later I was on my way home."

"All things happen for a reason," Max said.

"Tell me, does Miz Ark know what Fabrice did?"

"I told her. She will see to it that he gets his green card."

"I didn't mean that about Ray," Moe apologized. "I'm just worried about Marlene."

"Go to her, Mr. Rosen. As you see, the float is complete. You are not needed here."

"Thanks, but it's too early. Visiting hours don't start until ten. They won't let me in."

"Then ride with us to the staging area. We're leaving now. The troupe will be meeting us there."

"No, you go ahead," Moe said. "I'll close up here."

"Will we see you later?"

"I don't know."

Max seemed reluctant to go. He reached up and adjusted the red bandanna at his neck "Is there anything else I can do for you, Mr. Rosen?"

"Yes. You can stop calling me Mr. Rosen. My friends call me Moe."

"All right, Moe." Max offered his hand. "Please give my best to Marlene."

—◦◦◦—

Moe stood at the warehouse entrance watching the eighteen-wheeler slowly maneuver into the street. The parked cars on both sides were making the task extremely tricky. The truck ground its gears and raced its engine and spewed out huge puffs of black smoke as it inched its way back and forth. Moe gave a final wave, but everyone on board was involved in other things.

With one last look at his majestic creation, Moe turned and walked into the warehouse. He tried reminding himself that more than a million people would be seeing his designs today, but even that failed to cheer him.

Moe's footsteps echoed in the cavernous space. Someone outside on the float began to play a drum. Once again Moe found himself wondering if Marlene had known she was pregnant, and whether it would have been a girl or—

A noise, like the squeak of a door. Moe turned. The sound had come from over by that staircase. There was an oddly shaped little door Moe had never noticed before. His curiosity piqued, Moe walked over and squatted before it. It had a cheap little wooden peg for a handle, but when he pulled on it, the door wouldn't open. Setting his feet wide apart, Moe used both hands to grasp the peg. At first nothing happened, but when he leaned back, the door flew open so fast that he lost his balance and nearly fell.

Before he could right himself, something sprang from the darkness, banging into him and knocking him backward. The realization hit him harder than the concrete: Ray!

Before Moe knew what was happening, Ray was driving Moe's chin up with the heel of one hand so the other hand could stab him with—Jesus!—some kind of long needle!

Moe swiped at the arm on his chin with all his might, dislodging it but bringing Ray's full weight crashing down on him. The needle struck the concrete next to Moe's head with an ugly scraping noise that gave Moe the strength not only to hurl Ray off him but to throw a furious punch at his head.

It missed, but the momentum carried Moe into a roll that miraculously landed him on his feet.

Ray was ten yards ahead, sprinting for the street. With murder in his heart, Moe took off after him.

Ray headed out across the street, but nothing was there but a vacant lot surrounded by a high Cyclone fence. He swerved and began chasing the float. The float was halfway up the block, picking up speed. Moe understood instinctively what Ray was planning: he would throw himself under the long bed of the moving truck and roll through to the other side, creating a barrier between himself and Moe that would give Ray enough time to escape into traffic.

Moe ran with abandon, determined to stop Ray before he got there. The idea of calling out flashed through his mind, but with the drumming and the engine noise . . . No, he had to do this himself. He *wanted* to do this himself.

Ray caught up with the float as it neared the corner, dashing past the double set of rear wheels and heading for the front ones. Moe was gaining on him, but not quickly enough. He had closed to within a stride when Ray dropped into a crouch, preparing to hit the ground with his shoulder and roll through to the far side.

Moe went airborne, reaching out and grasping the back of Ray's shirt for just long enough to thwart his plan. Instead of rolling beneath the moving truck, Ray was forced to roll back out on Moe's side where, just inches from the path of the truck's approaching rear tires, he propped himself up on an elbow, pulled a gun from his waistband, and looked at Moe with an expression of such pure animal hatred that Moe, on his hands and knees, was momentarily frozen by it. Yes, Ray's eyes were saying, they may get me, but first I am going to have the pleasure of killing you.

The gun started to come up. Time seemed to have switched to super slow motion. Then, in the fraction of a second Moe had left to live, Ray's head, as if pulled by an unseen hand, was snapped sharply toward the pavement, placing it directly into the path of the oncoming rear tires. Ray's eyes went wild as he struggled desperately to free his neck, move his head, somehow get away from whatever was holding him there.

But there was no time. The rear wheels were bearing down on him. Just as Ray's mouth opened, his head was wrenched to the ground and the giant tire rolled over it, bumping only slightly but producing a hideous cracking noise, crushing Ray's head so flat that when the next tire arrived, other than for the spray of some matter the color of bloody bubble gum, its passage was disturbed hardly at all.

Moe, feeling faint, forced himself to go over. Ray's body lay on its back, with one knee bent and one hand in the air, its wrist displaying a gold Rolex. His head looked like a cheap prop from a teen horror movie. A long base-metal chain led straight from Ray's neck to a set of mangled keys. The keys, Moe reasoned, must have gotten caught under a tire and pulled Ray's head after them.

Moe heard drumming and looked up to see the float proceeding untroubled down the street. Liberty's arm was thrust majestically into the clear morning sky. Her torch was gleaming in the bright sunlight. Moe watched as it turned the corner and disappeared.

Ray's carcass was starting to attract gawkers. Moe avoided looking at what was left of the face as he bent down and retrieved his gun. Then he reached into his pocket, pulled out his cell phone, and checked his watch. Visiting hours wouldn't be starting for another hour and a half. He dialed 911.

EPILOGUE

The doctor saw Moe approaching and gave him a thumbs-up sign. Moe broke into a trot.

"She's showing signs of consciousness," the doctor reported. "And the swelling has stopped well short of the critical. Don't take it to the bank yet, Mr. Rosen, but it looks like she's out of the woods."

"Out of the woods," Moe repeated. He'd never heard a lovelier phrase. "Can I see her? Talk to her? What can I do?"

"I don't want her excited, but sure. Go in and hold her hand. Say a few words. See if she recognizes you."

They must have changed the dressing because there was no blood on the gauze. When she squeezed his hand, he bent over and kissed her nose, green tube and all.

—◦◦◦—

Moe emerged from the cool dark of the subway station into painfully bright sunshine. It was going to be a scorcher. He checked his watch. The parade would be getting under way soon.

The view down booth-lined Eastern Parkway brought back childhood memories. Moe remembered a time when there were stables in Prospect Park and the wide paths running along both sides of the parkway were used for horseback riding. Moe's father had taken him for his first pony ride here.

But the neighborhood had changed. The Jews had moved to the suburbs. The stables had closed. His father had died. The riding paths had been cemented over. It was a whole new world. Marlene was out of the woods.

Moe decided it would be fun to walk all the way to the Wedo's booth. He pushed his wallet to the very bottom of his side pocket and remembered that he'd turned his gun over to the detectives who'd responded to his 911. He checked the safety clasp on his moon watch, crossed the street and started walking up Eastern Parkway.

Police were manning the lines of barricades and keeping the parkway clear, but the paths on either side were filling up fast. Wherever Moe looked, he saw people streaming into the area, most of them black and many of them waving national flags. It felt like a benign invasion.

With each block, the crowd became thicker. The lines of food and souvenir booths seemed to stretch out forever. Every few yards he passed another vendor hawking something: cold drinks, plastic whistles, baseball hats, colorful banners and flags. On every corner, he passed kindly, middle-aged women in white dresses handing out prayer cards to people who promptly dropped them to the ground, making it look as if the women were standing in snowdrifts. He passed numerous groups of white-shirted, bow-tied, stone-faced black Muslim men standing behind bridge tables stacked with Nation of Islam newspapers, pamphlets, books, and posters.

It was fascinating at first, but after about ten blocks the crowd had become so dense that Moe's progress was reduced to a crawl. Competing files of pedestrians were winding their way through the stationary crowd like slow-moving lava. Moe had no choice but to become part of a particular flow and allow himself to be carried along.

Moe looked up along the parkway. The parade was in full swing. Floats and troupes and individual entries were backed up as far as he could see. The side paths were now packed to impassability. He would never have believed there were this many West Indians in the entire Western Hemisphere, let alone gathered in one section of Brooklyn. He felt a collective energy in the air, a kind of raucous joy that was so natural, so pervasive, so good-natured, that it had even the legions of uniformed police smiling. On his trek thus far, there had been no end of jostling and bumping and tripping and stepped-on feet and spilled drinks and dropped food, and yet Moe hadn't witnessed a single serious argument. The police function had been reduced to that of crossing guards. The sense of fun and fellowship was so strong—except from the black Muslims—that Moe had to keep reminding himself that he was a white man in the midst of an overwhelmingly black crowd.

He pushed on, moving along in fits and starts, breathing in the mixed pungent smells that hung in the sweltering summer air: beer and spices, marijuana and sweat, rum and perfume and frying meat. Everything began to blend together into a single, swirling sensory collage that encompassed the confusion of waving flags, the blaring of bands, the bleating of whistles, the endless flashes of flesh, the cries and cheers of the crowd, the dazzle of the costumes, the dancing of the troupes, the glare and the glitter, the trilling of the steel bands, the throbbing, insistent rhythm of the drums.

Then, just when he was convinced that the Wedo's booth must have been moved to a parallel universe, there it was. The giant snake. The rainbow. The silly fish. Sirene.

She didn't see him as he worked his way around to the back, squeezed in between the resupply truck and the line of drink coolers, and stepped up onto one of the wooden pallets that served as the booth's floor.

Sirene looked up from a metal box stuffed with money. "You best be here to work."

"Of course."

"*Bon*. Get two boxes of meat patties from the boy on the truck."

"Marlene's awake. She's out of the woods."

Sirene made that chirping sound. "We knew that an hour ago," she told him, her face breaking into a grin. "Now, where are those patties?"

"Where is Air?"

She gave him another chirp. He decided not to say anything about Ray.

Moe remained inside the booth helping out as best he could. Once he got the hang of it, he was allowed to take over cooking the meat patties, using the plastic tongs to slide the finished patties into wax-paper sheaths and refilling the rotating toaster shelves with cold patties from the box. It was mindless, repetitive work and, for some reason, enormous fun.

"How much am I getting paid for this?" he asked Sirene during a rare lull in the action.

"You already take my best waitress," she told him, straightening up the cash in the box. "That is not enough?"

"More than enough."

"Okay, everyone," Sirene called a few minutes later, clapping her hands. "Time for our break."

"How come?" Moe asked.

She chirped, gesturing toward the parkway.

In the distance, above the forest of bobbing heads and waving flags, the golden foil of Liberty's torch was just coming into view. All the Wedo's workers finished up with their customers and then grouped together in the booth to watch. Sirene came over and stood by Moe's side. It was cramped inside the booth, but not nearly as cramped as on the street outside.

When the float pulled even with the booth, it stopped. The band fell silent as the troupe, more than a hundred strong, shuffled into formation behind it. With their loose black capes and droopy black caps, they looked like a regiment of shades from the netherworld.

The crowd was becoming restless. Jammed together between the barricades and the booths, and baking in the heat, its tolerance for delay was minimal. The solid mass of bodies presented Moe with a skyline of hats, listless flags, and infants squirming on shoulders.

Suddenly the crowd sensed something. People shushed one other, craned to see, pointed. As the crowd quivered and became still, Moe heard the low, plaintive sound of a single drum. It was beating out a slow, strange African rhythm, insistent but somehow sad, a rhythm that seemed to pass through Moe's skin and resonate somewhere deep inside him. He looked up toward the bandstand on Liberty's crown and saw a pair of fluid hands. It was Fabrice.

Out in the street, in response to the drumming, the troupe began to move in unison, the simplest of movements: rising up on its collective toes and dropping back, but rhythmically, always on the same beat, accompanied by a single clap of the hands, as if they had all fallen under the drum's hypnotic spell. Moe watched as the crowd joined in with this elemental dance, the steady rising and falling and clapping suggesting a kind of collective respiration. The people around him in the booth had joined in as well. Moe felt the wooden pallets under his feet moving to the steady rhythm of Fabrice's drum.

Suddenly the drumming increased in both volume and pace, summoning the troupe to action. The front section of about two dozen dark-shrouded dancers began moving forward. They split into two groups, each group narrowing to single file and slowly mounting the ramps on either side of the float. Once on the float, the dancers became more animated, adding twirls and swoops to their movements as they made their way along the separate paths that wound around the crown and the dance floor before joining into a single path that led them into Liberty's massive upraised arm.

The drumming stopped, but its sound seemed to reverberate in the air. A moment later, high up in the torch, a golden door was thrown open and Air—with cape reversed and sequins gleaming, transformed into a tawny vision in red, white, and blue—stepped out onto the ledge. While the crowd cheered, she spread her arms and rained golden glitter on them.

The massed speakers exploded with sound as the entire band started blasting out an upbeat Afro-Caribbean tune. Air sat and rode the slide down to the plywood dance floor.

One by one, the other members of the troupe stepped through the golden door in their now colorful costumes, threw handfuls of golden glitter into the air, and slid down to join Air on the dance floor. When they were all there, they lined up and began clapping to the music.

Slowly but surely, under their combined weight, the one-inch plywood floor began to move until, like a trampoline, it was sending them high in the air, their capes flying, their Mylar streaming, their sequins glinting in the sun—all of them bouncing together, like bizarrely dressed Masai warriors celebrating a successful hunt. To Moe, it seemed an absurd clash of cultures, but no one else seemed to notice.

He glanced over. Sirene was clapping and swaying to the beat, giggling delightedly each time her daughter bounced high in the air.

Sirene bumped Moe with her hip, cupped her hand to his ear, and said, "You do nice work, Moses."

He smiled and nodded his thanks. His father had always called him Moses. Marlene was out of the woods. The float looked beautiful. Everywhere he looked, people were swaying to the music, waving flags, blowing whistles, cheering. He looked up at the bandstand on Liberty's crown and saw Fabrice pounding away on his big drum. His head was thrown back, his eyes were closed, and the smile on his face suggested that he had entered the promised land.